"Blast all who defy me!" the Shadowmaster roared, and lightning leapt from his eyes like two darting white flames, roaring across the dark chamber to swallow up his apprentice and the scrying portal with him.

Hastrim staggered back with a startled sob as his companion and their spell vanished into wisps of curling smoke.

"I did tell him not to mention the Great Foe again," the Shadowmaster said chidingly. Then he turned his head from the drifting smoke and said politely to Hastrim, "Please continue with the exposition your companion so abruptly abandoned. . . ."

FORGOTTEN REALMS
FANTASY ADVENTURE

THE SHADOW OF THE AVATAR TRILOGY
Ed Greenwood

Shadows of Doom

Cloak of Shadows

All Shadows Fled

Other Books by Ed Greenwood

Elminster, The Making of a Mage

Crown of Fire

Spellfire

All Shadows Fled

Book Three

The Shadow of the Avatar Trilogy

Ed Greenwood

ALL SHADOWS FLED

First Printing: October 1995
Printed in the United States of America.
Library of Congress Catalog Card Number: 94-61677

9 8 7 6 5 4 3 2 1

ISBN: 0-7869-0302-3

TSR, Inc.
201 Sheridan Springs Rd.
Lake Geneva, WI 53147
U.S.A.

TSR Ltd.
120 Church End, Cherry Hinton
Cambridge CB1 3LB
United Kingdom

To Jenny, for literally everything.

cha mhisd'a thig dhuit am boidag

Away, Shadows, away! I grow tired of slaying thee . . .
and presently I shall grow angry. *Then* you'll be sorry!
                    The Simbul, Queen of Aglarond
                Said in spell-battle before all her court
                            Year of Shadows

Prologue

Three living heroes and a ghost dared to take an enchanted blade out of the world, hunting shapeshifters in their ancient Castle of Shadows. . . .

For centuries, the Malaugrym had been dark figures of legend, fey sorcerers who could take any shape they chose. They came to Faerûn to impersonate kings and reavers and archmages, to entertain themselves with the havoc they could wreak—and to seize mortal women as breeding slaves, carrying them off across the planes to the place they called Shadowhome.

When the famous archmage Elminster of Shadowdale caught Malaugrym in Faerûn, they paid with their lives. Twice he journeyed to the Castle of Shadows to humble the House of Malaug . . . but no mere mortal had ever made such a foray and returned to Faerûn to tell of it.

Until Lady Sharantyr, Knight of Myth Drannor; Belkram and Itharr of the Harpers; and the ghostly remnant of Syluné, Witch of Shadowdale, went up against the shapeshifters armed with the Sword of Mystra. And with that sword, Sharantyr cut her way back from the brink of death and out of the Castle of Shadows, slaying many of the evil shapeshifters as she went.

Unfortunately, most of them still lived, and vowed revenge on four new foes. More entered Faerûn with the returning heroes and escaped to wander the

Realms at will.

Even worse, Faerûn was much as they'd left it: in the throes of the magical chaos, bloodshed, and lawlessness of the Time of Troubles, when the gods themselves walked the Realms, no magic could be trusted, and fire and fury raged across the lands.

It was a time for heroes, and the four who'd escaped the Castle of Shadows found Elminster, the Old Mage, waiting for them, with orders to undertake still more perilous tasks in the desperate work of saving civilized Faerûn.

And the Malaugrym were waiting for them, too. . . .

1
It Begins with a Flame

The wind rose and whistled through the stones of a roofless, ruined manor house on a grassy hillside in Daggerdale. The trampled slope was strewn with tentacled, jellylike, eye-studded nightmare bodies.

Three weary, wild-eyed rangers and a ghostly lady hastened up the hill from the monsters they'd slain, running like starving men to a banquet table. They hurried toward a man who sat in the ruins.

The gaunt, white-bearded old man sat on what was left of a crumbling wall and serenely smoked a pipe. He looked at them all, smiled, and spat out this smoke belcher. It rose smoothly upward to float by his ear, spouting wisps of smoke that curled away to be lost in the quickening breeze. "Ye deserve congratulations for one thing, at least," he announced.

After the silence had begun to stretch, Itharr sighed and asked in tones that were *just* respectful, "And what, Lord Elminster, would that be?"

"Keeping thyselves alive," Elminster told him dryly.

"I heard an 'at least' in there," Syluné put in. Her silvery tresses hung still around her eerily translucent face despite the gusting wind. Beside her, the blood-spattered lady ranger Shar shot her an amused look through her own wind-whipped hair.

Elminster glared severely at the ghostly Witch of Shadowdale. "There *is* a little matter of bringing a trio or more of Malaugrym into Faerûn, and allowing them to wander off untraced and untrammeled, to work their wanton wills across the land."

" 'Work their wanton wills' . . . I like that; 'twould fit nicely into a purple Harper ballad," Syluné replied serenely. "My choice, Old Mage, was between the lives of these three heroes—nay, no wincing, now; they've more than earned the title—and those of a few shapeshifters. *I* think my decision was the right one . . . and if you disagree so strongly, why did you not take action yourself? You must have been here watching us."

"Been here, aye. Watching, no," the Old Mage replied, eyes on the hillside below them—where, at his magical bidding, the horribly distorted bodies of the Malaugrym were rising into the air and catching fire. "I was tossing meteor swarms over the turrets of Telflamm, half a world away."

"By the gods, the bardic phrases keep flowing, like . . ." The ghost sorceress paused meaningfully.

"Nightsoil from a hurled bucket?" Belkram offered helpfully.

Syluné rolled her eyes and continued, "And your reason for this . . . ah, *fiery* behavior?"

El grinned. "I was feeding a wild magic area to make it grow into a shield against Red Wizards . . . so I could turn my attention closer to home."

Belkram caught the first whiff of burning flesh and spun around, raising the gory daggers he held ready in both hands. Seeing the source of the smell, he relaxed. A certain grim satisfaction grew on his face as he watched the bodies of their foes burn. Sharantyr gave the midair cremation a single quick glance and turned her gaze back to the Old Mage.

"I know you well enough, Elminster," she said levelly,

"to know that such words always lead us to another of your 'little tasks' . . . and I'd appreciate knowing what this one is without a lot of clever tongue-fencing. Several Malaugrym—one in particular—have about used up my patience for today." As she stared challengingly at the Old Mage, Shar flexed her aching jaw. Her mouth, scorched by a Malaugrym tentacle whose foul taste she could still remember, was throbbing painfully, and her tongue was a thick, numb thing.

As her companions looked at the usually merry Shar in surprise, Elminster inclined his head and said, "Plain speaking is wise in any case, Lady Knight. Know, then: thy swords and spells—and all of ye, with them—are urgently needed in the coming defense of Shadowdale. I'm here to send ye where ye're most needed in that fight."

"The Zhentarim?" Syluné asked shortly. It was more statement than question.

As if her words had been some sort of cue, the world around them was suddenly a cold place of endlessly streaming white flames, and her companions stood frozen amid the conflagration. The last thing the Witch of Shadowdale heard was Elminster's disgusted cry: "Ah, *no!* Not *again!*" And then his tattered words were whirled away from her, and all that was left was the ceaseless roaring. . . .

* * * * *

After what must have been a very long time, Syluné knew herself again. She was all that was left of the woman widely known as the Witch of Shadowdale. . . .

She was Syluné. Still a ghost . . . and still in Faerûn. Hanging in the heart of the roaring.

All around her, flames that did not burn streamed endlessly past her motionless friends and the crumbling stones of the manor. But she could move and think . . . though the cold white flames made her tremble uncontrollably as they roared through her.

Syluné found she could move, if she bent her will hard to the doing. Let us be doing, then.

With slow determination, she drifted nearer the Old Mage, sitting motionless on his bit of wall. His hands were uplifted and his lips open, wearing the disgusted frown of his realization that whatever it was had caught him again.

So they were in some sort of trap. A magical trap, though its flames—which didn't seem to harm anything—had withstood the wildness of magic stalking Faerûn for some time, it seemed. Some of the wildflowers growing amid the stones had bloomed and withered since the magic had begun. The companions had been here for days, then. Syluné wished she could sigh. I've not been a ghost long enough to learn patience for waits that may well take years.

She looked at the Old Mage's pipe, still floating beside his head where he'd left it, and saw that the flames bent around it.

They seemed to be avoiding it! Syluné stared at the spell-flames narrowly for a time; they boiled up out of nowhere on one side of the ruins, arced over her frozen companions, and then returned in an endless rush to nowhere on the far side of the broken walls. It was some sort of stasis field that avoided Elminster's small, curved, ever-smoking pipe.

So, the pipe yet radiated its own magic—and floated on its own, not frozen by the flames. She frowned. He'd once been able to teleport with it, hadn't he?

She drifted nearer, noticing faint wisps of smoke curling up out of the pipe bowl ever so slowly and rising to mingle with the onrushing flames.

She eyed it. This was probably going to hurt.

Mystra, if any part of you is still around to hear, she thought firmly, aid me now. And with the resolve still strong in her, she surged forward, thinning a part of her essence into the pipe.

Magics swirled and tore at her, defenses against tampering that bore Elminster's trademark spell-upon-spell interlacing. Gods, the pain!

Whirling around in a silent scream, Syluné found that the pipe could teleport vapor in and away, in an endless cycle—giving her an escape whenever she wished—and could also transport anyone who touched it and willed it, *thus,* from place to place.

Elminster sat frozen, but perhaps she could guide the pipe to him . . . yes! That very movement was a direction he'd given the pipe several times recently, so how to do it was displayed right in front of her!

Syluné swirled around the pipe and moved it down toward the Old Mage's mouth. The flames bent away from her, and grim satisfaction rose within her as she made the slow, drifting journey. This was going to work!

At last the pipe touched the Old Mage's lips, but he sat open-mouthed, unmoving, and she could feel no quickening of will within him, only the endless roaring. The magic was binding his wits, then. Of *course* it must be, or he'd have used spellfire to drink it down to nothingness long ago. Syluné wanted to sigh again.

Perhaps she could force a teleport by—oh, gods, this might well be the last thing she ever did, the last moment she knew.

Farewell, Faerûn, Syluné thought, and flowed back into the pipe. She must will it to take the Old Mage away from here, to the meadow. The meadow where Sharantyr had danced about with a glowing sword in the depths of the night—a lifetime ago, it seemed—in the meadow just over there.

And then white flames roared up between her ears and up her throat and the world exploded, whirling her away. . . .

* * * * *

Castle of Shadows, Shadowhome, Flamerule 15

"I have seen enough shadow weaving and clearing away of dead kin and rubble to last me many an eon," the gigantic horned worm declared in a voice that echoed in the far corners of the cavernous room, "and Shadowhome is rebuilt sufficiently to set my gorge at ease—for now."

With a rattle of huge chitin plates, he glided into the dim, shadowed chamber, and there dwindled into a bald, long-tailed, gray-scaled humanoid. Othortyn of the Malaugrym eyed his minions, a pair of tentacled lesser kin who peered into the flickering, floating light of a scrying portal at the center of the chamber. Othortyn shifted his tail and asked irritably, "So how've you two been wasting your time?"

"Watching what befalls in the world of the humans," Inder said boldly, "as you commanded." His quiet companion, Hastrim, nodded but said nothing.

"And what have you found?" Othortyn asked, settling himself on a crumbling stone throne that was almost as old as he.

"The ambitious humans who dwell in Zhentil Keep, bolstered by their god—or one who claims to be Bane—have gone to war," Inder said in a voice swift and shrill with excitement. "They've sent four armies into adjacent lands, the largest by road into Shadowdale . . . where the Great Foe dwells."

"And what befell this force sent against Elminster?" Othortyn asked quietly.

"Some local human mage called down lightnings and cooked many in their armor . . . and then the Foe turned a few thousand into boulders while they were camped at a place called Voonlar. No doubt he planned to transform them all, but—"

Othortyn blanched. "Mass transformation? You *dare* to tell me that the Great Foe can turn whole armies into toads? I've not heard that sort of nonsense since I was a youngling and pranksome elders tried to scare me with wild tales of human wizards!"

Inder met his master's gaze steadily. "Didn't you believe those tales?" he asked quietly.

Othortyn glowered. "So, just how many spells, oh wise apprentice, do these wizards hurl around that I don't know about?" he asked, voice heavy with sarcasm. As he eyed the younger Malaugrym, his tail curled out to open a door that had been secret for long years. He took out a dusty bottle from the dark niche beyond.

Inder shrugged. "Several thousand, perhaps."

"So, with all this magic to hurl about, reshaping worlds," Othortyn snarled, the end of his tail rearing back and lengthening into a hollow stinger, "why did oh-so-mighty Elminster stop making his rocks before the whole host was done?"

Inder frowned as his master pierced the cork of the bottle and drank deeply. The apprentice said, "His spell—as would any mighty magic, we believe—created an area of wild magic . . . which is still spreading. A wizard would see such a thing as the greatest danger of all, and would do nothing to aid its spread—nor dare to risk himself in its vicinity."

"So the Great Foe did not confront his own foes directly," Hastrim added, "fearing for his skin."

"He turned instead to the other armies, where only lesser mages stood against him," Inder continued, "and—"

"Speak no more of the Foe," the old Shadowmaster said sharply. "What has become of our kin who reached Faerûn?"

"Atarl, Yinthrim, and Revered Elder Ahorga survived the battle with the three accursed humans who came here," Inder said in more sober tones, "and seem to be roaming Faerûn in many shapes, learning its ways and uses."

"Others of our house have found their own, separate ways into Faerûn," Hastrim added. "We have scryed

Bralatar and Lorgyn, and seen one other, whom we believe to be Lunquar, get of Byatra. . . ." His voice trailed away, and there was a little silence.

"Is that all?" Othortyn growled. "I thought Jaster had gathered a dozen or more eager younglings around him!"

"He did," Inder said quickly, "but when Starner came to you with word that the Great Foe was caught in the loop trap you cast at their gate, you told him to gather all kin with spells to spare and make haste to—"

"Blast all who defy me!" Othortyn roared, and lightning leapt from his eyes like two darting white flames, roaring across the chamber to swallow up Inder and the scrying portal with him.

Hastrim staggered back with a startled sob as his companion and their spell vanished into wisps of curling smoke.

"I did tell you, Inder, not to mention the Great Foe again," Othortyn said chidingly. Then he turned his head from the drifting smoke and said politely to Hastrim, "Please continue with the exposition of events that Inder so abruptly abandoned . . ."

Hastrim stared at him in stunned silence, face pale. Muscles rippled around his mouth as he fought for calm.

"Feel free to be as clever as you feel necessary," the old Shadowmaster said soothingly.

Hastrim looked at Othortyn, and then his gaze fell again to regard the greasy curls of smoke that had been Inder. He swallowed.

"Well," he said unhappily, "perhaps it would be best to begin when it was first noticed that three humans—bearing a magic sword—had somehow stepped from Faerûn into the heart of Shadowhome . . . undetected."

"Good, good," the old, bald Shadowmaster said encouragingly, opening another bottle. "Would you like something to drink?"

"Er—" Hastrim began, and then added with sudden

firmness, "Yes," and a long, snakelike tentacle put a dusty bottle in his hand.

* * * * *

Faerûn, Daggerdale, Flamerule 15

"Easy, lass," a familiar voice rumbled as Syluné of Shadowdale slowly blinked her way back into awareness. " 'Twas well done, to be sure. Ye shattered a spell loop, a very nasty Malaugrym magic—and there were a dozen of them waiting with all the spells they could think of, for us to break out. It's probably best that Shar and the lads were stunned when ye hurled me elsewhere. It saved them from about forty mind-rending attacks, and left me free to use the sort of Art that was really necessary."

Elminster gestured down the hillside, and Syluné saw rainbow swirlings there, above torn earth and blasted stumps. The trees around the stream and the leaning bridge were no more . . . and no doubt the gate to the Shadowmasters' home plane was gone too.

"A wild magic area?" she whispered.

"I fear so," Elminster replied grimly, "but the gate is gone forever, and a score or so more Malaugrym with it."

Syluné shuddered and drifted up out of his hands. Except for the few stones where the Old Mage was sitting—well west of where he had been—the ruined manor was now a crater of mud and gravel.

She swirled back to face him. "How long has it been since we came back from the Castle of Shadows?"

"Nigh on a month," Elminster said quietly.

Syluné nodded grimly. "I thought so. Has Shadowdale fallen?"

Elminster gave her a twisted grin. "Not yet." He got up and trudged west, into the trees. "Come to the meadow."

Syluné drifted along beside him, suddenly reluctant to be alone. The old wizard had taken only a few paces before they emerged into a field of trodden grass where Belkram, Itharr, and Sharantyr sat, looking up with welcoming smiles.

"Thankee, and all that," Itharr said, his broad shoulders shifting as he smiled.

"All part of my orders," Syluné told him briskly, giving Elminster a meaningful look, "as enunciated by the tyrant mage here."

"Ah, yes," Belkram said. "I believe I know just how you feel."

"Yes," Sharantyr agreed crisply. "I think it's about time, Old Mage, that you told us what befell Faerûn while we were all caught in this magic."

"You might have revived us sooner," Itharr added darkly.

Elminster looked at the burly ranger. "It took me days to repair and rebuild thy bodies, all three of ye. I had to use necromantic spells I haven't looked at in ages . . . and I do mean ages." He lifted an eyebrow. "Perhaps I didn't get thy head screwed on quite right."

"I—" Itharr began, but Belkram interrupted him.

"If that's so, sir—why do I feel weary, and in pain?"

"Aye!" Itharr agreed.

"The only way I could save ye at all," Elminster muttered, "was to restore ye to exactly as ye were before the trap took us. As it was, I nearly lost ye more than once—ye in particular, Belkram, *five* times! The gods know I've grown used to never receiving the slightest thanks when I help folk, but betimes I think certain beneficiaries of my arts close enough to me—and perceptive enough, to—ah, ne'er mind . . . " He glared at the handsome Harper.

Belkram returned his look of anger.

"All right," Sharantyr said, looking from one to the other. "Enough. Tell us about the Realms, El."

Elminster's face grew calm as he nodded and said

briskly, "Zhentilar armies march on Shadowdale from all sides—and the avatar of the god Bane rides with them, leading the main body himself."

"Faerûn's flying dung," Syluné said crisply. The unaccustomed oath drew startled gazes her way. "Even if the dale can withstand such an assault," she said bitterly, "it'll be torn into smoking ruins in the doing." She turned to look south. "And after all these years, I'll see it destroyed after all."

"Be not so quick to surrender our home to the Black Gauntlet," Elminster said firmly. "*I* shall be there, fighting to the last . . . and I've sent Zhentilar troops running bootless away from Shadowdale more times than I care to recall."

"If three swords can make a difference in this, sir," Belkram said heavily, "things must be bad. Tell us in truth what's befallen thus far . . . where are the Zhents now?"

Elminster nodded. "Four armies are on the march," he said, all trace of testiness gone. "The one coming down through Voonlar is the largest, though my friend Perendra took care of a goodly number of the fools by calling up a lightning storm. Fancy marching through a downpour in full armor; some of these warriors must have cold iron *between* their ears, not just over them! Meanwhile, I dealt with a few thousand more."

"Oh? How do you 'deal with' a few thousand Zhent troops?" Belkram asked, shifting into a more comfortable slouch in the grass. The more he dealt with archmages, the more it was becoming obvious that their shared concept of 'haste' allowed time for thorough discussions of everything.

"Carefully, lad," Elminster told him predictably. "Carefully."

The two Harpers sighed together . . . and had many other opportunities to sigh as the wizard rambled on. At one point Belkram muttered despairingly, "Get *on* with it!" under his breath.

He'd spoken a trifle too loudly. The Old Mage's eyebrows rose, and Belkram gulped.

"Patience certainly seems to be the provision ye used up most in the shadows," El observed mildly as his pipe glided in to find its way to his lips. He blew a slow, spreading smoke ring and then banished his pipe again. "Teleportation is one thing that still seems reliable among all this chaos of Art, so I spent the better part of the highsun hours yesterday transporting a dozen monsters—hydras, firedrakes, wyverns, behirs, death kisses, and the like—into the camp of the second, central force, north of the Flaming Tower."

Belkram chuckled, but Shar looked troubled. "What's to stop their using spells to drive those beasts before them, south into the heart of Shadowdale?"

"Me," the Old Mage told her impishly. "I took care of their mages first." He watched another smoke ring drift away on the wind and added, "Some of the beasts I sent into their midst were rather hungry, too."

"Can't Bane teleport just as easily as you can?" Itharr asked quietly.

Elminster nodded his approval at such tactical thought. "Of course. He'll have to come to the aid of his Central Blade or lose the lot of them . . . but the doing will keep him occupied for a time, too busy to work other mischief." He ran fingers through his beard. "The same consideration governed my treatment of the smallest force. Fzoul's leading four hundred or so mounted men-at-arms past us right now, through Daggerdale."

"Four hundred Zhentilar?" Belkram asked, holding up his daggers. "You want us to take down four hundred warriors? Shouldn't we get horses to ride on, just to make it a little fairer?"

Shar and Itharr snorted together. Syluné reclined gracefully on thin air, as if sprawled on a couch, and awaited Elminster's answer.

The Old Mage shook his head and asked softly, "Bold

today, aren't we, friend Harper?"

Lesser men might have quailed before that tone, but Belkram merely shrugged, smiled, and waved at Elminster to continue.

Inclining his head in a mock bow of thanks, Elminster said, "That task is not yours." He lifted his lips in a mirthless grin. "I suspect a few orcs can do it better."

"*A few orcs?*" Sharantyr roared, her voice rising from deep and ragged tones, for all the world as if she were a burly male and not a lithe lady. "Elminster!" That last squeaked word of reproach sounded more like a lady's pique, and goaded Syluné into peals of tinkling laughter.

"Yestereve," Elminster told them in tones of injured innocence, "I approached several orc bands foraging in Daggerdale, and undertook to alert them that a well-provisioned Zhent force was entering the territory. That should make things a little warmer for Fzoul than he anticipated, and rob him of most opportunities to reach Shadowdale ahead of the other Zhent forces, hole up in the woods around Grimstead, and amuse himself by using his spells to harass the good folk of the dale."

"All right, El. You've been both clever and busy," Syluné reassured him, her voice soothing. Her next words, however, came out as sharp as the crack of a whip: "But so have we. My friends here grow stiff and tired and hungry. Armies march on Shadowdale from all sides, you said, and have told us of three, so what attack is coming from the south—and what is our duty in dealing with it?"

Elminster bowed his head again to hide a grin, cleared his throat in apparent embarrassment, and said, "I need ye four to deal with the fourth Zhent attack: the Sword of the South. It's a band of Sembian mercenaries and the covert Zhentarim agents who hired them. They've been assembling in Battledale for a month and more, drawn from all over Sembia and the eastern dales."

"They're going to try to march through the Elven

Court woods?" Shar asked, one shapely eyebrow raised. "That's not a wise tactic for any armed band."

The Old Mage shook his head. "Their orders are to take and subdue Mistledale, and without pause press on up the Mistle Trail, to drive into Shadowdale from the south." He smiled gently. "You will stop them."

"I thought we were going to defend Shadowdale," Belkram said. "*You* may be able to dance around the Realms with a thought and a wiggle of your hips, but we have to *walk* . . . and I don't feel like running back and forth between two dales, sword in hand, through gods know how many Zhent blackhelms!"

Elminster held up a quelling hand. "I said I'd come to send ye where ye are most needed. Right now Shadowdale is crowded with frightened troops bustling about. I don't want them to relax because the heroes have come to town, and I don't want them in thy way, or ye in theirs. *Mistledale* is thy battlefield. The defense of Mistledale will be the southern defense of Shadowdale."

"How strong is this fourth host?" Belkram asked suspiciously.

Elminster shrugged. "About seven thousand, when last I counted."

"Seven thousand!" Itharr burst out as jaws dropped all round.

Shar shook her head. "You love us, don't you?" she murmured.

El chuckled. "Oh, ye'll have help. All of Shar's battle companions, the Knights of Myth Drannor, are in Mistledale already, mustering the Riders."

"There are only thirty Riders, perhaps six more if the graybeards who can still walk and breathe at the same time come out of retirement, and another dozen if their sword apprentices ride with them, too," Syluné said softly, "and barely a dozen Knights, even if all who've retired or strayed off come running to Mistledale."

El frowned. "And ye, of course . . . isn't that battle might enough?"

"Ah, Old Mage," Syluné said gently, "you may not have noticed, being old and terribly important and even busier than usual . . . but I'm not . . . er, the woman I used to be."

El chuckled. "I've been spreading stories of the Ghost Witch of Shadowdale these last few months . . . I think ye'll find, on a battlefield, that ye're rather *more* than ye used to be."

Syluné glared at him, her eyes two white flames dancing in the air. "And just *what* does that mean?"

"I've had half Twilight Hall modifying their best battle spells since the seasons turned," the old wizard told her. "If it all works, they can cast them simultaneously through ye, so a dozen or more battle magics—which ye can aim—lash out from ye at once."

"And the catch?"

"The power involved will burn ye out from within, leaving thy body only ashes . . . killing ye."

"El, I don't *have*—oh. I see. As I'm dead already, I should survive the destruction of whatever body you're going to give me."

El nodded. "It's waiting for ye in Mistledale," he said quietly. "Not the last one I'll give ye if—gods willing—I survive this Time of Troubles."

Tears welled up in her phantom eyes, and he added quickly, "Ye'd best get down there speedily. Torm's been dressing the body—ye—in all sorts of black leather, red evening lace, and fishnet gauze apparel, most evenings, and seating ye in the porch window of the Six Shields to entertain the locals."

"Oh he *has,* has he?" Ghostly eyes flashed. "I think I'll just slip into this body of mine at an opportune moment and give him the fright of his life!"

Shar grinned broadly. "May I watch?"

"No, that's 'may *we* watch?' " Belkram corrected her.

"Of course," Syluné told them grandly. "This Six Shields place is unfamiliar to me, though . . ."

"A cheap rooming house east of Lhuin's tannery," El

told her in the manner of a pompous guide, "opened recently to house field workers, drovers, and others too cheap to stay at the Hart or the Arms."

Shar and the Witch of Shadowdale sniffed in unison. "It sounds like the sort of place where Torm would stay, tight-pockets that he is."

"Much as I'd like to watch ye roast Torm on a spit, just to see him wriggle for once, there is some haste," the Old Mage added. "By sundown, the scouts of the Sword of the South may well reach Galath's Roost."

"How can we possibly reach Mistledale in time, then?" Itharr asked—unwisely, as it turned out.

Sharantyr gave him a weary look. "He's going to mass teleport us," she said grimly. "It always makes me feel sick for hours afterward." She sighed and put one arm across her bosom and the other over her stomach, bracing herself. "Get on with it, then."

"Wait," Belkram said, brow wrinkling. "We haven't even—"

The last, fading thing the Harper saw as he struggled to finish his sentence was Elminster's cheery grin. Around him the world flashed and changed—into blue, swirling misty emptiness. Next came a sense of falling, for just one wrenching moment, and then they were standing on a bare board floor in a loft lit by two barrel-sized lamps that hung down on dusty chains from the roof beam. Frowning men in armor stood staring down at large maps whose corners were held down by daggers and gauntlets—or looking up at the newcomers in startled consternation, hands going to hilts.

Belkram and Itharr stood a little behind Sharantyr. Right in front of her was a tall, broad-shouldered and hard-faced man whose steely eyes raked both Harpers for a moment before he took a catlike step forward and crushed her into an embrace.

"Shar, by the grace of all the gods!"

The lady ranger's shoulders shook for a moment as she clung to him, her drawn sword forgotten, and she knew tears would be bright on her face when she turned to introduce them. Florin Falconhand did not give her the chance.

"I've missed you, little one," he growled, and as Shar reached up to tousle his unruly hair, he added, "but you've found companions on the trail, I see. Who are these two gentlemen you've brought?"

Eyeing the drawn blades crowding in around them, Belkram deemed the moment right. He bent his knee, parted the leathers at his throat to show his silver harp pin, and said, "Belkram and Itharr of the Harpers to fight alongside you, Lord Florin. Elminster sent us."

A good-natured grin split the famous ranger's face, and he reached one long arm around Sharantyr to clasp their forearms. "Be welcome! We have need of swords, good men to wield them . . . and adventurers brave enough to stand up to Elminster, too!"

"Pardon, Lord," Itharr said smoothly, "but shouldn't that be 'foolish enough'?"

There were chuckles from all around the room, and other men thrust forward their hands in welcome. They were accepted.

Shar tossed her silver blade under the table and put her freed hand on Florin's cheek to guide him down into a kiss. As their lips touched, she was overheard to be murmuring, "Well, here we go again. . . ."

2
Bodies, Fresh and Otherwise

Mistledale, Flamerule 15

It was horribly dark and somehow dusty, followed by a whirling moment of wrenching pain that became a red agony in her chest, rising up to choke her. Threads of pain rolled down limbs stiff from disuse to an aching forest of fingertips . . . and then light and sound suddenly burst and swam all around her. The Witch of Shadowdale found herself blinking back tears.

She had a body again!

Fighting an urge to shriek in triumph, Syluné clung to that thought: she had a body again! A body Torm had obviously just finished dressing in a black lace cutaway gown that left her bare there and there and *there*. . . . He stood with his back to her, humming a contented ditty as he held up a red silk garter before the lamp and surveyed it critically.

It *did* look rather splendid, but Syluné bent all her attention to making the still unfamiliar body move—pushing against the bed with utmost care to sit up silently, and then leaning forward into a quick barefoot step, slipping her arms around him. Her lips went straight to his ear, and before she kissed its hairy lobe, she murmured into it, "Torm . . . I've come for you! Torm . . ."

With a gratifying shriek, Torm leapt into the air, red silk flying. Syluné clung to his trembling limbs and made the leap with him, but the Knight twisted in the air to fling her free and grabbed at his belt dagger. The Witch of Shadowdale put one leg behind her, bounced on it, and lifted her other knee smartly between his, ere she bounded backward onto the bed.

Lord Torm of Shadowdale, Knight of Myth Drannor and thief of some skill, rose into the air once more, sobbing. His darkening eyes met hers for just a moment—with a look of mingled pain, terror, and disbelief—before he crashed face first to the floor.

Some minutes later, the figure sprawled on the furs beside the bed stopped moaning and writhing, and asked hesitantly, "Syluné? Is it you, truly?"

She stood up and walked slowly around the room, kicking experimentally to limber up stiff legs and toes. "It is, Torm . . . which is why you still live, I suppose."

Weakly, the thief on the floor began to chuckle. "Bits of me do. Others I'm not so sure about. I'm sorry, Lady."

"Apology accepted, lecherous scum."

He laughed openly this time, his whooping breaking off with a catch as the shaking brought him fresh pain. "Ohhh, gods," he said at last, rolling over. "I've not felt this much pain since . . . well, never mind."

"I hope she was worth it," Syluné said teasingly, and then asked curiously, "Why weren't you wearing one of your usual flamboyant codpieces?"

Torm looked hurt. "I wasn't dressed yet! Can you see me going downstairs in *this*?" He held his arms wide to fully display the patched and stained cotton undersuit that went under his fighting leathers. "Ladies first," he added, gesturing at her.

Syluné put her hands on her hips and gave him a level stare as she gestured, up and down, at herself. "This is your idea of 'dressed,' I take it?"

Torm gave her a sly look from the floor, and rolled up

to a sitting position, wincing once. "Well, you hadn't complained before tonight," he said, feigning innocence.

"Yet—as you may *just* have noticed—I'm doing so now," Syluné told him calmly. Then she snapped, "Take this frippery off me—at once!"

Torm bounded to his feet with an alacrity that belied the severity of his injury. "My pleasure, Lady Syluné!"

"I'll bet," she said dryly. "Try to keep your hands on the buckles and thongs, now, and when you're done, I'll need a neck rub. Hmm—my calves, too. This body is as stiff as old wood!" She struck a pose, pirouetted experimentally, admired herself in the burnished metal looking glass, and rubbed her nose. "You've taken some care with my hair," she said in tones of pleased surprise. "Diligent brushing, at the least. My thanks, Torm."

"Lady," Torm said seriously, reaching out a finger to stroke the silvery fall of her hair, "in all my life I'd never dared touch your hair, or Storm's, but I always wanted to. It's . . . truly beautiful . . . like spun silver."

Syluné laughed lightly and laid a hand on his cheek. "Why, thank you, Torm—this, from the maid-chaser of Shadowdale?"

"Lady, I meant it," the thief replied, and bowed. " 'Twas an honor caring for your body." A twinkle crept into his eye. "In fact, if you weren't so many years my senior . . ."

Syluné glared at him, and gestured again at herself. "You were hard at work removing all this saucy stuff, remember?"

Torm's gaze dropped—and he discovered the fallen garter. Plucking it up from the floor, he offered it to her mutely. Syluné gave him a withering look, so he shrugged and tossed it over his shoulder. Then he undid her sash, put his hands on her shoulders and spun her around lightly. He stripped her with a speed and expertise that told her he'd done this a time or two before.

"This bit's much easier when you're standing up and—er, with us," he commented. "Oh, by the way . . .

the stone that lets you occupy this body is implanted here." He touched the inside of her left arm, just above the elbow. Syluné probed cautiously, and thought she felt the magic stone deep within, alongside the bone.

"Mystra bless you and keep you, Old Mage," she breathed, "wherever she is."

"What about prayers for me?" Torm asked teasingly, fingers busy undoing the black silk choker he'd put around her throat earlier.

"You'll be needing more than I feel capable of giving," she replied with a chuckle. Then the Witch of Shadowdale reached out, caught hold of his chin, and kissed him firmly, darting her tongue into his mouth.

When she released him, Torm was smiling a little dazedly. "What was that for?" he asked in pleased tones.

She put her arms around him, smelly undersuit and all. "Torm, you rogue," she said feelingly, "do you know how *long* it's been since I've *held* someone? Kissed anyone? Tasted anything? Even your mouth is preferable to nothing at all!"

"Hey!" Torm said in aggrieved tones. "What's wrong with the taste of my mouth?"

"Nothing," she said tartly, spinning away from him, "except that it's the only taste you've got." She sat down on a chair. "Now, about that neck rub."

"If my taste is so bad," Torm said, delving hurriedly into a wardrobe, "how is it that you're in *my* bedchamber, out of a dozen more in this place? Hey?"

"That can be remedied," she said, rising.

Torm caught her wrist and sat her back down. "You're *not* going out into the hall like that!"

"Why not?" She gave him a deadly look. "After what I've heard about what you've been doing to this body before I got here, it could hardly damage my reputation— or yours—any further! Has Illistyl heard about this?"

Torm looked pained. "How did you—? Oh. Elminster."

She nodded in silent satisfaction. The thief looked at

her, found his eyes drawn to meet her own, sighed, reminded himself again that this magnificent creature was a woman old enough to be his great granddam many times over, smiled ruefully, and turned her around to face away from him again. "You wanted a rub," he said, "and you shall have it. Then you can go down those stairs and fight off the entire Zhent army doe-naked if you want . . . but you might catch cold before they get here."

"Not if all the men of Mistledale give me the sort of hot glances you've been throwing my way," she returned. Torm chuckled and tipped some scented oil out of the bottle he'd taken from the wardrobe, rubbed his palms together, and then laid gentle fingers on her shoulders.

Syluné stiffened. "What're y—oh. Ohhh." A few pleasant minutes later, she asked almost sleepily, "How did you know I love the scent of cloves? Did Elminster tell you?"

"No," Torm replied, sounding irritated.

"How, then?"

"Lady Syluné," Torm said carefully, "I *am* a thief."

He had to hold her up to keep her from falling off the chair as she bent over and shook with sudden, helpless laughter.

* * * * *

Daggerdale, Flamerule 15

Valaster's Stand had thrust lancelike into the eastern Daggerdale sky for an age and more, and bid fair to do so for a long time to come. Long before Valaster had chosen to die there, the stand had been an arrowhead-shaped ridge that rose sharply upward as it ran northwest, to end in a jagged, overhanging point of rock under which many a traveler had camped. Wiser folk kept to the thick stand of shadowtop trees that marched up its back, and so stayed hidden from the eyes of predators.

The trees on the edge of the rocky point were dead or dying. Their bare branches thrust up into the sky like the gnarled fingers of a dead man, a popular roost for birds of prey. Two large and dusty buzzards sat side by side there now. Many another raptor circled, squalling at the buzzards' refusal to leave, and then flew off in search of other perches.

The two dusty birds paid them no heed, for they were deep in conversation.

"We *can't* get back without a mage," one said in tones that threatened to become a wail.

"If we find one powerful enough," the larger buzzard added, "there remains the problem of compelling him to create a way between the planes—and yet keep ourselves safe against his treachery."

"To say nothing of the wrath of the elders of the blood if they hold us responsible for opening a way into Shadowhome any mortal can use . . . can you imagine armies of men in the halls of the castle?"

"I could tell them it's all your fault, Atarl," said the larger buzzard, sounding amused.

"I don't find this a matter for jesting," the other raptor said coldly, "even from you."

"We'd best begin lurking about cities and towers and the like, looking for wizards and trying to find out just who is mighty, and what interests drive them," the larger buzzard said. "This may take a long time."

"Aren't they most likely to be found in cities?" Atarl responded almost despairingly. "Yinthrim, I don't know how to look and act in a human city! We won't be able to learn anything if we're always running afoul of local laws and customs, and getting attacked!"

"How to begin, then? We—*'ware!*"

A large, dark bird was gliding down out of the high blue sky toward them, headed silently but purposefully for their tree. The buzzards watched it nervously, shifting on their perches. "An eagle?" Atarl guessed. "Do they eat buzzards?"

"Nothing eats buzzards, if I recall old Othortyn's teachings, except other buzzards," Yinthrim said tightly, "but if he was wrong . . ."

The eagle circled the tree, regarding them both with dark and knowing eyes. "Is this all you've managed to do?" it asked coldly. "Take bird-shape and sit around on dead trees feeling sorry for yourselves?"

"Ahorga?" Atarl gasped.

"Son of Yerga," the eagle responded calmly as it came to rest, wings flapping, between them.

"We were just discussing—"

"I know; it's how I knew you. Is this all you've done—flee into the wilderlands and then sit and talk?"

"Well, no—" Atarl protested, but Yinthrim interrupted.

"That's a fair summation of our doings, yes," he said. "I'd rather tarry now and plan wisely than charge into one blundering battle after another and awaken the attention of the Red Wizards, these Zhentarim, and Elminster's friends."

The eagle nodded. "Fair enough. Have you come to any conclusions as to what to do—as opposed to what not to do?"

"One question," Atarl said hurriedly. "How many more of us came through with the sword and . . . survived?"

"None I know of, but others of the blood seem to have found their own, separate ways into Faerûn."

"Will any of them join with us," Atarl asked eagerly, "in hunting down the three violators of the castle? Or the Great Foe?"

Ahorga turned a cold and glittering eye on the younger Shadowmaster. "Hot for revenge, are you? None of them—nor will I."

"*What?*"

Ahorga turned to see if the silent Yinthrim was as shocked as Atarl, but the larger buzzard merely shrugged and said calmly, "Say on."

Ahorga nodded. "Rushing into battle here is a very good way to get slain. They'd no doubt rather see what Faerûn has to offer before getting themselves destroyed . . . and so should you."

He looked back at Atarl. "Go after the three rangers if you must—you're likely to find them and the Great Foe in and around Shadowdale, southeast of here—but you'd better gather some rings and wands and suchlike that wizards here use to store battle magic . . . you'll need such power to take even those three. You'd best get some experience in impersonating mortals of Faerûn first . . . unless you *like* being burned, lashed, and transformed against your will by frightened wizards!"

"You make it sound as if every mage of this world can dispose of us with a wave of his hand," Atarl said bitterly.

"If you sneer at them and rush into battle with them heedless of what might befall," Ahorga told him, taking flight with a sudden, powerful wingbeat that almost tumbled them from the tree, "that's exactly what may happen." He circled around them. "Go softly, and make surprise your best weapon."

"Will we see you again?" Yinthrim asked.

"If you stay alive, almost certainly," the senior Shadowmaster said. "Remember, an ambush is your best tactic, and against Elminster, it's your *only* tactic."

"We'll practice ambushes, then," Yinthrim promised grimly. "The Realms around here, I think, are suddenly going to become much more dangerous."

"Now *that* sounds like a son of Malaug speaking," Ahorga said approvingly. Without a farewell, he flew off southwest.

Atarl watched him go, and then said in a small voice, "Are mortal mages really that dangerous?"

"No," Yinthrim assured him. "He was just telling us that overconfidence is."

"Words to live by? Hmmph," Atarl said, and turned one wing into a tentacle long enough to make a rude gesture into the southwest. Yinthrim chuckled and flew from the branch.

"Where are you going?" Atarl asked in sudden alarm.

"I'm going to practice ambushing something—anything," his fellow Malaugrym replied. "I'm hungry."

* * * * *

Verdant farms stretched away on both sides of the road, which ran like a sword blade down the length of Mistledale. Along the backs of those prosperous steadings stood the unbroken green wall of the encircling Elven Court woods. On this bright morning Mistledale was a beautiful place to ride, with a good mount moving strongly beneath the saddle—even if the rider rode in the midst of a solid ring of ebon-armored warriors, who took care to keep their armored forms between her and any possible attack.

For the third time, Jhessail Silvertree lost sight of everything but moving black-armored bulks and a forest of lances. She studied the small circle of blue sky visible above her—all she could see of the world around—sighed, and decided she'd had about enough. From the mutterings behind her, she could tell that her apprentice, Illistyl, whose tongue was apt to be sharper than that of almost anyone else, was clinging to her temper with grim talons. Jhessail smiled tightly, thanked Torm for his work in outfitting her with riding breeches—though her lack of armor was why the Riders were treating her this way—and swung her legs suddenly up underneath her.

She heard a startled, wordless exclamation from a Rider on her right as she spread her hands for balance and stood up on her saddle. She had time for a good look around before the Riders on either side of her were extending their lances around her like the bars of an upturned portcullis and crying out:

"Lady, get down!"

"Catch hold of my lance!"

"Careful, Lady!"

She folded her arms across her breast and waited for them to fall silent—and soon enough, uncertainly, they did. "Thank you for your kind concern, Gentlesirs," she said as the horses slowed to a rather jarring trot, "but both Illistyl and I find it rather hard to do any scouting or become familiar with the land around us—land you gallants already know well, but which we've seen only once or twice in passing—through a solid wall of plate armor."

"That's just it," the leader of the patrol rumbled, his deep voice sounding almost scandalized. "You wear no armor! What if a Zhent arrow came from the trees? How could we shield you better than we have been?"

"Kuthe," Jhessail said soothingly, " 'tis not your diligence or skills I reproach, but my lack of any good way to see around or through all of you. I'm saving my one 'long eyes' spell for any spying we need do in the forest. I know the risks of riding to war; I've done it before, remember."

"But to expose yourself needlessly," Kuthe growled, "is foolish, Lady."

"To a vigilant guard of his homeland, yes," Jhessail said, still standing on her saddle, "but I am an adventuress. One who plays with spells. An explorer of baatezu-haunted Myth Drannor. Wedded to an elf, remember? I've done far more crazed things in my life than riding out without armor, I assure you."

"But the little lass—" Kuthe said, gesturing helplessly.

"Call me that again, ironhead," Illistyl advised him sharply, "and you'll be chasing your teeth around the inside of that great helm of yours."

There were guffaws from the Riders, but one of them cut through the chorus of mirth. "Lone rider behind!"

Heads snapped around, and Jhessail turned, smiled, and announced, "It's Lord Merith. The reinforcements Elminster promised us must have arrived."

"Reinforcements?" Kuthe rumbled, looking up at her.

"We've heard nothing of this . . . How many, Lady?"

"Four," she told him sweetly, and there were more guffaws. Illistyl was sure she heard an angry snort as Kuthe's helm swung away from them, but a moment later Jhessail snapped, "Ahead—at Treesedge! *Look!*"

The eastern end of Mistledale, where the flanking arms of the forest met to form a narrow green tunnel around the road to the Standing Stone, had always been called Treesedge. The spot was marked by a covered well and the crumbling rampart of a tiny keep— well known to Riders on patrol who'd sheltered from downpours under its remnants. It was a beautiful spot to spend a night, but a bit lonely to be a grave site.

It seemed likely, however, that men were going to be buried there now. Crossbow quarrels were humming down the road from the east, raking the rear of a hard-riding band of merchants on lathered, stumbling horses fleeing west into Mistledale.

The strength of the merchant band was dwindling steadily. The bolts found easy targets. As Jhessail watched, a fat merchant threw up his hands with a strangled wail and pitched from his saddle, choking on the quarrel that stood out of his throat. On the other side of the road, a horse's head flopped and swung—and a breath later both horse and rider crashed and rolled in the dust, collapsing into the long silence of death.

Jhessail dropped into her saddle again a scant moment before the Riders spurred ahead into a grim, silent gallop, knowing they'd not be in time. Far behind them, Merith stood up on his own saddle, saw that strife lay ahead, and reached for his bow.

Lances leveled, the Riders of Mistledale swept east. "Get out of the road!" Kuthe snarled at merchants who could not hear. "Clear the way!"

"Kuthe! Halt your men!" Jhessail shouted. "*Now!*"

The great helm turned her way, the face within dark with anger. "You have some sort of plan?"

"Yes," Jhessail cried, leaning close to him as their

mounts thundered along side by side. "Just stop them!"

Kuthe gave her a long, slow look—and then reached for the horn at his belt.

After the horn rang out around them, the patrol became a confused mass of dust, rearing horses, and cursing men. Lances rang and rattled off armored shoulders, and Jhessail had to duck hastily to avoid being inadvertently unhorsed.

"Well, mage?" Kuthe demanded when he could be heard. His eyes were on the last merchants, dying up ahead . . . and at something moving on the tree-lined road beyond them. Their slayers.

The leader of the Rider patrol shot her a look. "*Well?*"

Jhessail's mouth was a thin, white-lipped line as she told him shortly, "Back away . . . Give us room side by side."

Kuthe waved one great gauntlet in heavy silence; Illistyl was already guiding her mount forward. Jhessail whispered to her, and they raised their arms together, spread as if in supplication to the sky overhead—and waited.

In tense silence as the Riders eyed them, they watched the road to the east. "Well?" Kuthe demanded. "Have you seen enough?"

"Wait until they come out," Jhessail said, her eyes on the road. "It'd be our death to ride down that firing tunnel, the gods know. Let them come out. If I'm right, they'll be the Zhents we're expecting . . . with orders to ride right on and take Mistledale. They probably killed those merchants just to stop them from warning us."

Kuthe nodded as the killers of the merchants rode into view: a band of mounted crossbowmen, clad in armor as dark as that of the Riders, streaming out of the road mouth and fanning across the fields of Treesedge. Around the two sorceresses, men swore at the sight of that armor.

"Zhent blackhelms, all right," Kuthe said, "and riding hard to encircle us . . . sixty of them, or more. What now, Lady?"

"Keep silence for a breath or two," Jhessail told him softly, "while we do what we have to. Let no man here ride forward until I give the word. When our first spell goes off, your horses may move by themselves; be ready to hold them back!"

"Whose place is it to give orders?" a Rider demanded gruffly.

Jhessail turned on him eyes that were dark and cold, and said, "It will mean death to ride forward. Disobey my *suggestion* freely, but leave word for your widow first."

More than one dry chuckle answered her from the men around, and Kuthe growled, "Right. We wait. Work your magic. Shields *up!*"

Crossbow quarrels were already hissing their way, though the range was impossibly long. Ignoring them, Jhessail spread her arms again and began the incantation, Illistyl chanting in unison.

Abruptly the air in front of the Riders was full of shadowy, moving forms—images that suddenly grew dark and solid; the gleaming black armored backs of Riders on horseback, charging away with lances lowered. More than one mount under the real Riders surged forward to join them, and had to be reined in, hard. The ground shook under the thunder of phantom hooves, and dust rose in a cloud as thirty dark horsemen raced away east.

"Gods," the Rider who'd challenged Jhessail whispered, watching the illusory Riders charge away into battle. "They certainly *look* real."

"Aye, but how can ghost Riders kill any Zhents?" Kuthe demanded as Merith Strongbow came up beside him, an arrow ready, and nodded in silent greeting.

"That's the next spell," the elf told him with quiet confidence. "I've seen this trick before." He thrust both bow and arrow into the startled Rider's hands. "Here—hold this."

As Kuthe gaped at him, he raised his own hands and joined in the gestures of the next spell, murmuring something the Rider couldn't quite hear.

Then he plucked bow and arrow back from the officer's hands and stared east, watching as the dust cloud behind the false Riders became a thick, swirling mass of yellow and green—and the two forces crashed together.

With startled speed, the Zhents plunged through the phantom Riders—into the thick of the yellow-green cloud. And men who rode into that cloud did not come out again.

"I hate doing that to horses," Illistyl said, her voice as thin and cold as a knife.

Merith's eyes, however, were on those who'd ridden wide. "*Jhess!*" he snapped urgently. As his wife peered past Kuthe, Merith drew his bowstring back to his chin, angled the ready arrow up into the sky, and loosed.

Kuthe had never been so close to a spell being cast before. He stiffened and swallowed as one slim and shapely arm brushed his breastplate in an arcane gesture, and a clear, musical voice spoke two distinct words.

She turned her head and winked at him. Kuthe blinked at her—and when he looked again at the sky, the arrow had already split into a dozen shafts, plummeting down on the hard-riding Zhents in a deadly rain.

All but two of the invaders fell in that volley. Kuthe glared at the surviving Zhents and snapped, "Orold—take them!" Six of the Riders spurred away without a word, waving their lances as they followed Orold into battle.

"It feels . . . unfair, killing men like that," Jhessail said quietly.

Kuthe stared at her, and then at the fading yellow cloud where only a few horses still choked and rolled.

"Lass, lass," one of the older Riders replied through his snow-white mustache, "there're still near seven thousand of them, if our scouts be right. When we face *all* of 'em, sweeping down on our homes, d'you think they'll turn their mounts back if we yell 'unfair' then? Aye?"

Another Rider spoke then. "I can even things just a trifle more."

Jhessail turned her head to see who'd spoken; the voice had sounded surprisingly old. The Rider guiding his mount toward her wore worn armor that had been recently burnished at the joints to quell creeping rust. The armor was of an older, bulkier design than what Kuthe wore, though most of it matched the ebon gloss of the other Riders' harnesses. The Rider doffed his helm—and Jhessail stared into the lined face of a very old man.

"Lead us if you will, Baergil," Kuthe said quietly.

"Nay, lad," the old Rider told him. "My commanding days are done. I know daily just how good I was—I order my cabbages about in the garden, and they heed me not a whit."

"Ho, Baergil," Merith said with a smile, and the old man matched it as his cloudy blue eyes met the elf's steady gaze. "I remember you."

"And I you, Sir Elf," Baergil replied. "Though it's been thirty years gone since then."

"Baergil led the Riders that many summers ago," Kuthe told Jhessail, "when I was but a lad. Then he turned to the worship of Tempus, Lord of Battles, and left our ranks."

"They're all dead," Illistyl told them bleakly; she had never stopped watching the Zhents die. "I guess we'll not need your spells, priest of the war god."

Baergil smiled. "Nay, lass; their deaths're what I was waiting for. There's a spell that raises the fallen. . . ."

"To do—what?" Jhessail asked quietly.

"In the hours before dawn," Baergil said, "if they ride as hard as I'll bid them, sixty skeletal reavers will ride into Essembra, striking at anyone with drawn weapons

—or who hurls spells at them. Those who offer them peace they'll leave be, but Zhents being Zhents . . ."

There was a roar of hard laughter. "Do it!" Illistyl told him delightedly, and the warrior priest nodded, watching Orold and his men return.

Then he turned back to them. "That should buy us the time we need," Baergil said with a certain satisfaction, "to make Galath's Roost ready to properly welcome Zhent butchers." The Riders around him laughed again—a chorus of low, quiet sounds that held no humor.

Jhessail shivered despite herself, and caught Illistyl's eye. The two of them shared a comforting look as the priest turned away.

As Merith moved up beside his wife and stretched out a long arm to embrace her, Jhessail felt a pat on her knee—and looked up to see Kuthe wheeling away from her.

"Well done, Knight," he said gruffly. "See you at the Roost!" He urged his mount into a canter, and all around Riders spurred their horses after him, heading for the distant trail into the trees that would take them to the Roost . . . to turn the ruined keep into a death-trap for Zhentilar blackhelms.

Merith and Jhessail's arms were around each other, and their kiss went on until Illistyl looked up at the sky and remarked brightly, "Beautiful weather we're having, isn't it?"

The sky seemed to know this already, though the two Knights beside her didn't seem to notice—or care. Illistyl sighed and rode away. In the distance, she saw dead men and horses rising in a stiff ring around the black-armored priest. She shivered, shook her head, and rode after the Riders.

See the Realms and taste true adventure, they'd said. Well, here we go chasing it again—and flashing swords to that!

3
The Dead and
the Living Both Ride

Essembra, Battledale, early hours of Flamerule 16

Gostar yawned and backed into another circular walk, keeping his eyes and attention always on the night to the north. As if his shifting had been a signal, his companions did the same. Those who fell asleep on guard duty or were judged careless often swallowed sword blades on the spot, but the long, cold hours made feet ache and limbs stiffen. It was best to keep moving in the last stretch before dawn, when the mists clouded bright armor and played tricks on eye and ear.

Now, for instance. A low rumble—Gostar could feel it in his jaw more than he could hear it—was rising from the ever-shifting mists ahead. A helmed head down the line inclined to listen; the others had heard it, too.

The noise was growing louder, becoming a continuous soft thunder, swirling over and around them with the scudding mists . . . and seeming familiar. He'd heard this sound before. In his saddle, on the rolling plains near Thentia . . .

Then he knew what it was, and ice clawed at his heart and throat.

Gostar shook himself, swallowed, and shouted,

"Rorst! Run back to rouse the camp!"

"And why'd I risk a flogging to do that, now?" Rorst asked in his usual, careless, I've-seen-it-all tone.

"Can't you *hear* it?" Gostar waved one gauntleted hand at the mists before them, where the sound had become a continuous choppy thunder. "Those're *horses,* man—half a hundred or more, at full gallop!"

Helmed heads were looking at him all along the line, now—and in the eyes, their whites flashing in the gloom, Gostar saw the grim realization that he was right. Swords gleamed and sang as they were drawn. Rorst took a few lazily shambling steps away from the line just to show that he didn't take orders from a fellow ranker, and feared nothing besides. Then he broke into a trot.

A line of fast-plunging horses leapt out of the north mists, like arrows seeking targets. Atop them rode black-armored warriors, drawn swords in hand.

Gostar yelled in fear and defiance and raised his own sword, whirling it around his head to get the speed he'd need to cleave armor and unhorse a foe. He sprang deftly aside as a charger galloped right at him, then leaned in to strike his blow. It wasn't until he looked up into eyes that were dead and dark that Gostar knew something was wrong, horribly wrong.

The face above his was Estard's . . . and Estard was up in Mistledale this night, with sixty fellow Zhentilar blades, carving out a claim there for the Sword of the South. Who, then, was this . . . ?

Bright pain burst through Gostar as Estard's sweeping blade cut through the light mail under Gostar's left arm and into the ribs and chest beyond—and the wounded man hung for a long, burning moment on that cruel edge of steel. The world grew dark around him as he flew free, the ground so hard and close and . . . more hooves struck him as he fell, crushing him into the turf, but Gostar felt them not. Nor anything else, ever again.

* * * * *

A raw scream split the night. Swordlord Amglar came awake, its echo ringing painfully between his ears. He'd been dreaming of gentler, softer, and more welcoming sounds, by far.

"What befalls, by the gods?" he growled at the darkness, feeling for his sword hilt. Horses were thundering through the camp, and the clash and ring of arms rose around him, mingled with shouts—voices he knew.

They were under attack by a large mounted force!

Amglar cursed, snatched up sword and shield, and stamped feet into his boots, but wasted no time on clothes. His sword squire was snoring like a contented whale at the far end of the tent, with all their armor racked beyond him. It might as well be a realm away.

Boots secure, Amglar spat a heartfelt curse and ran for the back of the tent, where the din was less. The attack was from the north . . . Hillsfar? Who else could muster enough mounted swords to get through the road guard? Elves never fought from the saddle . . . and even if every farmer in Mistledale could find a horse, scarce more than a handful'd be able to stay on it while swinging a blade!

Then he was out into the night, and war was all around him—Zhent blackhelm fighting Zhent blackhelm! Amglar stared around for a moment at running, half-naked men, horses plunging and trotting stiffly among them, stiff black-armored riders—stiff? The swordlord's eyes narrowed.

He ducked back out of the way of a cursing knot of men being dragged behind pikes buried deep in a rider who did not slow or fall from his saddle. The rider clung to the upswept forecantle with one hand while he swung a futile blade back and forth with the other. The horse struggled on under the weight of them all.

Undead. The attackers must be their own men, raised and sent back from Mistledale. Amglar stared around at Essembra, cursed with loud feeling, and started a perilous run toward the red-lantern house the mages had taken as their own. He hoped he'd make it there alive . . . and in time.

He was still running hard, dodging blackhelms who should be dead and frantic quarrels from his own terrified men, when Ondeler appeared at the close-curtained balcony of the Bold Banners and stared at the battle below. There was no hint yet of dawn, but the torches in their tripods still blazed, and in the dancing radiance they cast, the Zhentarim wizard could see the street was choked with struggling men.

"Bane's hand!" Ondeler cursed, amazed and fearful. Who could be attacking them here, in the heart of Essembra? Behind him, a lass appeared on the balcony and gasped. He turned and snapped at her, "My robe! Be quick!"

Scared eyes met his for a moment, and she was gone. Ondeler turned back to the street, crouching low behind the balcony rail, and watched the carnage below. Swordlord Amglar, still a distance off, ran toward the red-lantern house, and then Ondeler heard anxious breathing at his shoulder.

"Lord?" the lass whispered.

He reached out without looking, felt the familiar fabric of his robes, grasped it firmly, and said, "Go now and awaken Myarvuk—the mage with the curling black beard, who came in with me. Bid him come here: Ondeler commands. If he seems unwilling, tell him the seven talons await. Haste, now!"

"Lord, I will," she hissed, and was gone.

Ondeler smiled wryly as he felt for what he'd need. Why was it that ladies of the evening obeyed faster and more willingly than any of the Zhents under him? Perhaps he should take all the women of this house with him, to be his swordcaptains and envoys—if he still had any command at all, after this attack.

He gave up groping for the secret pockets and rose into a cautious crouch to put the robe on. Once it was around him, his fingers knew the places where this and that were stored, and came up with them.

He rose up to his full height, made the pass that touched the two crumbling substances together, and chanted:

"By dung of bat and sulphur's reek
And mystic words I now do speak—
Ashtyn orthruu angcoug laen—
Let empty air burst into—flame!"

As the components dwindled and left his hands empty, one end of the street below obediently erupted in ravening flame, in an explosion that hurled blazing bodies against walls in a gruesome chorus of thuds.

In the flickering aftermath of the fire, Ondeler could see some armored men fighting on despite the flames rising from their bodies. He felt a chill of fear; how—?

Undead. Ah, of course. Most were ashes, but a few were horses and men, bare-boned or burning, still moving, fighting. . . .

Through them stumbled a man with a drawn sword, who wore only boots and a furious expression. Swordlord Amglar had finally reached the red-lantern house. He was heading for the door beneath Ondeler and glaring up at the balcony as he came.

"Crimson curtains, wizard! Are you trying to burn all Essembra down, and us with it?"

"It does seem to work, Swordlord," Ondeler replied with a serenity he did not feel. "Nice uniform, by the way . . ."

Amglar made a certain rude gesture with his sword, but the wizard sneered and raised his hands as if to cast a spell. The Zhentilar snarled and hastened out of view, in under the railing, heading for the door.

"I am here, Ondeler," Myarvuk said from the chamber behind the balcony where the wizard stood.

"Good," said his Zhentarim master. "Did you bring my envoy with you?"

"Envoy?"

"The woman who came for you . . . Belurastra."

"The—?" Wisely, Myarvuk swallowed his astonishment and replied levelly, "She stands beside me, master."

"Get her some riding breeches, boots, a dagger—you know," Ondeler said, eyes still on the street below. "She'll be riding with us."

"Lord?" Belurastra asked in a low, cautious voice, as the apprentice mage hurried away.

"Aye, envoy?"

"I-I am unused to war. Are you sure you want to do this?"

"I am," Ondeler said flatly, watching a dozen men-at-arms hacking undead limb from limb across the street. An attacker rode toward them, and the wizard swept a stone from another hidden pocket, whispered a word over it, and held it out to make an intricate gesture.

An instant later, a boulder the size of a small cottage appeared above the undead mount and rider and crashed to the cobbles, crushing them both into a tangled, bloody mass. Ondeler nodded in satisfaction. "Another fireball may not be necessary," he announced.

"That's good news, wizard," the sour voice of Swordlord Amglar grunted from the room behind. "Your last fire spell sent at least seven of our swords to their graves . . . and a few more bid fair to join them before the day is full."

"Their surviving swordbrothers might just be able to deal with a few zombies," Ondeler said sarcastically. "Weight of numbers and all that."

Amglar ignored this, refusing to rise to the challenge. It was not the first time this arrogant Zhentarim had likened loyal troops of Zhentil Keep to pitiful inferiors not able to match wits or swords with the walking dead. He wondered idly if Ondeler would have dared to act thus if he'd known that Amglar was under orders to report regularly to Draethe, steward of the Inner Circle, on the wizard's performance. Well, no matter; one such report was soon going to be the last, featuring the sorrowful news that Ondeler's own incompetence had brought about his death in battle. Amglar had been considering elegant ways of wording that missive for some time now.

But enough; it was time to play the stone-skulled soldier again. "I've ordered all the troops awakened, fed, and made ready to march," he said heavily. "As soon as the last undead ones are hewn down and burned, we go north. They're probably laughing in Mistledale now, thinking they've the whole day to dig in and await us . . . I'd like to take most of that preparation time away from them."

"*All* the troops?" Ondeler turned, raising an eyebrow. "Even"—he gestured expressively at the boudoir around them, taking in the entire red-lantern house in his meaning—"the rest of the magelings?"

Amglar set his jaw. "The whole host," he said flatly, and held up his sword hilt, the black hand of Bane gleaming in obsidian on the pommel, in silent reminder that he held overall command of the Sword of the South, supreme even in dealings with Ondeler.

The wizard shrugged. "I am ready, as always." As Myarvuk returned with a bundle of clothing, his master said coldly, "Rouse the 'prentices in as much haste as is seemly. Our swordlord is impatient to find other battlefields than this town."

Myarvuk nodded in silence and withdrew, leaving Lady Belurastra curiously eyeing the belt, boots, breeches, and tunic.

"Put them on," Ondeler ordered her as Belurastra stood stroking one of the smooth-carved balls that surmounted her wooden bedposts. She wore a slightly bewildered expression, and made no move to take up the small sheathed dagger that lay atop the heap.

"If you ride nude," Ondeler told her coldly, "you'll be raw before the sun is bright, and of no use to me."

Belurastra raised large, dark eyes to meet his and

asked, "Lord, you are determined to do this?"

"Of course—and if I must tell you again, young Landras of my 'prentices will have the use of your backside to practice his firewhip spell tonight."

The lady escort sighed—it was almost a shiver—and said, "Very well," in a small voice as she undid the lace and let her shift fall to the floor. Ondeler watched it form a puddle of cloth around her feet and turned his head away in satisfaction to glare at the swordlord once more.

Amglar had raised his own blade as if to stare at its edge critically, but the wizard saw his gaze dart to the woman, and smiled. Brains in their codpieces, all of these swordswingers. 'Twas a pity that they were needed at all, to hold what the wizards of the keep won. . . .

The swordlord was a veteran soldier. After that first glance to see what she was doing, he kept his gaze resolutely away from Belurastra until it was too late.

Smoothly, the most beautiful woman in Battledale, senior escort of the Bold Banners house, twisted and pulled on the wooden bedpost ball. It came away, and she reached into the hollow interior beneath it and snatched forth a slim poniard. Tossing the ball on the rumpled bed, she used her freed hand to strip away a wax-sealed sheath from the weapon as she raised it.

In the lamplight, a dark green liquid gleamed on the needle-slim steel. Something—perhaps a momentary flash of reflection—alerted the wizard, and he whirled about to face Belurastra.

"I regret," she said firmly as she plunged the poisoned blade into his right eye, "that I cannot accept the position of envoy to *any* Zhentarim wizard!"

As she jerked the blade free, the swordlord leapt at her. Ignoring Ondeler's crumpling body, he caught her wrist in steely fingers before she could turn the blade on herself.

The deadly poniard hung bloodily just above her bare breast for a perilous moment as they strained against each other—and then the Zhentilar twisted and yanked. Belurastra sobbed in helpless pain, and the blade spun to the floor. It struck the floorboards and stood quivering there.

"Poisoned, Lady?" Amglar asked in low tones. "Bravely done—but to throw your life after his would be a waste . . . a foolish waste." He released her wrist, and the nude woman took a smooth step back.

"You'll not slay me?" she asked, rubbing her wrist.

The Zhentilar officer shook his head. "Nay, Lady, if you agree not to bury that little fang in me—though you'll forgive me if I neglect to mention your name or heroic deed in my reports. Best hide that blade after we're gone, somewhere that doesn't tie it to you. And neither of us speaks of this, or remembers it, for the rest of our days."

The lady escort's eyes widened in sudden hope.

Amglar regarded her gravely. "Well? Have we agreement?"

"We do," Belurastra said, eyes bright with unshed, grateful tears.

He smiled. The heels of his boots clicked together. "As to your query: slay you? Nay; I salute you. You've done something none of us dared to . . . and freed us of his idiocies just when we could no longer afford them."

A smile flickered across her face. Amglar realized it was because of his elaborate dignity—the boots he'd clicked together were all he wore. He grinned back at her, and said, "If you're so adverse to wearing breeches an' all, I'll see if they'll fit me."

Myarvuk came bustling in a few breaths later and looked sharply down at the body sprawled facedown on the floor, blood pooled about its head.

Amglar, resplendent in too short breeches, said briefly, "Spell went wrong. You're spellmaster of this sword now."

Myarvuk brightened. Then his eyes narrowed and he took a quick pace back, out of the swordlord's reach. "How can I be sure your next report to the steward won't contain a note of how I treacherously slew my master? I think I must know where we both stand . . . or if I must ensure that I'm very soon the only one still standing." He raised one hand threateningly, wriggling his fingers in a pantomime of spellcasting.

Amglar shrugged. "Save your spells for the foe, boy. Even if I did report that you killed Ondeler, 'twould not paint you ill in *their* eyes. You know that. Rest assured my reports won't say you had any part of it, unless you want me to write thus. Now stop prancing about trying to impress me, an' see what you can salvage of this carrion's"—he nudged the dead wizard with his foot— "magic, for your own use."

Myarvuk bent to his task eagerly, but stiffened a few breaths later when Amglar growled, "Just one other matter, Spellmaster. You don't need an envoy, an' Battledale doesn't need its best lady escort slain. If we are to have a deal, she stays here, unhurt—your witness, if you ever need one, that you weren't anywhere near when Ondeler so unfortunately left us."

Myarvuk nodded and shrugged. "No argument here, Lord." He bent gingerly to the body. "I don't suppose you—?"

"Nay, boy. Loot your own bodies . . . an' don't be all day about it. The Sword of the South rides out of Essembra as soon as it's light enough to see full quarrel range ahead. There'll be no scouting and creeping about, either. We ride looking for battle. Someone in Mistledale seems to want death, and I mean to bring it to him!"

* * * * *

Ashabenford, Mistledale, Flamerule 16

"Clever battle strategies?" Florin asked, wrinkling his brow. "What clever battle strategies, Torm, do you think a force of seventy—twenty of whom are untrained farmers—can essay on the field? Against seven thousand?"

The thief shrugged. "The mighty battle mastery of gallant Florin Falconhand is a legend from the Dragon Reach to the Storm Horns, and shiny-eyed maidens await, breathless, for whatever Florin may have up his—"

"Don't push it, Torm," Florin said dryly, and snapped his visor down. His next words boomed hollowly from inside his fearsome great helm. "Armed with my reputation, I'm sure we can take the field with sixty-nine rather than seventy."

As the Knights around them chuckled, the ranger stood tall in his stirrups and waved his blade. "Ride out!"

The cry was echoed by the captain of the Riders, and all the horses surged forward eagerly. They were so few that the road took them easily.

More than one watching villager shook his head in disbelief at the calm manner of Mistledale's defenders. One of the riders—the woman with silver hair, who'd sat asleep and nearly naked in the window of the Six Shields several nights running—even laughed merrily at something the thief said to her. The three rangers riding easily behind her exchanged glances and smiles, and spurred their horses to pass her by, giving the watching folk of Ashabenford cheerful waves.

The villagers were not heartened.

One spat into the dust of the road and rumbled, "A handful against thousands! We'd best be packing the night through and try for Cormyr, I guess. . . ."

"There's no safe place to ride to," the woman standing beside him said quietly. "I'll be staying on. They'll cut me down in my own fields, to be sure, but at least I'll die at home, on my own land, an' I'll not have run from anyone."

"Don't be daft! You *want* to die screaming, with half a dozen Zhent blackhelms laughing over you?"

"Nay, but the gods don't seem to care what I want—

an' I don't even know the road to Cormyr. This is as good a place to die as any."

"A thousand warriors, and a thousand more, and many more besides, that merchant said," another villager said softly. "The Riders'll all be slain, sure. Yet hear them laugh!"

"Fools," the first villager grunted. "I'm off to pack. Who's with me?"

"I'll ride to Cormyr with you," said another. "Even if the gods themselves took the field with our Riders an' these Knights of Myth Drannor, there's no hope they'll win against so many."

There were many silent nods at these words, and the villagers sighed and turned away from the road. In the distance, the riders were little more than tiny moving dots now.

The war band left Ashabenford behind in a few breaths, riding easily east down the dale. The morning was chilly but clear, and as Florin looked around at his battle companions and the tranquil, sun-splashed farms on either side, he was happy. Much blood lay ahead—perhaps the ending of all their bright days—and yet he was doing what needed to be done, and folk needed him to do it. What more can anyone ask than to be needed and wanted and free to answer the call?

The captain was guiding her mount closer to his; Florin sidestepped his charger to meet her. "Aye, Lady?"

Captain Nelyssa's gray-green eyes met his, and her thin lips relaxed into a rueful smile. "I fret still, Florin. I know what we must do, and yet, to ride away and leave Ashabenford with not a sword to defend it . . . What if a dozen of them—nay, three of them, with ready blades—sneak past us through the woods? Who will defend the old men and maids then?"

"Harpers, Lady of Chauntea," Florin told her gravely. "Almost twenty of them, come to us from Twilight Hall in Berdusk with all the magic Lady Cylyria can spare. They will fight to hold Ashabenford even if we fall—and they carry the means to farspeak Twilight Hall and call on swift spell aid."

"Aye." The lady paladin looked troubled. "And spells themselves have become chancy things of late."

"Not all spells," Syluné put in as she rode on Florin's other side, "else I'd not be here now."

"And you are very much here," Torm purred from the saddle beside her.

"Stow it, clever tongue," growled the fat priest Rathan, who rode on the thief's other side, saddle creaking under his weight. "Ye're worse than a boar in heat!"

Torm favored his best friend with a complicated gesture that had nothing to do with casting spells.

"Tymora forgive ye," the priest said heavily, crossing his arms disapprovingly across his ample girth, "but I do not. Seven nights of abstinence shall be thy penance, I vow!"

"You'll have to chain me somewhere to manage that—and, of course, catch me first," Torm told him mockingly, ducking his horse smoothly around behind Syluné's mount.

Rathan sighed and waved at him in mock dismissal.

The captain of the Riders watched with interest. "Can yon thief run at any speed?" she asked Florin.

"Watch him during the battle," Florin told her dryly. "There're few folk—even winged things—that can keep up with his retreat."

In reply to this, Torm treated the ranger to an even more intricate gesture. Nelyssa's eyebrows rose. "Droll fellow . . . did he succeed at thieving by outrunning guards?"

"No," Florin told her, not quite smiling. "Just by staying alive this long. And he did that by outrunning husbands."

Nelyssa rolled her eyes. "I can see we're going to have to watch ourselves," she said sarcastically.

Torm turned in his saddle, winked at her, and then

leered at the Shield of Chauntea until she curtly ordered to him to scout ahead.

Laughing, Torm waved and galloped away.

"I'd best go after him to keep him out of trouble," Sharantyr said to Belkram and Itharr. "Come with me?"

"Of course, Shar," they said together, and the three horses leapt ahead as one.

Syluné watched the three rangers pull away and sighed. "I've grown used to them," she told Florin. "See you at the battle." She urged her mount into a canter.

"We're only going to Swords Creek!" Florin said in amused protest. "Torm's probably reached it by now!"

"All the more reason for my being there in haste," Syluné told him severely. "The less time I give him on his own, the less I'll have to patch or set right!" And she was gone, galloping hard through the black-armored ranks of the Riders. Some of them amusedly watched her go; others cast appreciative glances at the silver hair that streamed out behind her as she crouched low over her horse's neck.

"Are your Knights always this pranksome?" Captain Nelyssa Shendean asked Florin quietly, visions of chaos on the battlefield rising before her eyes . . . chaos that could kill them all.

Florin gave the Shield of Chauntea a smile that had cold steel in it. "Usually far worse than this," he told her. "They're taking it gently so as not to upset you, I'd say."

Nelyssa sighed—and then her eyes widened in horror as she realized he wasn't jesting. Her hand went to the electrum earth pendant around her neck and brought it to her lips. "Mother Chauntea, preserve and shield us," she murmured feelingly.

An instant later, the ground rumbled under the hooves of the hurrying horses, rocking them all. As startled men cursed and hauled at their reins around her, Nelyssa looked around at Mistledale with a sudden, dazzling smile. Then she stood up in her stirrups, whooped, drew her sword, swung it in a wild, flashing salute to the sun overhead, and galloped off toward Swords Creek in tearing haste, scattering astonished Riders in all directions.

Florin met Rathan's gaze. He took in the priest's eloquently raised eyebrows, and shrugged. "We seem to have that effect on folks," he observed. "Tymora should be happy."

"Oh, she is," Rathan told him. "Wherever we go, the entire Realms around seems to be plunged into taking wild chances."

"I've noticed that," Florin said in dry tones. "It's not a state of affairs to everyone's taste."

The stout priest of Tymora shrugged in his turn. "Their loss," he said piously, "and Faerûn's gain. May Tymora smile upon ye in the battle, Florin."

"And upon thee, stout heart," Florin told him. Rathan looked sharply at the ranger's innocent smile, and found it not quite innocent enough. He snorted and spurred away, leaving Florin alone with the Riders of Mistledale.

The ranger caught a few questioning looks from the black-armored armsmen around him, and smiled. "Easy, lads. There's no need to rush into our graves. The gods wait for us all."

"There're going to be *gods* at this battle?" one of the Riders asked fearfully.

"Now, lad, let's not get our hopes up," an older Rider said with a grin. "You've got to save *some* excitement for your next battle!"

The younger Rider swallowed. "If I live to see another one," he whispered, "I'll begin to worry about such things, Ostyn."

"That's the spirit!" the older Rider told him. "Cast your worries aside, and ride on into battle!"

The young Rider looked at him with a very white face and said nothing.

"Keep track of kills, shall we, lad?" Ostyn proposed.

"See which of us can slay the most Zhents?"

The younger Rider stared at him for a moment—and then fainted dead away, his eyes rolling up as he slid limply from his saddle.

Florin made a grab for the falling Rider's shoulder, caught him, and snapped, "Get the reins, Ostyn!"

The older Rider did so, deftly, and they guided the mount to an ungainly halt.

The rearguard Riders caught them up. "One down already?" a fat, cheerful woman asked, looking at the limp form across Florin's lap. "We'll have to ask the Zhents to hold a thousand or so swords in reserve."

"You're volunteering to ask them?" Florin chuckled as they righted the young Rider in his saddle and shook him gently back to his senses.

"Never volunteer," Ostyn warned her.

"Actually," she said, indicating the reviving Rider with her sword, "I was going to nominate *him*."

The young Rider's eyes snapped open. He stared at her for a moment, face as white as a priest's vestment—and then, still staring, slid out of his saddle again.

They let him fall to the ground this time, stared at each other, and sighed.

4
Softly Come the Storms

"Hold up, there!"

One moment the road ahead was empty, but the next, a stern-looking, ragged crone with the largest, wartiest nose Torm had ever seen was standing calmly in front of his cantering horse, hand raised, bidding him halt.

Startled, the thief hauled hard on the reins. The war horse under him skidded in the dust as it reared, bugling, and came to a halt, lashing out with steel-shod hooves.

The woman regarded it calmly. "An excitable animal—and you must be the illustrious Torm that the ladies of Twilight Hall have told me so much about." She turned away, hands on hips, and then turned back to him and asked curiously, "Did you really get a certain part of your anatomy caught in a closet door in Zhentil Keep, or was that just a fireside tale?"

Torm sputtered. He'd just noticed that the woman, in her kerchief and ragged dress, was standing in midair, her muddy, ill-fitting boots a good three feet off the ground. A merry gale of laughter came from Sharantyr, Belkram, and Syluné as they reined their mounts in around him. Itharr merely shook his head in smiling silence.

"Well met, Margrueth," Syluné said, eyes dancing in welcome. The old woman looked her up and down.

"Got yerself a new body, have you? Hmmph. No one

offers *me* a new body to replace this old, aching barrel! I could get used to yours, really I could. Silver hair and all."

"You wouldn't want to go through what I have," Syluné told her softly. "Really, you wouldn't."

"Gods, girl—I know that!" Margrueth told her. "I'm old and ugly, not witless! Just envious, that's all."

"If you're a sorceress," Torm asked her curiously, "why don't you choose any looks you want?"

Margrueth glared at him sourly. "That would work for snaring a man for a night of pleasure—*if*, like some folk here, stolen nights of pleasure were what I wanted!"

She let the rebuke hang in the air between them, but Torm merely shrugged, so the old Harper went on. "Sooner or later, though—with my luck, sooner—the one I was with'd see the real me. I'd not hide it, mind; the real me is the one I'm proud of. Some of us value honesty over deceit."

"Some of us must be fools," Torm returned sharply, causing Rathan to chuckle as he slowed his horse to join the group of riders.

"Fool I may be," Margrueth told him, "but I could be in worse straits than this!" She gestured at her nose, and swept her hand down at her fat, shapeless body.

"How?" Torm asked, falling into the trap.

"I could have *your* looks," she told him sweetly, and turned away. Then she turned back again. "It did get caught in that door, didn't it?"

There was a general hoot of laughter, and Torm snarled and urged his mount forward—only to find that the stout old woman flashed through the air to block his way once more.

"I stopped you for a reason, Lord Torm," she told him severely. "Beyond this point our traps start, and the road ceases to be safe—even for thieves with clever tongues and more luck than Tymora gives anyone! Yonder is Swords Creek."

Torm looked at the little rivulet meandering its muddy way across the fields, and asked curiously, "Why Swords Creek for our stand? Is it just a place easily found among all these fields?"

"Mistledale tradition," the captain of the Riders said from behind him. She brought her horse to a halt in a wild thudding of hooves. "On these banks many battles were fought of old."

"And we Harpers've been here since yestereve, preparing it for one more," Margrueth added. "Water spells to make the ground sodden and turn wet spots into bogs to break Zhent cavalry charges, wild magic areas there and *there*—no, Torm, you can't see them— for the foe to halt in, and suchlike."

" 'We Harpers'?" Torm asked. "Aside from you, I can see only two men."

"Ah, that's because they're not done yet," the old woman told him. "The others're in hiding already."

"Hiding? Where?" Torm asked, looking around at apparently empty fields. "Are they all mages using invisibility?"

"No. Not one," she replied with a smile.

Torm shook his head. "There's not a man alive who could hide under my nose between here and that creek."

As the words left his lips, the thief felt a solid tap on his left boot—and his war horse reared again. Cursing, Torm wrestled to keep it from leaping forward; he was struggling to head the snorting beast around, away from the creek, when Captain Nelyssa's strong arm caught hold of the bridle. The paladin pulled and whistled, and Torm's mount quieted immediately—allowing the thief to cleverly fall off.

As he bounced on his belly in the dust, Torm found himself staring eyeball to eyeball with the grinning cause of his upset: a dust-covered man buried neckdeep in the earth, who held a sword, hilt uppermost, in one hand. It must have been what had tapped his boot. In his other gauntleted hand, the man held a shield that had been so thickly covered with turf and grass that it had served to entirely conceal the hole he was crouching in.

"Ye gods!" Torm gasped.

"No, even being one god'd be a promotion, I think," the Harper replied cheerfully. "Fine morning to be out on the grass, 'taint it, Lord?"

The riders all around them roared with laughter at Torm's expression—until the thief buried his nose in the grass and laughed along with them. He nodded to the Harper, rolled to a sitting position, and squinted up at Margrueth. "Right, then, I'll grant you the victory. So tell me how many more of these little holes have you scattered around Mistledale?"

Margrueth shook her head soberly. "That, I'll tell no one. Spying spells that listen to speech from afar aren't easily blocked out in the open."

Her words made them all look around—but aside from the two Harpers in the distance and Florin arriving with the Rider rearguard (one of them looking decidedly green), they could see no man or beast.

"But there's no one!" Torm said, waving a hand.

Margrueth shrugged. "There could be a small army of those mages using invisibility, young man. Think before you speak, and you'll not feel so often chastened."

Torm gave her a dark look, and then shook his head and grinned. "I begin to wish I'd had you as my mother."

"So do I, lad," Margrueth replied, "So do I. Your backside would've seen a lot more heat, and valuables belonging to others and good-looking ladies a lot less, in the years since."

"Hmmm," Torm replied with rueful eloquence, and there was more laughter.

* * * * *

"Oh, *bloody bats!* It's gone wrong again—and they're all *laughing!*"

"Not at ye," the older man said, watching the young man fling down the tangled trip wire in fury, his fingers trembling in agitated excitement. "Easy, lad," the gray-haired Harper ranger added. "Time for all that falling and dancing about an' all later—when ye've a sword in yer hand an' several hundred Zhents taking their turn at ye."

"How can you be so *calm* about it?" his younger companion protested. "We're going to *die!*"

Level brown eyes stared into his. "Aye, so? We all have to, lad, but there's nothing as says we have to behave like craven cattle first." The old man deftly disentangled the thread and held it out. "An' another thing," he continued, "I've been in about forty o' these little affrays before, an' them as came to kill me haven't quite managed the job yet. It might well take 'em as many tries afore they get ye, too! I've seen it all before, lad . . . take heart, and be easy, I say."

The young man stared into those level brown eyes, took a deep breath, and then bent and tied the trip wire—quickly and surely. Then he stepped back with a flourish, smiled tightly at the gray-haired Harper, and said, "Done. I hope you remember where our hide is."

"Here, under my boot," the older man said with a smile. "Another trick you'd do well to remember."

"Bloody bats to you, too," the younger Harper said almost affectionately, scrambling down into the pit they'd dug. The old man followed, waving to Margrueth as he reached for the turf-covered shield that would hide them from the world.

But Margrueth wasn't looking at him. She was looking up, frowning at a raven circling in the bright morning sky high above. She said something to Syluné, who lifted one shapely arm to hurl magic up into the sky—a spell that was never cast.

The raven came out of its lazy circle like an arrow, streaking south and east. But from the blue emptiness high above came another bird, a steel-gray falcon with talons outstretched. It struck like a hammer, and then flapped up and away in triumph amid a cloud of black feathers. For just a moment, the watchers below caught a glimpse of silver hair and tattered black robes, and then the slayer was a falcon once more.

Even as Torm gasped, "The Simbul!" the falcon's kill fell to earth, twisting and growing as it plummeted.

It was the broken body of a black-robed human wizard that crashed into one muddy bank of Swords Creek. The mage flopped bonelessly once, and then lay sprawled and still. One Zhentarim would never spy on Mistledale again.

The old Harper looked back up at the sky. "Well, I lied to ye," he said to the stunned young Harper beside him. "I hadn't seen it all before. I've seen gales and fog and lances of lightning leaping across the sky—but I've never seen it rain wizards before!"

* * * * *

Ordulin, Sembia, Flamerule 16

The morning sun sent bright rays through the casement of tinted glass, casting a many-hued image of light upon the floor furs. That meant it was past time for clients of the Winking Will-o'-the-Wisp Pleasure Palace to be gone so linen could be washed, ladies could bathe and sleep, and coins could be safely exchanged at the nearest bank for soft metal trade tokens stamped with the sunburst symbol of the house.

The occupants of the Red Sash Room on the third floor, however, could not have cared less about the hour—for very different reasons. One of those occupants was Baedelkar the Thaumaturge, rising hope of the Zhentarim, who held the Lady of the Red Sash in his arms as if he never intended to let her go.

Her milk-white skin was soft and smooth against him, and her kisses warm and sweet, with the faintest hint of exotic spices . . . nutmeg? Dunbark? Cinnamon? Ah, but it mattered not.

At that ardent moment, a fist fell upon the other side of the bolted door. It was an imperious fist, but the door was thick and carpeted to steal away sound, and the couple within, seated together on the edge of the large circular bed, did not want to hear it. Their lips met again, and clung.

The fist, however, was persistent. Another blow fell upon the door, and then another, and so on, until they were joined by a softly menacing, magically sent voice: "I know you're within, Baedelkar. The Inner Circle has need of us both, immediately. We've been ordered to join the Sword, somewhere north of Essembra, *right now*."

After a momentary, answering silence (during which the Lady of the Red Sash murmured and moved in Baedelkar's arms) the voice went on: "Neither High Lord Manshoon nor I am used to waiting . . . for an apprentice. Presently one or both of us shall grow weary of it, Baedelkar—and then it will be too late for you to continue as a Zhentarim . . . or anything else."

Baedelkar the Thaumaturge cursed in a soft whisper with feeling, and made as if to pull free . . . but the large, sapphire eyes staring into his pleaded with him, and sweet lips begged, "Just one more kiss, proud lord . . . a brief parting, until we meet again." Those lips lifted longingly toward his.

Baedelkar hesitated for only a moment before he bent his head hungrily forward. It was the last mistake he ever made.

The arms caressing his back seemed stronger and broader, the tongue in his mouth thicker. Starting to choke, the Zhentarim tried to pull away, but found that he was locked in an embrace as unyielding as steel, and tentacles were sliding around him. The eyes so close to his held a horrible flame of triumph as the flesh of her exquisite face bulged and moved, flowing up and over his own visage, covering his nose even as the cold and questing tentacle that had been a velvet-smooth tongue flowed down his throat, choking him. And preventing him from uttering even the simplest spell.

Baedelkar the Thaumaturge struggled in earnest, then, fighting with sudden desperation against the death embracing him. A red roaring rose up in his head, and creeping flesh rolled over his eyes, blotting out his last glimpse of Faerûn—a sun-splashed room and those malevolent, glittering eyes in a face that had become a nightmare of flowing flesh. . . .

Bane aid me . . . Bane aid me . . . Bane . . .

"*Right,* Baedelkar," the cultured voice beyond the door snarled, suddenly losing its drawling grace. "You've defied me long enough! I hope you'll still think she was worth it, after I do—*this!*"

The wizard's body began to shake violently, and pulse with light. The tentacled thing hurriedly flung it back onto the bed and flowed away across the room, to where the wizard's robe lay across a discarded body harness: a thing of leather straps that held a slim satchel of potion vials, several bulging pouches of sundries to spin spells, and . . . a small, well-worn spellbook with battered metal corners.

The creeping thing flowed up and over this heap of magic and, without slowing, turned and slithered along the wall. In its wake, the wizard's belongings were gone, the side chest bare. Meanwhile, the body on the bed jerked and thrashed in spell thrall, and then leapt up into the air once and crashed down in limp silence.

As tentacles hurriedly tore open the casements and let the chill air of morning into the room, there was a snarl of fury from beyond the door—and then a muttered incantation. It rose to a singing final word, and then came ominous silence.

The monstrous, shapeshifting mass flowed out the window and up the wall outside, disappearing from the room seconds before the gilded door of the Red Sash Room burst apart in a rain of dust and splinters.

Nentor Thuldoum of the Zhentarim stood in the doorway, blinking in incredulous rage.

"You worm! You disobedient ti—" Nentor's fury fled as he saw what lay on the bed. His jaw dropped, and he stared down in horror at the riven remains. His spell had scorched Baedelkar with a lashing lightning, but should not have eaten away body and brains from within, leaving behind a shriveled husk . . . and empty eye sockets.

* * * * *

Swords Creek, Mistledale, Flamerule 16

Thuds and splinterings resounded across Swords Creek as the defenders of Mistledale drove tree trunks into the ground in an outward curve west of the stream. A steady stream of wagons was creaking east along the road from Ashabenford as Riders watched the land to the east for any sign of the approaching foe.

"Leave openings there and *there*," Kuthe directed as Riders swarmed past him in pairs, carrying logs. Beyond them, more of the black-armored men were hewing the ends of the sloped stakes into sharp points. "I hope we'll need room to ride out into the fray in force."

"*I* hope the Zhents fall dead of the blistering plague and we don't have a fray at all," a farmer muttered, snapping his reins to begin the run back to town for more supplies. He stood up as the empty wagon rattled away, looking around the busy camp, and shaking his head. Not a hundred swords to defend Mistledale against—how many? Two, three thousand, or more? The word from Essembra was that they'd outgrown all the beds in the place a tenday ago, with not a third of the force mustered. The Sword of the South, indeed— and they'd have a Zhentarim wizard or three with them, too.

He looked back at the camp once more and spat

thoughtfully into the rising road dust. An army this small wouldn't delay the Zhent host more than an hour or two on its march to Mistledale. Death might well come for him before dusk today—but where was there to run? He couldn't pluck up his steading and stow it in a pack to take with him. Stand or fall, it'd be here, in Mistledale, where he'd lived his life. The farmer slowed the wagon to make his trip back down the dale as long as he could—it might be his last look around at the finest place to dwell in all Faerûn. He tried not to think about the likelihood that by sundown tomorrow it might also be the finest graveyard in Faerûn.

A steel-gray falcon circled high in the cloudless sky overhead, for all the world as if it was taking interest in the encampment taking shape by the creek. The farmer squinted up at it, spat again, and went down the dale toward Ashabenford, where the high councilor would be waving his black scepter and barking orders. Heedless of him, wagoners would load in haste and head east, and fleeing townsfolk would drive overloaded carts west.

The breezes died away to the softest of stirrings, what the folk of the dale called a ghost's kiss. By the banks of the creek, a tall, broad-shouldered man in gleaming plate armor looked around the palisade of wooden fangs and saw that it was now almost a full circle. He nodded in satisfaction and turned to where a farmer stood by his laden wagon.

"Bring the tents," Florin Falconhand said to the man. "We'd best get started."

Kuthe frowned at the tall ranger. "This soon?"

"I doubt they'll attack before dark," the Knight of Myth Drannor replied. "Before they could get here, it'll be sundown; they'd have to charge with the setting sun in their eyes."

Kuthe grunted his agreement and turned away. "No cooking fires until the tents are up!" he bellowed, "and don't drop those barrels of beer or I'll leave you to face the men who have to go thirsty!"

"Noisy, isn't he?" Torm muttered, critically inspecting the wicked-looking point he'd whittled on the end of one stake.

"A paragon of authority," Rathan grunted, taking a swig from his belt flask. "I've no quarrel if he's as much in evidence when we start hacking at each other in the mud and the blood." He took another pull at the flask, which gurgled.

Torm looked up at the sound. "Hey! Give that here," he suggested, extending a hand.

"What's this?" Kuthe growled, striding past. "Drinking?" His eyes flashed.

"He sees the flask and instantly knows what we're doing!" Torm gasped in mock fear. "Can no man stand against this tower of perception?"

"I fear not," Rathan growled. "He makes my boots quake, and me in them. Wits as keen as a sword blade—and tongue sharper, too!" Both Knights threw up their hands as if in awe and cowered, wailing.

"Bah!" the Rider officer snarled, and turned away. "Adventurers!"

"Bah!" Torm called after him, his mimicry perfect. "Stiff-necked local constabulary!"

Kuthe stiffened as more than one of the Riders around them chuckled, but did not turn around. After a moment, he strode on.

"Hind end of a blind boar," Torm muttered conversationally as they moved to the next stake.

"Torm's entertaining himself as usual, I see," Sharantyr observed to Syluné as they worked on their own stakes not far away.

The Witch of Shadowdale grinned. "He doesn't know it yet, but I volunteered him for digging the privies."

Sharantyr sighed. "*You* use the ladies' first, then. I've no wish to be the one who tries out his latest collection of 'humorous' traps."

"Does he do that to the pit for the men, too?" Itharr

asked, looking up from the fire pit he and Belkram were digging. Sharantyr looked over at him and nodded. "Ah, thanks for the warning," the Harper grunted, and knelt to begin lining the pit with stones.

A pair of men in black armor emblazoned with the white horse of Mistledale approached with two large, rope-wrapped canvas bundles. "Your tent," the Riders told Itharr, "and one for the ladies."

"One is all we'll need," Sharantyr said serenely, moving to the last unsharpened stake. "I'm used to the snores of these two by now."

The Rider raised his eyebrows and looked her up and down. Sharantyr raised her own eyebrows in reply, and said coolly, "I'm an adventurer, remember?"

The man rolled his eyes and turned away, face expressionless behind his bristling mustache. His companion growled "Lucky dogs" quite distinctly as they went on down the line of stakes.

"If you knew," Belkram said to the Riders' backs. "If you only knew."

"I heard that," Syluné said warningly, and both Harpers looked up at her with such looks of bewildered innocence that she giggled.

Sharantyr puzzled out how the ropes were tangled, and got the tent unrolled. She hummed a merry tune as she laid it out, shaking her head to clear her nostrils of the strong—and expected—reek of mildew. Such things were always put away damp. She critically surveyed the forest-green tent and its white horse blazon. "Does someone in the dale run a camp for bored Sembian nobles?"

"Aye," Belkram told her as the two Harpers came to join her, expertly plucking the poles out of the heart of the rumpled canvas. "But they're under the misapprehension that they're just housing the short-coin laborers who arrive each harvest to help get the crop off the fields . . . it's not until they see their hired help at work in the fields that they realize how many bored Sembian nobles they're carrying."

Sharantyr chuckled at that as Belkram held the tent up with one pole, and Itharr crawled inside to raise it from within. "I could get used to having both of you gallant blades around," she said affectionately, fielding the tangle of tent rope that Syluné tossed to her.

"Just two of us? Is that enough to keep up with you?" Belkram asked with a grin.

"On some mornings," Sharantyr said, thrusting over his head the emptied sack that had held the tent pegs. "On some mornings."

"Mmphffh," he replied firmly.

"Exactly what I was going to say," Itharr agreed, head emerging from the half-raised tent. "Mmphffh."

Sharantyr and Syluné sighed, smiled, and shook their heads in unison.

"Get him a bag, too," Torm suggested, pointing at Itharr as he walked past. "Me, too, and Rathan. After all, you know what they say—all men're the same with a bag over—"

"*Enough,* Torm!" Syluné said, and snapped her fingers. The thief vanished in midstep, and they heard his surprised "Hoy!" of protest from the far end of the camp as he reappeared, looked around, and started back toward them.

"Poor Torm," Sharantyr said, watching him. "I wonder if he'll ever grow into dignity and polite manners? I suppose he must grow up someday."

"For some of us," Syluné observed serenely, "it's a long walk."

*　*　*　*　*

Battledale, Flamerule 16

There was a sudden flash of emerald radiance from the empty saddle ahead, and Swordlord Amglar stiffened, hand going to the hilt of his sword—just in case.

Spellmaster Myarvuk rode ahead of the hitherto

unladen horse, the mount under him linked to it by a long lead. Now he was twisting around to see what had befallen, clinging to his saddle in an ungainly attempt not to fall off. Amglar watched him in grim amusement. These wizards all rode with the grace and balance of lumpy sacks of feed—and if the expression on Myarvuk's face was any guide, about as much comfort.

As both men stared at the green light pulsing and growing stronger in the saddle, Amglar watched the Zhentarim mage's tense face . . . until, suddenly, he knew the new thing he was seeing there: fear.

A second empty-saddled horse pulled its lead free and galloped off to the right. The swordlord's gaze darted to it, but no radiance or other sign of magic appeared. If the gods smiled, perhaps there'd only be one high Zhentarim joining them.

Of course, given what utter ice-hearted bastards all powerful mages of the Black Network were, one was more than enough.

The emerald light had built into the shape of a seated man now, and the swordlord sighed amid the endless thunder of hooves. The rest of his time with the Sword of the South was not going to be enjoyable—and might well encompass the rest of his life, given the ruthless and sensitive nature of senior Zhentarim.

The green radiance flashed and faded, revealing a richly cloaked man who sat his saddle as if he'd always been there—and was already looking grimly about, his face as black as old night.

At least this one could ride. Amglar forced a grim half smile onto his own face as the Zhent wizard turned to look behind him.

"For the glory of Zhentil Keep," the swordlord said in formal welcome. The wizard merely nodded curtly and turned his head away. Oh, joy. Getting this one to take the slightest notice of orders was going to be nigh impossible. Best start wading into the blood now, then. Amglar reined his horse in beside the galloping wizard.

"Lord Manshoon sends his greetings, Spellmaster Thuldoum," Amglar said loudly, keeping his voice calm and unhurried. Young Myarvuk had lost his title, of course, the moment his superior here had arrived.

"Give me his message," Thuldoum said in bored tones, extending a gloved hand. "I *do* hope to find it still sealed."

"No message," Amglar returned calmly as they thundered on up the road toward the Standing Stone. "Manshoon farspoke me, and bade me pass on his feelings." If this warning had no effect, things were going to be a royal muddle from now on.

"I see," the senior Zhentarim replied in tones of clear disbelief. Amglar shrugged, letting the man see his gesture. Of course, most Zhentarim would see such nonchalance as the bravado of a fool, not the confidence of a man secure in his power. He was just going to have to educate this one differently.

"Myarvuk," the new arrival snapped grimly, obviously short on patience, "Baedelkar will not be joining us. Your duties will now include his."

The younger Zhentarim nodded in expressionless silence; Amglar knew he was wondering if this cheerful newcomer had been the cause of Baedelkar's disappearance—and if one Myarvuk would be the next wizard to drop out of sight forever when Nentor Thuldoum grew displeased.

He'd never worked with the man before, but knew that Thuldoum had been deadly in battle while riding out of the Citadel of the Raven against brigands, Thentian freebands, and all manner of goblinkin and monsters of Thar. Later the senior Zhentarim had come to Zhentil Keep to train battle mages for the Network; "Dull Doom" he'd been to his apprentices, due to his dry, studious manner and the short, ruthless temper it concealed. Not a man to cross. Nonetheless, Myarvuk, son of Thaelon, was going to do just that. Starting, in a small way, now.

"What was Baedelkar's fate?" Myarvuk asked, with the most casual 'I'd better know' tone he could muster.

"Dead," Nentor said shortly, "slain in his bed by"—he shrugged to indicate that his next words were a guess—"something he must have tried to summon." His mouth shut like a falling portcullis, making it plain that no more would be forthcoming about his absent apprentice. Then he turned his head to glare at Amglar again.

"Swordlord," he snapped, making it sound as if he'd been asking for it repeatedly and was growing impatient, "I await your report of the doings of the Sword thus far. Come up here where I can see you."

Amglar inclined his head in slow, silent acquiescence, and spurred his mount forward. Yes, it was going to be a *long* road to Shadowdale. . . .

5

Glorious Victories Are
Elusive Things

Tower of Ashaba, Shadowdale, Flamerule 16

"Snug, my lord?" Shaerl asked, tightening the straps
that held the plates around Mourngrym's upper thighs.

"Keep your fingers on the buckles," the lord of
Shadowdale told his wife with an affectionate grin,
reaching down to tousle her hair. They were alone in
their bedchamber in the Tower of Ashaba, hiding
Mourngrym's wounds from the wagging tongues of
rumor. He didn't want half of Shadowdale fleeing because they'd heard he was dead.

It had been a very near thing. Without Elminster,
Storm, or Syluné to hand, with the temples already
crammed to the rafters with wounded, and with Lhaeo
busy ransacking the heavily trapped cellars of Elminster's Tower in search of healing potions and weapons,
there were few people left in the dale who could deal
with wounds caused by poisoned blades. A white-faced
Shaerl had spent a long evening cutting open her lord,
tears and his blood mingling together on her face as she
brushed errant locks of hair out of her eyes and bent repeatedly to her grisly task.

Mourngrym winced as she forced a sideplate over the

quilted undertunic on his ribs, which bulged where they shouldn't because of the bandages beneath. "Sorry, Mourn," she muttered, feeling his muscles tighten under her hands.

The lord of Shadowdale let out a sigh. "Don't be. Without you I'd be dead right now, and the dale fallen."

Shaerl made a rude noise. "Such dramatics! Do you think I'd flee or put a dagger in my heart if you died, when your killers and those who sent them will come marching into my reach in a few days?"

Mourngrym smiled and put out a hand—the one without the gauntlet—to the side of her face, tilting her jaw up so that he could kiss her.

His wife, the fiery temper of her noble Rowanmantle upbringing lurking not far behind her eyes, kissed him with ardent passion, locking her fingers in his hair to ensure that this wouldn't be a brief brush of lips.

"*Try* not to get carved up this time," she chided him when she released him at last. "I don't want to spend another night like yestereve."

"As the dancer said to the high priest," Mourngrym murmured. Shaerl sighed at this, her lord's habit of lame Waterdhavian humor, and handed him his helm, sword, and remaining gauntlet.

Nodding in acknowledgment, the lord of Shadowdale said, "Now I really must get to horse." He strode away—but before he'd taken three paces, she'd slipped around to bar his path, a slim but imperious hand slapped hard against the Amcathra arms emblazoned on his breastplate.

"Sword and gauntlet on and in place before you go out that door—and the helm before you set foot outside the tower. I don't want to be married to a headless man. They're not quite talkative enough."

Mourngrym sighed, smiled, and did as he was bid. It was easiest to comply, as always, and his sharp-tongued mate was right—as always. Who was to say a Zhent agent, or merely someone in need of the coins they'd pay, wasn't lurking a bowshot away from the tower, or in a balcony above the courtyard, awaiting his chance?

These past two rides Zhent raiders had kept Shadowdale's defenders busy fighting off several attempts to burn the dale's smithy and granaries. There had also been the setting of several fires along the roads into the dale, no doubt to widen them and rob defenders of any cover; the attempt to taint the River Ashaba upstream by dumping carrion into it; and the poison dumped into the well of the Old Skull Inn—which had forced Lhaeo to call on the Simbul and endure her acidic lecture on placing a guard over basic necessities. The problem was that Mourngrym had too few competent guards to do that, let alone hold Shadowdale against thousands of well-equipped Zhentilar troops led by gods-knew-how-many Zhent priests and mages.

"Wouldn't it be nice," he asked Shaerl as he settled the sword on his hip and she surveyed the result critically, "if some mad god or other would just crush Zhentil Keep to rubble for us?"

"I'll see to it," she told him briskly, "but I'd take it more kindly if they'd settle for simply crushing the hosts on their way here to slaughter us . . . and if I knew where Elminster was just now."

"Boo!" breathed an all-too-familiar voice on the back of her neck.

Shaerl shrieked as she leapt forward into Mourngrym's arms. The lord of Shadowdale began to laugh helplessly, shaking his lady—and she broke free and spun like a dancer on one small bare foot to confront the Old Mage, her eyes snapping with anger.

"Must you always creep up on folks invisibly and then try to startle them with grand entrances?"

"Everyone needs a hobby, look ye," Elminster said, regarding her with eyes that sparkled in amusement, "and that's one of mine."

"Well, find another! Gods! My heart's still—feel it! It's—"

"No, love," Mourngrym said hastily as the gleam in Elminster's eye grew brighter, "you don't want to make that sort of offer! Not with Elminster!"

Shaerl turned on him. "And *you!* Laughing at my discomfort, like a boy playing in the street! You ought to be—"

"Somewhere quieter," Mourngrym said sarcastically, striding past her, "like the heart of a battle with the entire Zhent army!"

Shaerl made a gesture in his direction. Mourngrym waggled one steel-clad finger at her in mock admonishment, and went out.

The lady of Shadowdale sighed away her exasperation and turned back to Elminster. "Be welcome, Old Mage," she said softly. "I'd appreciate a chance to talk about what lies ahead for us, if you've the time."

" 'Tis why I came," Elminster rumbled, "now that my work at the Standing Stone is done: three arrow swarms, and a little something extra." He went straight to Mourngrym's most comfortable chair and sat down with a grunt of pleasure, swinging his feet up over one of its massive arms.

Shaerl smiled at that and started toward the sideboard where the decanters of wine awaited—but she'd taken only a few steps before a full goblet of her favorite vintage came gliding up to hang in the air in front of her. She took it, turned, and saw Elminster raising an identical drink in salute. "To a lady who does not take serious contributions from idiots," he announced.

Shaerl grinned, shook her head slightly, and returned his toast. "To a wizard who takes more delight in misbehaving than does a small child—and is all the more welcome here for it."

They both drank. Shaerl discovered the bottom of her glass, shrugged, and continued to the sideboard to take up the decanter. She had a feeling she was going to want a lot more of this before they were done. . . .

* * * * *

The Standing Stone, the Dales, Flamerule 16

"Dusk comes swiftly," Swordlord Amglar told the two wizards, pointing at the red sun glimmering low in the west.

"We press on," Nentor Thuldoum told him coldly. "If we try to camp at the Standing Stone, we'll be in the trees or strung out along three roads—and we can be attacked along each one."

"So much is common knowledge," Amglar agreed calmly. "I merely wish to point out that if we press on to Mistledale, it'll be dark by the time we ride out of the trees—ideal conditions for our foes to ambush us."

The spellmaster turned on him with menacing slowness. "Are you trying to tell me what to do?"

"Yes," Amglar said evenly, locking eyes with him. "That's exactly what I'm trying to do. Manshoon *does* expect you to take orders from me; his description of you, as I recall, was 'a fool, but a biddable fool.' Shall I report to him that he was wrong?"

Thuldoum held his eyes for a long, cold moment as their saddles creaked under them. Myarvuk, riding just ahead, hummed a tune, trying to pretend he could hear nothing of this. Thuldoum said softly, "I'm watching you, Swordlord. Watching and waiting for the slightest slip, the smallest excuse . . . be careful. Be very, very careful."

Amglar raised his eyebrows, but his face remained expressionless. "I always am," he said, and the spellmaster could have sworn that the warrior's eyes held a glint of mocking laughter.

Then they were slowing to round the turn onto the Moonsea Ride under the watchful bulk of the ancient Standing Stone. There was a brief confusion as mounted Zhentilar armsmen looked back expecting orders to halt, heard nothing, and rather tentatively continued, heading west toward Mistledale.

The rings on the spellmaster's hands winked with sudden radiance, and the air all around was filled with humming arrows. Shafts leapt from the trees on their left, hissing into startled men and their mounts alike, easily piercing black Zhentilar armor.

"We're under attack!" someone bellowed.

"Dismount! Into the trees there—*charge!*" Amglar shouted, pointing with his sword. "In at them!"

His orders made Spellmaster Thuldoum turn to him, and Amglar saw that the wizard was staring down at his rings in astonishment. As they looked at each other, the rings flashed again—and another volley of arrows came hissing out of the trees on the other side of the road.

Amglar's eyes narrowed as he ducked low on his horse's neck, but it was too late to stop the rush of furious armsmen into the trees, charging in as he'd ordered. Horses screamed and reared, and men toppled from saddles everywhere in the tangled intersection. The swordlord fought to stay in his saddle.

"Back, mages!" he bellowed, waving with his sword toward the Standing Stone itself. "Back!"

By some favor of the gods, neither Zhentarim had been hit; they spurred their horses after him, ruthlessly riding down armsmen in their haste. "Swordcaptains, to me!" Amglar roared as he reached the trees to the east, his eyes on the woods to the north. If his hunch was right, there'd be no more arrows from there—nor any other attack.

"Is this *your* doing, mage?" he snarled when a frightened-looking spellmaster rode up to him.

"No!" Thuldoum barked. "If these arrows are spellborne, it's not a magic I know! I—"

His rings flashed once more. He was staring down at them in horror when the trees on the eastern side of the road erupted in clothyard shafts! An arrow took Amglar through the shoulder, and another three thudded into his charger. Yelling in pain and fury, he flung himself free as it bucked and went down, crashing over backward atop an unfortunate armsman.

He hit the road hard and bounced in the dust, winded. Myarvuk slid from his saddle, half a dozen shafts standing out from his body and a glazed, lifeless stare in his eyes. Gods spit on it—the truly biddable mage down already!

As Amglar fought for his breath, arrows flared into flames and then nothingness around the spellmaster, who must have some sort of magical shield against them—of course, Amglar thought sourly. But the volley tore into the officers turning in answer to his call. The intersection was full of rolling, maddened horses and sprawled, trampled bodies . . . in just a few breaths half an army had been reduced to bloody chaos.

"Halt!" Amglar roared, struggling to his feet, arm and shoulder burning. He ran into the path of the second 'lance,' just as they came thundering up the road to see what had occurred. "Halt!"

He staggered hastily back—a thousand cantering horses can't stop immediately—tripped on a body, and with a roar of pain fetched up against a tree.

"Sir?" A swordcaptain asked, beside him. Through red mists of pain, Amglar set his teeth and looked up. Blood was coursing down his arm, bright red on the black armor; he clutched at his arm and snarled, "Get a horn and call the rally and retreat to those I sent into the woods. They'll not find a foe unless they run on all the way to the dale! Then relay the order to halt! On your way, send three or four more captains to me!"

The man nodded and hurried away, wasting no time on salutes or words. Amglar glared after him. Good. At least one Zhentilar knew how to be an officer; he'd have to remember that man's face.

Feeling the spellmaster's eyes on him but paying no attention, Amglar strode to meet the officers who were hurrying toward him. "Clear this place," he ordered.

"Drag everything up the north road, and set torches; we'll strip the bodies later. Slay any horse that can't stand on four good legs. Let no man touch the fallen mage—that task is for the spellmaster alone." Without turning his head, he snapped, "Thuldoum! Be about it."

The Zhentarim said nothing, but Amglar heard the creaking of leather as the wizard dismounted, and a snort of irritation from the man's horse as someone else took the reins.

"I want you to know," the spellmaster said in a low, fast voice, "that I had no part in this attack. It was not my doing—and nothing I carry has any power to hurl arrows anywhere!"

"I know, mage," Amglar said shortly. "It was some sort of arrow spell—three spells, belike—set to go off when something enchanted passed by: your rings. They're probably rolling around laughing in Mistledale right now. See to your dead comrade."

He walked away without looking at the Zhentarim and headed to the front of the lance that had halted on the road. He would tell them to dismount and set a watch in the trees in case there were archers or rangers lurking out there.

Dead men lay heaped underfoot. Someone was groaning weakly under a pile of bodies off to the right. Amglar scowled. A swordlord's lot is not a happy one.

* * * * *

Swords Creek, Mistledale, Flamerule 16

"Who goes?" The challenge came out of the night. The voice sounded young and eager, and its owner was probably holding a loaded crossbow. Jhessail sighed and spoke quickly before Illistyl or Merith could say anything smart. "Owls are blue tonight," she told the darkness calmly. "Kuthe's patrol, with three Knights of Myth Drannor. I am Jhessail of Shadowdale."

"Pass, Lady," the voice said, sounding suddenly respectful, even wistful.

An admirer, then, probably a Harper. Merith laid a hand on his lady's thigh and squeezed. Leaning close, the elf whispered, "Men who lust after you are everywhere in the Realms, it seems. Truly I am fortunate to have arrived in your arms first, and—"

"Oh, do belt up, dear," Jhessail said, grinning.

"Aye," Illistyl's sharp tones came out of the close darkness on Jhessail's other side. "And forthwith, before I spew!"

"If ye can stand the company of the two blades she's picked up, who both fancy themselves clever—Belkram and Itharr of the Harpers—Sharantyr's left room and a warm fire for ye," the gruff tones of Rathan came to them out of the night.

"Kind of her," Jhessail said, "but we're going right back out after we feed and hobble our horses. We're going to be a little surprise in the Zhentarim backside on the morrow!"

"Ye'll probably lift a few eyebrows hereabouts, too, if ye try charging on hobbled horses!" Rathan chuckled.

"We're leaving the horses here, you dolt," Jhessail told him affectionately. "Where's Torm?"

"He felt restless, and wanted to go 'exploring,' as he put it," the burly priest replied. "So I gave him a little too much wine and smote him one. He'll wake before dawn, in *just* the right mood for a good battle."

"I'm glad it's you who shares a tent with him," Illistyl said feelingly.

"I'll be only too happy to surrender my sleeping furs to thee, gentle maid," Rathan said eagerly, "and I'm sure Torm won't object in the slightest!"

"Ah, *ha!*" Illistyl agreed flatly. "I doubt he'd mind, indeed." She rode on, turning to add, "I'll save my furious defenses for the fray tomorrow."

"I rather think we all will, lass," the elderly voice of a dale farmer came gruffly out of the nearby darkness.

"Or we'll be dead before another night comes down on the Realms."

* * * * *

The Standing Stone, the Dales, Flamerule 16

"Galath's Roost is the only logical place to camp for the night—that's the problem," Swordlord Amglar said to the silent ring of officers around the map.

"What problem?" Spellmaster Thuldoum said sharply. For some hours now, he'd been trying to overcome his own fright and whispers of incompetence or disloyalty by playing the sharp-tongued aggressor. Everyone in earshot was tired of it.

"I mean, wizard," Amglar explained in wearily patient tones that brought secret smiles to the lips of a few swordcaptains, "that it's the place our foes expect us. Just as they knew we'd pass by this spot."

He waved at the road behind them and the dark and silent bulk of the Standing Stone beyond. Three hundred armsmen and six score war horses lay dead along the north road, heaped cottage-high under the stars . . . and already the wolves were howling, nearer each time. Amglar tried not to think of the fallen. The dead were beyond his orders; it was the living he had to worry about.

"So?" the Zhentarim said coolly. "They hardly have enough blades to hold a ruin against us, even in the dark. And my spells can make it bright as day, so our archers can keep to the night and strike down well-lit targets as they please."

"I'm thinking there'll be traps there, not defenders," Amglar said heavily. "I don't suppose you can see into the place from here, can you? Or better: let our veteran swordcaptains look at things. They'll know traps better than either of us." To say anything else might make this spellmaster hurl spells in a fury, and after what had befallen so far, that would be all the Sword of the South needed.

The Zhentarim was shaking his head. "No, it's much too far to send an eye. I'd have to have seen the hold before with my own eyes to scry it with any of the other magics I carry."

"You've *nothing* that can help us?" One of the three lancecaptains said, not bothering to keep the contempt out of his voice. The spellmaster made a silent show of looking him up and down and committing his face to memory, but all of them knew any hostile move the wizard made in this gathering would result in his death. Not a few of the personal belt daggers around the map would be poisoned, too.

"You're a brave man, sir of the lance," Nentor Thuldoum said in silken tones, "if a foolhardy one. A wizard of the Network *always* has something that can be turned to use, and it's always more than his foes—and others," he added pointedly, staring around at the impassive soldiers' faces, "expect. I have a spell ready that can create a beast to explore the ruins for us . . . but only I will be able to see through its eyes."

"And if there's an enemy wizard at the Roost?" Amglar asked quietly. "Will such a one be able to see you through it—and send any magic through you, to strike us here?"

"No," the spellmaster said. "In fact, it's unlikely that any wizard who meets my creature will escape alive."

"Cast your spell, then," Amglar ordered, his voice riding over a murmur of disbelief at the wizard's words from the officers. "The sooner we know, the sooner we can act."

"Stand back," the wizard said curtly. "All of you." He drew himself up and glared around at the black-armored men—and their sullen faces. "Let no man disturb my casting, on pain of death. Lord Manshoon's standing orders apply here as in the Keep."

By the time the last of those words left his mouth,

Nentor Thuldoum stood alone in the center of an open space perhaps twelve paces across, ringed by a warily silent audience. He looked around at them and smiled. Good; the more who saw this, the better.

From the safe pouch at his belt, Thuldoum drew a small sphere of blown glass that held a veined, gelatinous mass trapped in its heart. He held it on his fingertips, and for the benefit of the assembled soldiers murmured an incantation that was far longer and more impressive than it needed to be.

Then he made a dramatic and totally unnecessary gesture, and blew the sphere gently out of his palm. It plunged to the hard-trodden earth in front of him and burst with a tiny singing sigh.

A drunken man's nightmare boiled up from where it had been, growing with frightening speed, rearing up until it was larger than a horse. Men gasped and backed away in gratifying alarm; the spellmaster smiled tightly at them and pointed west and a little south, into the trees. His creation gathered itself up and drifted obediently off across the road, soldiers scrambling to get out of its way.

It was a shapeless bulk of translucent gray-white jelly that swam and flowed constantly. Countless staring eyes and silently snapping mouths slid across its changing outer surface, appearing and disappearing with bewildering speed.

"A mouther!" one of the veteran armsmen gasped. The drifting thing did look like the deadly gibbering mouther of yore . . . though no gibberer had ever risen man-high off the ground and flown about at a wizard's bidding, so far as Thuldoum knew.

Then it was gone into the trees, and his world became a place of dark trunks and branches and shifting shadows, looming up before him, thick and tangled. . . .

"Bring me a seat," he said, not breaking his vision from his creation, "and something safe to drink. Someone who knows traps and castles should stand by me, too—we'll both have questions to ask each other when my creature reaches the Roost."

* * * * *

Galath's Roost, Mistledale, Flamerule 16

Galath's Roost had been blasted apart four centuries ago by mages who knew their business. Since that day, the small keep atop its stony height had been swallowed by the forest. Massive duskwoods and cedars rent what was left of its walls and yet held them up, their trunks cupping chambers that were open to the sky and walls that ran to nowhere. Their leaves all but hid the riven keep from view . . . but if one stood a little way off and in just the right spot, the faint flicker of a fire glimmered through the trees.

The room whence the fire came had one wall open to the night—but the two pilgrims who'd built the fire and now huddled around it had good and prudent reasons for not choosing any of the better-preserved rooms in the Roost. They were discussing that now.

"A good job, they did," the taller one said grudgingly.

"You're certain they left this room safe?" asked the other, clutching his expensive talisman of the god under his chin. The gilded image of Tyr's warhammer and scales shone back the firelight, serene and unchanging.

"All but *that* door," the first one replied, pointing. "If you go out that, a very large crate of rubble will fall on you."

"Ah," said the other. "I'd best go water the gods' gardens out the way we came in, then." He sipped from a battered tin cup, making no move to get up, and added, "A good thing we found that cellar, or they'd have seen us, sure."

"That was no cellar," his tall, lean companion chuckled, scratching under his much-patched tunic. "That was the castle cesspit."

"What?" the shorter pilgrim said, staring down at his boots and then at his elbows and his cloak—but finding no foulness. "Is my nose as bad as all that, then?"

"After four hundred years," his companion told him kindly, "dung is just dust."

"Huh," the shorter pilgrim agreed, and launched into a dry chuckle that ended in a fit of coughing. "I guess the Realms're covered deep in old dung, then. Urrrgh. Aiiuh." These last two comments accompanied a grunting attempt to rise—an attempt that ended in a disgusted wave of one dirty hand, and a return to a more or less comfortable lounging position against a pile of moss-cloaked rubble.

In all the activity, neither devotee of Tyr noticed a dark, many-eyed bulk slithering silently out of the night, over the stones in the ruined end of the room. As they decided aloud that a prayer to the Lord of Justice might be prudent before they wandered off into the woods to relieve themselves, the thing of eyes and jaws crept unnoticed toward them.

" 'Tis your turn to begin the devotion," the shorter pilgrim mumbled.

"Do it be in truth, Jarald? Or've you just forgotten the words to the Call of the Just again?"

"I've not! I remember them well!" the shorter pilgrim said heatedly. "Will you plague me with the misdeed of one night down all the years to come?" Behind him, unseen in the flickering confusion where the firelight played on a broken end of stone wall, something that swam with many eyes and hungry mouths reared up, looming darker and larger, drifting tendrils of itself across the ceiling to hang above the two oblivious pilgrims.

"I don't rightly know," his taller companion said, with a slow grin. "How long did you plan to go on living?"

From the darkness above came a sudden swift movement. . . .

6
War Comes to Mistledale

The fire was dying down; he'd have to make this swift. The taller pilgrim cleared his throat, lurched forward from a seated position to his knees, and began. "Hear us, O Great Balance, as we hear thee! From our knees we cry to thee*eee!*"

His words ended in a surprised cry as he raised his eyes to the firelit ceiling—and found himself staring at an oozing, descending blob of jelly that swam with jaws and eyeballs! And all of those eyeballs were staring at him!

The horrid thing lunged at him, seven or more sets of fangs biting the air hungrily as they came. The pilgrim flung himself backward and to his feet, out of reach, and the thwarted reaching thing turned with fearsome speed and struck at the other pilgrim.

The shorter man was already on his feet, watching the monster with a surprisingly calm expression of curiosity on his face. He sidestepped the attacking tendril—and found a second questing arm reaching down, almost upon him. He was trapped between them. As they reached in, he shrugged and grimaced.

An instant later, the many-fanged mouths opened wide for their first savage strike—but the pilgrims were gone. Two clouds of dark, whirling globules stood for an instant where the men had been. And then the jaws bit down. On nothing.

The globules crashed to the floor in a red rain that spattered the stones and put the hissing fire out. Amid the sudden smoke of its dying, the floor ran with small puddles that moved together with purposeful speed.

The many-fanged monster peered suspiciously around the room and came slowly free of the ceiling to gather itself into a floating sphere of questing eyes and gnashing teeth. It echoed the dumbfounded astonishment of the distant Zhentarim who'd created it; he'd never seen anything of the like before. Was this a spell? Were the two pilgrims of Tyr doppelgangers who'd learned a new trick? Or . . . something else?

The floating monster glared around the ruined chamber, but nothing moved except the thick, dark red fluid on the floor. Two holy symbols lay amid the moving gore, and tin cups and scabbarded swords and knives leaned where the pilgrims had left them, but their clothes were gone. The monster bent its gaze again on the moving liquid.

Slowly, as if with great effort, the red fluid was gathering, joining into two ever-widening pools. The creature watched for a long time; the pools became two rising, glistening red humps. Purposefully the fanged thing flew across the chamber to hang above one pool, and extended a forest of mouths with questing tongues, intending to suck up the pool.

With surprising speed, the pool leapt upward to meet it, roaring in a red column that plunged into all the waiting mouths. The fanged creature darkened, shuddered—and flew apart in a wet explosion of staring eyeballs and slime.

Gelatinous fragments of its riven body were flung to the far corners of the rubble-strewn room . . . but before they could stain the walls or floor, these wet remnants faded silently away into the air, as if they had never been.

* * * * *

The swordcaptains standing around Nentor Thuldoum nearly swallowed their tongues in startled fear when the wizard let out a sudden raw scream, clawed blindly and convulsively at them all, and then flung himself back in his seat, clutching at his head. The wordless wet gargle in his throat rose again into a screaming, a high keening that went on and on . . . and men pulled back from the reeling Zhentarim and drew their blades. They shivered.

"What should we do, Lord?" a swordcaptain asked, hurrying to where Swordlord Amglar sat watching, his back against the ancient bulk of the Standing Stone.

The commander looked up expressionlessly at the anxious officer and shrugged. "Either this passes, or it doesn't. If the latter, we'll put arrows through him from well away until he falls silent, and then burn the body." Amglar reached for the wineskin and goblet that sat on the grass beside him, and his lips curved into a mirthless grin. "Wizards are all like that, inside," he told the swordcaptain softly. "If their control is ever broken, all the screaming and wide-eyed raving bursts out, for us all to see."

The man shivered. "What does that to wizards, Lord?"

Amglar shrugged. "It's but magic sweeping away restraint. Mages are just men and maids like all the rest of us. The problem with our kindly Zhentarim is that they all seem to forget that."

* * * * *

In a ruined chamber deep in the night-cloaked woods, two columns of dark, glistening liquid grew slowly darker and more solid, shifting into manlike shapes. One sharpened into the likeness of the shorter pilgrim while the other was still a glistening humanoid, eyes and mouth just swimming into view on a face of red slime.

"That body?" the unfinished one asked disgustedly.

"Again?"

"You'd prefer this?" The shorter pilgrim flickered and slid, its clothes and bristles melting away into ivory-skinned voluptuousness. A breathtakingly beautiful female human caressed itself provocatively, posing with its hands in a magnificent fall of flame-red hair.

"Where'd you see *that?*" the unfinished one asked.

The second Malaugrym smiled. "Well, it's a long story. . . ."

* * * * *

Tower of Ashaba, Shadowdale, early Flamerule 17

"Is there more moongleam?" Elminster asked hopefully, holding out his goblet.

Chin on hand, Shaerl shook her head. "Not this side of the cellars, and I'm in no state to climb stairs now. Not after—gods, Old Mage, it's been six bottles! Doesn't wine touch you?"

"No," Elminster told her. "I just like the taste."

Shaerl rolled her eyes. "Of course. Silly of me even to think you'd get tipsy, or take headaches from wine, like mere mortals."

"Look ye, lass, it took me the better part of a year to get the spell right—and after all that, Mystra laughed and changed me with a wave of her hand! I could have saved myself hours—nay, days—of painstaking research!"

"Aye," Shaerl agreed dryly. "I can see how long and hard it would have been, drinking every night away to see how long it took you to start reeling, and if 'twas different than the night before."

"That's *not* how I did it, lass!" Elminster growled at her.

Shaerl spread her hands in apology and sighed. "I'd have more sympathy, El, if I didn't look in the mirror every morn and see myself getting older, fast. Not all that long ago I was ordering my gowns slit thigh-high to catch the eyes of young blades at feasts, and having gowns made to match so my parents wouldn't see until the coach was around the first bend, and I could strip them off! Now I couldn't even get into any of those gowns . . . if I still dared to dress like that!"

"Why don't ye dare dress like that?" the Old Mage asked, trying to peer around the edge of the table to see her ankles. "A few years and a child don't ruin one's legs!"

"But they do add to one's belly. Never mind about me . . . you know what I'm talking about, Old Mage. You've had centuries—and may well have centuries more. I'll be lucky to see sixty summers."

" 'Tis not the shining thing ye think it, this longevity," Elminster told her gravely. "I bury friends every day, it seems . . . and one grows so *tired* of it all. If ye didn't need me so sorely in the days ahead, 'twould be so easy to just bid it all good-bye and lie down in a tomb somewhere to dream the ages away . . . but ye always need me."

"I do?" Shaerl asked challengingly, but hastily added, "No offense, Old Mage."

Elminster waved a dismissive hand. "Not ye personally—thou art one of the bright spots, lass. Cormyrean noble ladies who can think for themselves are rarer than they should be! I meant the Realms in general, and Shadowdale in particular. There's something here that the gods need very badly just now—and I must guard it from them."

"Ah, with us caught in the middle, as usual," Shaerl said sarcastically. "Wonderful."

"Ye wanted adventure when ye left the castle of thy father," Elminster reminded her. "So ye took the oath to Azoun and joined Vangerdahast's service, were sent to Shadowdale and promptly married the man ye were sent to spy on . . . so here ye are. Too late by far to criticize the bed ye made for thyself, dear."

"I *know*," Shaerl replied in exasperation. She got up, leaning on the table for support, and then strode restlessly about the room. "It's just—"

She threw up her hands in surrender, whirled around, and ran to the old wizard, flinging her arms around him.

"I'm just so scared, El," she said, tears standing in her eyes as she stared into his. Her lower lip trembled. "Every time Mourn goes out that door, I think it's the last time I'll see him alive. Zhentil Keep attacks us every gods-be-damned spring . . . and now the entire world seems torn apart, with gods everywhere and orcs and brigands, and magic going wild! Mourn needs me to be strong, I know, when what I want to do is run *away* from it all, just the two of us, and—"

"The two of us? Ye and this old wizard? Miss, I'll remind ye that ye're married!" Elminster said primly.

"I meant Mourngrym, you dolt," Shaerl said scornfully, voice wavering on the edge of tears.

"I know ye did, little one," Elminster said. He folded her gently into his arms. That brought the explosion of sobs he'd known it would. He held the lady of Shadowdale, murmuring comforting promises and stroking her hair until her tears were spent.

She lifted her head from his breast at last, red eyed and wild haired, and blinked at him tremulously, morose thanks in her eyes.

"Ah, ye're done!" Elminster said brightly. "Now, how about that wine?"

"Ooohh!" In mock rage Shaerl snatched up a cushion from the chair and belted him with it.

"That's better," the Old Mage said gruffly, through the rain of blows. "Beat the wits out of the only archmage left to defend Shadowdale, *that's* a smart girl."

Shaerl let fall the cushion as if its touch suddenly burned her fingers. "Sorry," she whispered, turning her head away.

Elminster chuckled and clapped her shoulder. "I was jesting, lass. Why don't ye settle into a slightly more cozy position on my lap—one in which thy knee *isn't* pressing hard into this old bladder, mind—an' I tell ye all the wild tales about which avatar is walking where in Faerûn, and what a mess they're making of things. When ye're thoroughly scared, I'll pass on to news of the main Zhent army, currently being warmly entertained in Voonlar by several hobgoblin bands I sent thence . . . ah, dropped literally atop their camp, actually."

Shaerl giggled. "I wish I'd been there to see *that*," she said. "Has it thinned the Zhent host appreciably?"

Elminster nodded. "Moreover, I'm not done yet. It's taken me until now to locate my favorite hobgoblin tribe—the Nose Bones—so they'll be er, dropping in on our Zhent friends just before dawn."

"Taken you until now?" Shaerl said in mock alarm. "Why, whatever have you been doing?"

"Holding the Realms together, lass," Elminster told her rather grimly, "and fighting off various old foes who've decided to take advantage of the Fall of the Gods to conquer or destroy as much of Faerûn as they can seize—the Malaugrym, in particular, have been troublesome."

"Those Who Walk in Shadow?" Shaerl asked, eyes grave. "Storm and I have talked about them several times, after one attacked you at the inn and you wouldn't tell us anything. They sounded deadly, indeed."

"Ah, but I've acquired three heroes to deal with them now," Elminster said, holding out to her a goblet that shouldn't have been full.

Shaerl stared at it suspiciously, sipped it, and then peered into it again. It was still full—or rather, full again. She gave Elminster a look.

The Old Mage spread his hands with an air of innocence.

The lady of Shadowdale sighed. "So who are these three mighty ones?"

"Sharantyr and two Harpers; men who came to Storm for training."

Shaerl stared at him, mouth open. "The three

rangers? Against spell-hurling shapeshifters? El, they'll be *killed!*"

Elminster shrugged. "That fate could well befall us all in the days ahead. I can't be everywhere, especially now, with bindings failing and magic twisting awry all across Toril. My valiant three've done well enough thus far, I must say. Even if they all perish forthwith, they've dealt the House of Malaug a shrewd blow."

"Will you write that on their tombs?" Shaerl asked quietly.

Elminster shrugged but said nothing. After a long silence, the lady of Shadowdale whispered, "What will you write on ours?"

The ghost of a smile stole across the Old Mage's face. "Perhaps: I should have been laid to rest here long ago, but I'm still busy defending Shadowdale."

"Oh, no," she said quietly, shaking her head as the bedchamber door opened and a weary Mourngrym strode in, tossing down cloak, helm, and sword. "That's what *your* tomb should say."

"It already does, lass. Ask Lhaeo to show ye some time—on the morrow. It's a good place to hide with thy heir, if the dale's overrun. Oh, in case he forgets to tell ye—don't mind all the floating eyeballs that'll drift around after ye. They do no harm . . . and if the food runs out, they're good eating."

"Is he teasing you about fried eyeballs again?" Mourngrym asked as he strode into the room. Without slowing to hear Shaerl's reply, he bent over the chair to kiss the top of her head, and then looked up at Elminster as the soft fingers of his wife stole up to stroke his cheek. "And what's this about 'hide'? And 'overrun'? With you here holding the dale against all invaders?"

"We must all fall sometime," Elminster replied very quietly. "That's why I've been grooming every hero I could find these last ten years or so. Someday, defending Shadowdale without me will be your task. Perhaps someday soon."

* * * * *

The Standing Stone, the Dales, Flamerule 17

The spellmaster's screams broke off suddenly, and he slumped forward in his seat. Hesitantly one of the swordcaptains took a few paces toward the wizard, sword drawn, and then looked back to the swordlord for instructions. Other officers with ready weapons were also gathering cautiously around the seated wizard.

"Is he dead?" Amglar asked bluntly. The swordcaptain turned to see, taking a few paces closer—and then shrank back in horror as sudden radiances flashed and spun around the body, jerking it convulsively.

Amglar's eyes narrowed. Contingencies, perhaps . . . not attacks visited from afar, no.

His judgment was confirmed an instant later as the Zhentarim shook himself and stood, looking around irritably at all the grim faces and raised swords. "Put away all this steel," he snapped, "and find something useful to do—such as getting me a hot meal. Spellhurling's hungry work."

The swordcaptain Amglar had just given orders to turned back to the swordlord and spread his hands in a silent question. Amglar waved at him to 'hold hard' for the nonce, got up, and strode over to Thuldoum.

"How are you, mage?" he asked, putting his hand on the hilt of his sword.

"I'll live," Thuldoum said coldly, "and my wits are my own; you need not hack me down for fear I'll turn on you all."

"The Roost's defended, then?"

"No," the spellmaster said. "It's deserted. A little overgrown and tumbledown to be an ideal camp, but safe enough."

"Safe? Why the screaming then?"

"My creation encountered two beings who can shift shape. They were camped in one of the rooms."

"Doppelgangers? If they impersonate our swordcaptains, they can play merry death and chaos with this Sword!"

"These weren't doppelgangers," Nentor Thuldoum said grimly. "One of them tried to merge with my monster, destroying it. I was held in thrall, and saw into its mind. It was old, very old, and it hates Elminster of Shadowdale more than you or I do; possibly more than High Lord Manshoon does. They've been feuding for centuries."

"And so?"

"It also hates three other humans I don't know; they looked like rangers. It thinks all of them are in Mistledale right now . . . and was headed there to feed on them, the moment it was satisfied the human shape I saw it in—a pilgrim of Tyr—was good enough to fool them."

"You think these two shapechangers are on the way to Mistledale by now?"

"Yes," the Zhentarim said flatly. "I couldn't break free until it ate the monster's mind, but the last thought I overheard was that it was eager to get to its prey."

"Then we'll be just as urgent in our advance on the Roost, once you set us a directional spell so we can get there through the woods, and not have to use the road and the open dale."

"The moment I've eaten," the spellmaster told him coldly, "you'll have that spell. The drink, I think, is even more important right now."

Wordlessly Amglar unclipped a chased metal flask from his belt and held it out. The Zhentarim regarded it and then him suspiciously, then in sudden resolve undid the stopper and took a sip—then a long pull.

When he could stop gasping, the spellmaster wiped at his numbed lips and asked, "B-By all the gods, what *is* that stuff?"

"Firewine," Amglar told him, surprised. "You don't get out much, do you, wizard?"

"Enough," Thuldoum told him darkly. "More than enough."

"Spellmaster?" A swordcaptain was hurrying up with a covered platter that trailed wisps of steam. "Your evenfeast!"

"Ah, that's better," Thuldoum said, and turned to Amglar. "You see, Swordlord? Properly treated, I will deal with you properly in return . . . just like any man. You might remember that."

"Aye," the swordlord said, remembering Myarvuk's still, staring face as they buried him. "I will keep it in mind—always."

* * * * *

Mistledale, Flamerule 17

The larger of the two owls fluttered down to a branch on the edge of the dale, and grew a human mouth. "Best be wary," it said to the owl alighting beside it. "They may have us spying spells set—and a single arrow could slay us in these shapes."

"Take on something larger, Yinthrim?"

"No," the larger Malaugrym said firmly. "That'd just invite discovery and attack . . . and they'll have mages about. No, Atarl, just take care. After we avenge the despoiled honor of the House of Malaug, let us return here and await the dawn. On a battlefield, amusements will be many."

* * * * *

Swords Creek, Mistledale, Flamerule 17

"Yes?" Syluné inquired, turning from her lamp and mirror and raising an imperious eyebrow. On either side of the tent door, Belkram and Itharr stared out and raised their blades warily, waiting.

"Your servant, Lady," said the voice outside. A man's voice. A familiar man's voice.

"Yes, Torm?" Syluné asked, a trifle wearily. The two Harpers relaxed, trading grins across the dim tent mouth. "Come to undress me? Or just to collect all your lingerie?"

"No," the thief said in a low voice. "May I come in?"

Syluné turned to Sharantyr, who nodded. The three Harpers were sleeping in all but their boots, drawn swords to hand, and had already lain down. The Witch of Shadowdale was sitting up before a mirror, looking at the body she might well lose again on the morrow. "Yes—but leave your pranks outside the door. I'm not in the mood."

"Your command is my wish, as I believe Elminster once said," Torm said with just a hint of his usual impishness, looking warily into the tent. Belkram and Itharr saluted him silently with their blades; he answered them with a sardonic lift of his brows, and stepped into the tent. He was holding something behind his back.

Syluné turned on her stool to face him. With the candlelight behind her, lighting her silver hair into flame, she looked unearthly as well as beautiful. "Well, Torm?"

"I . . . ah, I came to do your hair," Torm said, bringing a fistful of combs and a tiny scent bottle into view. All four folk in the tent stared at him, and his face grew pinker. Looking down at his hands, he said, "I seem to have grown used to it." He looked up at Syluné. "If you don't mind?"

The smile that the Witch of Shadowdale gave him then took his heart away. Torm swallowed as she stretched forth her hands to him. "Mind? I am honored. Please!"

As Torm stepped forward, eyes shining, Belkram said kindly, "Haul your tongue in, there's a good boy. We've done the tent floor already, and you'll look more sensible with it safely stowed away."

Sharantyr shot her comrade a sharp look, but Torm did not even turn around.

"I know it's been said before," he said calmly, "but if you go around giving folk a piece of your clever mind, Belkram, soon enough you'll have none left for yourself."

Belkram spread his hands in apology. "Aye, it's the real Torm. Sorry for shattering your gesture, sir. With all these shapeshifters around, one can't be too careful."

Torm rounded on him then. " 'Too careful'?" he asked, incredulously. "You folk make berserkers look like timid moles! When you discover what the word 'careful' means, come and tell me! You certainly haven't displayed any great store of it thus far! I doubt Elminster'd dare to do what you have . . . let alone *this* thief!"

"He's right, you know," Sharantyr said with a chuckle.

"Of course he's right," Itharr told her. "We've just been charging ahead as fast as we could into peril after peril, hoping the gods, our foes, and ourselves alike wouldn't notice what reckless fools we're being, and pay us off for it! And now he's gone and spoiled it, and on the eve of battle, too! Bad thief! Naughty, naughty *bad* thief!"

The tent erupted in helpless laughter. In the night outside, two Rider sentries exchanged wondering glances, and shook their heads.

"Harpers and adventurers . . . crazed wits, if you ask me," one said feelingly.

"No argument here," his fellow replied, watching the darkness around warily. Something glided past—and he tensed to shout and hurl his spear—until he saw that it was only an owl. Another owl flapped along in its wake. Now that was something rarely seen.

The guard frowned at the two birds as the night swallowed them again. He shrugged. As long as they weren't arrows, dragons, or flying wizards, things in the sky were no concern of his. He yawned and peered all around again, seeking real danger.

* * * * *

Galath's Roost, Mistledale, Flamerule 17

"The wizard said it was deserted, and safe," the Zhentilar swordcaptain grunted, "but we know all about wizards, don't we, lads? Swords out, watch wary, and be ready for the worst!" He glared around at the Zhentilar soldiers and told them, "I don't want to lose one of you because someone wasn't looking, or was thinking about his mistress back at the Keep, or how many coins this or that jack owed him. So take yer time, and let's do this the right way. Torches and mage lights to the fore."

There was a creaking and rattling, and the men moved as one. Then the only sound was the soft whisper and rustle of disturbed foliage. The first scouts of the Sword of the South advanced up the steep, thickly forested slope toward the ruin of Galath's Roost.

When the foremost man was an easy ten paces from the overgrown stones of a wall, he turned and shrieked like an owl, thrice. In response, the mage lights drifted silently forward, over the helmed heads of the soldiers, into the dark and hollow places of stone ahead.

Nothing moved. There was no sound that could not be put down to small things that flap or scuttle in a forest by night. Cautiously the Zhentilar moved forward, swords out, probing the ferns and brambles ahead for spring bows, trip cords, and pits. They found nothing.

From here and there along the edges of the ruin, double owl hoots rang out as scout after scout signalled his safe entry into the keep. Files of men bearing torches began to work their way through the trees in answer to the calls.

A scout halted in a dark chamber, hearing the stony scrape of something moving to his right, through an archway thick with vines and mottled moss. "Be that you, Baeremuth?" The whisper was cautious, and the reply was quick and low.

"Aye. Fflarast?"

"Me," Fflarast confirmed, turning his loaded hand crossbow aside to prevent any accidents. "Anything of interest?"

"Lots of rubble, and something's nest . . . vole bones an' the like. I think this place really is deserted."

"Good. Crazed orders, hacking through the woods in the dark just to camp in a ruin, but . . ."

"Better'n trying to fight our way into Mistledale down that bow-shot throat, if we'd taken the road. They must have at least a dozen archers—an' a dozen's all they'd need, Fflar, to take down four hundred or more of us, for sure. This way, we can strike out of the woods all along the south side of the dale. Those farmers'll run themselves crazed trying to be everywhere at once to stop us."

"You plot like a swordlord," Fflarast muttered. "We'd better get on, or Dellyn'll be running his blade up our backsides and bellowing at us for being a pair of craven laggards or spies for the enemy."

"Huh. He sees spies under every stone, that one," Baeremuth replied, and suited actions to words by turning over a rock that was suspiciously damp among dry, dusty ones.

There was a sudden rush of rubble and a crash that shook the room. Fflarast cursed and staggered back, trying to keep his feet, but ended up sitting down hard on rubble. When he'd scrambled up and could see again through the rising dust, his mouth went suddenly dry.

Baeremuth Asanter lay under a fallen block of stone nearly as large as a pack mule. Thin rivers of blood were running out from beneath it—and Fflar could just see the tips of the fingers of one hand, reaching vainly for aid. It would reach forever now.

7

Death Grows Impatient

Fflarast Blackriver peered again at his comrade's remains and then backed away *very* carefully. The rockfall hadn't been accidental.

Someone had gone to a lot of trouble with wooden wedges and spars and balanced stones—and even flung dust around afterward to hide their work. The wedges were the bright hue of newly cut wood; this had been done within the last day or so.

"Oh, Bane preserve us," Fflarast whispered, backing out of the chamber. At that moment, a heavy booming off to the right marked the discovery of another trap. It was followed by a faint, raw screaming that went on for a long time before ending suddenly in a gurgle. Fflarast knew those sounds. Someone had put a half-crushed man out of his agony with a quick sword thrust to the throat.

"Ye gods and small creeping things hear my plea," the Zhentilar warrior whispered, invoking the old, old prayer of desperate warriors. He wasn't facing half a hundred orcs alone on a crag, like the legendary Borthin had been when he roared out the invocation, but dead is dead, and Fflarast Blackriver had only one life to lose. Moreover, he valued it just as much as Borthin had his own.

There came another rushing of stone off to the left,

and startled cursing. Ah—one trap had missed. Good; that meant they were probably all clever feats, and not magic. Maybe—just maybe—Fflar would see the end of this day.

There came a ringing of steel from behind him. "What's ahead, scout?" a self-important swordcaptain snapped. Pelaeron himself, scourge of lazy soldiers. Oh, joy.

"Traps, sir," Fflarast said, indicating the fallen block and Baeremuth's arm. "I'm deciding how best to safely proceed."

"Well, hurry up about it," the officer snapped, prodding Fflar's mail-covered backside with his sword tip. "We haven't got all night, you know." A file of warriors was crowding into the room behind the swordcaptain. Fflarast looked at them—and at Pelaeron's steely eye— and then swallowed, shrugged, and carefully climbed over the rubble to the left of Baeremuth, on into the darkness.

Darkness where there should have been light. The torch had been with Baeremuth, and no mage lights were near. "Torch," Fflarast rapped out, keeping his voice as laconic as possible, and reached back.

The swordcaptain curtly waved an armsman with a blazing torch forward. The man reached to hand the torch to Fflarast, shuffled amid loose stones, tripped, and measured his length on the rubble. Stones shifted—and Fflar flung himself backward into unknown darkness as hard and fast as he could.

An instant later, armsman, torch, Pelaeron, and all vanished in a roaring and tumbling of stone as two carefully balanced blocks collapsed sideways, and the floor of the chamber above came down.

Fflarast landed hard on his tailbone on rough-edged rocks and lay there groaning. The chamber he'd come through was now a new-sealed tomb in front of him. He was lying in a cross passage—and listening to fresh crashings off to the left as heavy stones dropped and rolled. Tortured metal shrieked briefly as it crumpled, a man screamed for an instant, and then there were only echoes. Echoes that faded slowly into silence.

Fflar shuddered. He snarled wordlessly. Gods take all wizards! Save my bruised behind! Grunting, he rolled slowly and carefully to the left, to his knees, and felt for his sword.

There was another rolling crash in the distance, and shouts. Fflarast found his sword and clutched it, not moving as he fought down fear. He was alone in chill darkness with death waiting all around him. For the greater glory of Zhentil Keep, whose proud lords would not even know that Fflarast Blackriver had died in the service. Or care one whit, if someone told them.

"Hungry beasts take them all," Fflar told the darkness softly, and stayed on his knees, wondering how long it would be until dawn . . . and if he'd dare try to find his way out of the ruin even then.

Far down the passage, many torches glimmered and danced, and a voice said, "There—that's armor!"

"I serve Zhentil Keep!" Fflar shouted desperately, flinging up his arms in case someone was very eager to fire his crossbow. No quarrels answered. The voice came again. "Who are you, soldier?"

"Fflarast Blackriver, of Pelaeron's Mace." He cleared his throat and added, "I'm alone. Pelaeron and most of his swords lie under stone beside me. We've struck two traps already."

"It seems a contagious habit," the voice responded dryly. "Stay where you are. I'm going to throw you a torch."

A moment later, fire *whup-whup-whupped* end over end through the darkness, trailing sparks, and fell amid rubble, showing Fflar a row of archways on one side of the passage, and doors or fallen walls on the side he'd come in by. A boot—still twitching feebly—could be seen in the fall of rubble beside him. Fflarast swallowed and turned his back on it, looking through the nearest arch.

"What can you see, soldier?" the voice asked.

"A huge chamber—probably a great hall," Fflarast answered. "It has balconies around its inside walls, and the roof's gone somewhere. There's moonlight at one end."

"Off to your left—my right?"

"Aye," Fflarast called. "It looks open—big empty stretches."

Voices murmured down the corridor. The officer called, "Can you get to the torch?"

Fflarast struggled over rubble for a few sweating moments, half-expecting the ceiling to fall on him, but reached the guttering torch safely. "I have it," he called, and swung it high.

"Good. We're going to throw you another. Pitch it out into this large hall of yours and tell us what you see."

Fflarast did so. The chamber rivalled the main hall of the Black Altar back in Zhentil Keep. He'd stood honor guard in that dark temple more than once, and knew this hall was fully as large. He told them so.

"Can you say anything of interest?"

"No . . . broken tiles . . . heaved and stained flooring, but open. The torchlight doesn't show it all. Nothing moving or alive that I can see."

"Good man. Stay where you are. We're coming to join you."

Fflarast sighed heavily and stood as still as he could, watching the slow and cautious advance of a long file of black-armored men.

It seemed half the Sword of the South was in the passage. Someone had cut a long, bent sapling and lashed a torch to it, and was lighting the high ceiling as they came, finding holes and old rockfalls. There were also two shafts that presumably let light and air down into the keep, but as the soldiers of Zhentil Keep cautiously passed beneath them, nothing swooped down or fell from above. Soon the Zhentilar reached Fflarast, and a swordcaptain—another officious one—curtly ordered him to stand aside.

A torch was tossed on down the passage. Its flickering light revealed that the corridor was blocked completely not far beyond where Fflarast had entered it. An entire room seemed to have fallen from the floor above, pouring a high mound of broken stone across the passage from wall to wall, and almost to the ceiling. Fflar looked at it and shuddered.

"This great hall it is, then," the swordcaptain ordered, turning away. The man at his elbow—the swordcaptain who'd thrown the torch to Fflarast—peered into the vast chamber and murmured, "I have a bad feeling about this room."

"I think we all do!" the other officer snarled, fear lacing his blustering voice. "So let's just get on with it! Men—out swords and advance, the first dozen of you! Stop and report if you see anything of import—especially moving bones! I want to get that mage in here fast . . . and then maybe we'll all get some sleep!"

Men moved reluctantly into the chamber. Fflarast stood silent, glad he wasn't among them, expecting to hear another heavy crash at any moment.

Minutes passed, and the men standing still and tense in the passage could hear each other breathing, hoarse and fast. But no cries or falls of stone came, and soon a man whose armor bore the red shoulder emblem of a sword came back to the archway and reported crisply, "No danger, sir. Molds and rubbish down one end, where a lot of water's come in, but there's nothing else in the place except two stairs up to the floor above and a high seat—of bare stone, nothing in it—on a raised bit at the far end. The place is huge; there's room for a good two thousand blades to bunk down, though I'd not want to be close in under some of the balconies; they look none too safe."

"Well done, sword. Set men to guard all doors and archways into the place; we'll move in. Swordcaptain

Aezel, go out and tell the swordlord. Request that the spellmaster be brought in, forthwith—and if the wizard objects, request it again."

There were a few dry chuckles in the safe anonymity of the gloom, and then men were on the move. Fflarast Blackriver came to a sudden decision. He handed his torch to a passing armsman and took up the straight, back-to-the-wall stance of a man on guard duty. He wasn't going into that great hall unless directly ordered to.

Thankfully, the officious swordcaptain passed on into the great hall, and the bulk of the soldiery followed, leaving a few wary veterans standing in the passage with Fflarast. "Neatly done, lad," one of them hissed, and grinned. Fflarast gave him a grin back, and they waited in the darkness together until a bright blaze of torches and the shuffling of many booted feet told them the main body of the Sword had arrived.

Men in black armor seemed to file past forever, until at last the black battle robes of the spellmaster could be seen sweeping majestically down the passage. He was escorted by two swordcaptains and the swordlord himself.

The supreme commander of the Sword of the South halted close enough to Fflarast to touch him, and said to the wizard, "The men want you to look around and set them at their ease that there's no magic or hidden, lurking things about. Do that, but we haven't time for you to send them haring down every passage in the place in hopes of finding magic treasure that was likely taken away long ago. I'll be outside, supervising the perimeter watch; send Swordcaptain Tschender here out to me if you want anything."

The spellmaster nodded impatiently, seeming eager to get into the room, and the swordlord stepped back, rolled his eyes behind the wizard's back, and strode off back down the corridor, leaving behind at least six veterans struggling not to chuckle as the Zhentarim stepped grandly through the nearest arch.

By unspoken, common accord the men in the passage

all moved to stand where they could look through archways, and watch what befell in the great hall. Wizards of the Black Network were not loved—but they were always a source of entertainment, if one could keep safely out of the way.

Spellmaster Thuldoum strode grandly across the vast chamber, head high, looking slowly from left to right and back again. When he caught sight of the throne, he bent forward in eagerness, and his pace quickened.

"Gods spit down on 'im," one of the soldiers muttered. "He's going to sit on the throne!"

For a moment it appeared that the wizard was going to do just that—but prudence came to him at the last moment, and they saw him ordering a reluctant armsman into the seat instead.

Gingerly the soldier sat down—and from the ceiling above, a ring of boulders on chains crashed down, smashing the vainly leaping man to bloody ruin on the stones. One stone, rebounding from the impact on its chain, nearly beheaded the startled wizard, who staggered backward, arms flailing, as armsmen watched in horror. The soldier who'd been a shade too slow in vacating the throne lay where he had fallen, a broken figure in a pool of blood.

"What did I tell ye?" a soldier said, who hadn't in fact spoken before, all that long night. "Stupid buttocks-brain."

It seemed the wizard wasn't done. He'd caught sight of something behind or beyond the throne that only he could see, and was casting a spell. With all eyes upon him, he made a show of it, gesturing dramatically as he brought the invocation to a ringing climax—and a door slowly appeared in the blank wall behind the high seat. Magical radiance shone blue and silver, brightening to a soft white glow, and spread slowly along an arched frame to outline a large door.

As Zhentilar stared at it and Spellmaster Thuldoum

grinned in triumph, Fflarast felt the tense prickling of hairs rising on the back of his neck. Oh, no . . .

The Zhentarim brought his hands down with a flourish, pointing at the door, and shouted the last word of the spell that would open it.

The door winked out. Blue-white flashes ran all over the ceiling of the chamber as a web of magic discharged, and Galath's Roost fell in on itself with a roar.

Fflarast saw the ceiling begin to fall and the wizard stare up and then vanish. He did not wait to see a thousand of his fellow warriors crushed, but turned and flung himself headlong down the passage, running as he had never run before.

There was an earth-splitting crash of stone upon stone, and Fflar was flung off his feet. He landed rolling amid dust and falling stones as the castle shook around him. The entire armor gallery had fallen into the great hall.

"Gods!" one of the old soldiers in the passage gasped. "The floor, too!" And with a slow, gathering thunder, the overloaded floor gave way, dropping in huge pieces down into dark cellars beneath.

By then, Fflar was sprinting toward the moonlight, sweat almost blinding him. A last leap over rubble— and he was out, tumbling in the ferns and coming up running, to get well away from the walls.

"Easy, soldier," said a swordcaptain, putting out a hand to stop Fflarast's frantic flight. "What befell?"

Fflar clung to the man, panting, unable to catch his breath—and from the ruined keep behind him came a slow series of smaller crashes.

They listened together, and then the officer shook Fflar by the shoulders. "Well?"

An old soldier came into view out of the same rent in the wall Fflar had used. It was one of the veterans who'd stayed in the passage. He was walking slowly and stiffly, ignoring the occasional falls of small stones from above, and the officer strode toward him with a snarl, dragging Fflar along.

"What befell?" he snapped, eyeing the old man's gray whiskers.

The old warrior looked up at him and said, "Don't bluster, lad . . . ye're an officer, remember?"

The swordcaptain roared out his anger and snatched at his sword—and Fflar hit him in the side of his neck with one mailed fist, as hard as he'd ever hit anyone in his life. He got in two more good blows before the body reached the ground—and stayed there.

"Easy, lad . . . ye've broken his neck, there's no need to dance on his bones," the veteran muttered, bending over Fflar. "Now ye'd best get away from him and practice looking innocent, afore the next officer happens along."

"Too late," a deep, grave voice said above them both. Fflar and the veteran looked up into the cold, tired eyes of Swordlord Amglar. "But by the sounds of things, I've just lost too many blades to waste two more because cruel, spoiled nobles' sons make bad officers. Consider this—accident—forgotten, and so long as you have no more, scout, I'll continue to forget it. Now tell me in truth what's befallen in there."

Fflarast and the veteran looked at each other, and then Fflar spoke. "The spellmaster cast a spell to open a door behind the throne, and—I think—set off some sort of magical trap. The whole ceiling came down at once . . . but I think I saw him vanish before the stones hit. I ran, then . . . that's all I saw. Before that, though, my unit—Pelaeron's Mace—and a lot of others I heard die, but didn't see, were crushed in rockfall traps . . . the keep's bulging with them."

The swordlord nodded soberly. "The spellmaster's magic brought him safely out to us here," he said, his lips twisting bitterly, "and dearly though I'd love to put him to death for this blunder, we need him in the battle tomorrow." He leaned in close to them, and his next words came in a whisper.

"Don't raise a hand to him this night, whatever the provocation . . . but if either of you survives the coming battle, and he's still breathing at the end of it, I want either or both of you to slay him. He may have contingencies, mind—try to dismember the body and then burn it." He looked from Fflar to the veteran, and then back to Fflar. "Understood?"

"I understand and will obey," the old soldier whispered, and Fflar echoed his words. The swordlord nodded. "Good." He looked at the veteran. "So the ceiling fell . . . what did you see after that?"

"The floor an' all went down into—cellars, I'd guess—below, breaking off and sliding slowly; in bits, ye know. Then the balconies broke off and fell in on top of it all, one by one. I saw spell flashes before each fall . . . the whole thing's one huge trap, sir, if ye ask me. I'd sooner sleep in the hot heart of an enemy campfire tonight than go back in there, sir." He jerked his head to indicate the ruined castle behind him.

The swordlord nodded grimly. "We've been duped by a clever foe—and an arrogant, careless wizard." He sighed and added, "Gods curse all wizards. If things in Faerûn were all decided by the strength of a sword arm and not sneaking spells, we'd all be a lot better off!"

Rising with another sigh, their commander pointed toward a campfire. "Go and report to Shieldmaster Tesker; you're part of my own mace now, both of you." He turned away, and as they stammered their thanks, he turned back and added, "Oh, and tell him from me that you're both swords now. If we've any armor so blazoned that fits, you're to wear it tomorrow."

"May the gods thank you more than we can, sir!" the old veteran gasped.

Amglar smiled thinly. "You'll probably be cursing me on the morrow. Save your delight for when all of this is over, and we're standing proudly on the battlements of Zhentil Keep again. Then I'll thank the gods too . . . just how fervently I do it then, mind you, will depend on what they've done to us since."

All three of them laughed together, the grim laughter of fighting men who shared the same peril—and the same jaundiced view of the world that had put them there. Then they clasped forearms and parted.

On his way to the fires, Fflar stopped for a moment as he realized something the other two had already known—most soldiers keep warm with the memories of such moments.

* * * * *

Swords Creek, Mistledale, Flamerule 17

Syluné of Shadowdale lay awake in the darkness, as she did every night. When one no longer needs to sleep and one's friends are in danger, there is no better way to guard them than to lie among them, feigning slumber, with a watch spell set.

Through its invisible web she felt Itharr stir, plagued by dark thoughts, building his killing rage for the battle tomorrow. Later, Syluné sent soothing visions to Belkram when a dream made him start in terror and almost awaken. Sharantyr needed no such kindnesses; she lay in peace, her dreams deep.

They were fine battle companions and good friends. Syluné smiled up at the dark roof of the tent overhead. She closed her eyes again and turned her thoughts to the many folk and places and things she must check on and watch over during this Time of Troubles, if the Realms she loved were to survive, and not some shattered, twisted remnant of Toril. At least the hours when others slept gave her time enough for reflection, to consider and anticipate all the consequences and probable unintended effects of her every action. It could truly be said of the Chosen that, more than any other thinking creatures of Faerûn, they knew exactly what they were doing at all times.

Right now, Syluné was thinking over the battle tomorrow . . . the battle that would probably cost her this body. Jhessail and Rathan both carried fragments of stone from her hut should anything befall the one within her now, and—something was amiss!

A scrying spell swept over the tent, seeing who lay within. Its primary dweomer paused above each sleeping face as Syluné pretended to slumber, but it did not seem to sense the spell web, and withdrew without any disturbance. Yet, that is. Now someone, probably a Zhentarim mage, knew who was in this tent. While most folk still believed that the Witch of Shadowdale was long dead, only a Malaugrym had any reason to view these four sleepers as greater foes than the mightier Knights of Myth Drannor sleeping in other tents.

Syluné let out her breath in a long gasp and rose from her physical body as a ghostly, shadowy image, questing out into the camp around for any signs of fell magic. She could feel the frozen fire of magic items lying immobile in the tent Jhessail and Merith shared with Illistyl and a lady Rider, and a few faint dweomers from enspelled glow daggers riding on the hips of watchful sentries around the edge of the camp . . . but as long moments passed, no hostile spells came out of the night. Far away to the northeast, near ruined Myth Drannor, a wolf howled, but nothing nearby answered.

Yet a single fireball could do a lot of damage to a force this small. Perhaps she should raise a spell shield. Syluné glanced out of the tent into the still moonlight. To do so over the entire camp would be a punishing drain on the little life essence she had left; she really needed a living being to power such a magic—and to do it for long would leave the creature weak and quivering. Not a sword arm could be spared from the battle, though, so . . .

Something was disturbing the spell web! Syluné whirled back to face into the tent in time to see two dark, serpentine bodies rise up through the floor, making the softest of tearing sounds. Their heads, which had parted the canvas so swiftly, were deadly steel blades atop undulating, scaled coils, but they rose up in the darkness, growing swiftly larger.

Malaugrym!

The Witch of Shadowdale sent a shrieking warning through the spell web to awaken her companions as she hurled her ghostly form back across the tent. She had to reach her body! Very few of her spells were available to her in this ghostly form, when she could hold nothing solid.

One serpent-blade was arching over her own body, and the other was rearing above Sharantyr, whence it could plunge itself down into her sleeping breast. Syluné cast a curving shield of force over the lady ranger as she swept past.

Just in time! The blade came down at Sharantyr's face and was struck aside by the invisible barrier, trailing a line of white sparks.

The other serpent-thing struck at Syluné's body before she could slip into it, throwing its coils around her throat and wrists. The rest of its body extended toward Belkram, blade rearing back to strike.

She'd warned all three rangers to keep silence and find their blades as they awakened, and as the serpent-thing stretched over toward him, Belkram came boiling up out of his furs, hacking at the thing savagely.

Its hammer strike burst through his frantic parry and almost pinned to him to the tent floor, laying open his shoulder as he twisted desperately aside. He roared in pain. Sharantyr tried to scramble to his aid, and found herself a prisoner under the shield, but Itharr came leaping across the tent with his blade gleaming, bellowing, "Aid! An attack! Knights of Myth Drannor, to us!"

Syluné slid into her body, heedless of the strangling coil about her throat. She did not need to breathe, and so could take no harm from the crushing constriction of the Malaugrym—whose constraint prevented her from hurling spells. She gathered her will as ironlike coils tightened about her, and hauled her shield of force away from Sharantyr. She angled it up to wall herself away from the rest of the tent and shoved the Malaugrym's blade away from Belkram in the process.

The shapeshifter simply extended its body farther to strike at the Harper once more, but Itharr slashed it aside—and with her companions safe behind the shield, Syluné unleashed a spell that made steel shards burst from her body.

The Malaugrym took them all, convulsing in agony and flailing about the tent, sweeping her body off its bed and hurling Itharr to sprawl atop Sharantyr and the other serpentine Shadowmaster. Belkram sprang upon it and drove his blade home, but it writhed under him, not mortally harmed by his steel, and tried to shake him off. He sat on it, stabbing it repeatedly, so it grew fangs and bit his thigh.

Sharantyr and Itharr rolled around among the furs with the other Malaugrym, hacking and stabbing at it in a frenzy—and then the tent flap burst open and the Knights of Myth Drannor charged in.

Florin had doffed his armor for the night and wore only breeches, but his stout sword was in his hand. He dived without pause onto the serpent-thing on the beds, hacking at its blade-head with a flurry of blows, trying to sever the serpent's dark steel. Torm took one look at Syluné, who struggled upright with coils thick around her throat, and howled in fury, leaping across the tent with his dagger flashing.

Syluné kicked out one foot, trying to touch him, and Rathan saw what she was doing. He pushed past the thief and grasped Syluné's ankle firmly. What she said to him mind-to-mind he shouted aloud: "Malaugrym! Use silver on them to slay! They're shapeshifters! Use silver!"

At the door of the tent, Jhessail and Illistyl both nodded grimly. As Merith dived past them and buried his silver-bladed dagger in the Malaugrym that was battering Belkram all around the tent, they ran to where Itharr and Sharantyr were stabbing the other, and murmured spells as they slapped their hands at the blades, heedless of sharp, flashing edges.

The weapons glowed blue-white as Jhessail snatched her hand back, shaking drops of blood from it. When the glow faded, they shone silver . . . and the wounds they made did not close. Sharantyr and Itharr set to work chopping with frenzied speed, gasping their thanks.

Florin severed the blade-head of the other Malaugrym with a last blow and grabbed at the gory serpent-form, trying to hurl it away from a groaning Belkram. It grew many fanged mouths as he pounced on it, and one of them shot forth on a long stalk to snap at Torm, who ducked his head aside. Rathan raised his hand to cast a spell—and the jaws expanded with lightning speed to envelop it, biting down with cruel force.

The fat cleric doggedly intoned his spell, sweat running down his face—and fire from his hand burst forth within the Malaugrym, causing it to recoil with a roar of mingled fury and pain.

Illistyl's eyes narrowed as flames gouted from the beast. She dug a hand into her purse, snatched a silver coin, and snapped out a cantrip that crumbled the metal to powder in her hands. Flinging the powdered silver into the flames, she leapt back.

The explosion that followed was spectacular. The coils around Syluné spasmed, flinging her free—and then smashed into her body with the force of a charging war horse, hurling her like a rag doll against the side of the tent. She struck, tumbled, and came to rest atop Torm, who madly stabbed the Malaugrym and sobbed with rage.

"It's dead, Torm," Syluné told him gently, putting a hand on his shoulder as she looked over him at the gory lumps that had been the other Malaugrym. "And so's the other one."

"Gods," the thief hissed, eyes blazing, "they could have killed you!"

"Yes," Syluné agreed, "but they did not, thanks in part to you." She put up her hand to wipe the sweat from his brow, then leaned forward and kissed him. He stared at her for a moment, and threw his arms around her, weeping uncontrollably.

"It's been rather a long time since any man got this angry for my sake," she murmured into his shoulder, "but try not to get yourself killed defending me, Torm!"

"Why not?" the thief said when he found enough control to speak. "Have you seen what they did to your hair?"

8
The Ring of Skulls

Swords Creek, Mistledale, Flamerule 17

Sharantyr shades her eyes again and is sure of it.
Another flash, there . . . and another. And then Zhents
are pouring out of the woods in a hundred places, the
bright morning sun glinting on ebon armor.

There is a stir along the banks of Swords Creek, and
the short bark of Kuthe's order off to the right. The Riders of Mistledale move amid a growing thunder of
hooves, hurrying along the southern edge of the dale to
meet the invaders. Lance tips glitter as they sweep
down.

Restless, the lady ranger hefts her own gleaming
blade, licks her lips, and watches Kuthe's lance lowered
with menacing force. He flicks it expertly, taking out
the throat of a Zhentilar as he passes, and with bright
blood still trailing from the tip, buries it deep in the
face of the first Zhent horseman to appear out of the
woods.

The man crumples as he's flung back out of his
saddle. A score of crashes follow up and down the edge
of the trees as Zhent maces and spears find shields or
the Riders behind them and a horn sounds from just behind Shar, calling the retreat.

Horses wheel and rear. Zhentilar soldiers race in to

gut the retreating warriors as they turn away. One Rider tarries too long, and Shar sees him go down, hacking frantically with his blade at a dozen foes as they drag him to ground and stab him. The riderless mount in fear lashes out with its hooves, leaps wildly into the air, shedding broken Zhent armsmen like rag dolls, and lands running west down the dale to where Kuthe is rallying the Riders.

Arrows hiss past Shar's shoulder as the farmers of Mistledale, faces set in fear and determination, strike their own first blows against the foe. Only a few black-armored figures fall, and now they're streaming out of the trees by the hundreds, a glittering black carpet of death that advances west with casual confidence. More than one of the watchers along Swords Creek gasps or retches in fear; there are thousands of Zhents!

"Gods," a man nearby mutters in despair and disbelief, "have they been breeding armsmen like rabbits? *Look* at them!"

* * * * *

Certain death was coming for them, and they all knew it. Shar traded tight grins with Belkram and Itharr as they heard Torm's voice lifted in jaunty song:

> *"Come, oh, come play with me!*
> *Bring, oh, bring your sword, and*
> *We'll be three!"*

The Riders had succeeded in keeping the foe east of the creek. Secure in their numbers, none of the Zhentilar had moved to outflank the paltry line of waiting warriors . . . yet. Nor were they bothering with any sort of tight formation, merely gathering in mobs around a dozen steadily advancing standards.

Shar's lip curled in derision, and then she shrugged. Outnumbering us hundreds to one, what do they need of discipline or battlecraft?

The Sword of the South came on without pause or parley. Shar looked again at the Riders, wondering if they'd mount another charge to disrupt the steady Zhent advance. Kuthe's helm turned; the white-horse blazon caught the sun as he looked back at her. And then his helm jerked sharply back east again.

There was a murmur from the defenders of Mistledale as they all saw what Kuthe had espied the casting of, from his high saddle: eight tiny balls of fire spun up into view and roared across Swords Creek, howling through the air and growing in size and fury as they came.

The line of defenders raised their shields and shifted uneasily as the roaring conflagration spun nearer—but then the spinning flames and sparks rippled, pulsed . . . and were gone. Swarms of birds and smoke spread harmlessly across the sky. The unseen wild magic shields in front of the defenders had worked.

A shout of satisfaction arose from the defenders—but it was answered by a ragged cry of excitement, rising from the Zhent ranks. A trumpet blared, and the Sword of the South charged forward. They lowered their spears and trotted into the creek, a sea of soldiers flanked by two bands of mounted armsmen. The horsemen to the north splashed slowly down through the creek, avoiding the road—no doubt fearing traps. Their comrades to the south spurred across the creek in a spray of waters, and gathered speed as they hurtled up the west bank toward the Riders.

Shar looked from one forest of black helms to the other . . . and back again. Was it going to be all over in the first few breaths? *There aren't enough of us to stand for more than one charge . . . and that only with luck.*

The screams began. The Zhent horsemen to the right were raising frantic shields or toppling from their saddles as a storm of blades twinkled and flashed around them at faces and throats.

"First blow to Chauntea," Itharr murmured, watching them plunge on into oblivion. None of the Zhentilar horsemen reached the leveled lances of the waiting Riders, and few managed to pull out of that storm of steel to flee.

Lighting cracked and flashed low over the Zhent ranks, stabbing at the defenders of Mistledale . . . but became a stream of red rose petals, and drifted away on the quickening breeze. There were chuckles up and down the line of defenders. The sweat of quickening fear was making Shar's blade sticky; she shifted her grip on it and snatched a last glance to the north before the first Zhents reached her.

The northern Zhent cavalry had crossed the creek and were lowering their lances to meet a single line of Riders that had come out of nowhere to bar their path. With an exultant roar they swept down *through* the phantom forms of the waiting Riders . . . and plunged into the spike-lined disemboweling pits. At about the same time, the arrows of the best archers of Mistledale found them.

A spear cast out of the Zhent lines clipped the edge of Sharantyr's shield, and she found herself in the midst of what all battles become: a crowded, confused whirlwind of hard-plied steel crashing down on shields and armor, skirling off opposing blades—and sinking into screaming men.

A Zhentilar armsman swung a huge morningstar at her. Shar threw herself to her knees. As the weapon rattled past overhead, she struck upward with her shield, hurling her foe off-balance. She swept her sword up into the throat of the next charging armsman, who staggered on, dead already, and ran his blade into the armpit of the man with the morningstar. They crashed down together, and Shar shook their blood out of her eyes and took a hasty step aside to put her blade into the neck of a tall armsman who'd engaged Belkram, and was straining to overwhelm the snarling Harper. The man reeled and went down, spraying her with more blood. Belkram gave her a fierce grin of thanks as they faced the next Zhents shoulder to shoulder.

Arrows were still hissing past; there were so many Zhents that the dale farmers could fire over the heads of those in the fray and yet find targets in plenty. A horn rang out, calling the defenders of the dale to retreat to the second line of standards.

In answer to its call, Shar smashed her way free of a tightening knot of Zhentilar and backed hastily from the creek. One of the orange standards that marked a gap in the wild magic shields fluttered off to her left, and she saw Jhessail and Illistyl crouching by it, behind Merith's raised sword and shield. Their hands wove in spellcasting gestures.

Shar slashed an overly enthusiastic Zhent across the face, and as he went down, watched the spell of her fellow Knights take effect.

Upended helms full of metal shards and salvaged arrowheads were rising from the ground with slow, menacing force—one, three . . . six in all. Zhents were backing uncertainly away from them, but one man hacked at a helm with his blade.

He was the first to fall, ripped apart as the magic erupted, transforming the helms and their contents into pinwheel sprays of arrows that tore into the Zhent host on all sides.

Zhentilar blackhelms screamed in chorus and fell in great swathes, as if harvested by a gigantic, invisible scythe. Shar felt her gorge rise. She turned away from the sight and hastened back to the rallying standards, Belkram and Itharr at her side. There were still thousands of Zhents left; the Sword of the South was surging on across the creek, heedless of the cost. As the defenders gathered at the standards another horn call rang out from their midst.

This one was meant for the hidden Harpers. Trip

wires hidden among the trampled grass were tightened now, and . . .

As it happened, Shar watched the first shield rise, spilling a startled Zhent forward—and revealing a Harper with a loaded crossbow. He discharged his quarrel into the face of the nearest Zhent officer, dropped the bow, and snatched up his spear to ward away a charging armsman. That gave the other two Harpers in the hole time to scramble out, gain their feet, and begin their race through the Zhent rear, hacking and slashing at the full run.

Men and women in leather boiled up out of the ground in two dozen places or more, and there was much shouting and chaos. Shar had a brief glimpse of a furious-looking man in robes—a Zhent wizard, she realized—stumbling hastily away from a seeking blade. Then she was much too busy to look at anything but the foes all around, their blades falling on her own with the force of hammers.

The Sword of the South rolled into the defenders again, a wall of grim men wielding blades and maces. They pushed the outnumbered dalefolk slowly back to higher ground. Another horn cried out from just behind her, and Shar flung herself flat.

An instant later, arrows hissed over her in a deadly stream, and the front rank of Zhents melted away, hurled to the ground like torn thorn bushes. A brief blip of the horn indicated it was safe to rise.

Sharantyr found her feet and stared across bloodsoaked ground at the Zhents . . . over the frightened faces of the Zhentilar rearguard, back across the creek. There, Harper swords flashed, message runners fell, and Zhent officers shouted and flailed in disarray. A rolling ball of flame told her at least one Harper spell had worked—a lone Harper paused, tossed sweat-soaked hair out of his eyes, and lashed half a dozen pursuers with a bright net of fire.

The Harpers were pitifully few. Most of those fighting

south to a rallying point were going down, attacked from all sides by enraged and fearful Zhents. Shar saw one armsman catch his foot on the edge of an open Harper hole and fall helplessly away from the ranger he was attacking. The man leapt across the hole, breaking free of a ring of Zhents, and raced toward a banner that had been set alight as a rallying point.

Not far behind Shar, Margrueth muttered an incantation. A flying Zhent spear headed past her, and she dived sideways to smash it down with her shield, for fear it would reach the sorceress.

It skidded into the dirt, and an instant later came Margrueth's short bark of satisfaction. A wall of twinkling swords blinked into solidity in the air around the surviving Harpers, chopping down pursuing Zhents. Men jerked and fell in that deadly whirlwind.

A black-robed Zhentarim wizard strode toward the wall of swords, careful to keep in the lee of a trio of large shields held high by armsmen. He raised his hands and gestured grandly—but was answered by fearful shouts as his magic went wild. Instead of fading away, the blades flew in all directions, butchering Harpers and Zhents alike.

A strident horn call began another Zhent cavalry charge, striking at the Riders again along the southern edge of the dale. The ground shook as sixty or more horsemen gathered speed, heading west. The Zhentilar foot soldiers advanced, too, striding purposefully to overwhelm the few defenders.

Shar caught a seeking sword on her dagger, warded it away, and drove her own blade into the man's throat. As he spun away, clutching the spraying gore, she sprang to meet the next man, leaping high to put all her weight behind the downstroke. Her steel glanced off the guards of a slow parrying blade and sheared through its wielder's jaw. He fell back, choking, and was trampled by his fellow soldiers in their hunger to get at her.

"Hold the line!" she heard Rathan Thentraver roar, somewhere to the left.

A Harper fell against her leg and went down, a sword in his face. Only Belkram's swift blade saved Shar, and they retreated together, Itharr striking aside Zhent blades from one side.

"Kiss my steel!" Torm shouted defiantly nearby, and was answered by a short scream.

Shar reeled, found her footing again, and glared wildly around. The defenders of Mistledale were reduced to a few knots of struggling swords—themselves and the Knights of Myth Drannor. The gaps in the line were so large now that the farmers, back behind the fray, could loose shafts freely through them—and only that paltry but deadly fire was keeping the Zhents from sweeping forward to surround and rout them.

The horns called anew. The defenders fell back again, seeking another line of standards as lightnings danced briefly among the Zhents. The creek was far off now, across a sea of bobbing black helms, and the iron taste of grim despair rose in Sharantyr's mouth.

They were all going to die here, today, swept away by a thousand Zhent blades, sent to their deaths by Elminster in this dark time on Faerûn. . . .

With a crash that shook the battlefield, the Zhent cavalry and the Riders of Mistledale rushed together. A breath later, something flashed across the sky. The Zhentarim spellmaster tried another futile spell—and was answered by Jhessail and Illistyl, who sent a dancing serpent of flame through the ranks of the advancing armsmen.

Shar heard Syluné's voice rise in sudden passion. An instant later, a knot of Zhentilar armsmen levitated into the air, waving weapons in futile horror, lofting high above the battlefield.

Some of their fellows were too slow witted to avoid walking beneath the shouting spell victims and were gawking up at their fellows aloft when the Zhentilar plunged back to earth. They crashed down like so much spilled kindling to smash into bloody ruin on the earth and raised blades below.

The Zhent advance faltered. In the sudden lull, a man in old and shiny black Rider armor pushed past Shar and strode into the Zhent ranks, a shimmering arrowhead of force preceding him, cleaving men who stood in his way.

"Here me, Tempus, Lord of Battles!" the man roared as he went, hands raised and empty. "Let the old warriors rise, if it pleases ye! Raise a ring of skulls, I entreat ye! Oh, Tempus!"

It was the old Rider, Baergil. A Zhent, drawn sword in hand, ducked around behind the old priest's magic and raced in. As he jerked back the white-horse helm and drew his sword viciously across the exposed throat, there came one last, bubbling cry of "Tempusss!"

The spell was complete. Baergil's body blazed with sudden blue fire. His slayer fell back in awe. The dead priest hung upright in the streaming flames, hands uplifted to the sky, and men murmured at the sight.

Cries of awe and fear came as the trampled turf under the Zhents erupted. Staring things of mottled green and brown bones burst up out of the soil . . . rising through the horrified armsmen to form into a silent, floating ring of skulls just overhead. Many battles had been fought by the banks of Swords Creek, and countless warriors had fallen here, to lie under the earth until called up by so mighty a magic.

The eyes of the skulls flared into sudden fire, the same cold, eerie blue flame that blazed around Baergil. Zhentilar cried out in alarm and began to run—but nothing could flee fast enough to escape the rays of chill light that lanced from the skulls through the Zhent host.

Where those blue rays touched the running or striding armsmen of the Sword of the South, flesh melted away, leaving only bones. Skeletal warriors rushed on for a pace or two, and then collapsed.

The Zhents on the far side of the creek and the defenders of Mistledale alike stared in horror as thousands of armsmen died.

When no man was left standing between Baergil's corpse and the creek, the skulls turned until the rays that streamed from their glowing sockets met in the heart of the field of bones. Blue light pulsed and built to almost blinding fury, and gauntlets were raised to shield eyes all over the battlefield. An armored form strode along in the heart of the radiance.

It had been striding forever, it seemed, fearless and patient, a figure twelve feet tall and clad in a full suit of gleaming plate armor, visor down. As the rays began to fade and the skulls sank back to the earth in silent unison, the armored figure was suddenly among them, treading on Zhentilar bones without a sound, walking toward Baergil.

"The War God," someone whispered. The defenders of Mistledale fell back at the armored giant's approach.

In eerie silence, two flaming blue gauntlets reached out and took up the priest's body, cradling it against the massive chest. The Knights of Myth Drannor parted in respectful silence. The helm turned slowly from side to side to survey them, and for just a moment Shar felt the scorching weight of eyes that blazed like two red flames.

In silence, Tempus strode on, west toward distant Ashabenford, bearing Baergil's body in his arms. To those who watched, it seemed the body began to burn, blazing its own miniature pyre.

The implacable avatar vanished over the hill . . . and left the handful of weary men and women to defend Mistledale against several thousand shaken Zhentilar soldiers.

What was left of the Sword of the South stood along the east bank of Swords Creek, still more than enough armsmen to crush the few who resisted them. Their hireswords and booty brothers were among the fallen; those who remained were veteran Zhent blackhelms. In fearful, sullen silence, they eyed the field of death before them, but orders were shouted, and officers ran about brandishing maces . . . and reluctantly, the soldiers of Zhentil Keep began to advance.

"It must be now," Sharantyr heard Syluné say quietly.

In the distance, there came a sudden burst of radiance as the Witch of Shadowdale appeared in the heart of the Zhents . . . in the small space between Swordlord Amglar and Spellmaster Nentor Thuldoum. The men broke off their arguing to gape in unison at the beautiful woman who stood between them, the glow of her magic fading around her.

"Well met indeed, gentlesirs," Syluné told them softly, raising her lithe arms in glee.

The magic missiles that streamed out of her riddled both men, even before the fireballs and bolts of lightning leapt forth in their wake.

Amglar and Nentor of the Zhentarim died screaming.

Syluné sang a terrible, wordless song of rage and sorrow for the body she was losing, and her slim-hipped form blazed white with the fury of the magic coursing through her.

Zhentilar stared at the dancing, burning figure in their midst, and then perished in the whirlwind of unleashed spells that sprayed death in all directions from the woman.

Florin swallowed what might have been a sob as he watched bright flames gout from Syluné's eyes and mouth, streaming across scorched turf to immolate shouting Zhentilar, whose vainly hurled spears vanished in that inferno.

There came a quickening of the spell fury, and Syluné's head was gone, blown away with the awesome energies pouring from her. The headless body turned as if it could see, and raised its hands to burn fleeing

Zhent horsemen from their distant saddles. Flames streamed from her neck and hands . . . and before she turned away, her hands were gone, and spells were now leaping from the stumps of her arms.

Someone was rallying the Zhentilar as the stream of spells flickered, and then ceased . . . and men in ebon armor charged across the smoking ground, blades raised to slay the swaying, disintegrating Witch of Shadowdale.

"No!" Belkram roared, waving his own blade in sudden fury. "For Mistledale! For *Syluné!*" He rushed across the strewn bones, his sword held high. Itharr and Florin raced to catch up to him. Sharantyr was moving before she thought about it, following her companions into a band of scattered, dazed-looking Zhent blackhelms still several hundred strong.

Beside her, Shar saw flashing legs and a bouncing bosom, and turned to see Jhessail sprinting along, weaponless, with Illistyl running at her heels and Merith moving with fluid grace and drawn sword.

"Wait!" Rathan puffed, behind them. "Save some Zhents for me!"

They were almost at the stream and the grim-faced foremost Zhents who stood there when what was left of the Witch of Shadowdale vanished in a burst of snarling flames that threw men headlong or sent them fleeing wildly back toward the trees.

Then Belkram, Itharr, and Florin splashed across the stream, roaring out their grief together. They fell upon the Zhents like three maddened reapers mowing wheat. It was the last such harvest that their foes needed to see: the shattered Sword of the South broke and fled, an army no more.

Belkram ran on toward the dying flames that had been Syluné, and Itharr and Florin paced him, swording the few blackhelms foolish enough to get in their way. Sharantyr tried to catch up, but her lungs were burning; she'd never seen men run so fast before.

By the time she reached the spot where Belkram knelt, the Harper was on his knees amid the smoldering ashes, weeping.

The stone cradled so gently in his gauntlets had cracked in the heat. "Lady," Belkram sobbed despairingly, "leave us not!"

But there came no reply but the creak of cooling stone. The Harper raised a face that streamed tears and cried to Florin, *"Do something!"*

The Knight smiled down at him and undid the last buckle of his chest armor. As it fell open, he drew forth something he wore on a chain. A lump of stone. All of the gathered adventurers saw a streak of ghostly radiance arc from the shattered stone to the good one.

The stone winked once with its stored fire, reassuringly. Florin took off the chain and handed it to Belkram. "Yours, I think," the Shield of Shadowdale said quietly. "I think she's grown tired of Torm's tricks."

Belkram's eyes shone. He was still struggling to speak when the Riders of Mistledale swept past with lowered lances, ruthlessly riding down fleeing Zhents. "For Baergil!" they bellowed as they went. "For Baergil!"

Kuthe was in the foremost saddle, swaying and pale, blood all down his front from a deep wound in his shoulder. "Kuthe!" Jhessail called as he spurred his mount past. "Have done! They're beaten!"

He rode in a wide circle back to her, face set, and said, "The field may be ours, Lady, but Mistledale is my home. Every Zhent who can still walk by sunset is a sword that can strike from darkness when we sleep! I'll not rest until they're all dead and done!"

Fflarast Blackriver and the old Harper who'd seen the sky rain wizards for the first time yesterday lay side by side under the very hooves of Kuthe's mount as he snarled those words, but they did not hear him. Dust lay on their staring eyes and still faces, and the darkening blood spilled under them both was the same hue:

one could not tell which was the Harper's, and which belonged to the Zhentilar.

The leader of the Riders spurred away, the weary hooves of his mount trampling both bodies. Florin watched him go. "Where is the captain of the Riders?" he asked quietly.

"Who?" Rathan asked. "That lady paladin?"

"Aye," Florin replied, "I've known her a long time."

"Oho," Torm spoke up, "an old lady friend, eh? May—"

His crowing words ended in a sharp gasp as Illistyl thrust a sharp hand into his gut. "Someday, clever tongue," she warned him, "you'll say just one word too many. . . ."

"Uhhh," Torm agreed, doubled over.

"Indubitably," Rathan translated, looking at the breathless thief with interest.

Florin, ignoring them all, was striding across the field and looking for Captain Nelyssa.

He caught sight of her at last, hard by the trees on the southern edge of the dale, well behind the last standard the defenders of the dale had rallied around. A mound of Zhentilar lay heaped about her and the sprawled bulk of her horse. A band of blackhelms had tried to outflank the fray—and paid for their cunning with their lives. There'd been over thirty of them, though, and it seemed the veteran Zhentilar armsmen were the measure of one paladin of Chauntea.

In a small lake of blood at the heart of the heaped dead lay the hacked and twisted form of Nelyssa, captain of the Riders of Mistledale, her armor torn open down the bloody mess of her front, and her notched and broken blade still clutched in her hand. Even as Florin broke into a run and shouted, lifting the heads of Harpers and farmers who knelt by the still form, he knew he was too late.

Nelyssa's face was unmarked, but bone-white; she looked very like the young lass Florin had known so long ago . . . but her eyes were dark and sightless. The ranger stared into them as he sank down beside her and let out a long, shuddering sigh of grief. Was this madness of strife going to claim all the best hearts and minds before it was done?

"I need your sword, noble Falconhand," said a voice as rough and sharp as the skin of its owner. Margrueth of the Harpers laid her hand on Florin's own. The ranger looked up at her, finding it suddenly hard to drag his eyes away from Nelyssa's frozen face.

When he did, he was shocked at what he saw. The fire of life had gone out of the Harper sorceress, too. She was gray to the lips, and her skin was sunken and shriveled so that it seemed a skull thinly draped with flesh. Only the eyes told him the feisty Margrueth still lived, eyes dancing like two lively dark flames. "You will aid me in this, Knight. I must have your oath on it."

"My oath?" Weary and sad as he was, Florin still found that he could be startled. He looked around at the wondering farmers and the grim-faced Harpers, leaving him alone with the living woman and the dead one. They looked back at him. His oath. Whatever for?

And then, because she was old Margrueth and she was a Harper—and because he was Florin Falconhand—he turned to meet those wise old eyes. Holding her gaze, he lifted his voice to say clearly, "In Mielikki's name and mine own, I, Florin Falconhand, born of Cormyr, Lord of Shadowdale and Knight of Myth Drannor, promise on my honor to aid you, Margrueth, on this day and on this field, as you would command me."

"Nicely done," Margrueth said with a smile. "Now this is what I'll have you do—and swiftly, for the spells I wove today burned much life from me . . . I'd not live to see sunset whatever befell. Know for your own comfort that I act freely in this, and my wits are mine own."

She laid herself down, wheezing a little, atop Nelyssa's body, face to face. "Count four breaths, noble Florin, and plunge your blade into my back. Mind that it goes right through me, and into the lass beneath—

and that you hold it thus for a breath, no more. Do this." And with that order, she put her lips to the paladin's mouth.

Florin stared down at her, swallowed, and then said hurriedly, in the two breaths left to him, "You shall be remembered with honor, Margrueth!"

As he'd been bid, he brought his blade down in a clean thrust, right through the old sorceress, and into Nelyssa beneath, where her armor was all riven away down her front. Margrueth jerked once under his steel, and blue-white light, like many tiny lightnings, crackled and danced around the joined lips of the two women.

Florin drew his blade out carefully. For a moment, the same radiance clung to its suddenly shining length. It looked as bright and sharp as it was when new, the scrapes and nicks of battle gone from it.

Yet more wondrous far was what befell where it had been. Margrueth's body was twisting and contracting into a thing of curling smoke, to the accompaniment of one last, dry chuckle.

That sound faded, and Nelyssa's revealed body stirred, color returned to her face, and a light came into her dark eyes. She slowly sat up.

"Florin?" she asked softly as the Harpers and farmers around cried out in wonder, gasped, or wept, "Have I slept? Is the day won—or lost?"

And Florin Falconhand cast aside his blade and knelt to take her in his arms. "Won for some, Captain . . . won for Mistledale. And yet lost for others, lost forever. Margrueth traded her life for yours."

The captain of the Riders turned pale. "No!"

"Aye, Nelyssa," Florin said gently, "you must know this, and hear the truth. She chose freely, and worked a magic I did not know, binding me under oath. Mine was the blade that took her life, and gave it to you. She was at the end of her life, drained by this battle . . . and brought you back to us."

The paladin of Chauntea flung her arms around him

and wept.

* * * * *

"Hmmph," Torm said to Rathan as they trudged across the field, taking up the best weapons and tossing them on a farmer's sledge to bear back to Ashabenford, "women never do that to *me*. My arms await—see? Here they are, two of them, and fairly well matched to each other, too—and do ladies sob their sorrows away into my breast? No! Is it the cut of his chin, d'you think? The wave in his hair? His strong, manly bearing? Those gleaming teeth?"

"All of those," his friend agreed. "Now give me a hand with this halberd—*three* dead ones draped over it, look ye; three—and take comfort in the fact that ye've probably been in almost as many strange beds as he has . . . an' that ye're better far at stealing things."

"Umm," Torm agreed, looking again at the woman in Florin's arms. His eyes fell to the dark, sticky puddle of blood they shared, and he swallowed. So much blood. . . .

"When we get back to the Six Shields," he told Rathan fiercely, "I'm going to get very drunk!"

"Oh? Don't forget that ye lost the bet with Syluné! We won the battle, so ye have to wear the scanties ye were putting on her, an' go sit in the window!"

"But she's . . . dead. You won't hold me to—"

"Oh, but I will," Rathan said softly. "In memory of her, ye *will* sit in that window this night, if I have to break thy limbs to get the fripperies onto ye."

Torm tore a gorget free of a Zhentilar who'd not be needing it anymore, and flung it with a clatter onto the sledge. "I'm going to get very *very* drunk!" he said fiercely, "first."

"Hmm," Rathan said, lifting a body into the air with one hand to pluck daggers free with the other, "that'll make the dressing an amusing affair. May I watch?"

* * * * *

"He'll be too drunk to stop anyone from watching," one buzzard commented to the other, shifting a little on a low, bare branch as a nearby farmer gave them a dirty look, bent to pick up a fallen bow, and then shrugged and turned away, knowing he couldn't hit the tree, let alone two watchful carrion birds.

"Faerûn certainly affords more entertainment than Shadowhome," Bralatar said, remembering the battle as he looked out over the ravaged field.

"And because the peril to and consequences for us are the less, one can really enjoy it," Lorgyn replied, watching Merith and Jhessail embrace, and Illistyl, after a moment, turn and look around the battlefield for Torm.

"I *cannot* understand the thinking of Yinthrim, to throw life and all the unfolding chances of this world away just to try to avenge kin who may well have plotted his own death, had they lived."

"Atarl, yes," Lorgyn agreed, "would always plunge into battle, given the slightest of excuses, but such folly is unusual for Yinthrim." He looked at the site of the tent where the two Malaugrym had perished the night before—now a trampled sward strewn with sprawled bodies. He shrugged. "I guess battle hunger overtook them."

"Battle hunger? Attacking three sleeping humans is something done out of 'battle hunger'?" Bralatar had a fine, showy grasp of sarcastic incredulity when something aroused him to it. He shifted on the branch, fluttering his feathers in irritation. "Admit they liked to slay folk, and fatally misjudged the fervor of these mortals, and have done with it. Two fewer fools to breed will make our house that much the stronger."

"A phrase fit for a speech of any Shadowmaster High," Lorgyn acknowledged, bowing his head. "So when, in your judgment, would it be best that we make *our* strike against the three who dared to intrude into

Shadowhome, and slay so many Malaugrym?"

"When those three rangers are much older, and we've seen far more of this world—or at least, not now," Bralatar replied with his usual sharp humor. "Those two maids over there—Jhessail and Illistyl, if I heard aright—still have spells left. And who knows how many of those Harpers are mages? I'm not descending into the midst of a battlefield where one old man called down a *god* not long ago!"

"And the Lord of Battles at that," Lorgyn agreed. "Now is not a good time."

" 'Now' is never a good time," Bralatar said dryly.

* * * * *

"At first light," Florin ordered, looking around the map-strewn room, "we ride north to Shadowdale, where our swords are sorely needed."

Kuthe nodded grimly. "Haste must be our course, yes." He looked at the cot where Nelyssa lay, nodding weakly.

"I shall ride to Shadowdale on the morrow," she said firmly, "and any man who shouts at me not to go will serve me as a replacement mount!"

Kuthe closed his open mouth stiffly, and turned his head away, then swung it around again, opened his mouth to speak, caught her eye—and closed his jaws once more.

Torm and Rathan, scratching at their rough, stiff bandages, sputtered with mirth and went out hastily.

"Ah, 'twas worth all that jabber to see Lord High-and-Mighty's face!" Torm chuckled. "Now, let's be finding that drink I was talking of . . . "

"I'll go with ye," Rathan said grimly. "Too many friends fell this day. I want to feel a small fire in my belly this night."

Torm raised his eyebrows. "And why not? You do that every other night; why change things now?"

Rathan favored him with both a weary look and an unpriestly gesture.

* * * * *

Just after the two Knights had wearily passed around a corner of the street, a door swung open, and Illistyl hurried, white-faced, out into the waiting night. Her mind yet burned with the sight of a Rider's crushed leg being amputated, the grim faces of sawing surgeon and patient, the Rider's rolling eyes. Illistyl shook her head as she stumbled along in the darkness, but could not shake the images away. . . .

Suddenly something was rising within her. She fell heavily to her knees and vomited into the dark grass.

A weary Rider turned his head at the sound, watched her sobbing out the contents of her stomach, and turned back to sewing up a comrade's slashed arm.

"Hmm," he said thoughtfully, "it seems great adventurers are human after all."

His older companion winced as the needle went in again. "Oh, they're human, lad . . . all too human. That's where most of the trouble begins."

9
Even Wizards Must Die

The mists of morning were still drifting off the river as the Knights of Myth Drannor and the Riders of Mistledale rode north together, leather creaking loudly among the riverbank trees. They pressed on, stiff and sore from yesterday's fighting, but more than one Rider wore a wondering smile as he looked around at the awakening forest on this bright morning he'd not expected to see.

"Such a victory," one man muttered to his companion. "Thousands we sent to their graves. 'Twas the favor of the gods, to be sure, that we weren't all sent to the Deathrealms in their first charge, and Mistledale laid waste before highsun!"

"Aye, we place much store in the favor of the gods," his comrade replied, "or we'd not be riding straight into another battle!" He pointed ahead. Plumes of smoke rose into the sky to the north.

Shadowdale was burning.

The Knights and Riders pressed on up the Mistle Trail, urging their mounts to greater haste.

Torm waved a hand at the smoke and said loudly and bitterly, "Look! We'll get there in time to join the Zhents at their fires, with the dale pillaged and burned and not a man or maid left to fight for!"

"Say not so!" Merith told him, but Kuthe and Nelyssa nodded slowly.

"We've taken this way in haste before," the captain of the Riders said, her eyes very dark, "and spent more than a day in the forest . . . and that was a few riders on fresh, swift mounts—not a force this large that fought yesterday."

Belkram was frowning and holding his head to one side, as if listening to something. He straightened in his saddle and said, "There is a way to take us there more swiftly."

Florin Falconhand, who rode at the head of the column, turned his head. "You mean magic," he said grimly. "Is that wise, given the chaos ruling sorcery?"

Belkram listened for a breath longer, and then shrugged. "Syluné says teleportation seems unaffected—it served her even on the battlefield yestermorn, passing wild magic shields to do so."

"Without a body, she can't cast any spells," Kuthe pointed out. "What good is it if the Lady Jhessail here hurls one of us on ahead? A lone rider makes a better target than a relief force!"

"There is a way to take us all," Belkram replied slowly, passing on the words from the stone that held the Witch of Shadowdale. "Elminster taught it to m— her."

The ranger nodded. "There is a risk," Florin said; it was a statement, not a query. He looked around at the others, holding up his hand for a halt. "Are you willing to take on that danger? All of you?"

The Knights nodded without hesitation. Among the Riders were some swift glances back and forth, and shrugs. One leaned forward and asked Florin, "Are you?"

The Shield of Shadowdale shrugged. "Of course."

"He's a Knight of Myth Drannor," Rathan explained as if to a child.

"Which is to say, he's a reckless idiot," Torm elaborated in a stage whisper.

The men of Mistledale were still chuckling when Captain Nelyssa said crisply, "I will undergo this magic. Let us be about it."

"We'll need some space," Belkram said, and pointed into the trees. "That glade there."

Nelyssa nodded. "Let all who are unwilling to chance this spell stay here on the trail." She turned her horse's head and guided it into the trees.

As they followed, Belkram looked at Jhessail. "You must do the casting."

She wrinkled her nose at him. "So I'd gathered."

No one stayed on the road. When everyone was arrayed around Belkram, he took off the chain and gave it to Jhessail. She held up the stone, and grew still for a moment as she listened. Merith, who'd been in such castings before, slid deftly from his saddle and lay on the ground, taking hold of one hoof of his horse and one of his lady's ankles. Florin edged his mount over to take a firm hold on Merith's horse, and Sharantyr, Itharr, Belkram, Captain Nelyssa, and Kuthe followed, creating a human chain.

Jhessail smiled her thanks, and said, "Draw in close, everyone—to touch at least one other person or their mount. Remain that way, and don't pull free until we're elsewhere."

She drew a deep breath and put the stone into her mouth. Closing her eyes in concentration, Jhessail followed Syluné's guidance in the casting. The loop of chain dangling from her chin rattled as she moved. After a brief series of gestures, she threw both hands high into the air and froze.

A blue mist raced out from her body to swirl around them all. It rose, growing thicker and winking with small flashes of blue light . . . light that was suddenly blinding, blotting the world out in an shifting, drifting swirl . . . that faded away to show Faerûn again.

They were in a different clearing—a larger space littered with felled trees and stacked firewood. To the north was daylight, where the woods gave way to the first fields of Shadowdale. Through the cloaking trees, they saw the stone bridge over the Ashaba, where a watchful guard always stood.

A guard of three frightened old men, whose spears trembled in their hands as they shouted in alarm at the sudden appearance of so many horsemen. Florin took his hand from Merith's horse to raise it in a reassuring salute.

Jhessail shuddered and collapsed silently onto her husband, the stone falling from her mouth.

"Is she—?" Belkram and Itharr said together, leaning anxiously down. Merith cradled her as he reached out, plucked up the stone that was Syluné, and held it up to Belkram.

"Drained, not dead," the elf said softly. "A mass teleport is something far beyond her Art. Though Syluné gave direction, my Jhess worked the spell."

"We must still make haste," Nelyssa reminded.

Illistyl frowned. "Florin! Come back here!"

The ranger, who was halfway to the bridge, acknowledged the relieved greetings of the dalesmen before he turned questioningly.

"I haven't Art to equal Jhess's," the younger sorceress said, "but I can manage something you should use now."

Florin was already hurrying his war horse back to her. Firefoam had paced restlessly back and forth behind the lines of the battle yesterday, and was eager to get into a proper fray; he snorted and tossed his head as they approached Illistyl, fearing he would be relegated to stand and watch, again. The diminutive sorceress stood looking up at him as his great muzzle lowered to her nose.

"How would you like to fly?" she asked softly.

Firefoam's bugle awoke echoes from the trees around and made many of the other horses stamp and whinny.

"Fly ahead," Illistyl said, looking up at Florin, "and see where we're needed. Rally folk, and return if you need us anywhere in particular—otherwise, we'll just charge on up the road and kill Zhents!"

"A shrewd grasp of tactics," Captain Nelyssa said dryly.

Illistyl cast her spell with deft speed.

Florin scooped the limp form of Jhessail from Merith's arms and settled her against his own chest.

"Done! Get you gone!" Illistyl cried, waving her hands; Florin smiled his thanks and saluted as Firefoam bounded aloft—and was gone across the sky, heading for the distant Tower of Ashaba.

As they hurried across, Jhessail asked the first old farmer on the bridge, "How goes the battle?"

"Not well," he rasped. "Too many Zhents!"

"A problem we're familiar with," Torm agreed grandly, urging his horse off the bridge.

An instant later, the ground rocked and thundered. Riders fought to control snorting mounts and stay in their saddles as they gaped at a huge ball of flame that rose up, up into the sky over Shadowdale.

"The tower?" Illistyl gasped, white to the lips. "Florin?"

"Not the tower," Jhessail said, shaking her head. "But close by, west and south."

"The temple of Lathander," Rathan grunted, "or I'm an idiot."

"You *are* an idiot," Torm pointed out.

Rathan's reply was a certain wordless gesture with his mace as he hauled on the reins, taking his horse to one side of the cart road and gaining room to gallop. Torm cast a quick look back to see all the Riders doing so, and pulled his mount to the left, catching a glare from Kuthe for his tardiness.

"Ready, all?" Captain Nelyssa asked crisply. *"Forward!"*

At her yell, they nudged their mounts into a gallop

and swept north into the heart of Shadowdale.

The smoke lay like a haze in the air here, drifting out of the trees to the east, and the fields around them were green and deserted. Up ahead, they could hear the swelling sound of shouts and screams and the clangor of steel on steel. Here and there a blade flashed as it caught the sunlight through the smoke and swirling dust.

The crossroads in front of the Old Skull Inn was heaped with dead. The twisted mounds were so high the Zhentilar, advancing in a great horde from the east, had to scramble and climb. The grisly, slippery wall was being held against them by desperate dalesmen wielding axes and blades.

Among the dusty defenders were Storm Silverhand and her sister, Dove, both clad in battered and scorched plate armor but bareheaded, their silver tresses swirling as they fought. Storm leapt into the air and smashed aside a foe's blade, her other hand snaking in to take him by the throat. Muscles rippled in her arm as they crashed back down to earth together. The Zhent blackhelm struggled for a moment in her iron grip— then fell limp, his neck broken. Two of his fellows scrambled up the mound of dead, waving blades to get their chance at the Bard of Shadowdale.

Dove Falconhand took that chance away, rushing along the line of defenders to thrust one Zhent desperately aside into the other armsman. Off-balance, the blackhelms stumbled among the corpses. Storm dumped the man she'd just slain atop one, and kicked the other in the face with her boot. He fell down the heap, head rolling limply, and was smashed aside by more Zhentilar rushing up to challenge Storm in their turn.

"That's the problem with Zhents," Rathan growled as they turned their horses toward the black-armored host crowded up against the wall of dead. "There're always too many of them."

"Lances *down!*" Nelyssa cried, and led the charge.

Through the thunder of pounding hooves they heard someone of Shadowdale cry, "The Riders! The Riders of Mistledale!"

"And the mighty Torm, too!" the thief shouted back, just before they crashed into the Zhent lines.

Men reeled like broken dolls under the impact of hooves and lances and thundering war horses, and when the press of bodies slowed their progress, the Riders let go their lances and laid about themselves with swords and maces.

"Shadowdale!" Dove Falconhand snarled, leading a charge from the ridge of slain.

There were screams of agony and frustration from the Zhents, packed too tightly together to raise weapons or move from the blades.

A desperately wielded spear sought Torm's thigh; he sprang from his saddle and vaulted into the fray, drawn sword extended between his boots. He came down atop a Zhentilar and rode the man to the ground, stabbing viciously with the dagger in his free hand. The man convulsed and lay still; by then Torm was two kills away, his slim blade and dagger sliding in and out before the close-packed Zhents could react.

With a wall of corpses around him like a shield, he struck out from between their bodies, swift and sure, thrusting, dancing away from blades . . . until the crash of a felled Rider and his horse cleared some space, and the dead began to topple and slump all around.

Into the opened space leapt Storm, clapping a gasping Torm on his shoulder. "Bravely done!"

"Ah—all for . . . you . . . Lady," Torm huffed, trying to essay a courtly bow—and slipping in gore so that he lurched to one knee. The fall saved his life; a whirling axe meant for his head flashed harmlessly through empty air.

Storm hauled him upright. "The battle's *this* way," she said helpfully, pointing with a sword that was red to the hilt.

He gave her a fierce smile in answer. Then his jaw dropped. "By the gods, look!" he bellowed, pointing. Storm turned in time to see Belkram, Itharr, and Sharantyr advance another pace through the ranks of Zhentilar. Fighting in unison, standing close together in a human arrowhead, they were dealing death with furious speed.

"The Rangers Three," Storm said, watching her pupils in admiration.

The hesitant gangliness she'd seen all too often the day she'd fought Belkram and Itharr at the farmhouse was gone. Now they moved like dancers, deft and quick. Sharantyr was the key. Her smooth style had drawn the two Harpers into a team. Storm began to believe their survival in the castle of the Malaugrym was more than good fortune bolstered by the aid of Mystra and Elminster. She shook her head in pleased admiration and threw herself into the battle once more, coming up alongside the Rangers Three in their bloody foray into the Zhent ranks.

The Rider charge had cleared space enough to fight, and the easy killing was done. Fresh Zhents were pressing forward for their first chance to fight, and there seemed no end to them.

They'd struck at Shadowdale from the west, and from the north. Some fell magic had wrought a great explosion and fire westward, hard by the Twisted Tower. There was fighting all over the dale, and the day might still be lost—but this welcome, unexpected aid had come from Mistledale, from whence she'd expected only more blackhelms.

"Azuth be with us," she breathed, feeling fresh sorrow at the thought that Mystra was no more.

Storm swept her notched long sword up to strike aside a reaching halberd. Catching hold of it as the man rushed helplessly forward, she pulled, sprawling him to the turf in front of her. A dalesman stabbed the Zhent in the face before he could rise, and from somewhere near at hand Storm heard the deep laughter of Bronn Selgard, the smith. Dove must be rallying the last folk from the inn to join this push, to drive the Zhents back into the trees.

There was a ringing sound as the great iron-headed hammer Bronn wielded crashed down on some unfortunate Zhent's helm. The winded Rangers Three began to fall back. A spell hurled bodies in all directions, tearing a breach in the wall of corpses behind her.

Storm turned, frowning—creating a breach for the Zhents to pour through? What simpleton had birthed such a plan?—and then laughed aloud in delight.

"For Shadowdale!" came the roar from beyond the wall. Warriors in full plate armor rode through the breach, lances gleaming. At their head, three figures rode abreast: Florin; Mourngrym, lord of Shadowdale; and Shaerl, his lady.

" 'Ware!" Storm yelled to the Rangers Three, waving them aside.

Dove sprang acrobatically across the path of the charging horses, somersaulted in a clanking of protesting armor, and fetched up beside Storm. Just then, the lances of the charging dalefolk came down, crashing into the massed Zhentilar in a great screaming of men and horses and tortured metal.

As first, the horses were slowed by the sheer weight of blackhelms standing against them. The mounted armsmen of the tower spurred out and around them, striking at the foe on either side. When the last horseman had charged, the Zhent lines had fallen back a good twenty paces—a distance marked by a carpet of black-armored fallen.

The dale riders pulled back to spare their horses from Zhent blades, and a cheer went up from the weary farmers and merchants who'd held the wall of dead so long against the forefront of the Zhent army.

A little space opened up between the defenders and

the army of Zhentil Keep; Dove stared across it and hissed, "Oh, for some arrows . . ."

"All gone, hours ago," Storm told her, and they embraced wearily, eyes on the foe. Both sides had paused to catch breath, it seemed, staring at each other across the fallen, but making no move to attack.

"Gods, look how many there are," Shaerl murmured. "Can we hold them until sunset?"

"We must," Mourngrym replied shortly, looking around at the dead. "And dark'll bring the wolves and wild dogs out to feed, too."

"Well fought, you three," Storm called to Belkram, Itharr, and Sharantyr, who'd sat down together on some dead Zhentilar, rubbing at aching shoulders and bruised forearms.

"Of course," Itharr replied. "After all, you taught us."

Storm chuckled. "To dance with your blade, aye, a little—but fighting as one is your own doing."

"They're coming again," Dove said, striding forward. " 'Ware, all!"

She swung her sword in wide, wild arcs to loosen stiffening muscles, and set herself to meet the Zhentilar attack; a cautious affair this time, with two or three blackhelms moving against each defender.

"This could be bad," Belkram murmured.

Sharantyr sighed. "Just try to stay alive . . . I need you both."

"You do?" Itharr asked, adopting Torm's manner of mock astonishment.

"I do," Sharantyr growled back at him. "We've got those Malaugrym to catch, remember?"

"Gods," Belkram cursed as he caught a hard-swung Zhent blade on his own and was driven a pace back. "Do Elminster's little tasks never end?"

"Where is Elminster, anyway?" Itharr panted, slashing a staggering Zhent across the face and bringing his blade up into the throat of the blackhelm fencing with Sharantyr.

"Off saving some other corner of the Realms, no doubt," Belkram said, driving his foe back with a few solid swings.

"I don't care about other corners of the Realms," Torm called to them, "only the one I'm in."

"An essentially selfish philosophy," Dove scolded him.

"But one that all lesser mortals must needs cling to, if they want to cling to life," Torm returned archly. He threw the blade in his hand into one eye of a snarling Zhent, who was charging in beside the one he was fighting. The man crashed down, and the thief leapt high to avoid being knocked over. His Zhent opponent wasn't so nimble, and toppled sideways, whereupon Hammerhand Bucko, the wagonmaker of the dale, calmly crushed the man's head with a sledgehammer.

"Thank you," Torm told him politely.

After gaping at him for a moment in amazement, Hammerhand grinned.

A trumpet rang out, the Zhents pressed forward, and the defenders of Shadowdale became all too busy to talk.

A tortured scream topped the fray as Nelyssa's mount reared up, three blades in its belly, and went down. The paladin threw herself clear at the last moment. Only some desperate bladework by Storm and Dove, sparks dancing from their furiously plied blades, kept the captain of the Riders alive until she could find her feet and fight on.

Kuthe grunted in pain and went down, a spear through him, and a moment later the Rider beside him fell, transfixed by three Zhent blades.

"Too many of them!" Merith snarled in frustration, swinging two swords in deadly, whirling unison. "What price sundown now?"

"There's too many! We can't hold them!" Illistyl shouted, swinging a sword awkwardly.

"We *must* hold them!" Mourngrym snarled back at her from the heart of a knot of Zhents.

"Where in the name of the Seven Dancing Gods is the Old Mage?" Storm raged as she carved her way to the lord of Shadowdale. "Especially now that we need him—for once."

"The temple," a wounded priest of Lathander gasped from behind her. "He stood alone there—or with a woman, some said—against Bane himself!"

Storm turned and stared at the rising column of black smoke that marked the distant temple. "No," she whispered. "Oh, no." She leapt clear of the fray, scant inches ahead of a Zhent blade, and sprinted away across the heaped dead.

Sharantyr turned, hacked through a Zhent blackhelm twice her size, and saw Storm spring into the saddle of a dale war horse. It leapt into a full gallop like an arrow shot from a bow, heading west.

Though Shar whirled back to face another foe, she still saw Storm's anguished face in her mind. No one should look like that. Nothing should ever happen in Faerûn to make the Bard of Shadowdale look like that.

She parried the Zhentilar blade and spun away to run after Storm's racing dapple gray, heedless of the heaped dead.

Uncertainly, Belkram turned to follow, but Itharr shouted in alarm.

"Look you!" He pointed the other way, east beyond Krag Pool, where new plumes of smoke were rising through the green leaves of the trees.

"Gods," Shaerl gasped, her face white, as she stared east into the blazing forest. "The Zhents have fired the wood! The dale may become our pyre yet!"

The defenders of Shadowdale, too few and too weary to fight a blaze, stared at the quickening flames in horror.

"Now," Dove said firmly, " 'tis time!" She held up the blade she bore and called, "Ea*nam*orrath!"

Lighting leapt from its suddenly blazing length, crackling along the line of blackhelms to strike the blade Lord Florin wielded. His sword flashed. Florin hissed at the shock of the bolt surging through the weapon, and then the lightning leapt back, sinking back into Dove's blade as if it were an errant phantom returning home.

In its wake lay a blackened path of dead Zhentilar, sprawled wherever the bolt had danced, and the air was sharp with the smell of the strike that had felled them. The surviving Zhent warriors drew back in disarray, leaving the defenders alone with the dead.

"Florin!" Itharr shouted. "Lord Florin!"

The Shield of Shadowdale turned his head.

Itharr called, "We must pray to Mielikki for a downpour!"

"But if all the gods are cast down and powerless . . ." a Rider leaning on his sword nearby said.

"No! He's right!" Illistyl snapped. "Mielikki and Eldath dwell in Faerûn; their power is sourced here. Shaerl! Is your maid, Jenna, anywhere about?"

"I—I sent her to help Jhaele tend the wounded at the Old Skull," Shaerl said doubtfully, wiping sweat and tangled hair out of her eyes. "Why?"

"She worships Eldath," Illistyl snarled. "Come!"

"And what of the Zhents?" Mourngrym bellowed. He waved an arm to indicate the hundreds of Zhentilar still facing them, though the blackhelms seemed to be retreating to the trees at the edge of the dale.

"Fall back," Illistyl told him. "Back to this ridge of bodies. You can see the inn from there, and Florin and the Rangers Three can join Jenna in prayer. If the woods burn, we are all lost, whether we fight for Shadowdale or Zhentil Keep!"

They all stared at her a moment, then scrambled to take up new positions among the mounds of fallen. Belkram, Itharr, and Sharantyr found themselves trotting toward the inn, panting, while Florin ran on ahead, feet racing as if he were rested and fresh. Shaerl and Mourngrym ran along behind them as rearguard, and the stout priest Rathan puffed after the hurrying band.

"Gods," Belkram said, stumbling as his throbbing feet sent fresh lances of pain upward. "I don't think the gods meant me to be a hero! Being one of those sleeping temple guards seems more within my grasp!"

"Here, now!" Rathan Thentraver said in offended tones. "Dost thou slander the holy?"

"All too often," Itharr told him as they picked their way among the wounded laid on blankets, restless in their pain. Someone was wailing in grief, and blood-soaked bandages—and flies—were everywhere. "What does this Jenna look like?"

"Just look for Florin," Belkram instructed, pointing at the open inn door. "He must be in th—"

The ground heaved. A deafening howl of rage and grief smashed into the ears of everyone in Shadowdale. Thrown to their knees, the three rangers looked back east, from whence the sound had come.

A sphere of raging flames hung high in the air over the burning trees, spinning. The flames from the woods below were being drawn up into it. It pulsed, becoming almost blinding in its fury—but against the bright whirling flames a figure could be seen standing in its fiery heart; a wildly leaping figure clad in the black tatters of a gown.

"Oh, sweet gods spare us!" someone gasped.

The woods were dark and hissing now as the last fire soared up out of them. The sphere spun once more before it hurled its fire down in a ravening beam of utter destruction, into the Zhent soldiers crowded along the Voonlar road. They did not even have time to scream before they were tumbling ashes. The scouring flames lashed the very stones into ruin.

The Central Blade of Bane's Black Gauntlet was no more.

"Who—?" one of the Riders asked in awe, staring up at the figure who stood on empty air above the trees, all her flames spent now.

"The Simbul," Shaerl whispered. She turned, swept a tankard off a table, and drained it at a single gulp.

"The Witch-Queen?" the man gasped. "The Shield Against Thay?"

"The same," Shaerl replied bitterly, and turned into Mourngrym's arms with a sob.

"This can only mean one thing," the lord of Shadowdale said grimly, holding his shaking, weeping lady. "Elminster is dead."

10
Time to be Truly Heroes

The Castle of Shadows, Shadowhome, Flamerule 18

In a deepness that very few Malaugrym know, in the ever-shifting cellars of the Castle of Shadows, there was a place where thinking shadows glided endlessly through the gloom, vast and slow. These ponderous phantoms circled a grotto where shapeshifters who bore the title Shadowmaster High had been wont to hide the bones of rivals and others they'd deemed expedient to make 'vanish.'

The grotto was a cold cavern of rough rock where waters dripped endlessly among the pale, chill glows of fungi, but at its heart two seats faced each other—seats carved out of the flanks of massive, ancient stalagmites . . . and these seats each bore a curious graven symbol believed to be the sign of Malaug himself. It was a rune found in few places in the Castle of Shadows, and all of its occurrences were well known in the lore of the House of Malaug—save these two.

There was not much else to see in the bone-white glow but tumbled rock and bones . . . but there was much to feel, hanging heavy and watchful on all sides.

Even the youngest Shadowmasters had heard tales of locales in Shadowhome where mighty magics slumbered, which only the Shadowmaster High could perceive and wield. This was one of those places.

The young and ambitious Malaugrym Argast and Amdramnar had recently discovered the grotto in separate, private explorations. Both had been guided in their wanderings among the shifting shadows by the writings of Shadowmaster High Melvydur. Dead these thousand years and more, Melvydur mentioned the grotto as the place where the dynasty he founded was conceived—and where he laid to rest the bodies of all his sons who rebelled against him. His writings end when the last son succeeded in destroying Melvydur.

This secret grotto of silent bones and uncaring rock was a gloomy place . . . but it was a place of power. Ancient magic lay heavy in the air, awaiting the right word or gesture to awaken it. And more than anything else, those of the blood of Malaug hungered after power.

Argast and Amdramnar were rivals, and perhaps the best of the younger generation of Shadowmasters. Certainly they were the most subtle, patient, and polite in their dealings—and so commanded the most respect, not to mention fear, among their elders. Those elders would have been most surprised to see them sharing any place in relative peace.

Indeed, as they sat facing each other, their faces were grim and wary, their fingers very close to hurling slaying spells and wielding powerful and deadly items. Yet they sat, and did not move to rend and slay. Their elders were right to fear them.

"Have we agreement?" Argast asked.

"By my name, we do," Amdramnar replied. "Have we agreement?"

"By my name, we do," Argast responded as they watched the drops of their blood slowly flow together into the vial.

They rose as one, and Argast took the vial and stoppered it, handing it to Amdramnar to place on the seat he'd vacated. What befell one Shadowmaster would now also afflict the other—until the vial was broken by someone using the right spells to prevent grave damage to them both.

"If this agreement is to end, we must both meet here to quench it," Argast intoned, continuing the old ritual both of them had read about, but never witnessed.

"Agreed. When we meet, each of us may bring with him one other of the house—no more, and no other beings," Amdramnar responded.

"Agreed," they affirmed together, and walked away from the heart of the grotto, to where the cloaking shadows slid endlessly by.

"Were it not for so many destroyed," Argast said as their eyes met again, "I should never have agreed to work with you in anything. And yet now I welcome the prospect."

Amdramnar inclined his head. "I, too, hope that trust, even friendship, can grow out of this. Whatever befalls, we must work together to destroy the three beings who dared to strike down so many of our blood. They have done it once, and could well come again . . . and what if they brought the Great Foe with them this time, or an army of lesser mages?"

"You befriended them," Argast said, "seeking to learn their ways and secrets. Do you think they will seek to return?"

Amdramnar opened his mouth to reply, then sighed, shrugged, and shook his head. "I know not. Their deeds and words did not always strike a good match together—and they were accompanied by some sort of vigilant sentience of greater sorcery than I command."

"Elminster, of course."

"No, I think not. A gentler, more neutral regard . . . less knowing, less . . . afire with humor, let us say. I touched this intelligence only fleetingly."

Argast lifted his own shoulders and let them fall. "As you say, you have had contact with this mysterious other, and I have not. It is not Elminster, then." He hesitated as they stepped together onto the back of the flapping shadow they'd been waiting for. It bore them away into roiling dimness, and Argast added, "Please do not take my next query as anything more unfriendly than a desire to know if some future use can be made of it. You fancied the woman as a mate?"

Amdramnar regarded him expressionlessly. "I did, and do."

"Have you any knowledge of her feelings toward you?"

"She did not know what to make of me. I was not the menacing scaly thing she expected—but she never relaxed, though she did trust me so far as to open herself to attack on several occasions . . . at least once to see what I'd do, I am certain."

"And what would you do if you met her again?"

"I do not know. I must learn more of her true powers, aims, and loyalties. At present I still desire her as a mate and as part of our house. Although the damage done by her weapon was . . . unprecedented, she was acting at first to defend herself even as you or I would against treachery from a fellow Malaugrym. That she and her companions came here to do us harm is, I think, likely. That they did not know us is certain, and so I must conclude that they came here on principle, or following the orders of another."

"Elminster? If not the Great Foe, then who?"

"That is one of the things we must learn."

The shadow bore them into brighter and more tranquil surroundings, a placid blue pool wreathed in mists, and Amdramnar added, "Yet if the need arises, I would strike to slay her and her two companions without hesitation. The men must die in any case, for the honor of our house. If the woman proves less than I believe her to be, death can come to her whenever her usefulness in breeding the next generation of Shadowmasters is done."

He turned his head to regard Argast. "On the other hand, she is but one of many countless maids who walk

Faerûn right now . . . and many of those, I'm given to understand, have a strong talent for sorcery."

"More suitable mates may await both of us?"

"And many of our fellows, perhaps. We shall see. Faerûn awaits."

"So many riches . . . denied to us for so long."

"At the command of the Great Foe, remember—bolstered by craven Shadowmasters High who feared both his magic and the access all of us would have to things not under the control of the Shadow Throne."

"This is truth," Argast said softly. "Even I've seen more in the great scrying portal over the years than Dhalgrave intended, and I am one of those who pays little attention to intrigues and watching over other planes. It is no wonder some of our elders—Milhvar comes to mind—spent much time and effort on covert expeditions into the realms of Faerûn, seeking magic."

"And mates," Amdramnar said with the ghost of a smile, "if the rumors are true."

"He has offspring in Faerûn?"

"Ignorant of their heritage, and perhaps weak in their shapeshifting, no doubt," Amdramnar replied, "but yes—several, I believe."

Argast frowned. "Unknown offspring aside, how many of our kin walk Faerûn right now?"

"Whoever survived battle with Sharantyr and her companions, when the sword took her back to Faerûn. Ahorga, I have seen . . . and two others who took many shapes, but are possibly Atarl and Yinthrim. There are others: two working together, and at least one more. I cannot believe all of these fled the battle; some of the kin must have seized upon the emptiness of the Shadow Throne to defy the standing decrees and make their own ways into Faerûn."

"Bralatar and Lorgyn have both vanished from their chambers," Argast said quietly, "and have been absent for more than a dozen feastings."

"So," Amdramnar replied, one side of his face lifting

into a smile, "let us do likewise, you and I. To Faerûn, to take the shapes of others, and watch patiently, and learn before we move against these mortals. In the chaos ruling Faerûn right now, we dare not rely on magic. Any foray there now will be very dangerous—but what opportunities for hunting!"

"I feel its attraction more strongly as the years pass and we visit it not," Argast replied. "I begin to understand why so many of our elders defied the Great Foe even when they knew death awaited them."

"Shadowhome and the planes we can readily reach never felt limiting in any way before," Amdramnar said quietly. "Faerûn seemed to be no more than some sort of fanciful land of beasts where the restless of our house went to play, and when careless got hurt there. But now . . ."

"Let us prepare," Argast said, eyes shining. "I want to be in Faerûn without delay!"

The shadow glided to the place it always did, and they stepped off it and went on up a dusty stair choked with the skeletal remains of dead and forgotten servants, into an undercrypt several stairs beneath the Hall of Griffons. There they parted, ascending into the castle proper by different ways so as not to be seen together by interested eyes.

The gigantic shadow that had been their steed drifted on to a place the two Malaugrym did not know. There it rose into a different form and called forth four spherical stones of winking blue fire to orbit one of its wrists endlessly.

"And so two more of the restless of our house go to play," it said in amused tones, "one at least formally welcoming the prospect! Interesting times in old Shadowhome, indeed!"

And as it chuckled, it did something else in the darkness, and vanished to other, deeper places. There were many locales in Shadowhome that neither Argast nor Amdramnar had ever visited, or known about. That lack of knowledge, though, didn't seem likely to prove fatal to either of them. Yet.

* * * * *

Faerûn, Shadowdale, Flamerule 18

The serene radiance of Selune fell upon ravaged Shadowdale as it did on all the rest of Faerûn this night. Bright moonlight gleamed on both the armor of weary dale sentries and the bloodied gear of the dead. There was no sound but the howling of wolves and the bawling of cattle whose dead masters would never return to milk them. The two women who stood in a lonely place of scorched stones were as silent as the night breezes.

One was the Bard of Shadowdale, Storm Silverhand, her face grim and smudged with dirt and old, dried blood that was not her own. She still wore her armor, and leaned on a sword that had seen much use this day. Had she not recently drunk of a certain well-hidden decanter in her kitchen, she would be trembling with weariness now.

The other woman had no body left to tire—she was a thing of ghostly radiance, a softly curved bright shadow in the night. She floated upright above the stones of her long-burned hut, face lifted to the stars, and began an invocation to Mystra more ancient than she was . . . and *that* was old indeed. No one disturbed them, or came near; such doings at the ruined hut were why the folk of the dale still called her the Witch of Shadowdale, and shunned this place.

"Great Lady of Mysteries, hear me," the ghostly lady said into the night, picturing the dark, star-filled eyes of the goddess. "Your servant Syluné entreats."

She and Storm both knew well that Mystra was no more, but perhaps the one who had taken her place would hear . . . or steadfast Azuth, the Hand of Sorcery.

Her call fell into silence, and she stood there in the moonlight feeling more lonely than she had for years. "Mystra, hear me," she said at last. "Azuth, hear me."

From out of the darkness of vast distances, a voice echoed. A voice she knew. "Azuth hears, little sister."

"Lord of Spellcraft," Syluné breathed, almost shuddering in relief, "does Elminster live?"

There came a twinkling of lights in the air above her, soft green and blue radiances that sparkled as they spun slowly about each other. From out of the heart of this occurrence came the deep, confident voice of the god Azuth. "I did not feel him pass . . . but I cannot feel his mind now, either. Much is in chaos; I cannot be sure of his fate."

"I stand in Shadowdale," Syluné told him. "We have resisted the work of Bane here thus far, at great cost."

"Aye, great cost, indeed. Mystra returned to us, and was lost again forever. She and Elminster fought Bane for possession of a Celestial Stair."

Syluné closed her eyes in despair, but forced herself to say on. "I need your guidance, High One. We face another peril: shapeshifters who call themselves Malaugrym, who came into Faerûn when the Sword of Mystra brought three heroes back to us, three who went to the shadow realm of the shapeshifters to do Our Lady's work. They are loose in the land, working mischief."

The great voice seemed to hold a tone of bitter amusement. "These days, it seems half the multiverse is loose in Faerûn, working mischief . . . one Azuth among them. My powers are twisted and lessened. 'Tis all I can do to hold the Realms together, with all the irresponsible spell-hurlers active. Red Wizards, Calishite lords, Zhentarim, and near a thousand ambitious lone wizards whose magic is mighty. Gods and mortals alike are trying to take advantage of the widespread chaos. And without Mystra, magic is truly unreliable. I work constantly to keep the fabric of all from being torn utterly by these ignorant wielders of Art so that Toril will not be dashed apart in utter destruction. You have my sympathy, Sister, and my regrets . . . but you must contend with the House of Malaug on your own; I dare not intervene. Gather your allies, and work as you have never worked before. 'Tis time to truly be heroes."

Syluné stood motionless. "May you succeed in your task," she said softly.

"And may you find the good fortune Our Lady Mystra could not," the god replied, "and prevail. Know that I love you, Syluné, and would aid if I could. Look not to seek divine aid again until this Time of Troubles is past." And the small storm of twinkling lights melted silently away, leaving the night sky above the stones empty.

The ghostly figure of the Witch of Shadowdale stared up at the empty air where Azuth had manifested, then turned toward her sister Storm and reached out.

"Take me away from here," she pleaded, her voice on the edge of tears. "Take me back to your kitchen, and the fire, and your arms."

"Of course," Storm said quietly. She bent to take up the stone Belkram had surrendered, and Syluné saw that her face was wet with tears.

They walked south and then east together, taking a long route around the heart of the moonlit dale to avoid challenges and the worst of the dead.

"You heard all?" Syluné asked grimly.

Storm sighed. "Aye, this dale is going to be very different if Elminster is no more."

"He was a father—and a friend—to you more than any of us," Syluné said softly. " 'Tis I should be comforting you."

Storm shook her head wearily, as if to clear it. "I did not feel him die. I can't be sure . . . he may still live."

"And if he does not?"

"Then it is as Azuth told us: time for us—all of us Seven—to truly be heroes, without his comforting aid and guidance . . . and vigilance for our safety."

Syluné sighed. "I never thought I'd be alive without him to turn to. He seems as permanent a feature of the Realms as Mount Waterdeep, or Anauroch, or the Shaar." They climbed a stile and descended into a field of parsnips. Halfway down one of its long rows, she added, "Sharantyr is beside herself! I thought she'd tear the two prisoners apart with her bare hands."

"She gave her blade to Mourngrym because she feared she'd want to use it," Storm said softly. "My own fury is past. El told me how tired of life he'd become more than once this last season."

"Should we let those two go?"

"Mercy has ever been our watchword here, and yet . . ."

Storm's voice trailed away, and with slow deliberation she sheathed the blade she held. "I may come to feel the rage Sharantyr holds again, tomorrow. Since Doust became lord, we have always shown the people that justice by fair trial holds sway in Shadowdale. So we will have a trial and justice, and Mourngrym will have the hard task of sentencing."

She was silent for a long time before she added in a whisper, "I am glad of that, because I don't feel like holding trials at all . . . I want to go out and kill things."

* * * * *

"Your sword arm?" Sharantyr asked, watching Itharr wince and reach for his shoulder.

He nodded. "I've worn it out these last two days."

"And seen enough death to last several lifetimes," Belkram added quietly, handing him a goblet. Itharr took it in his good hand and hastily sipped at it to prevent a spill.

Sharantyr dug her fingers into the muscles of his shoulder, and he shuddered uncontrollably. He handed the goblet back to Belkram hastily.

"Thanks . . . I'll want the rest of it when this long-taloned beast here stops tearing my shoulder apart!"

Sharantyr managed a playful snarl, but then fell silent again, her face sad. She shook her head when Belkram offered the decanter to her, and asked him, "When will you get Syluné back?"

"In the morning, Storm said." Belkram poured himself a goblet and drained most of it at one gulp. "I imagine they're meeting to talk about what they must do to defend the dale now that Elminster's gone."

"That's a meeting we must have, too," Itharr said, looking up. "Whither now, for the three of us?"

"What have we to jaw about," Sharantyr asked with sudden fierceness as her fingers worked on his stiff shoulders with iron tenderness, "until we've dealt with the Malaugrym? Elminster gave us a task, and it's unfinished. Harpers—and Knights of Myth Drannor—don't walk away from their duty. Not now, not ever!"

When she caught Belkram's look of wonder, she blushed, turning her head away. "I'm sorry," Shar mumbled, her voice quavering for an instant. "I . . . his dying . . . I'm too upset to make sense."

"No, Lady," Belkram said, advancing to take one of her hands in his own. He knelt and kissed it in one smooth movement. "You make perfect sense—now, and always."

Sharantyr turned her head away again from the rising fire she saw in his eyes, and tried to blink away her sudden tears, tears that would not stop falling.

* * * * *

Uncaring crickets were chirping as the Bard of Shadowdale turned in at her arched gate. She brushed past its roses and stumbled in her weariness. Syluné drifted with silent grace at her shoulder.

The door ahead of them was open, and the lamps were lit. Storm sighed and reached for her blade again, wondering if she really felt up to another fight against some sinister Zhent intruder . . . then relaxed with a heavy sigh of relief when she saw the short and familiar figure of Lhaeo come out to greet them.

"Tea is made, Ladies," Elminster's scribe said in a small, forlorn voice.

"Oh, Lhaeo," Storm said, touched, and held out her arms to him.

A moment later, the last prince of Tethyr was weeping into her breast, clutching her as if she were his last anchor in a storm-racked sea. "El told me I'd know if he died," he gasped when he could speak again, "and yet I *don't* know! The touch of his mind is gone!" He burst into fresh tears, weeping uncontrollably.

Storm stood in the moonlight, holding him in silence. There was nothing she could say. Her silver hair bent over him as her own tears began to fall. They wept together, and the ghostly form of Syluné hovered over them both, her spectral hands reaching out to console . . . in vain.

There was nothing at all she could do.

11
There's Always Revenge

It was a bright morning in fair Shadowdale. The tower, the inn, and the streets were still buzzing with talk of the disappearance, a day and a night ago, of Adon and Midnight, the two prisoners convicted of the murder of Elminster of Shadowdale. Some said they'd been spirited away by agents of Zhentil Keep, lurking in the dale even now; others that they were archmages, foul fiends, or Bane and Manshoon themselves, who wore false shapes and escaped by magic as soon as they were bound in the dungeons. Shadowdale had lost its greatest protector, a wise old uncle—albeit a cantankerous and mischievous uncle—to just about everyone who'd lived in Shadowdale.

Nor was he the only man mourned in the dale. Many a family wept over sons or fathers who would come back only on a shield, to be buried by an honor guard led by the grim-faced lord of Shadowdale. No one could spare the time for full mourning rites or long nights of grieving, however; there was too much that had to be done.

Magic still spun wild in Faerûn, and news of strife and god-caused devastation came to Shadowdale with every new, heavily armed caravan. The Zhentarim could strike again at any time, and Daggerdale was an open battlefield roamed by hungry wolves, orcs, and worse. To keep such perils at bay, the few warriors still able to fight were standing guard on all four roads out of the dale, fervently hoping not to see blackhelms in the distance.

In the dale, dead Zhents and horses lay everywhere, some half devoured by bold night scavengers. The returned priests of Lathander were busily blessing the dead to ensure that they would not rise undead to stalk Shadowdale in the years to come. The old women of the dale were stripping the bodies of anything that could be used again, and the foresters surveyed the burnt woods with an eye to replanting.

Yestereve, six full carts piled high with weapons and helms had groaned up the road to the tower. The clangor of their being stockpiled had gone on all night, wherefore this morning Lord Mourngrym had a headache that felt as if someone were repeatedly stabbing a dagger through the top of his head.

"*Why* must I get up?" he asked Shaerl. "I'm lord of this dale. Can't I lie abed just once in a year?"

"You did," she replied sweetly, "three months back. We were trying for a daughter, remember?"

Mourngrym growled something wordless about her cheerfulness and rolled up to a sitting position on the edge of their bed. His arms and ribs were gold and purple with bruises, and two raw scars marked his forearm where Zhent blades had split through his best armor.

Shaerl hissed in sympathy as she traced one of those scars with a slim finger. She handed her lord a tankard of steaming bitterroot tea.

Mourngrym sipped it, made the same disgusted face he always did, and rose, handing the tankard back to her. "Here—*you* drink the stuff. It should cure your confounded cheerfulness!"

He took from its peg the silken robe she'd made for him. As always, he admired the blazons she'd sewn so carefully. The arms of the dale shone on one breast, his own arms on the other, and a target prominently on the back—their private joke: he'd been her target when

Cormyr sent her to Shadowdale to gain influence here.

Mourngrym smiled at the robe in his arms, leaned against the smooth-carved corner post of the bed, and mouthed a silent prayer to Tymora. Swinging the robe around his shoulders, he made his way across the bedchamber.

He winced as each step made his head pound—he hadn't had *that* much to drink last night, surely—but doggedly pursued his goal: the curtained archway that led into the morning room. There he would break his fast on the great table whose glass top covered gloriously hued maps of the dales. He loved those maps, a wedding gift from the Rowanmantles, and peering at their exquisite details never failed to cheer him.

He shouldered through the curtains, sniffing the welcome aroma of sausages and melted cheese and eggs on bread, and froze midstride.

"Storm! Well met and welcome, but *what* are you doing sitting in the middle of the table?—Oh, war council time again, is it?"

The Bard of Shadowdale smiled at him and tossed her head in greeting; her silver hair cascaded down one shoulder, and Mourngrym swallowed at her beauty, remembering the last time she'd sat on the table, wearing rather less, and the wild war council that had followed then. It was too early in the morning for all this. . . .

Eyeing the sausages on the platter beside Storm's boots, the lord of Shadowdale went to the long sideboard, took up a flask of firewine, and drained it at a single gulp.

When his eyes came back into focus, Storm was shaking her head. "You'll regret that, you know."

"My head already feels like a blacksmith's anvil," Mourngrym told her. "Is there any more of this stuff about, do you know?"

"End drawer down the window end," Storm and Shaerl said together, then broke into chuckles (Storm) and giggles (Shaerl) of mirth. Mourngrym gave them both a look of long-suffering disgust and went to the drawer indicated.

"It's too much," he told the Realms at large. "No man should have to deal with such cheery females. Haven't either of you heard of respectful silence?"

There was no reply. Mourngrym had taken the decanter back to the table, sipped from it without bothering with a flagon, and lifted his fork to deal with the sausages before the silence registered. He looked up—into Storm's impish eyes, dancing with mirth as she regarded him, lips pressed tightly together. He shot a look along the table to Shaerl, who had seated herself with dignity and was regarding him, chin on hand, in equally amused silence.

Mourngrym opened his mouth to say something, but closed it again and shrugged. "That's certainly more peaceful," he told the first sausage as he raised it.

"*Un*hand that sausage!" a voice bellowed from somewhere very near.

Mourngrym choked, tried to spring up, arms flailing, and toppled sideways, gabbling for breath.

He and the chair met the flagstone floor with a solid, head-ringing crash amid an explosion of laughter. Mourngrym found himself then face to face with Rathan Thentraver.

The stout priest was crawling out from under the table. He winked, deftly plucked the sausage off Mourngrym's fork, bit into it, and said, "Umm. Very good! Thank you for offering me this excellent viand!"

"I am going to kill someone," Mourngrym announced calmly to the ceiling, "and probably soon. How long have you been under here?"

"Not long," Rathan rumbled cheerfully. He emerged. "How long do you plan to sleep in every morning? Not turning into a vampire, are you?"

"No," Mourngrym told him shortly, and rolled to his feet. "No fangs to you."

"Ah," Storm said, "that's better. I was afraid you were

going to play the grim stone-headed tyrant all day." As she spoke, the wall gong chimed.

Mourngrym looked at it sourly and sat down again. "And what does that signify?"

" 'Tis the signal that you've finished your morning feast, my lord," Shaerl said sweetly, "and that yet another Realms-shaking war council is about to begin."

"But I *haven't* fin—" Mourngrym began. He snatched his platter to his chest just before Storm plucked it away. He brandished his fork at her. "Keep *back,* woman!"

There was laughter from the doorway. Belkram and Itharr of the Harpers stood there, staring delightedly into the room. "Now *that's* a sight worth walking here from Berdusk to see! We battle the Bard of Shadowdale with blades . . . but great lords use sausage forks on her!"

Mourngrym sighed, backed away to the sideboard, and set his plate down. Picking up a sausage, he pointed at the chairs ranged around the table and said, "Pray enter, Lords, Ladies, and Gentles, and be seated. There, there, and there . . . ah, and I believe that seat's available too . . . very good." He glanced at the gathering: Knights, Storm, a swirling radiance by her shoulder that must be Syluné, the two Harper rangers, Shaerl, and—who was missing?

Elminster, of course, and Lhaeo . . . not surprising. He bit into the sausage thoughtfully. Ah!

"This room's too quiet by far," he announced grandly. "Where's Torm?"

"I thought you'd never ask," the smooth voice of the thief replied from the doorway. "While you've been snoring, *I've* been working. Pretty soft being lord of a dale, isn't it?"

"You?" Mourngrym snorted, making a rude gesture with what was left of his sausage. "*Working?*"

"Indeed," Torm replied with dignity, "I have just returned from a dawn foray—a bold and brazen foray, let me say, fraught with peril and shining bravery—into the road camp just south of Voonlar, looking for certain things our departed Zhentish friends may have left behind!"

"*More* women?" Merith asked slyly. "Torm, how many can one man have?"

"The answer, Sir Elf, would surprise you," Torm said loftily, "but that is a matter for converse at some more relaxed time. I speak of the Central Blade's pack train . . . sixteen wagons of it, at any rate."

"Thieving still?" Shaerl sighed. "Torm, in case you haven't noticed, there's a war on! Must you indulge in petty thievery?"

Torm's eyebrows rose. " '*Petty* thievery,' Lady? You wound me to the quick! What did you think your surviving troops would eat? And be paid with? Starving men"—a dagger spun from his hand to transfix one of Mourngrym's sausages, and the thief jerked on the silken cord affixed to the hilt and snatched the food away from Mourngrym's hasty grab—"who feel they've been cheated tend to make unsafe guardians, particularly when they're also well-trained warriors."

"Belt up, well-trained warrior," Florin suggested kindly as Torm reeled in a dusty sausage and bit into it with satisfaction. The ranger looked around the table to address them. "We're here to talk some things out and decide how best to proceed, given the perils abroad in the land and . . . our lack of Elminster." In the silence that followed, he added, "In the absence of the Old Mage, Syluné is the eldest here, and should speak first."

"My thanks, Florin—I think," the ghostly Witch of Shadowdale said dryly. "For my part, I have unfinished business Elminster set me to. Sister, will you hand my stone to Itharr of the Harpers? He is the only one of our Rangers Three who hasn't borne me yet."

"I will," Storm said gravely, drawing the chain from her neck and rising to carry the stone around the table.

"The Rangers Three? Sounds like a chartered adventuring band," Torm commented. Itharr took the stone carefully, a little awed. The thief added, "Or a traveling minstrel show."

"Torm, dearest," Sharantyr said sweetly, "Tell me: do these idiocies just tumble out whenever you open your mouth—or do you actually sit there and *think them up?*"

"Thinking?" Torm frowned at her. "Who said anything about thinking? Kill first, then loot . . . and the thinking part is that unpleasant shouting business at the end when it all has to be divided. It makes brains hurt."

"Mine certainly does," Mourngrym said with feeling, "but I believe Syluné still has the high tongue in this round of converse."

"For my part," Syluné responded, "there is no more to say. I am a thing of ghosts and shadows. My will is bound to duty."

"Yes, but what would you *like* to do?"

"Find my sister the Simbul and beseech her to do as Elminster did," the Witch of Shadowdale said very quietly. "That is, make me a new body."

There was an embarrassed silence at the raw longing in her voice. Florin stepped into it by saying, "Next senior among us is my lady, Dove. What say you?"

Dove smiled at him and looked around the table. "My first duty—*our* first duty—must be to defend the folk of the Dales against brigands, Zhents, roving monsters, and the like. Otherwise, there'll be no crops, and starvation come winter. Time of Troubles or no, the work of daily life must go on. We have to find all the Zhents scrambling around the woods and deal with them, discover who or what else is lurking about to prey on our people, find and tend all the wounded, and rebuild what was ruined in the fighting."

"Well, that takes care of the council," Torm said lightly. "Let's be getting on with it. Mourngrym can make us all more sausages—*I'm* certainly hungry enough—and we can meet again when the snows fall."

"Rathan? Gag him, will you?" Illistyl snapped scornfully. "To think that I once bedded *that!*"

"Once? From what I recall, twi—"

"Enough, Torm," Dove said firmly, "or have you forgotten the fish bucket?"

"The fish bucket?" Mourngrym asked, leaning forward with interest. "Is this some sort of torture device fine upstanding noble lords can use on annoying thieves?"

"After he made a particularly crude remark," Jhessail explained, "Dove held Torm's head under water in the bucket of live fish she was bringing to the tower for evenfeast . . . until he ran out of bubbles."

"Ah, *that* explains what happened to his wits," Merith said delightedly. "They got soaked through and grew mildew. . . ."

"Gods in their palaces," Belkram said to Itharr in low tones, "are all their council meetings like this?"

"Oh, no, no," Storm assured him cheerfully. "Best manners this morn . . . because of you. Usually we just shout Torm down and get on, and no one speaks in turn."

"Strange you should mention that," Florin said with a smile, "as seniority brings us now to you."

"Aye, indeed," Storm said with a smile. "I concur with my sister Dove, but be aware that aside from Shar, Syluné, and my two Harpers here"—Belkram and Itharr smiled around the table and swept mock bows—"this assembly is just going to have to abandon chasing Malaugrym for the time being."

"Malaugrym?"

"The shapeshifters who attacked us in the tent, the night before the battle in Mistledale," Sharantyr explained.

"Those weren't doppelgangers?"

"No, something far worse."

"Oh . . . one of Mourngrym's speeches?"

"Stow it," Florin ordered with a grin and a sigh.

"Because some among us can't resist the urges to be clever, these little get-togethers are always *so* much fun."

"Hold hard," Shaerl said, leaning over the table with a frown. "Do I hear you rightly? *Chasing* Malaugrym? Are there a band of them?"

"A family, actually," Storm explained softly. "An ancient clan who kill those who know about them—so guard your lips. For centuries Elminster has slain any of them who dared to enter the Realms."

"So with him gone . . ."

"Chasing may no longer be necessary. They'll probably find *us* soon enough," Sharantyr observed.

"Is there any way—short of magic that may go wild, and blow this tower apart, or cover us all in cow dung—of knowing they're not here in this room, right now, taking the shape of one of us?" Torm asked sharply.

"No," Storm and Dove said in quiet unison.

"Well," Rathan joked, "You *did* come in late, Torm. . . ."

"Oh, no, you don't," Torm said warningly. "No one's opening me up to see if I'm really a scaly monster!" There was suddenly a dagger in his fingertips, and he waved it meaningfully.

"You're safe, Torm," Jhessail said with a smile. "No one could impersonate that debonair manner, that outrageous tongue, that—"

"Utter stupidity," Illistyl told the ceiling.

"As to the internal defense of the dale, and helping our folk set things to rights," Storm added, "journeyman Harpers will shortly gather in Shadowdale from all directions. To prevent the Zhents and . . . others from sneaking agents in among them, they all will report to Dove, who will cast a spell that marks them with a visible badge, a spell that contains nasty surprises for anyone trying to duplicate it. To get such a badge, of course, the Harpers will submit to mind-reading magic, allowing us to weed out ambitious Malaugrym."

"So this band of confirmed Harpers helps rebuild the dale," Torm said, "freeing us to do—what?"

"Ride patrol through the Elven Court woods, southeastern Daggerdale, and the other lands around Shadowdale, scouring it of brigands and monsters, giving us warning of attack from Zhentil Keep, Daggerdale, or Hillsfar. I've heard rumors of fell beasts leaving the ruins of Myth Drannor to roam the woods, and even talk of some wealthy merchants in Sembia hiring small armies in hopes of seizing a dale or two as private estates."

"What?" Torm laughed. "Armies, yes . . . but ambitious Sembian merchants? Show me the fool who'd dare challenge the famous Knights of Myth Drannor!"

"Look in yon mirror," Jhessail advised him in dry tones, pointing across the morning room. "You challenge us all too often."

"Vile slander!" Torm said severely, waving a finger at her. "May the gods look down and—"

"Gift thee with an egg, valiant Torm," Shaerl said. She swept a peppered plover egg up from Mourngrym's plate and thrust it whole into Torm's mouth.

"Nnn*mumph*," he protested.

"I agree completely," Rathan replied earnestly, patting the thief's hand (the one without the dagger). "Thy every word is as a pearl of wisdom, glistening among the dull pebbles of other oratory!"

"Oh, *please*," Illistyl said. "You're as bad as he is!"

Rathan gave her a hard look. "I prefer to say 'as good as,' young miss—'tis more charitable, far."

"If the free entertainment could subside for a moment," Merith said patiently, "perhaps we can hear the rest of Storm's plans."

Storm grinned at him. "We'll send two patrols equipped for long forays. The Knights will ride to Daggerdale; the Rangers Three with Syluné will circle Voonlar, the woods near Myth Drannor, and Mistledale. Both bands should make sure the Zhents haven't rallied anyone else in the south and deal with any trouble before it reaches our battle-riven dale. The dalefolk are too exhausted to deal with even sneak thieves."

"Fine, sounds sensible. Let's be doing it," Illistyl said, rising from the table. "I weary of talk. Merith, have you found me a horse?"

"What's wrong with your palfrey?" Mourngrym asked.

"Killed in the battle," Storm informed him curtly. Illistyl nodded, her eyes bright with sudden tears, but said nothing.

Across the table, Torm was in full flight again, leaning around Belkram to smile at Sharantyr.

"*Good,* my lady," the thief said with a leer, his eyes bright, "I could see my way clear to ably guard so beautiful a flower of the dale! Wouldst thou permit me to accompany thee on patrol?"

Sharantyr almost smiled. "I've grown used to Belkram and Itharr, thanks," she said crisply, taking the arms of the two Harper rangers seated on either side of her.

"I did not mean merely myself, Lady," Torm said, his manner suddenly serious. "Three blades and a disembodied voice isn't enough battle might for what you might well run into."

"I'll be going with them, Torm," Storm said quietly.

Heads turned in surprise all around the table, but the Bard of Shadowdale was looking at the three rangers. "If you'll have me?" she asked quietly.

"Right gladly, Lady," Belkram said, glancing quickly at his companions for confirmation, and receiving it.

A frown had come onto Mourngrym's face. "Torm may have a point about strength of arms. I was thinking of sending you Knights out on the first patrol east; there's word of a Zhent mageling rallying forty or more Zhentilar in the woods."

"I'll look forward to meeting them," Storm said in silken tones. More than one person around that council table shivered at the sound of the bard's voice.

"Are we agreed?" Mourngrym asked, standing up and looking down the table. There was a general affirmative chorus, and he said briskly, "Good—now get gone, all of you, so I can bathe and get dressed and have some food that clever Knights don't snatch off my plate!"

Chuckles and mocking salutes answered him.

Mourngrym made for his bedchamber, shook his head, and reflected—not for the first time—how untenable a position he held, the junior member of a band of adventurers who handed him the lordship of a dale after they were finished with it, but stayed around to drive him witless!

Growling faintly at the thought, he pushed back through the curtains, Shaerl in his wake.

The morning room cleared quickly. When it was quite empty, something moved under the table—something that looked like old and dark wood, but *flowed* downward to the floor, peeling itself free of the table's underside. It stretched like a hungry snake, slithered out from under the furniture, and rose swiftly, taking on the shape and appearance of one of the tower servants.

The Malaugrym glanced quickly around, but no one was in sight. The servant who was not a servant paused for a long moment to survey the table admiringly. Ahorga had always liked maps.

* * * * *

Elven Court woods, Flamerule 22

The embers crackled and glowed ruby red. The two women sat with their backs to it, facing outward on watch, listening to the faint scuttlings and hootings that mark any forest by night. They were in the Elven Court woods, well south of Voonlar, most of the way through their first night on patrol.

Itharr and Belkram had turned over watch duties to them not long ago, and were well and truly asleep, snoring faintly into their cloaks.

"How many nights have you spent thus?" Sharantyr asked quietly.

Behind her, Storm laughed softly. "Hundreds."

The ghostly tresses of Syluné turned, from where her disembodied head floated at Sharantyr's shoulder. "Thousands, Sister," she corrected.

"That's right—emphasize how old we are," Storm said, amused. "I try not to make people feel uncomfortable or lessened in any way."

"I was the Witch of Shadowdale, remember? Making people wary of me was the best way to hold power over them without ever harming anyone," Syluné replied.

Sharantyr sighed. "You seem so carefree," she said, shifting the naked long sword that lay across her thighs so that moonlight caught it at one end, and a faint red glow from the fire touched the other. She flicked it idly, watching the play of light on the steel. "Is it because you've both seen it all before?"

"Partly, Shar," Storm replied, "and partly because we've learned to try to enjoy *everything*, from being whipped in chains as a slave to being wooed by well-endowed princes."

"To clinging to the spar of a ship breaking apart in a storm," Syluné put in, sounding amused. "To lying paralyzed under the probes of a drow mage trying to determine if your powers lie in organs he can remove, or if you'll have to be bred to drow to give them your abilities."

Sharantyr shivered. "Don't speak of drow, please . . . "

"My apologies, Shar," the ghostly head beside her said quickly. "We both spoke of moments from our own experiences—I forgot that you'd been a captive of the drow, too."

Sharantyr turned her head. "You were a slave?"

"For years," the Bard of Shadowdale told her. "Not entirely bad years, either . . . though I never did develop any enjoyment for being whipped."

"What do you mean, 'not entirely bad years'?" Shar

asked incredulously. "How can you enjoy *anything* about being a slave?"

"That's what we were trying to say, you see," Syluné said softly. "It's not what the gods hand you in life that matters so much, nor what your strivings achieve or fail in the attempt. Whatever befalls, the best way to view life is to savor every moment of it, no matter how sordid or unpleasant . . . for one thing, the gods give us all only a certain span of time, and time wasted—in misery, despair, drunkenness, or casual inattention—is time gone forever."

"I see what you're saying," Sharantyr said slowly, "but you'll forgive me if I take some time getting to enjoy fighting in great battles, or falling into cesspits, or listening to Torm."

Trying not to laugh aloud, Storm shook with deep, bubbling laughter for a long time before she found breath enough to speak again. "Well said," were her first words. "Do you feel like talking about what befell in the Castle of Shadows?"

Shar chuckled helplessly. "I-I suppose so. What do you want to know?"

"Do you recall Elminster's burning the bodies of the Malaugrym you slew, back at the ruined manor in Daggerdale?" Syluné asked.

Shar nodded, but realized they couldn't see the gesture in the dark, and said cautiously, "Yes."

"He wasn't simply being tidy," the ghostly figure told her. "He was using a spell that destroys the bodies of the recently dead even as it yields up their last few moments of thought. In one of the Malaugrym was a strong desire to slay you—because another Malaugrym, who did not enter Faerûn at the time, wanted you as his mate. Another of the dead Malaugrym was reluctant to attack you for the same reason; the Malaugrym who favored you was his ally."

Sharantyr drew a deep, shuddering breath. "I see. You're wondering if I pine after some Malaugrym lord, or perhaps even carry a little shapeshifter-to-be within."

"No," Storm said sharply. "Even if either or both of those conditions were true, they are your affairs. We merely meant that it's apparent to us all that some adventures befell all three of you that went beyond 'See Malaugrym, slay Malaugrym, run run run.'"

Shar giggled. "*That* sounds elegant."

"Indeed," Syluné agreed dryly. "So give, Lady Sharantyr. What did you learn in the Castle of Shadows? And I don't mean about Malaugrym, or shapeshifting, or the nature of ever-shifting Shadowhome. I mean about yourself."

"About myself?"

"About Belkram and Itharr, then," Storm said gently. "How are my two half-trained Harpers?"

"Very good companions and able protectors. Belkram has a touch of Torm in him, I think."

Shar heard Storm's silent amusement at that observation, and went on, "Itharr is quieter, and there's a darkness in him. H-He needs to kill, sometimes."

"And how would you look upon spending several years adventuring with them both?" the lady bard asked. "Just the three of you, not a part of the Harpers or part of the Knights of Myth Drannor."

"I'd enjoy it, I hope," Shar replied, then added quickly, "but I fear the Shadowmasters will soon strike back, and—"

"And?" Syluné asked quietly.

"And I'll lose one or both of them," Sharantyr said. Her voice sank almost to a whisper.

"You are fond of them both, then?" Storm asked quietly.

"Aye, I—" Sharantyr's voice sharpened. "Why are you asking me this? Do you want me to shout from the tower turrets that I love them?"

"No, Shar," Syluné said softly. "We want you to admit it to yourself."

In the little silence that followed, Belkram snorted

softly in his sleep, and at the comical sound something inside Sharantyr suddenly rose into her throat, and she wept as quietly as she could.

The radiance of Syluné was suddenly all around her, and she felt a gentle, chill touch on her forehead. The ghostly kiss left a tingling behind, and her somehow calmer.

She sniffed away the last of her tears, and said in a small voice, "I'm so afraid of losing them."

"That's why I came along," Storm said softly, "to lend one more sword to the fray and make all of your chances for survival that much better."

"Malaugrym are everywhere!" Syluné intoned in tones of mock horror.

"Don't *say* that!" Sharantyr told her fiercely, turning her head to stare into eyes that were two serene white wraith fires.

"Why not? Face your fears as you should face everything else in life—openly. Name them, and they become things you can handle, after a fashion."

Sharantyr laughed, a little ruefully. "I didn't expect to spend my time staring into the night talking about my loves and fears," she told the two age-old sisters.

"Why not, Shar? What could we possibly talk about— in all our lives—that's more important than what we love and fear?"

* * * * *

Sembia, Flamerule 22

"I love to smell their fear," the man with the head of a panther said, raising bloody jaws from a villager who would never again flee screaming from anything.

"Now how could I tell that?" replied the man whose arms split into tentacles. A choking merchant struggled in the coils of two of those tentacles.

The Malaugrym shook the merchant, much as a

hunting cat shakes a rat in its jaws, and tightened his tentacles with lazy strength, tearing the man's head off. Blood sprayed in all directions as the corpse convulsed, wriggling in its final agony.

"Well? Are you going to eat this one?" Bralatar asked, his hands lengthening into talons to tear the man's body apart. He licked his lips in anticipation of the feast.

Lorgyn took one bite, then tossed the headless body aside. "No. I'll find something a little more succulent." He looked across the night-shrouded garden where they stood, at a building whose distinctive red lanterns marked it as a brothel. "In there."

"No wonder old Elminster wanted Faerûn for himself!" Bralatar said, watching his comrade reach up with a small forest of tentacles and swarm up the side of the building. "It's a neverending love-feast and brawl!"

"Aye," Lorgyn called down, heedless of whose attention they might alert, "only better!"

A man's head suddenly appeared out of one window. "Hoy!" he snarled, "what're—doppelgangers! Call the Watc—"

A tentacle descended in a slap that carried the weight of falling stone, breaking the man's neck as a child snaps a twig. He fell onto the sill, and said no more.

The Malaugrym's tentacles were busy at a higher window. He reached in to a bed where a fat merchant was rolling among slippery silk sheets, pretending he couldn't find the giggling owner of the bed, wriggling around beneath them.

"Not here!" the merchant hollered, clutching at a pillow. "*Where's* she gone? Oh, sweet merciful gods, help me . . . my partner'll be furious when he learns how much I spent for an hour of pleasure, and then couldn't find the wench for the size and opulence of her bed! Are there *other* men lost under here, I wonder? That wagon of mine that went missing last moon, perhaps? I'll just have to see! May—"

"Oh, be *silent!*" Lorgyn snarled in exasperation, snapping out a tentacle to wrap around the man's jaws.

The fat merchant suddenly grew a mouth as wide as a horse and caught the tentacle; an extra mouth appeared in his forehead and hissed, "Get your own plaything!"

Lorgyn recoiled in amazement. "Who—?"

The grotesque mouth spat the tentacle back at Lorgyn and shrank away to nothingness, dwindling into features the Malaugrym at the window recognized. "Lunquar!"

"The same," the older Shadowmaster replied, ignoring the sudden terrified scream from the bedclothes beneath him. He pinned the woman down without sparing her a glance, and said, "I've been watching you two break necks and hurl bodies about for days now; why such a bold rampage?"

"Fun, Lunquar, fun!" Lorgyn said exultantly, using one long tentacle to snatch up the man whose neck he'd just broken and shake him as a trophy. "See?" There was a scream from the window below.

"That's just what I mean," the Shadowmaster on the bed said. "You left that one dangling half out of a window! Hear the screaming now!"

"So?"

"So why rouse half of Faerûn when a little subtlety could win you thrones?"

"What fun is that?" the voice of Bralatar came floating up to them. "You can rule just as well through fear . . . in fact, whenever we've the time to spare, we should spread a little more fear!"

"Your style, perhaps; not mine," the older Shadowmaster replied. "I'm saving my fury for when I meet up with one of Mystra's Chosen!"

"Aye," Lorgyn agreed, his voice menacingly soft. His eyes glowed a sudden emerald green in the gloom. "If you want reasons for rampaging, there's always . . . revenge."

12
Whistling, the Wizard Met His End

Sembia, Flamerule 23

Birds called and fluttered in a wood where moss grew green on old, proud trees, untouched by a woodsman's axe for three hundred years. A stone wall as high as six men kept errant axes out, for the wood was part of a private estate in the fair uplands of Sembia—an estate that saw few visitors, and even fewer uninvited ones.

Yet one can never be too careful, and trolls may lurk anywhere. So it was that the war dogs Warhorn and Bolder wandered the grounds diligently, carrying two hundred pounds of taut muscle each behind their spiked war collars. Their jaws closed often on squirrels, and they suffered nothing larger than that to live—except men they knew.

No man they knew smelled quite like the peculiar odor now in Warhorn's nostrils. The mighty war dog growled a deep warning to Bolder and advanced cautiously toward the smell, questing from side to side like a soldier.

Bolder caught up to him, stiffened, and rubbed his flank alongside Warhorn to signify he'd smelled the scent, too. They went forward soundlessly together on stiff, alert legs, lips drawn back to bare huge teeth.

The smell grew strong indeed, prickling in their throats. Of a sudden, they broke apart and rushed around either side of a great shadowtop tree, a forest giant big enough to hide four dogs behind. They went with eyes aflame and jaws agape, feet scrabbling on the mossy turf—and vanished.

All that the listening birds heard was two wet snapping sounds, then a brief thudding, and shortly afterward, a rustling of leaves as something large climbed the forest giant.

"Never fear, never fear,
For my smiles are all for thee."

A man in a bloodied apron sang ere he struck the brass gong that hung by the door.

"So come away, lady fair,
And we will married be!"

He set down the metal basin of meat scraps, wiped his hands on his hips, and waited—but the expected hungry canines did not come.

The man struck the gong again. "Warhorn? Bolder? Gone deaf, have ye?"

The words had just left his lips when the two war dogs raced into view, running hard . . . and yet without their usual fluid grace . . . almost as if they weren't used to loping. The man stared hard at them for a moment. He crouched down and asked merrily, "So what have ye been into, my hearties? Highsummer mushrooms again?"

He leaned forward to pat Warhorn, and barely had time to notice a strange golden fire in the old dog's eyes before the tentacles took him. Snakelike they coiled up his patting arm and shook him, and he was still struggling for breath to shout when they broadened and slapped over his nose and mouth.

His frantic struggles were brief. His slayer rose slowly to an impossible height for a dog and held the dangling corpse upright. The other dog cocked its head for a moment, surveying the limp body. The canine form began to melt and flow, shifting slowly into an exact duplicate of the unfortunate servant.

Delicate tentacles undid the apron and held it out while Bralatar continued surveying the dead man critically, noting tiny scars, pimples, and precisely where hair grew. He shifted himself to match. He took the apron, careful to knot it as the man had worn it, and announced, "Done."

Lorgyn nodded and passed over the man's belt and ring of keys as he sank back down into dog shape atop the dead man. His tentacles coiled and squeezed, trembling with sudden effort.

When he was done, a bloody, boneless mass was all that was left of the servant. Tentacles dragged the gory thing behind the nearest tree and became digging claws. Soon all trace of the murder was gone.

Bralatar hummed the tune the man had been singing as he went to a wrought and fluted metal gate. One faithful war dog trotted at his heels.

In the small garden beyond, svelte nymphs and winged women of weathered stone posed in frozen wantonness among fountains and pools and floating lilies . . . and Dorgan Sundyl strode through them unseeing, bored to the depths of his being.

His muscles gleamed with oil and the vigor of this morning's workout, and his uniform shone back the sun. A bejewelled sword swung at his hip, and his movements had a lazy grace as one long-booted foot glided forward, followed—as always—by the other, taking him around a grassy path that he'd walked a thousand thousand times before. He would dearly love something to fight.

Dorgan sometimes prayed to the gods to bring an intruder into the garden—a man that he could bait a while before engaging him in furious swordplay, and subsequently slaying him and presenting him to the master. Even a little man would do.

He would have been surprised indeed to learn that the gods—the thoughtful gods—were finally, this morn, about to grant his wish.

It took three keys before Bralatar found the one that opened the gate—and by then, the magnificent-looking guard in the garden beyond was suspicious.

"How, now? What ails Areld?" Dorgan mused aloud as he strode toward the gate, hand going to sword and eyes flicking watchfully about to be sure that only one man stood there, not a concealed band of brigands.

Another thing . . . the dogs were never allowed in the garden! What was old Warhorn playing at?

"Areld?" he challenged, sword grating. "What befalls?"

Areld swayed, one hand on the opened gate—but fell, toppling forward into the grass without a sound. Dorgan raced to stand over him, blocking passage through the gate, looking warily around for an archer or anyone waiting to rush in . . . but the woods beyond were empty of all but birds. Warhorn stood, patiently watching him.

Dorgan held the sword up between him and the dog, point out, just in case, and bent over Areld. "Are you sick, man? D—"

Those were the last words he ever spoke. Something slammed into the small of his back and drove him into a sprawling fall onto the servant. Arms of flesh curved up to envelop his head, smothering him with ruthless efficiency.

Soon after, Dorgan and Areld carried a limp, pulped mass back out into the grounds, to the base of a certain tree where the turf was torn as if by a recent upheaval. "You should have dug a large pit," Areld said with dark humor. "I'm sure we'll be able to fill it if this mage is as suspicious minded as most. There'll be beasts and human guards every few paces ahead of us now to keep intruders from ever breathing the same air as Lord Magnificent the Spell-Hurler."

Retracing their steps, the guard and the servant passed through the garden, coming at last to the only way they could see into the castle: a stone door carved into the shape of a snarling human face, with two outstretched hands beneath it to serve as handles.

"Warded, or I'm a war dog," the man who was not Dorgan muttered. "I don't like the look of those hands."

"So we slide past," the one who was not Areld murmured, extending a ribbon-thin tentacle to point. "Here—see?"

It took some time to flatten themselves out into creeping things thin enough to slip through a tiny gap between the crumbling stone and the old, slowly warping doorframe, with its carvings of satyrs and bunches of grapes and flirtatious sprites, but they passed through without incident, and without being seen.

They stood in a high, vaulted hall whose open bronze doors showed another, loftier hall, with a gallery at its far end, and many doors opening off it here, there, and everywhere. To the left, and nearby (by the smell) was the kitchen; the location of other features they could only guess at.

Wherefore the two men dwindled hurriedly back into the shapes of the two war dogs and padded into the hall with apparent aimlessness, sniffing as they roamed. The doors they passed were closed, but a broad, red-carpeted spiral stair ascended at the far end of the hall, and up this they went—on the theory that most wizards like to look out loftily over the lands around.

Partway up its ascent, the stair paused at a sunny landing, and Bolder slunk over to the small forest of ferny plants there. He peered through, uttering a short *whuf* to signal Warhorn that he'd found something of interest.

The two Malaugrym had retained their own eyes, far keener than those of a dog, and could readily see a small, slender, rather plain stone tower outside.

The tower was ringed by a moat over which tiny lightnings of amethyst hue flickered from time to time— some warding magic, no doubt. The moat in turn was surrounded by a strip of lawn. Flagstone paths led to the edge of the moat, but there was no sign of any drawbridge, and the paths also ran in a great arc in both directions, around the tower and out of view, flanking the walls of a gigantic building . . . the one in which they stood.

"Rich indeed, this wizard," Bolder growled. "Look: this house goes all the way around."

Warhorn growled a wordless reply of exasperation. How long was it going to take to find a safe way out of this vast house, into the inner garden with the tower?

Not long at all, as it turned out. A two-headed panther, black and deadly, stalked into view on the circular lawn, and a door swung open as if it were expected. They saw a man, a goad in his hand, standing in the open door, and the great cat moved fluidly toward him.

"Feeding time for everyone," Bolder grunted. They turned away from the window to hurry down the stairs.

A little distance along the passage they saw two women carrying bundles of linen. The maids frowned at them but did nothing beyond exchanging the question: "What are the dogs doing in here, I wonder?"

Wagging their tails, the dogs passed on by, proceeding to a place where a momentary shift of a paw into a human hand opened doors that were not locked, skirted a strong smell of cat (they heard a questioning growl from the other side of a door they left closed), and found their way to the inner garden. No one shouted an alarm as the dogs pawed the door open and stepped out onto the lawn.

Strong magic tingled around them, and they looked this way and that in some haste. The lawn seemed deserted.

A huge, curved stone bench adorned the edge of the

moat, and beyond it Bralatar saw what he was looking for: the top arc of an old, massive grating in the tower wall, moat water lapping into it. A privy chute.

"Come," he said. He headed straight across the lawn. On the edge of the moat he shifted shape to grow flippers and tentacles, and heard Lorgyn's snort of alarm behind him as the stone bench suddenly shuddered and rose, stretching out hammerlike arms. A golem!

By then Bralatar was in the inky water, and too busy to worry about guardians on land: what felt like large hungry eels with teeth like daggers were savaging him. He grew tentacles, thrust one down an unseen gullet, and expanded, tossing bony spines out and through his foe until the water turned a dull red and the biting went away. He served another eel with same tactic, and another. By then, massive stone arms were crashing down into the water, and Lorgyn was splashing frantically to keep clear of their strength.

Bralatar made an eel-thing of himself and wriggled through the grating, ignoring a few nips from another unseen moat dweller. The stone chute ahead of him was as slimy and noisome as he'd expected, but rose clear of the water straight away. He wormed up it hastily, becoming a snakelike ribbon as he went in case the wizard was thorough—or crazed—enough to have traps partway up a dung chute.

Behind him, Lorgyn splashed around for a breath or two more before he was clear of the water. Bralatar spared him no attention, but spiraled steadily up the shaft, sending feelers ahead to probe for traps. Somewhere above them, someone was cheerfully whistling a very old bawdy tune.

He found nothing, but as his most cautiously questing tentacle rose a trifle up out of the privy seat to peer into the dark chamber beyond, a calm, soulless female voice said: "Turn back," and a radiance began to grow around the top of the shaft. The whistling broke off abruptly.

"Hurry!" Bralatar snapped, placing suckers on the stone around him and heaving hard. He catapulted up out of the shaft like some sort of flying squid, and thumped to the floor; he'd not yet begun to grow when a second thump heralded Lorgyn's arrival.

"Now who can that be?" an annoyed voice came to their ears through the chamber door. It sounded very near, and approaching. The mage was almost upon them!

Lorgyn laid a tentacle on Bralatar's shoulder and hissed, "Distract him—those two women in the green tapestry room at the brothel; unclad, holding hands, and amazed at somehow ending up here. . . ."

They shifted shapes with lightning speed, twisting, writhing, and arching like maddened things—and were done, linking their slim fingers together and adopting amazed and fearful expressions just as the door opened by itself, and a balding, beak-nosed man peered in at them over a leveled wand.

"By the Seven Mysteries, who are you?" he gasped.

"Please, sir," the blonde woman breathed, entreaty in her green eyes, "where are we? What place is this?"

The wizard dragged his eyes up from the ivory curves of her bare body, swallowed, and blinked.

"You're in my tower—the Tower of Mortoth," he said gruffly. "Er, that's me." He took a step into the room. "Perhaps you've heard of me?"

The taller of the two women parted her raven tresses to display a figure fully as spectacular as her companion's, and husked, "Nay, Lord . . . but pray, tell us about yourself. Pleasing great men is our business—and our pleasure."

And as Mortoth goggled at her in astonishment, two tentacles appeared over the shoulder of the blonde maid and shot out with terrifying speed. One grasped the wand, twisted, and snatched—and it flew from the stumbling wizard's bruised fingers.

"Rivals!" the wizard snarled as he caught his

balance. Blue-white bolts of force were already streaking from his fingers in a hasty burst of magic missiles.

Those missiles curved home, and he saw the two intruders flinch, but one had grown fleshy wings, and the other had dropped into catlike form, and they sprang at him before he could do anything else.

The room crashed and spun for Mortoth as heavy bodies slammed into him and bowled him over. Suddenly flesh was enveloping him. He struggled, trying to spit out something that was probing into his mouth, and failing.

Lorgyn, his eyes like two copper coins catching the sun, encased the wizard's head and hands in folds of flesh, invading his mouth with a firm tentacle to keep him from speaking spells, and leaving him only small nose-hole for breathing.

"Do you want the portal right here?" he asked.

Bralatar shrugged. "Why not? We know a way into this room, and I don't want to risk wandering around among waiting spells and enchanted items and possible traps looking for a better place. Get the thing done first."

Lorgyn nodded. "The decision is wise." He held the wizard securely as Mortoth's struggles ceased and his body started to tremble.

Bralatar paced out the space he'd need and began the casting, moving slowly and carefully, his body half voluptuous maiden and half panther. White, cold fire that blazed but did not consume sprang up where he gestured, building into two open rings—both about as far across inside as a man is tall; one horizontal and the other vertical—linked by a webwork of complex lines and runes.

"Place him," he ordered. Lorgyn spun the helpless wizard deftly to a spot where Bralatar bound him about with the same cold fire before Lorgyn released the binding of flesh.

Mortoth blinked. He could suddenly see again and

opened his mouth to shout a spell, but found himself staring into a pair of cold, uncaring eyes for just an instant before his vision vanished abruptly. The same white, endless fire that had taken it whirled into his mouth, and all he could do was hum. . . .

Bralatar stepped back with a satisfied air, surveying the magical gate he'd created. The wizard hung spread-eagled and helpless in the upright circle; anyone stepping into the other circle, blazing just above the floor, would set foot in Shadowhome.

To use the other end to come to Faerûn, a rival Shadowmaster would have to stand in exactly the right spot in the Castle of Shadows, and utter the secret word Bralatar had bound the casting with. There was a small chance that one of the blood of Malaug might be standing near when the gate formed—it did not become invisible until complete—but in the spot he'd chosen, in a place as large as the Castle of Shadows, it was unlikely.

Necessary though it was if he and Lorgyn were ever to return home, Bralatar had no intention of testing his creation. Each use would drain the wizard of some of his life-energy, and they'd need another magic-wielding being to replace him. Most mortals could power the passage of only four beings before they died, the last life stolen from them to leave behind only shriveled husks.

It was a pity the senior Malaugrym never revealed the locations of the ancient gates in Faerûn built or discovered by the early blood of Malaug. Worse still, neither he nor Lorgyn had the use of a scrying portal to search either Shadowhome or Faerûn from afar. If there were gates enough and in the right places, they could have avoided this entire undertaking . . . and left important, bustling little Mortoth of Sembia in peace.

"At least we're putting this wizard to good use, not just slaying him and seizing his magic, as Lunquar did to all the Zhents he could find in the brothels of Sembia,"

Bralatar commented, watching cold fire race up and down Mortoth's motionless limbs.

"Lunquar's gathered a lot of magic, don't forget," Lorgyn reminded him.

"Yes, but the risk!"

"The Great Foe is dead! What is to stop us ruling over all?"

"So why did Lunquar counsel us to subtlety?"

"It's his way. Lunquar's always been a fierce loner; he refused to work with Dhalgrave himself, once. He's as bad as Ahorga."

"The probable difference between them is that to get home, Lunquar's going to have to do what we have—or use our gate, at whatever price we set—and old Ahorga can no doubt travel freely back and forth between Shadowhome and Faerûn. He must know the old gates and the traps our kin set on them ages ago."

"Are there any gates known to our kin, that we've not trapped?"

Lorgyn shook his lovely blonde head. "Not so far as I know; the doing was deliberate and absolute, to prevent the use of all gates known to us by any being not familiar with our guard spells."

* * * * *

The Castle of Shadows, Shadowhome, Flamerule 23

"And we intend to keep things that way," said Amdramnar softly, staring through his hastily cast scrying portal. He'd only caught this utterance and the last few words of something about Ahorga, but it was clear which of the kin were involved: they'd found Bralatar and Lorgyn.

It had been sheer chance that he and Argast had passed through the little-used Hall of the Eyes to avoid the well-traveled Hathtor's Gallery. The gate had appeared right in front of them, lines of white fire drawing themselves in the air.

Amdramnar was fast with his magic, but he was more used to hurling slaying spells in haste than spinning a scrying portal at speed. It had taken some time to call up a view of the other end of the unfolding magic.

"So we know of four kin active in Faerûn now: Ahorga and Lunquar, operating independently, and these two," Argast mused aloud. "Shall we place a slaying trap on their gate?"

"I think not," Amdramnar replied. "Given the right spell—I'll have find it in my librams—we can divine the trigger word Bralatar used in the casting. Then it can serve us as a route that Ahorga and the other elders don't know about, if we have to bring someone into Shadowhome undetected."

"A mate, for example," Argast said softly. "Your lady of the sword."

Amdramnar regarded him, unsmiling. "You seek a lady too, I know. With a world open to me, Sharantyr may not be my choice."

If the two Malaugrym who stood beside the scrying portal could have used it to look into each other's minds, they would have seen that Amdramnar burned with the need to have the mortal Sharantyr—and no other—and that Argast had a deeper need. His mother had fled the Castle of Shadows long ago and successfully hid, somewhere in Faerûn, from the seeking magic of the House of Malaug. She was then pregnant; Argast son of Halthor must have siblings now. If one could be befriended and manipulated, or bred with . . . a new dynasty of Shadowmasters could rise to rule the shattered House of Malaug. . . .

But it was very much a good thing that scrying portals—and most other magic, even wielded by kin—couldn't pry at the thoughts of Malaugrym.

"Let us go to your chambers," Argast suggested. "I'll wait without while you prepare your spell, and we can return here without delay."

Amdramnar nodded. He passed a hand across the scrying portal; it rippled and was gone, leaving the Hall of the Eyes dark and apparently empty.

* * * * *

"I have little liking for hunting mage after mage for their magic," Lorgyn said carefully as they stood in the room with the helpless wizard floating between them, "but we should take steps to ensure that this one doesn't have an apprentice or three who'll find and free him."

"Hah—if I know apprentices, more likely they'll slay and rob him, and take away all the magic they can." Bralatar replied.

Lorgyn looked thoughtful. "That brings to mind another thing," he said slowly, frowning. "There have always been rumors that Malaug left powerful magic hidden on Faerûn before he came to Shadowhome. It was one of the reasons old Stannar grumbled so much about the prohibition on forays into Faerûn. If we can find it . . ."

Bralatar lifted an eyebrow. "Is that why you ransacked Candlekeep?"

Lorgyn smiled faintly. "You know about that? Aye, but I found nothing there . . . not even in the minds of the eldest whitebeards. Are Malaug's writings truly lost, or forgotten—or are they just hidden in some grasping wizard's tower?"

"Elminster's tower, of course," Bralatar said grimly. His eyes alight with a sudden dark fire. "And with Elminster destroyed . . ."

13
Out of the Shadows

Shadows roiled around them, sliding past in an endless murmur of green and gray motes, streaming between the massive stone pillars. Each pillar, some of the kin whispered, held an unfortunate Malaugrym, entombed alive as part of the cruel magics Malaug employed. These traitors thus kept the very foundations of the Castle of Shadows from being swept away by shadows.

Argast and Amdramnar both suspected those whispers held truth. There was something eerie about the Undercrypt. One felt the scrutiny of an unseen presence here. As the Malaugrym stood facing each other in the stream of ever-shifting shadows, they could feel it very strongly. Was the watcher all that was left of Malaug himself? If it was the First to Walk Shadows, he must be truly ancient . . . and he never broke silence or gave any sign that he knew what befell his descendants. Other Malaugrym believed the castle itself was sentient, that the Undercrypt was where it was most truly awake and aware.

"I am ready," Argast announced calmly, "but I have one question: how much greater is the risk to us, traveling to a place neither of us has actually been?"

"Oh, but we have," Amdramnar said with a smile. "That's the beauty of it. Moreover, when we visited, I let fall a focus token there. The risk is vanishingly small."

Argast frowned. "You say I have been to this place?"

"Yes. We stood in the sky hurling spells down at the Great Foe and the three rangers with him when they were encamped in a ruin, and—"

"There? The ruin?"

"It's as good a place as any," Amdramnar said. "Close to places we've viewed, but in the wilderlands. We're not likely to be seen arriving, nor be swiftly called upon to shift shape or act at being something we're not—until we choose to do so. Let us smell and feel Faerûn first."

A faint smile crossed Argast's face. "Good points, all. Let us be going, then. I have waited a very long time for this."

"I, too," Amdramnar said, and reached out his hand to touch Argast's shoulder. He spoke a single word, there was a momentary falling, spinning sensation—and they were suddenly standing in the long grass of upland Daggerdale, with the ruins of Irythkeep around them.

"See how easy it is?" Amdramnar said, shaking his head. "It seems incredible that all of our clan has been kept from this for centuries, for fear of one old man!"

A helmed head promptly bobbed into view above a section of crumbling wall, and a voice roared, "Enemy mages! Strike—strike to slay, for the greater glory of the Dead Dragons!"

The two Malaugrym exchanged startled looks, then ducked away in opposite directions as a ball of flame hissed through the air, divided into two smaller balls, and chased them.

"By the blood of Malaug, who've we stumbled into *this* time?" Amdramnar snarled, somersaulting over a jagged wall and falling down the steep drop-off beyond with a jolt that rattled his very teeth. A moment later, there was a flash and a ground-shaking roar. The fireball struck the wall and blew it apart; it promptly toppled, burst, and plummeted down on top of him.

The furious Malaugrym grew one long leg and leapt—crazily off-balance—from under a huge pile of rubble that thudded into the turf where he'd lain a moment before.

He landed, rolled, and came up facing back where he'd been, in time to see a large war bird that must be Argast flap into view, rising sharply. A robed man who bore a gleaming staff stood on the edge of the drop-off. As Amdramnar hastily backed away, the man discharged the staff, spitting a beam of flame at Argast that scorched him all along one flank and startled him into a fall.

Another man took up a dramatic stance, a wand raised in his hand. He peppered Argast with magic missiles, sending him down to a hard landing on the rubble pile.

Argast got up shrieking in fury, but his Art was feeble. He could do little against wizards of power. He fled desperately downhill, changing shape into a large, bounding jackrabbit for greater speed—and outrunning a web of crimson bolts from the staff.

Very soon Amdramnar fetched up beside Argast, his eyes blazing. "Somewhere quiet in the wilderlands? By the fist of Malaug, what're the *cities* like?"

"Someone else must have decided this ruin would be quiet and secluded, too—or they wouldn't be so eager to throw away powerful magic on two men they haven't even spoken to yet," Amdramnar said calmly. "Let's withdraw."

"There seems little point to it," Argast said grimly, pointing at another swarm of bright bolts headed their way: magic missiles, unavoidable and painful. "Who are the Dead Dragons, anyway? An adventuring band? Some of the Great Foe's apprentices, out for some fun?"

Amdramnar suddenly chuckled. "No, I think they're some sort of cult that were always bothering the Great Foe . . . idiots who worship skeletal undead dragons."

Argast gave him a disbelieving look, but gritted his

teeth as the swarm of magic missiles struck home, hurling them both onto their backs in the grass. "Let's move out of sight," he said, sounding sick. "That hurt." Keeping low, they crawled over a ridge and became two wolves, trotting in a wide circle around the ruin.

"Shall we go elsewhere?" Amdramnar asked.

"Revenge first," Argast said in iron tones. "No one should try to slay Malaugrym out of hand and get away with it!" They trotted on. "So what does worshiping undead dragons have to do with hurling spells at everyone you glimpse?"

Amdramnar shrugged. "They seize treasure to offer dragons," he said slowly. "Perhaps they thought we were thieves come to take it."

"They walk around heavily laden with killing magic all the time?"

"Perhaps the Shadowmasters High were not such fools as we thought to ban entry into Faerûn," Amdramnar said mildly.

"Bah! Bralatar and Lorgyn still live—and have done well here. If those two overconfident lackwits can thrive in Faerûn, we certainly can!"

"Talking wolves?" A man's voice said from behind them. "Shapeshifters, more likely! 'Ware a trap!"

Without bothering to look around, the two Malaugrym broke into a run. The fireball, when it came, exploded just above their heads.

Somewhere in the red, roaring inferno of the fireball's fringes, Argast fetched up very hard against a boulder and felt many things snap. He saw Amdramnar hurtle helplessly past, turning over and over in midair, so racked with pain that he was losing wolf form. Tentacles and a misshapen gray mass wobbled and thrashed the air just before he landed in a cloud of dust.

"A fireball!" snapped the first voice they'd heard. "They must know we're here! *Attack!*"

As the two Malaugrym lay in pain among the smoldering grass, forty or more mages and warriors boiled up over a ridge ahead of them and raced past, to the place whence the fireball had come. The sounds of battle arose from thereabouts.

When Argast had fought down the pain and shifted shape into something resembling a long-limbed crocodile, he moved hastily away. He was just in time. A whirling cloud of flashing blades suddenly twinkled into being above the rocks where he'd lain, clanging and crashing off stone—then turned into slowly drifting white butterflies. Not far away, they heard someone curse all gods and wild magic.

Amdramnar managed to slither to where Argast lay panting. "What befalls?" he hissed.

"The dragon idiots were waiting for these others, and thought the fireball cast at us was an attack meant for them. They rushed the ambush they were planning and are attacking here and now. Who these others are is yet beyond me; *you're* supposed to be the expert on Faerûn!"

Amdramnar winced. "Truly said. Let's try to work our way over to the ruins. From that higher ground we can look back at the fighting."

"And get attacked by all the dragon worshipers who aren't quite so eager to get killed as these here are," Argast said sourly. "I await the experience with eager glee."

"Ah, be easy! Magic's starting going wild here anyway—see those blades turn to butterflies?"

"I'm not overwhelmed with joy," Argast said coldly, "at the prospect of starting my exploration of Faerûn as a butterfly! Or as anything else twisted or shackled by sorcery, strange as it may seem!"

"I'll admit my idea of coming to Irythkeep has turned out badly," Amdramnar replied quietly, "but we've seen a wand and a staff in use already, and magic is a large part of what we came here for. Why flee from it now that we know what we face? Why, they're busy battling each other!"

As he spoke, lightning cracked into the sky, split apart into three bolts with a spectacular crash, and leapt to earth, one striking quite close. Their hair rose, and their bodies tingled.

Argast said dryly, "*That's* why. Have you experienced enough yet? Can we go somewhere safer?"

"The ruins," Amdramnar insisted, "where we first appeared—if these Cult of the Dragon fools were preparing an ambush, they must be camped there. It's the only landmark in this stretch of country; the people they're fighting must have been planning to camp there, or at least use it to keep on the route they intended, and pass close by."

"What shapes do you suggest we take? Fireballs, so we can pass unnoticed, perhaps?" The sarcasm in Argast's tone was venomous; it was clear he suspected Amdramnar of having deliberately sent him into danger.

"Trust me, Argast," Amdramnar said firmly. "This fray was not of my doing. I've been hurt as badly as you. We'll both be spending some time healing. We'll need a large blood meal as fuel for it, too."

"What if we bite unknowing into a wizard and trigger nasty contingency spells?" Argast said warily. "What then?"

"We're a long way out in the uplands; they probably all came here on horses," Amdramnar replied patiently. "Now let's move . . . looking like horses ourselves might not be a bad idea. Someone might try to catch a horse, but they're hardly likely to waste a fireball killing it!"

"Now you speak wisely," Argast said, beginning the shift into equine form. Amdramnar sighed in relief and did likewise. He had begun to fear there was some sort of curse afflicting this foray into Faerûn.

They trotted in a very wide route, keeping to easy ground and almost out of sight of the ruined keep to be sure of avoiding the attention of anyone who might have a spell to hurl. They approached the ruins in the lee of a stand of trees, and made their hooves soft and pliable to keep as silent as possible. When they were near enough to hear voices and see men moving, they began to graze, drifting slowly around into view, hoping they'd be taken for mounts belonging to the camp.

"We'll take losses now, for sure," someone was grumbling. "How could they have seen us from so far off?"

"Mayhap they did not," a deeper voice replied.

"Mages don't waste fireballs on nothing, or throw them across grassland at a whim! That's sheer foolishness!"

"I've known some wizards whom the mantle of 'fool' would fit right well," the deep voice responded.

"Don't let Chaladar hear you say that! Some of the dragons like to chase and eat human warriors who put up a fight, you know!"

"Aye, I do know," the deep voice replied calmly. "Why do you think we asked you along?"

"What? How can you be—did Chaladar tell y—oh, gods! My horse . . . all unsaddled . . . sweet Tymora, aid me now!"

"That's not a very judicious prayer for a *faithful* follower of the Scaly Way, wouldn't you say, Malarnus?"

"Quit baiting the lad, Ornthar . . . you'll have him running into things and shrieking in a breath or two! Sit *down,* Felus! He was merely jesting with you!"

"Now what have you done with your wand, boy?" Ornthar growled. "Dropped it, no doubt, while running around like a man who can't find the privy seat and babbling to Lady Luck!"

The Malaugrym exchanged a look and moved closer.

"Here it is!"

"That's *my* wand, idiot!" Malarnus told him. "Where did you walk, Felus, and where've you been sitting? Go back to all those places and look for it, and—there!" There came a thud and a groan. Malarnus added sarcastically, "See how easy it is to find things when you trip over them?"

"Dolt!" Ornthar added helpfully.

Amdramnar took a step nearer and had a sudden idea. He began to shift shape, turning into a scorched-looking man, hairless and blackened, clothes hanging in tatters. When he was done, he turned to Argast and gestured for him to do the same. Argast gave him a doubtful look for a moment, but complied.

Amdramnar gestured to Argast to follow. He staggered around the last few trees and right into the camp.

"By the Dragon! Keep back!" a scarred veteran in half armor said, raising a wand in one hand and holding a blade in the other. Ornthar, no doubt. Seated on either side of him were an anxious youth and a sleek man with a spade beard. Felus and Malarnus.

"I-I . . . help us," Amdramnar gasped, staggering a pace closer. "Fireball . . . "

"Who are you?"

"Followers . . . we were to meet Chaladar here," Amdramnar husked. "All dead now but us. . . ."

"Felus," the seated man rapped, "get them some water." Malarnus indeed, by his voice. How generous.

Amdramnar staggered right over to the lad as he reached for a saddle skin, and Argast followed. Ornthar kept his eyes and his wand trained on them all the time. Malaug's curse on all well-trained warriors, Amdramnar thought, and worked magic that called forth fire.

Flames flared up right behind Malarnus, who heard the hiss and crackle, looked around with a frown, and jumped up with an oath. "Fire! Magic!" He spun around, eyes narrowing. "There's none here but y—"

He was, of course, too late. A tentacle whipped lash-like around his throat, jerked, and broke his neck. He joined Felus and Ornthar, who'd been distracted for one fatal moment by Malarnus's shout. All three lay broken on the ground.

"Take anything that looks magical," Amdramnar said. "We can discard things later. We'll ride two of their horses."

"And eat them later, too," Argast agreed, bending to the work of feverishly examining the camp.

They found three wands and an old cup . . . and that was all. If this Cult of the Dragon band carried heavy magic, it was in use beyond the ridge, where green smoke was drifting and the bright flashes of spells could still be seen.

Figures ran toward the ruined keep, now! Three . . . more . . . a dozen, but still small distant dots. Time to be gone.

"Come," Amdramnar snapped. He turned toward the nearest horse.

Argast hesitated for a moment, looking as if he was about to refuse and go his own way. Then he peered back at the running men, shrugged, and followed.

Amdramnar frowned, and was not gentle with his horse.

* * * * *

"I'd guess he's taken with some scrying spell and we won't see him until dusk," the younger and louder of the two men said.

"Peering at wenches in the brothels of Ordulin, most likely," the older man grunted. He ran a finger down the script in a thick and dusty book.

"Turnold!" the third apprentice in the library said sharply. She scowled. "You know I don't like to hear talk like that!"

The older man sighed. He replied without bothering to look up from his book, "You've got to learn about human nature and the ways of the world *some*time, Irendue. You must notice how he looks at you."

"That's a private matter between the master and myself," was the even sharper response, "and no concern of yours!"

"Oh, I'm not concerned," Turnold said easily. "If I were in your place I would be, but he's not interested in me."

"For your information, Master Prentice Turnold, he's not interested in me in the manner you so crudely allude to, either!"

"Oh? And just when I thought I'd got right the scrying spell the master taught me ten years ago! I particularly like the black-and-gold gown, by the way. . . ."

"You *worm!*" Irendue shrieked, leaping to her feet, her face white to the lips. "You utter . . . spying snake!"

"Oh, I was following the master's instructions . . . as was Lareth here. The master told us we might learn something. . . ."

The door banged furiously as Irendue left, and Lareth, who'd blushed as red as his scarlet robe, coughed uneasily. "You shouldn't bait her like that. You know she'll just run to the master and there'll be trouble."

"*We* have to pay for our training," Turnold said calmly, "and pay dearly. She pays in another way. I don't mind that; I'd just like her to be honest about it and not play the prim and prissy high lady with us."

"Why should she be honest?" Lareth asked, amused. "She's training to be a mage, not a hermit priest!"

"I could probably tell you things about hermit priests," Turnold replied calmly, turning a page.

"My, you have been busy with that scrying spell," Lareth returned. He held the grimoire he'd been frowning at under Turnold's nose and pointed at a notation in one margin of a battle spell. "Oparl's hand, do you think?"

Turnold shook his head. "Too spidery. Jamryth's, for a gold lion."

"I'll not wager with you, Turnold," Lareth said ruefully. "You're too often right!"

"That has always been my trouble," Turnold agreed calmly, eyes on his own book again.

"Thirsty work, this," Lareth said. He set down his book and flipping its spine ribbon to mark the page 'with Jamryth's notes. "I'm for a flagon. Join me?"

"Plenty of time left to get drunk today," Turnold replied. "I'll be along later."

"Right," Lareth said with a grin, and swept out.

Only a moment later, he added a scream.

By the time Turnold got out into the passage, wand in hand, Lareth had joined Irendue—and the master!—in a web of cold white fire that seemed to fill the privy chamber. Two women he'd never seen before—no, men wearing the faces of wenches—were standing in the passage facing him, with wide and ruthless smiles on their faces.

As he swept the wand up, Turnold felt the horrible strength of the tentacles that were falling on him from all around the door frame . . . tentacles that trailed back along the floor to join up with the men-women's bodies!

The wand was slapped from his hand, but a horrified Turnold scarcely noticed. He was trying desperately to scream, but discovering, as tentacles crowded into his mouth and slid coldly up his nostrils, that it was much too late. . . .

* * * * *

Daggerdale, Flamerule 23

"I begin to think Lunquar's approach is the right one," Argast said as his exhausted horse collapsed under him. "Hide as much as possible. Keep to crow shape and the like, take human form only when another shape will win suspicion. Lie low and learn."

"We'll have to lie low for a bit to heal fully," Amdramnar grunted. "Kill these now and eat?"

"Why not? They're too weak to be of any other use!"

The Malaugrym had ridden across half Daggerdale without a break; Argast's mount had collapsed on a steep slope in the rolling hills of the southeastern dale, hard by the woods that stretched to Shadowdale.

"I think the most important thing is to hide ourselves from the common folk," Amdramnar said slowly. "They seem very swift to call on adventurers when they see something amiss, and this world does have crude shapeshifters. . . ."

"Doppelgangers, yes, I remember all the tales about how Malaug must have bedded one and thus given us the power."

"It matters little now. I just want to hunt down this Sharantyr woman and the two men who came to Shadowhome with her."

"And kill them, slowly and painfully?"

"The two men, yes. The woman's fate depends on what she agrees to. . . ."

Argast shook his head and mouthed the words: then I'll kill her. He was careful to turn his head so that Amdramnar had no chance to see his lips.

Then he felt a tentacle brush his leg. He was about to strike it away angrily when he saw that Amdramnar was sinking down into the shape of a horse, and lying as if dead in the grass . . . and that his lone tentacle was pointing urgently across the valley.

Argast crouched down. He had already begun to take horse shape when he saw them: a dozen or so men and women in drab leather armor. Dirt-caked weapons hung in their hands, and they crept cautiously through the trees. A patrol.

Someone's patrol. Argast made himself as much like the real horse beside him as possible and lay still.

It seemed a very long time before a voice said, low-pitched and near, "They're still warm . . . this one, at least, still lives. Ridden to death."

"So their riders must be close by . . . hiding from us, no doubt."

"Zhent troops, for a gold lion."

"That's a wager I'll never take, Yheldon. If we find them and they have arrows, we'll end up just as dead as the mighty Elminster—and the Zhents'll be picking the gold coins out of both our purses!"

Argast twitched in excitement. The Great Foe dead!

It was dark before the two Malaugrym dared move again, coming up to clutch each other and hiss excitedly, "Elminster, dead!"

"We must confirm this," Amdramnar muttered. "I've heard tell men have thought him dead many times before."

"Of course," Argast agreed, "but if it be true, we can hunt freely!"

"Don't forget that woman back at the keep who turned our kin to mushrooms and slaughtered us like cattle! He's not the only one in Faerûn we must beware of."

"Aye, but he was the one who watched and waited for us. Moreover, with magic gone wild and gods walking Faerûn and everything in confusion . . ."

"You're right," Amdramnar acknowledged with a sigh, turning to look east.

"You sound disappointed that he's dead."

"I am, a little. I was dreading having to face him . . . but to strike him down myself! The honor of our house demands it! Someone has robbed me of the chance to fell the Great Foe." Amdramnar shook his head, and chuckled. "With Elminster gone, whatever will the elder kin blame their failures on now, I wonder?"

"They'll find something," Argast said. "They always do. I think skill at finding targets for blame is part of the wisdom of being an elder."

* * * * *

Near the Standing Stone, the Dales, Flamerule 24

"There's a large party on the road south of the Stone," Sharantyr said. She leapt lightly down from the lowest bough of the tree. The others were already loosening weapons in sheaths and taking up their gauntlets.

"Did you see lots of armor?" Belkram asked eagerly.

Sharantyr shook her head as she unlooped the reins of her mount. "No, bold warrior. I saw horses, men's heads above them, and dust. At least twenty horses, and probably more." She vaulted into the saddle and looked to Storm.

The Bard of Shadowdale smiled. "It's always good to have a look at the Stone before one rides there. It avoids a lot of surprises."

"Could it be another Zhent army?" Itharr asked as they guided their horses cautiously around roots, down mossy banks, and out onto the Hillsfar road.

Storm frowned. "Blackhelms riding openly, no. Some of our people"—they knew she meant the Harpers—"would have brought me word of any such force gathering or on the move through Sembia. Zhent agents could well have sponsored some hireswords—but on the other hand, were I an honest merchant in times as troubled as these, I'd travel in a large band with plenty of bought blades to defend me, too." A faint smile crossed her face, and she added, "So, as usual, we'd best be ready for anything."

They rode in wary silence past the ancient Standing Stone, seeing the glitter of steel in the forefront of the travelers coming north toward them. It was soon evident that the front rank consisted of five hard-eyed mercenaries with ready crossbows and full armor. They came on without stopping, loading and leveling their bows as they saw the armed rangers.

At the sight of those preparations, Storm said, "Stay well back, all of you. With magic unreliable, I can't protect you against crossbow bolts."

Itharr made a small sound of protest, but Syluné's soft voice said, "Heed her. Your death can be avoided this time if you act wisely, so why not avoid it?"

In the silence that followed, they watched Storm ride to meet the oncoming band.

"Stand aside, brigand," one of the hireswords ordered

shortly.

"Surrender your names and business to me, mercenary," Storm replied calmly, unmoving.

"Stand aside, I said!"

"Is anyone in this mounted assembly of a more reasonable mind?" Storm asked mildly. "Most travelers on these roads are well aware that the Knights of Myth Drannor patrol here; if your business is lawful, our encounter may be brief and pleasant . . . but an exchange of information is expected."

A crossbow snapped, and a quarrel flew. Belkram growled and made to launch his mount forward, sword flashing out.

At his ear, Syluné said in a voice of iron, "Stand and watch! You may even learn . . ."

Storm calmly plucked the crossbow bolt from her breast, examined it critically, and held it out, looking at the gaping man who'd fired it. "Yours, I believe?"

"Who are you?" another of the mercenaries snapped, face pale and voice sharp with alarm.

"Ah," Storm replied pleasantly, "the words you should have spoken first. I am Storm Silverhand, Bard of Shadowdale, and am accompanying a road patrol ordered by Lord Mourngrym of Shadowdale and the Knights of Myth Drannor to keep peace on the roads in these perilous times. Again, I ask you your names and business."

She tossed the crossbow bolt, underhanded, back to the man who'd fired it. He juggled it but dropped it to the road, and started to dismount.

"What's the delay here?" a man in rich robes called, urging his mount forward.

A man in a yellow cloak, who rode behind the mercenaries, answered, "Some sort of road patrol asking our business."

"Ignore them; we're in a hurry."

"A hurry to go where, goodsir?" Storm asked quietly.

"Ride her down!" the man ordered the mercenaries

curtly. Seeing one of his men out of his saddle, he shouted, "You heard me! Get up and get on!"

"Lord," one of the mercenaries said, "this w—"

"I'll hear none of it! Onward!"

"Hireswords," Storm asked quietly, "is this most audible man your master?"

A smile flickered on more than one face along the line of armored warriors before one said, "Aye, Lady. Rethuld of Saerloon."

"Thank you, good warrior," Storm said politely. She raised her voice. "Rethuld! I would speak with you!"

"But *I*," the man spat contemptuously, "would not speak with you! Anyone blocking the high road is a brigand, and I slay brigands, not bandy words with them!"

"By the treaty of the Stone in whose shadow we stand," Storm said quietly, "any dale lord is empowered to send patrols out on the roads—and all travelers on the road are bound to obey such patrols and surrender to their queries and examinations."

"That treaty is centuries old! We pay no attention to it in Sembia!"

"Old it may be," Storm replied calmly, "but I was there at its making, and I was also present not so long ago as all that, when the young land of Sembia in turn signed it to gain trade access to the Moonsea North and grow to its present wealth. You would do well to pay continued attention to it if you are a merchant of Sembia. Treaties ignored may be revoked—and with the roads closed, what are the prospects for your wealth then?"

"You said the dales were unprotected," the man in the yellow cloak said to Rethuld, frowning. "You said we'd be able to—"

"Silence! I am *not* prepared to discuss our private business dealings on the high road! We can speak of this later—if there is to be a later for you, Jasten!"

"I think," Storm said quietly, "this has gone far

enough. I've no wish to see blood spilled this day, so I think we'll have a little truth here." She made a gesture.

Another crossbow bolt hummed past her, but missed, and Storm completed her spell. She looked slowly around at the row of mercenaries and the half a dozen merchants crowded behind them. There were wagons beyond, with a dozen or more additional mercenaries flanking them . . . and presumably a rearguard. "If there's no harmful intent in this man's replies, you'll all be free to proceed—but I will look unfavorably on men who try to slip past me, or offer violence to me, before I am done. That means *you*, sir, trying to stay unseen in the trees . . . come out where I can see you!"

A man shouldered sullenly out through the brush, astonishment on his face and a sword in his hand. "Who—what are you, Lady?" he demanded.

"I am Storm Silverhand. Do you believe nothing in Sembia of the tales of Those Who Harp, or of the Seven Sisters? Or do you dismiss them as idle fancies and turn back to the hard, grasping work of stacking coins ever higher?"

"Minstrels tell many wild tales of the barbaric backlands of Faerûn," a fat merchant snapped from behind the line of mercenaries. "If we believed them all, we'd not dare leave our bedchambers for fear of flying dragons and dark elves in the streets and Red Wizards behind every tree!"

"Tell me," Storm asked, widening her eyes, "is your bedchamber tastefully furnished?"

"What?"

"If, as you say, you spend so much time there . . ."

There were chuckles from the men around, and the fat merchant sputtered in anger. "I—kill her!"

"Lord," one of the mercenaries replied, not turning to take his eyes off Storm, "I don't think that's possible. Not for us. Let's just hear her out, and—gods willing— we can proceed."

Storm gave him a dazzling smile. "Thank you, good-sir. It is always a pleasure to know one is in the presence of patience and good sense."

Then she turned to Rethuld, who sat silent and pale, beads of sweat suddenly thick on his forehead, and said gently, "While my spell lasts, you will be able to answer direct questions only with the truth. I ask you now: for what purpose was this band formed?"

Rethuld licked his lips, and his face contorted for an instant before he said, "To gain property in the Dalelands."

"Why?" Storm asked, "and why now?"

"Sembia grows unsafe . . . without watch spells, thieves and brigands are free to loot, kidnap, and slay as they like. I gathered men whose business, like mine, can be run from any locale, and we came north to find a better place to bide until the strife be over."

"How did you plan to find this 'better place'?"

Rethuld looked around helplessly, sweating, and said, "S-Search, until we came upon one to our liking."

"And what sort of place would be to your liking?"

"A stout keep or defensible manor." The words came out of Rethuld reluctantly, as if he were fighting hard not to utter them.

"Such places are seldom deserted," Storm said mildly. "I can think of only four that stand empty at present, and those are isolated ruins infested by monsters—extremely primitive and dangerous accommodations. How were you planning to take possession of a suitable place?"

"I-I . . ." Rethuld looked trapped, his eyes darting wildly from side to side, his lips trembling. When he spoke again, his voice was low and despairing. "Ah—seize it by force of arms."

There was a sigh of resignation from the men all around, and swords grated out, but Storm sat still in her saddle and said calmly, "I thought so. Tell me; was the idea your own?"

"Ah, no, Lady," Rethuld said, his voice rising to a sudden, desperate squeal, " 'twas brought to me by another."

"And the name of—?"

Rethuld sobbed suddenly; a blade that seemed to be made of bone protruded from his chest. He shook, mouth working, looked down at the bloody point in horror, and slumped over. The bone slid out of him from behind.

"I thought so," Storm said calmly, ignoring the blades that were slashing through her. "Malaugrym."

The man behind Rethuld suddenly writhed and dwindled—and a falcon sprang into the air, leaving an empty saddle behind. The bird darted south.

The blades were passing through the Bard of Shadowdale as if her body was made of smoke. She said to the men wielding them, "Submit to the others who patrol with me, and you shall have peace," but the fearful hacking continued unabated as the stone she wore between her breasts flashed with sudden blue fire. She rose from her own saddle and flew after the falcon, still in her own form.

"Gods," Belkram said as they ranged their mounts across the road to meet the oncoming mercenaries, "how can she take so many wounds?"

"She wears a gorget that protects her with ironguard magic," Syluné replied. "Metal weapons pass through her as if she were . . . as insubstantial as I."

Lightnings blazed out from her, and mercenaries cried out, reeling in the shadows and dropping their weapons.

"You heard the Bard of Shadowdale," Sharantyr cried, standing up in her saddle. "Turn back to Essembra, in peace!"

As they stared at her, the ghostly head of Syluné drifted forward, its pale glow reflected back from swords and armor all around. She added briskly, "Battledale holds manors in plenty left empty by the Zhents. I'm sure their rightful owners would be happy to sell them to you. Those who are adamant in their determination to press on will, before this day is out, find themselves sharing a grave with *me*."

That was all the Sembian band needed to see and hear. They wheeled their mounts in hasty terror and fled from the ghostly female head that flew toward them trailing long, silvery hair. They galloped south as fast as they could, leaving their wagons behind.

Belkram laughed aloud. "That was the easiest fight I've ever been in!"

Syluné turned. "Be not so quick to laugh; your work is just beginning."

"It is?"

"These wagons must be taken up the Stone, turned around there, and driven back to their owners, wherever they may flee to. I'll fly ahead to Essembra to get us enough drovers."

"Flying around like that? They'll flee just like all these hardened warriors here did!" Itharr protested.

"Not the Harpers," Syluné replied without turning. "The wagons, gentlesirs." She flew away down the road like an arrow shot from a bow.

Belkram sighed. "Why do we always get the sweat work, eh?"

"You're Harpers," Sharantyr reminded him sweetly. "Such unpleasantness provides meaning and purpose in your lives." Itharr shot her a grin, and she added, "You should be grateful: many folk *never* find meaning or purpose in their existence."

"Huh," Belkram grunted, climbing up onto the boards of the foremost wagon. "Why can't they all come and do this for us, then?"

14
High Evenfeast at Low Rythryn

The falcon winged frantically southward, trailing feathers in reckless haste as no real falcon would dare do—and growing new ones as no real falcon could hope to do.

Storm followed in its wake. Her fly spell thrust her steadily on through the air. She kept low above the trees so she might survive her tumble to the ground when the magic failed or went wild, and to make sure the falcon could not veer off or descend suddenly without her seeing just where it went.

The falcon's flight was southeast over the forest until Essembra lay on their right. Once past the town, it heeled westward, passing south across the road to Sembia and the outlying farms of Battledale, heading for the distant silver ribbon of the fast-flowing Ashaba, where it left the Pool of Yeven. Long before it got there, the falcon turned north again, flew a little way, and dived suddenly to earth.

Storm hurriedly swerved behind a tree to avoid being seen; as she'd expected, the shapeshifter halted its descent to skim along the stone walls of an estate, and peered into the trees all around as it went.

The falcon completed its circuit of the walls. Apparently

satisfied he was alone, the Malaugrym sank down beyond the wall.

Storm hastily flew nearer, working her way through the trees; she wanted to be inside the walls too, when her spell ran out. Even if this turned out to be a garden of deadly Malaugrym.

Beyond the wall was a cluster of towers, one of the many walled villas that rich Sembians and wizards had built for themselves. They were enclosed for safety against the monsters and brigands that roamed these lush wilderlands. The road past the gate would be one of the long, winding lanes that fed into Rauthauvyr's Road just north of Blackfeather Bridge.

She dare not tarry or work her way along the wall to avoid detection; her spell would run out in moments. Darting over the wall, Storm found herself over deserted gardens and a small ornamental pond. She turned sharply to keep herself over dry land, and dived hastily down, righting herself to land feet first. It was good she did. She was well above the turf when her magic gave out, and she fell precipitously to earth.

"Once more to embrace the soft lips and bruising talons of adventure, friends," she murmured to herself, quoting a ballad she had written hundreds of summers ago. She got up and dusted herself off.

The placid waters of a small garden pool showed her a rather fierce-looking lady in leathers, so she stripped off her clothes and sword, bundled them up together, and said a soft word over them.

They vanished obediently—at least that small magic had worked right; now for the next one. She checked that she still had the dagger in its sheath under her hair, at the back of her gorget band. These days, a lady never knew when she'd need a good sharp knife. The gorget itself, stuffed with coins, bore a chased design that was elegant enough to accompany the attire she planned. To it, then . . .

Standing nude above the pool, she worked a magic

she'd not used in quite this way for years, creating an ornate off-the-shoulder gown that would pass muster in the most exclusive circles in Sembia, and elegant high sandals to go with it. Her silver hair would do as she bid it, so she gave herself a sleek fall of tresses over one shoulder, and an elaborate braid over her brow. 'Twould do, indeed.

Taking a last look around to mark the place she'd left her gear, Storm strolled languidly across the gardens, eyes missing little despite her relaxed manner. She spotted the spatters of fresh blood beside a stone bench in a little bower, about where the falcon had landed, and wondered which inhabitant of the household was now a broken, unrecognizable boneless thing hastily buried nearby.

The Malaugrym awaited her somewhere inside these walls, all right. Storm strolled ahead as if no such peril was near, enjoying the gardens. A winding path girt with fragrant flowers took her to two small bridges that hopped from islet to islet across the large pond, to a terrace where stone urns stood in floral ranks along low, scalloped stone walls. Within those walls she could see folk moving—liveried servants.

Calmly she strolled up the path, ascending a broad stair to where a grizzled, monocled man of graying years and mustache was enjoying a row of flagons, each containing a different wine. He stared at her in amazement for only a moment before springing to his feet and saying, "Great lady, be welcome in Low Rythryn Towers!"

He bowed, offered her his hand, and indicated a vacant chair beside his own. "I am Lord Thael Sembergelt, once a battle commander of Sembia, but now lord only of this house. I am delighted the gods have brought me so noble and—dare I say?—beauteous a guest! Pray, make known to me your name."

"I am Storm Silverhand, called by many the Bard of Shadowdale," Storm replied with grave charm, "and I must tender my apologies for arriving uninvited. My spell travels brought me here unintentionally."

"No apologies are needed, not at all! In truth, you filled me with delight, strolling up through the gardens like that as if you were some hidden nymph come to greet me! It seemed this house were showing me one of its treasures!"

"Gallantly said, my lord," Storm said with a twinkle in her eyes. "I fear I've upset the calm tenor of your days. You must have few guests."

"We see few welcome guests in these troubled times," the old lord agreed gravely, offering her an empty goblet and silently beckoning a servant over. "But my house is honored by your presence. I heard you sing once in a tavern in Selgaunt, when you danced on a table for a room of weary soldiers. I'll not forget that."

Storm inclined her head in thanks. The servant, bearing a silver platter of decanters, glided to a stop between them.

"Pray take wine, Lady Storm," the old lord said earnestly, leaning forward in his chair. "I dearly hope you can stay for evenfeast, or even grace us for a few days. My house is yours."

"I would be delighted to dine with you tonight, my lord," Storm replied, watching her host trying to keep his eyes away from where her plunging gown was designed to make him look, "and see the morning sun rise with you. But as for longer, I cannot say."

"I quite understand," Lord Thael rumbled. He questioningly indicated the array of decanters.

"The glowfire, I think," Storm said, and enjoyed watching the gnarled old hands unstop and deftly pour.

He placed the goblet gently before her. "You are my fourth guest this even! There seems to be much strife on the roads in Battledale just now; we seldom see so many travelers this far off the road. You'll meet them at evenfeast."

"We?" Storm asked, raising her glass in salute. "You have a family, Lord Thael?"

"Only a nephew, Oburglan," Lord Thael said gruffly. "You'll meet him, too."

Guessing that the lord's nephew was no family prize, Storm savored the delicate bouquet of the glowfire for a moment, exchanged smiles with her host over the rim of the glass, and sipped. Yes. She kept her face pleasant and drank the wine with apparent relish, trying to ignore the burning sting of the poison as it slid down her throat. . . .

She'd chosen the drink herself. Thael had poured it, a servant had brought it . . . ah, gods above, the Malaugrym could be anyone!

As dusk came, Storm was still grimly trying to decide which of the folk of the manor was the shapeshifter. The servants came to call them in to evenfeast in the candlelit great hall of Low Rythryn Towers.

The waiting had been pleasant. Lord Thael, obviously enchanted with her, had treated Storm with all the courtesy he knew, discussed politics with a keen worldly interest, laughed appreciatively at her mimicry of dale lords, and gave a shrewd summation of the directionless self-interest that governed Sembia.

Now he escorted her to the best seat at the board, at his right hand. A lady of rank, Storm bowed as an equal to him, and endured a daggerlike glare from a thin and sour young man. Probably Oburglan, furious at being displaced at table in front of guests.

"Well met, gracious lady," said Thael's expressionless seneschal, Burldon Hawklan. "Even in this isolated hall, we have heard of the valiant deeds of the Bard of Shadowdale, and Those Who Harp at her command."

Storm smiled back at him. "Minstrels tend to overflower what they sing of," she responded gently, "but I thank you for your kind words." Hawklan bowed stiffly and took his place at the far end of the table; to Storm's eyes, he was every inch a professional soldier—one who did not consider himself retired.

The other guests were less impressive. One was a

smooth-faced, saturnine trader in spices and pelts from Ordulin by the name of Loth Shentle; the second was a young and handsome priest of Tymora from Selgaunt, Dathtor Vaeldeir, who professed to be very excited at the chaos now reigning over the Realms; and the last was a grim and dangerous-looking man, Thorlor Drynn, introduced to her as a trade envoy of Hillsfar.

The dinner was excellent, consisting of roasts of just about everything that could be roasted, smothered in a variety of gravies and sauces, with spiced greens served as garnishes. And wine, of course . . . much wine.

There was poison in her goblet again. Storm took a certain dark amusement in the fact that she could go on drinking it all night without ill effects because of what Mystra had made her into. She let her eyes wander up and down the table, wondering which of the eyes meeting hers belonged to a shapeshifter—and how soon it would be ere the Malaugrym grew restive and attacked.

The conversation began with talk of trade difficulties in these lawless times, and came around to unreliable magic and priests rendered helpless or mad and the Fall of the Gods. At that point Thael declared he'd heard enough about gods and their doings, and diverted talk to the future of trade in the Moonsea lands and the Dales, and the difficulties Zhentil Keep's aggressive nature was causing to all traders.

The grim envoy of Hillsfar spoke up. "For my part, my lord, we in Hillsfar are resolved to meet force with force. For too long the Zhents have taken advantage of the absence of strong nearby opposition to force their will on other folk and territories not their own—in fact, to behave little better than the brigands we universally detest.

"I do not speak of the times they raise armies and march on one of us—which, by the way, seems to happen at least once a spring, ruining harvests—but of their open attempts to control how and where ore is brought out of Glister, and anything at all out of

Daggerdale. They try to dictate where and when ships may sail the Moonsea, on what terms we must all trade in the region . . . and even if we may trade at all with their rivals Cormyr and Mulmaster."

"Bullies will always be with us, sir—if not one, then another," Loth Shentle said smoothly. "The trick is to anticipate their moves and take trade advantage of the side effects; a shortage of food here, rising prices of scarce items there . . ."

"As a fur dealer, you profit well out of Zhentil Keep's aggression, aye," Thorlor Drynn said coldly. "It has kept the prices of furs falsely high these ten years or more."

"I deal with the world as it is," Loth Shentle replied easily, "not as others might wish it to be."

"Yes, yes," the priest of Tymora said excitedly. "Deal with what the gods hurl your way, taking chances whenever you strive for something that is not the most obvious or easy!"

"But surely, my lords," Storm said quietly, "one should *not* accept the world as it is. Deal with it, yes— but strive always in one's dealings to get something in return, to make the world give a little . . . to nudge it in the direction of one's dreams."

Loth Shentle snorted. "I dream of vaults full of coins, Lady Storm," he said wryly. "Have you any that you can yield unto me?"

"Dreams are just that: dreams. Warriors must deal with the real world, with all its harsh brutalities and cold truths," the seneschal said.

Storm turned to look down the table. "I do not see the gulf between dream and reality, Sir Hawklan. We must fight Zhents because they actively pursue their dreams. In Shadowdale, we have fought them army to army, not merely poison in flagons"—she looked up and down the table, but saw no telling expression in the faces turned to her—"and daggers in the dark. Seven open battles these past ten summers. We should all pay very great attention to dreams."

Thorlor leaned forward. "Well said, Lady. I'd say the lords of Zhentil Keep have done quite well in their dreaming. Voonlar is already their vassal town, the Citadel of the Raven, which was to belong to us all, is firmly in their grasp, and Teshwave and Yûlash lie in ruins because of them . . . to say nothing of the harm done to the once-proud cities of the Moonsea North, Daggerdale, the Border Forest, and west along the trade route to far Waterdeep."

"Aye," their host said gruffly, setting down his heavy flagon. "*There's* a dream: the trade route from here across half Faerûn to the Sword Coast. An awesome undertaking, however base the motives and bloody the doing. What say you, Nephew? You once told me you wanted to see Waterdeep."

"I wonder at what tolls I'll have to pay," Oburglan said sullenly, "if I wait for the Black Gauntlet to finish this trade route. I heard there was a Zhent takeover in Loudwater—and some dealings in Saerloon, too . . . something about a lady sorceress." He looked across the table. "What do you know of this, Lady Storm—as a sorceress yourself?"

Thael turned a look of reproof on his nephew, brows bristling, but Storm smiled across the table at the resentful young man. "I'm hardly a sorceress, Oburglan, though I can cast a spell or two. I leave that to my more capable sisters. As to what befell in Saerloon, the sorceress who seduced those merchants and turned them to stone statues was an agent of Zhentil Keep. Over the years I've never found such tactics to have lasting success."

Someone chuckled, well down the table, and Oburglan's eyes were murderous as he raised his flagon to cover his mouth.

"Stone statues do furnish a garden, though—as Burgusk of Selgaunt found," Loth Shentle joked.

"Not this garden," Lord Thael rumbled. "I'd be too afraid of the spell wearing off and discovering I've got some mad Netherese sorceress at the far end of my pond—and more: that she's furious and happens to have a spell or two that can level mountains! What would I say to her, eh?"

"Care to dance, my lady?" Dathtor suggested. There were roars of mirth.

"How about: my name is . . . and my ransom is forty thousand pieces of gold?" Loth Shentle suggested.

"No, rather: my name is . . . and my next of kin are . . ." Thorlor put in.

Lord Thael looked at the only woman at his table, and his chuckles died away. "I forget that you *have* freed folk from stone, Lady Storm. What did you say to them?"

Storm looked into her glass, and answered, "I usually told them where they were, that I meant no harm, and what year it was. They always wanted to visit the privy after that."

That innocent and truthful observation brought a general shout of laughter.

When it started to die Storm added, a twinkle in her eyes, "But if I met the Netherese lady you mention, I'd probably say: I've had mornings like you're having!"

Everyone hooted, even Oburglan. Storm mused briefly to herself about the effects of too much wine on folk—it made them laugh, or cry, or rage all too easily. She plunged the table into awed silence by adding, "The only memorable Netherese mage I did meet was a man, and his body had withered away to almost nothing . . . so he tried to take mine."

"Gods," Hawklan mumbled after a very long moment had passed. "How did you escape?"

Storm shook her head. "I'm sorry," she said gently, "but that's a trade secret I keep as close about as any merchant guards his own. Ask Mystra to tell you—it is hers to reveal."

Oburglan sputtered. "That's right!" he protested. "Say something like that, then turn all mysterious!"

"Oburglan!" Thael rapped out. "You speak to a great

lady; do so civilly, or leave this board."

His nephew's face flamed, and he brought his goblet crashing down. "Right, then—" he began, placing both palms on the table to shove himself upright.

"Oburglan," Storm said softly, catching his angry gaze, "please stay. You are right to be angry . . . 'tis a maddening tactic we old wielders of sorcery use, to tell half a story and then fall silent when you want to know all. I would say more if I could, and I apologize for mentioning the Netherese at all."

Oburglan stared at her for a moment. He fumbled for his goblet. "How old are you, then?" he mumbled, eyes surveying Storm's curves. "I mean . . ." he looked away and scratched at the lip of his goblet in some confusion, "I don't see any wrinkles."

Down the table, someone sighed, someone else loudly stifled laughter, and Lord Thael covered his eyes.

"I apologize for this wild-tongued kin of mine," he rumbled. "Pray, forgiveness, Lady Storm!"

He turned blazing eyes to Oburglan. "Lad, lad, one *never* asks a lady her age, unless perhaps you're her suitor and must needs know what ground you walk upon! And even then, 'tis best to ask her brother, or father, or *any*one else!"

"Your advice is good, Lord, and should be followed by all men of breeding," Storm agreed cheerfully, "and yet there are exceptions to every rule . . . and I am one of them."

She caught Oburglan's eyes again, and gave him the easy grin of a sister. "Never trust a minstrel or bard who speaks of times and ages, for they're always stretching a year here and a year there, speaking of long-ago battles or fair ladies as if they'd witnessed them themselves. But this once, and before all this table, I'll tell you truth: I am half a dozen years shy of my six hundredth summer."

Oburglan gulped, stared at her, started to sneer . . . then gaped. "You're serious," he whispered.

Storm nodded. With one slim hand she indicated the shoulder that her gown left bare. "Not bad, eh?" she said in perfect mimicry of Lord Thael's gruff tones.

The table erupted again, and this time Oburglan joined in the general mirth. Lord Thael was practically weeping with laughter, his head nodding almost into his platter.

At the other end of the table, Hawklan saluted her with his goblet and said, "Remind me never to say anything before you, Lady, that I would not want to hear parodied!"

"A good rule for every man, Sir Hawklan, when dealing with any man or maid," she returned, raising her own glass. Did his eyes rest on it just a trifle too long?

Ah—no. They were fixed a little lower down. This gown hadn't been such a bright idea after all. But then, sophistication has its price. Moreover, if all of us change what we are and what we do because of the threat of Malaugrym attack, shapeshifters have won the victory without ever having to fight the battle!

"In that time, I have seen Hillsfar governed in many ways," Storm said, turning to the envoy as the laughter started to die. "I'd be interested to hear what you can tell us of Lord Maalthiir's publicly stated aims and intentions."

Thorlor Drynn inclined his head. "I thank you for your diplomacy and understanding, Lady Storm, in the wording you just employed. In reply, I can say only: very little. Lord Maalthiir has often promised to make Hillsfar great and to cleanse it of all hardship, suffering, and corruption. Laudable goals that none, I daresay, could seriously contest. By his actions, I think you can safely add to those general aims his intent not to let Zhentil Keep have possession of Yûlash, nor to suffer Mulmaster or Zhentil Keep to have control of the river Lis, or Moonsea shipping in general. For what it is worth—my words as a mouthpiece of Hillsfar being, of course, suspect by definition—I see no great preparations for armies to march, nor intentions on my lord's part to seize any other city or territory of Faerûn."

"I'm relieved to hear it," Loth Shentle said dryly, "as should be all neighbors of Hillsfar. Two cities of rampaging warlords are more than enough hereabouts."

"You speak overcautiously, Sir!" the priest of Tymora told him, refilling his own goblet for perhaps the fortieth time, his face flushed with its effects. "Strife brings change, and change is the natural order of things. It makes men and maids able, and quick, and alert! Bold, and—"

"Forced to rely on Lady Luck," the seneschal put in from the end of the table. "I've heard the litany a time or two before you were born, good Dathtor!"

The priest turned his red face around slowly to fix Hawklan with a bright-eyed gaze. "Then you should know e'en better than I that 'tis true!"

"I know no such thing," Hawklan said firmly. "I am a simple soldier; I swing my sword, obey orders to the letter, and let others worry about causes and outcomes and grand strategies."

"And on your off days, you drink too much and wench too much—beg pardon, Lady—and let life carry you on, on to the grave without disruption or excitement," Loth Shentle said.

"A summation that sounds familiar, Nephew?" Lord Thael said meaningfully. Oburglan flushed.

"No, Uncle! I mean—" his eyes darted to Storm, then back to Thael with an almost pleading look.

"Don't embarrass me in front of the lady, Uncle?" Storm asked the youth. "Is that what you want to say, but dare not find the words?"

Oburglan stared at her, opened his mouth, and shut it again, turning ruby to the tips of his ears.

"Oburglan," Storm said, setting down her goblet to lean forward, "*never* be embarrassed to admit truth, or think and talk about life, in front of anyone. I'd be more embarrassed to lie about my life or refuse to admit that

things are as they are. *I'm* not upset to learn that you're
drifting the days away here—it's not my life wasting
away. If you're upset talking about it, that shows you're
not satisfied in doing so, and *that's* gods-be-damned
good."

Heads turned along the table at her language, but
Storm kept her eyes locked on Oburglan's. "What you'd
best do, when we're all gone, is take a walk in that
beautiful garden out there with your uncle, and talk
about what you want to do in life. Not to do what he
says, but to decide for yourself. We all have to, sooner or
later. If it makes you feel better to hear it, I'd passed
away almost seventy years before I stopped my wild,
witless pursuit of fun and started wondering what I
wanted to do for myself."

Oburglan gulped. "Seventy years?" he said faintly. "I
didn't know there *was* that much fun."

The table roared with laughter once more. When
Lord Thael could speak again, he slapped Oburglan's
arm. "Well said!" He turned to Storm and added quietly,
"And *very* well said, Lady. I don't think I've a tongue
nimble enough to thank you rightly for saying those
words. I've never heard it said better, in all my . . . er,
sixty-eight years."

Storm smiled at him. "Shall I come back in two years
to ask you what you've decided to do with your life?"

There were uneasy chuckles around the table, and
Thael shook his head with a rueful smile. "I'd forgotten
that the tongue can be sharper than a sword."

"I think you have the quotation wrong, Lord," the
priest offered jestingly, but Storm turned on him with a
smile.

"What, Hand of Tymora? You stand in service to a
goddess and don't know for yourself the truth of that
maxim? Truly, you must be a very good priest! All the
clergy I know would much rather face the swords of
foes than the lashing tongues of their superiors!"

Dathtor Vaeldeir winced. "I begin to see the truth of

another maxim, Lords and Lady: 'If thou art captured, do and say anything to keep yourself from the hands of your foe's womenfolk.' "

Deep laughter rolled out around the table, and more than one eyebrow in the room rose to see Storm laughing as heartily as the others.

She raised her glass of newly filled, still-poisoned wine, her heart light, and bid the night continue long.

When the table did rise, her wish had been fulfilled; they'd talked away most of the time until dawn, and the first shift of servants had been replaced at table by a second. Most of the men were stumbling with drunken weariness as they sought out the jakes; Dathtor the priest was roaring drunk, and Oburglan had been emboldened enough by his imbibing to ask her how one best chose a wife. Storm was still smiling and shaking her head over that as she went to the women's garderobe—which, of course, she had all to herself.

No one attacked her there. Afterward, she went for a walk in the gardens in the last faint moonlight, avoiding the torchlit areas. Someone at that friendly table was a shapeshifter . . . and a Malaugrym dare not leave her alive, when she could call down the Simbul upon him or point him out to half a hundred wizards. The poison raging through her veins was proof enough of that.

No, an attack would come. She kept to the shadows as Loth Shentle strolled past, a little unsteadily, singing an old familiar ballad about ladies fair and fey. He startled her a few steps farther on when he paused on one of the bridges, announced, "*Gods,* but she's beautiful!" and proceeded to vomit his evenfeast helplessly into the pond.

Someone else was walking among the far fern beds, impossible to identify in the gloom. Storm sat down on a bench in the lee of a spiky bush, only then discerning the seneschal, Burldon Hawklan, who strode softly past, hand on sword, eyes sober and alert, taking care to make little sound.

Storm rose thoughtfully and watched him vanish into the night. In one hand, she hid the small thing she'd taken out in the garderobe.

"Out takin'—tak*eeng*—air, pretty lady?" said a loud voice by her elbow. The drunken priest of Tymora tried to lean against the tree, missed, and went for a short stagger before finding his balance again. Storm brought her hand to her mouth to cover her smile as he grinned loosely at her, sketched a shaky salute, and said, "Doan—doant—don't you worship the Lady Tymora, e'en as I do? C'mere!"

He was upon her, and the smell of wine was strong, and triumph blazed up in his eyes as he embraced her. His arms tightened . . . and seemed to be changing shape.

This was it. Their lips brushed together, and Storm worked her small magic in careful haste.

An instant later cruel claws raked her back, tearing away her gown and the flesh beneath in ribbons. Storm gasped and stiffened at the raw pain—but instead of trying to pull away from the Malaugrym, she leaned into his embrace, deepening their kiss. His savaging of her back slowed in astonishment, but Storm clung to him with all her own great strength, holding him firmly as her tongue thrust her saliva into his mouth. With it went the powdered silver from the coin she'd dissolved with her spell.

The shapeshifter spasmed in sudden agony, fear, and desperation. The silver was as poisonous to him as the liquid he'd been feeding Storm all night. Had she not been one of Mystra's Chosen, she'd have died hours ago, after the first sip Lord Thael offered her. She kept that in mind as she drew her mouth away from his and watched him closely. The creature who was not Dathtor Vaeldeir shuddered in her arms, convulsed, and died.

When she was sure he was dead, Storm swung his body over one shoulder, letting the claws that still dripped her blood dangle, and carried it grimly toward Lord Thael's kitchen wing, where there should be firewood enough to burn it.

She was most of the way there, crossing the great flagstone terrace, when many doors opened in the manor walls and a score of servants rushed out with lit torches, enclosing her in a wide ring.

Lord Thael stepped out last and faced her, sword in his hand. "What have you done, witch?" he bellowed, monocle dangling. He peered at her, and asked, "Or . . . is that you, Lunquar?"

Storm met his eyes coldly. "You know what I've done, Malaugrym. And what I must do." She lifted one side of her mouth in a mirthless smile, and asked, "Just to save time, tell me—how many more are there of you in this house?"

"I need no aid to deal with the likes of you, mortal woman," was the cold response. "With your precious Elminster dead, there's no one to watch us . . . and no one to stop us!" His teeth glinted in the torchlight as they lengthened into fangs, and he added with soft smile, "Faerûn will be ours!"

One of the servants screamed. Lord Thael was turning slowly into a thing with a tail and hunched shoulders of corded muscle. He came forward in a slow, careful crouch, eyes gleaming.

Storm let the body fall from her shoulder, kicked off her high sandals, and walked barefoot to meet him in the bloody tatters of her gown.

When she was only two paces away, the Malaugrym sprang and brought his blade around in a vicious arc. Storm strode right at him. His blade whistled through her as if she were smoke, and she grappled with him.

The Malaugrym ducked away and hacked at her again, saw that the blade really could not touch her, and flung it away with a snarl. It was still clanging across the flagstones amid sparks when he flung himself on her.

They strained together in the torchlight, two sets of rippling muscles gleaming. The shapeshifter seized her shoulder and wrist and pulled, roaring triumphantly.

He'd intended to tear her limb from limb, slapping her awake and making her scream for mercy—but he strained and pulled with all his might . . . and she resisted him easily, smiling all the while, and whispered the words of an enchantment.

The Malaugrym grunted in amazement at her strength, then felt his mouth and tongue moving of their own accord—no, *her* will!—to utter the single word "Ahorga."

Her magic had forced him to name himself! Enraged, Ahorga grew his neck to eel-like length and his fangs into snapping jaws, and he bit savagely at the smiling face of his foe. She turned her head away and forced his own arm up into the way of his jaws—such strength! He darted his head down and sank his fangs deep into her left shoulder and breast.

Now the screaming would start, and she'd plead for mercy . . . but no. This Storm woman hissed in pain but did not shriek or collapse. He bit deeply again, and twisted his head to tear a great gobbet of flesh free. Her blood fountained over them both, running freely to the flagstones, and he raised his head to roar exultantly at the high, glittering stars.

Then he felt pain such as he'd never felt before, greater than the fire spells that had scarred him in his youth. He writhed helplessly in his torment. Silver flames licked along her spilled blood, fire the same hue as her silvery hair, blazing up into a pillar now—and he was burning with it!

It was in pain and despair that Ahorga of the Malaugrym roared, struggling to break free of her grip, and failing. He stared once into her face, and saw that her eyes were two silver flames, too.

"Nooo!" he screamed. "Mercy!"

"I shall give you, Ahorga, the same mercy you gave to

Lord Thael Sembergelt," was the calm response. "The same mercy Malaugrym always afford mere mortals . . . none. This is a cleaner death than you deserve." The silver flames roared up to claim him.

When the body was a burnt husk, Storm cast it down atop the body of the Malaugrym Lunquar, and watched them both blaze. The flagstones beneath them cracked and shivered with the heat, and more than one of the servants fainted away, torches toppling to the terrace to gutter out. Storm stood motionless above the pyre until ashes were all that remained of the two shapeshifters.

She looked up, half-naked, front and back in bleeding ruin. Oburglan and the seneschal, Hawklan, gazed white-faced at her, swords in their hands.

"Lady," Hawklan asked, "what are you?"

"One of Mystra's Chosen," Storm answered him wearily. "These were two fell shapeshifters; the real Thael Sembergelt and Dathtor Vaeldeir are dead."

The seneschal licked his lips and asked, "Was that, then, Mystra's silver fire?"

Storm smiled wanly. "It was . . . pray that you never see its like again."

"Lady," Oburglan asked, his voice husky with fear, "are you . . . will you be all right?"

"I will be fine soon enough, Lord Sembergelt," Storm said to him. "I grieve for your uncle. I would have liked to come to know him well."

Tears spilled from both their eyes, then, but Oburglan's trembling lips shaped the wondering words, "Lord Sembergelt? You called me . . ."

One bloody hand came up to trace his chin. He did not raise his blade or flinch away. "You are Lord Sembergelt now," Storm said to him, "and if ever you need comfort or guidance or the aid of Those Who Harp, come to me—or tell any Harper." A trace of a smile came to her lips. "We even help spoiled Sembian lords." She stepped forward and kissed him.

His face was covered with her blood as she drew

back, but his eyes shone with a new light through the tears.

"Lady," the seneschal said haltingly, stepping forward, "if there is anything we can do . . . any aid we can render . . . " His eyes fell to her wounds, then rose again to her face.

Storm shook her head. "My thanks for your offer, noble Hawklan, but no. I'll be fine. I'll be even better if I know your new lord enjoys the same loving guidance you gave his uncle."

"Lady," Hawklan said quietly, "it shall be so. If you'll permit me?"

And he took her hand, went to his knee, and kissed her bloody fingertips.

Storm smiled at him. "As I bid Oburglan, so also I ask you: Call on me if there is need."

She stepped back from them, looked around at Low Rythryn Towers and the ragged circle of torches, and shook her head.

"One good thing has come of this, at least," she told the two weeping men. "Lord Thael lies where he would have wished: buried in his garden." She smiled at them again, then turned away. It was a long walk back to Shadowdale—and she'd need all that time to heal herself.

15
Travel Far, See Much— and Try To Survive

In a place of shifting shadows, behind hidden doors, in the heart of the ancient castle of the Malaugrym, was a light. The bright, glowing eye of a scrying portal floated in the murk, reflected from the tentacled face of a watchful figure bent over it . . . a figure whose skin was as dark and ever-shifting as the sliding shadows themselves.

His eyes, however, were two bright flames, and the doomstars winked brightly as they spun endlessly about his wrist. He stretched, watched them dim momentarily as they passed through a dark drift of shadow, sighed, and murmured, "Fools . . . this house is breeding fools by the score. Lunquar and Ahorga both gone—and they deserved it."

He turned again to the light, watching the wounded Storm walk through a merchant camp and wave away someone who rose to offer aid. Studying her kind, weary smile, he sighed again and passed his hand across the portal.

It rippled, then lit with tongues of leaping fire: a bonfire, this time. Steel flashed back its light as three figures in leather armor battled with twice as many men in black. They fought in a clearing—the camp of the black-armored ones—and the three in leather were winning. As he watched, a black-armored figure took a blade in the face and fell back into the fire, throwing out a shower of sparks. Small wonder; if those three could fight their way alive out of the Castle of Shadows and leave more than a score of the blood of Malaug dead behind them, a few Zhentilar armsmen should prove no trouble for them at all.

Wearing a smile that did not mean he was amused, the figure let his scrying portal fade away, stood up, and melted into the shadows. It was time to do what had to be done.

* * * * *

Faerûn, northwest Elven Court woods, Flamerule 26

"How many?"

"Seven Zhentilar and one orc," Belkram said, counting on his fingers. "Oh, and that snake."

"Oh, yes—mustn't forget the snake!" Syluné said merrily. She turned to grin at Sharantyr. They rolled their eyes in unison.

"I," Itharr said triumphantly, "stand ahead of you. My valiant blade has accounted for eleven Zhent deserters, one brigand, and three fingers off the left hand of another brigand!"

"Men will be boys," Sharantyr murmured. A ghostly giggle answered her from just ahead of her left cheek. She winced; Syluné had become invisible again.

They were tired, filthy, footsore—gods, how did anyone stay in armor more than a day? The *itching*, to say nothing of the small things crawling in their matted hair. They hadn't expected the last four Zhents, and had wasted a day chasing them—a day more than their rations. Empty bellies were groaning now, too.

All in all, it had been a successful patrol.

They trudged thankfully past the familiar beauty of

Harpers' Hill. Passing it meant warm baths and familiar beds were only paces away.

"Daylight!" Itharr broke into a trot.

Sharantyr gritted her teeth and managed a sprint, her raw joints and blistered feet shrieking in protest. Catching up to Itharr a bare three paces from Treesedge, she snarled, "Walk across someone's crops, and they'll kill you! We go *that* way until we strike the road!"

She pointed, and Itharr gave her a dirty look. He sighed and began to trudge in the indicated direction. "You never spared two breaths about turnips before!"

"I was never hungry enough to eat raw turnips before!" Sharantyr snarled back at him.

Behind them, Belkram chuckled wearily and waved a hand. "Lead on, the pair of you . . . and talk to me of roast goose, and gravy and old ale . . . ham and dressed pheasant and stuffed snake—not gods-be-kissed *turnips!*"

"Ye gods!" Itharr cried, slapping his forehead. "The snake! You forgot to bring the snake!" He turned reproachful eyes on Belkram. "We could've eaten that snake!"

"No," Belkram corrected, "*You* could've eaten that snake. I saw all the human skulls in its lair."

"Death, death, death," Sharantyr muttered. "Is that all adventurers talk about?"

Belkram gave her a look. "Well, let's see—there are other topics: butchering monsters for the stew pot, burning helpless villages, pillage, ra—"

"Death it is," Sharantyr said firmly. "Only a few hundred more paces now. Talk to me of death."

"Only a few hundred more paces?" Itharr gasped. "Good! Go and make them for me, so I can fall asleep right . . . here. . . ."

"*Oh* no, you don't," Sharantyr said, pulling hard on his hair as he sagged. "Come on—I'm sure that tree wants to grow to reach the light, and it can't if you're draped all over it, snoring like a flatulent bull! *Move!*"

"Yes, *sir!*" Itharr responded sarcastically, moving smartly forward for all of three paces before sinking into a weary walk once more.

"Gods above preserve me," Sharantyr said through clenched teeth. "Men!"

"Oh, dear," Belkram said to Itharr. "She's noticed! I guess that means we have to go way off into the bushes, now, whenever we have to . . ."

"What she hasn't noticed," Itharr retorted, stumbling in the weariness of utter exhaustion, "is that the gods *aren't* above anymore—that's what this whole trouble's about . . . as Elminster said."

"Good old Elminster," Belkram said sadly, putting one foot in front of the other and almost falling out into the road.

"Well, granted I look bad this morning," growled the wispy-bearded guard who caught hold of his shoulder to steady him, "but I'm sure I don't look *that* bad. No, Elminster's dead, friend . . . and so will ye be if ye don't convince me of thy rightful loyalty—and fast."

He gulped as the ghostly head of the Witch of Shadowdale came floating out of the trees to hang in front of him. "Well met, Guthtar," she said softly. "You remember me, do you not?"

"A-Aye, Lady," the guard stammered as Itharr and Sharantyr came out of the trees. "And her, too!" The six guards behind him fell back to get weapon room, eyeing all these sudden arrivals warily.

"Aye," Syluné said dryly. "I've noticed you never forget a fair-looking female. You are going to let Lord Mourngrym's patrol pass, aren't you?"

"Of course, Lady! Uh, begging thy pardons, sirs and Lady—uh, Lady and Lady . . . ah—oh, *dung!*"

"And a pleasant good morning to you, too, Guthtar," Syluné said with a smile, floating serenely past the sputtering guard. Belkram met Guthtar's eyes, spread his hands in silent commiseration, and followed. Itharr and Sharantyr trudged along in Belkram's wake, leaning on each other.

"Oh, gods," the lady ranger yawned. At a weary stagger, she neared the crossroads. "We must never let ourselves get this tired again!"

"I *tried* to tell those last four Zhents that," Belkram told her, "I really did! But they just kept on snarling and waving swords at us, and, well. . . ."

"Back from patrol, I see," Hammerhand Bucko called cheerfully from his doorway. They waved at him—the gesture almost made Itharr fall over—and went on, not daring to stop now for fear of collapse.

"Lhaeo? Lhaeo!" Syluné called, her head dancing up and down in the air to snare the scribe's attention. "Lhaeo!"

Elminster's scribe was a morose figure, trudging along every bit as wearily as they were walking. He looked up at Syluné's call, brightening visibly. "Well met, friends!"

"Itharr, give my stone to Lhaeo, will you?" Syluné floated close to the scribe's head and asked him, "Could you take me to Storm, please, good scribe? We have much to talk about."

Lhaeo blinked at her as Itharr handed him the stone. "Of course, Lady—'tis where I'm headed." He turned his head to look at the unshaven ranger, and said, "You folks look tired."

"No, really? And I spent all morning doing my hair!" Itharr told him with weary sarcasm. He set off grimly toward the tower.

"Fare you well, Lhaeo," Sharantyr added.

The scribe smiled wanly and waved. The three rangers nodded wearily to him and walked the last stretch of road to the Twisted Tower.

"Ohh, I'm so *tired!*" Sharantyr wailed. "And my feet hurt *so much!*"

"At least you've still got feet," Belkram said darkly. "Mine wore off about ten hours back."

"Try scratching all your itches," Itharr said without turning. "It helps to keep you awake."

"Could we *ride* on patrol next time?" Shar asked as they turned up the tower path.

"Through all those trees? We'd be wanting some eel-horses, I'd guess," said Belkram.

"Just a few more steps, friends," Itharr mumbled. "Just a few more steps . . ."

Then he noticed the row of gleaming breastplates and crossed forearms blocking their way. His eyes traveled up to the hard faces above them, but he recognized no one. Seven guards he'd never seen before were ranged across the open doorway of the Tower of Ashaba. They wore splendid chased armor and light helms in the hot summer sun, and their hairy forearms and corded thighs glistened with sweat. They were not moving aside.

"Stand aside, friends," Itharr said wearily, "before we fall over."

"And who are you three?" the centermost guard asked coolly. "Travelers generally stay at the Old Skull Inn—at the crossroads, down there. Beggars had best go to the temples . . . there's a house of Tymora just across the river, there."

As he'd spoken, Belkram and Sharantyr had straggled up to face the guards. Shar sighed and let her head sink into her hands. No. No, not now. Her knees sagged, and Belkram put his arms around her to hold her up, swaying himself.

"We have chambers awaiting us in the tower behind you," Itharr said quietly, taking two steps to the right so he could lean on the nearest hitching post.

"Oh? How so? Are you, then, lords and ladies of Shadowdale?"

"She is," Itharr said, waving a hand. "The Lady Sharantyr."

"Sharantyr? It's not a name known to me," the guard-captain said jovially. "Any of you heard of a Sharantyr, lads? Eh?"

There was a general chorus of chuckled nays. Itharr regarded them with dull eyes. "You're all new hires, aren't you?"

"Thurbal engaged us some days ago," the guardcaptain said a trifle stiffly. "We hail from Westgate."

"Belgard's boys?" Belgard was a retired mercenary whose school turned out guards known for their efficient cruelty and alertness; his graduates had gained swift popularity among the merchants of Sembia, and generally cost a client food, accommodation, armor, and over five silver pieces a day.

"Yes," the guardcaptain said shortly, "and we've been hired to keep brigands and Zhentilar out of this tower, see? So clear off, all of you—now!"

The three bedraggled figures in leather made no move. A light, rhythmic sound came from the female among them—the sound of snoring.

One of the guards snorted in amusement, and stepped forward. He bore a long baton in his hand, and used it to rap Sharantyr none too gently on the shoulder. "Hey! Wake up and clear off! You've heard the order. Now go!"

"Stand back, friend," Belkram suggested gently, "or I'll awaken enough to grow annoyed."

The guard cocked his head to one side, hands on hips. "Oh you will, will you?" he said sarcastically. "I quaver at the prospect!"

"Are you lot going to stand aside?" Itharr said. "We'd very much like to report in to Mourngrym."

"Lord Mourngrym's out riding the northern reaches," the guardcaptain told him silkily, "as all in Shadowdale know. I don't think you're anything more than brigands looking for a chance to slip inside. If you don't move on, it's brigands' chains you'll be feeling."

"In one of the cells where we can lie down?" Sharantyr asked sleepily.

"No," the guardcaptain said with a cruel grin, "our orders are to hang brigands from the dangle-bars."

"We're not brigands," Belkram said sourly, dragging Sharantyr to the hitching post on the other side of the path and draping her over it, "and you'd do well to let us into the tower!"

"We're not hired to do well," the guardcaptain said. "We're hired to follow orders. You're not getting past, and you've spent enough of our time. We're supposed to watch who passes on the road, not waste words with ruffians on our doorstep. So get you gone, now, or there'll be trouble."

"There will indeed," Itharr said, from his post.

The guardcaptain looked at him coldly, then turned his head back to catch the eyes of the guard with the baton, who stood menacingly close to Belkram, and said pleasantly, "Aldus, pray dispose of these petty annoyances."

"Gladly, Captain," Aldus replied, raising his baton and reaching forward to take Belkram by the throat.

"Have a care, Aldus," Belkram said softly to him, "that's my Harper pin you're hauling on."

"So?"

"A Harper pin should mean something to you, Aldus."

"Oh, aye." The guard stepped back and turned to the guardcaptain. "This one's stolen a Harper pin, Captain!"

"Hit him and take it, then!"

"Gladly, Captain!" Aldus spun around and brought his baton around in a wicked arc. Belkram stumbled back with inches to spare, and the guard rushed forward, pulling his baton back for another blow.

It never landed. As he charged forward, a slim hand rose from the post, caught hold of his arm, and pulled. Aldus's head rammed the post with all the strength of his charge, and Sharantyr stepped back, turned to survey the line of guards witheringly, and asked, "Who's next, dolts?"

There came a roar of anger, and five men started forward. "Hold hard!" their captain roared out, but none of them paid him heed.

Two reached the Lady of Shadowdale first, batons out—and she dropped to the path and flung herself at their boots. They went over her with a crash.

The third man in snarled a curse and kicked at her; Shar grabbed the boot flashing past her and hauled sharply upward. With a ground-shaking crash, the man fell on his rear. Then the batons of the fourth and fifth were raining down on her—for a few instants, before Belkram hit them from one side and Itharr from the other, and two helmed heads rang together.

Itharr fell on his knees atop the groaning third guard. The man emitted a sort of strangled whistle and thrashed around, struggling for breath enough to shout out his pain. Itharr rolled away, letting the senseless fourth and fifth guards fall on him.

The guardcaptain started forward hesitantly, seeing only two of his men left. They were rising with murder on their faces and swords in their hands.

Shar got to her own feet in time to face them, her hands empty—but by then Belkram had smashed aside the captain's hastily drawn blade and run the man up against the lintel, hands on his throat.

"Call your men off attacking the Lady of Shadowdale," the Harper snarled at him as they strained eyeball to eyeball, "or so help me I'll tear your throat out!" Iron fingers dug deep into the man's flesh to back up those words, then loosened enough to let the man whimper.

"Aid!" he called out in a raw voice. "An attack!"

Disgusted, Belkram bounced the man's head forcefully off the stones. The captain's eyes rolled up for a brief instant before he slid to the ground, but the Harper was already snatching the captain's blade out of his hands and whirling around.

The retreating Shar had fallen back over the tangled trio of unconscious guards, and Itharr was crouched over her, trying to ward off two jabbing blades with a pair of batons he'd snatched up.

Belkram snarled an oath and charged around the pile of bodies. He lunged at the two guards, waving his captured blade. They turned to meet him and fell back to force him to come between them. Belkram obliged, swerving at the last instant to bind the blade of one with his own. He grabbed the man by the armpit, swung him around into the path of the other guard's blade, and with his free hand smashed the man across the throat.

Gagging, the man fell. Belkram clubbed the back of his helm and sprang back.

The last guard's blade flashed through the leathers at Belkram's wrist, and the stolen sword spun away from the Harper's numbed fingers. The guard's face widened into an unpleasant grin. He sidled a foot or so, still smiling, as a stool Itharr had snatched up from inside the door struck the side of his head and carried him a pace to the south . . . into the realm of dreams.

The two Harpers looked wearily at each other, went to pick up Shar from the tangle of sprawled bodies, and trudged into the tower.

They'd almost reached the end of the long central passage when Shaerl and Thurbal, captain-of-arms of the Twisted Tower, strode briskly across it. The Lady of Shadowdale was speaking. "Well, I don't think those new men are trained eno—"

"I couldn't agree more," Belkram snarled, cradling Sharantyr's head against his shoulder.

"Aye," Itharr agreed, casting a guard's sword to the tiles at Thurbal's feet. "Next time you hire seven dolts from Belgard, be sure he remembers to send their brains along with them!"

Thurbal gaped at the three of them, but Shaerl turned to her captain-of-arms and snapped, "Get fresh guards for the doors—and send all the servants you can find here, as fast as they can move!"

She guided the three rangers to a bench and rang the nearest gong furiously. To the first servant who appeared, she snapped, "Send everyone here at once! Then fill my lord's bath—the new big one, and mind the water's hot! Get help, but do it fast!"

To the second she snarled, "Three carry-chairs, and men to bear them, back here as fast as you're able!"

Then she turned her head as the kitchen door opened. "Purk? Bring whatever you have roasting—and all the breads and cheeses you can lay hands on, and the best wine you can get—to my lord's chamber at once!"

"Impressive," Belkram murmured to her just before he fell asleep.

"Indeed," Shaerl told him gently. She looked down the hall to the doors, where armsmen were carrying in seven limp armored forms under Thurbal's coldly furious eye.

Itharr woke once on the stairs, swaying in his chair to murmur, "Killed a lot of Zhents for you . . ."

"Eat first," Shaerl told him, guiding the chair across the parlor. "We'll talk later."

"Bathe first," Sharantyr announced firmly.

"Nay, Lady," one of the armsmen said gently as he set her chair down. "For ye, it's sleep first." The lady ranger's head lolled to one side as she began to gently snore; she heard him only in her dreams.

"Get this armor off them," Shaerl told the armsman, unbuckling and tugging at Sharantyr's body for all she was worth.

"Haste or care, Lady?"

"Care for them . . . haste otherwise," she replied briskly, hurling a vambrace across the room. It struck the far wall with a crash that made a serving girl wince—and when the armsmen enthusiastically followed Shaerl's example, the maid covered her ears and fled. The air quickly filled with flying pieces of armor.

Amid the clangor, puffing relays of servants speedily filled the gigantic copper tub. Shaerl herself added the soap and wyverntail oil, then turned back to the armsmen. "Get some rope," she ordered the nearest one. "I don't want them drowning."

"Aye, Lady."

Striding to her wardrobe, Shaerl snatched the doors open and took the first three garments off their pegs without looking. Sliding them under the arms of each ranger—gods, the reek!—and across their chests, she flipped the ends of the three gowns up for the armsmen to tie the ropes to, noticed that one garment was a favorite of hers, shrugged, and began to disrobe.

An armsman hovering uncertainly nearby gulped, looked away, and a sash slapped into him. He caught it reflexively, then looked up to see his Lady's gown coming his way, mastered a calm expression as he fielded it, and stepped forward to take the rest as they were offered.

The Lady Shaerl was stepping unconcernedly into the hot depths of the tub as the other armsmen rushed back in with coils of rope, goggled at her for an instant, and wisely set about their task without comment or delay.

"More soap!" Shaerl ordered briskly as servants scurried, "and that scratcher!"

The wooden back scratcher was handed to her, and she set to work. Lice floated away almost immediately atop the scummy water. "Bethra," she said, without looking up, "Draw Lady Sharantyr's hair out over the edge, put a bowl under it, and start washing! Use my seafoam ointment!"

So it was that when Purk bustled up at the head of a procession bringing platters of hot fowl from the kitchens, he found three rangers, grimy and snoring, slumped over asleep in the huge bath, and the lady of the tower in their midst, as bare as the day she was born, scrubbing and rinsing for all she was worth.

"A feast is served, my lady," he announced with quiet dignity—and was most startled a moment later when Shaerl looked up at him through her dripping hair and snapped, "Well, off with your clothes and get in, Purk!

Wake them up and feed them—the others can pass you the platters as you need them! And have wine ready so that no one chokes—ah, gods, give a bottle here first! This is thirsty work!"

A grinning kitchen-boy uncorked a bottle and handed it to his lady, who winked at him and said, "You're small enough! Pick up a brush, off with those, and get in here!" She took a swig of wine, gasped in satisfaction, looked at one of the armsmen, and snapped, "More hot water!"

Hastening down the stairs to obey, the armsman met one of his fellows hastening the other way with a basin slopping in his hands. The first said, "The lady's passion for bathing is crazed! Have they all washed their wits out of their heads in Cormyr? What's wrong with just going down to the millpond when your stink starts to drive the dogs away?"

The other shrugged. "Overcrowding?" he jested innocently, and went on up the stairs, redoubling his speed as they heard the faint but imperious call:

"Where's that water?"

* * * * *

Tower of Mortoth, Sembia, Flamerule 26

Bralatar and Lorgyn stepped back into the privy chamber of the Tower of Mortoth and exchanged coldly triumphant smiles. "Worked perfectly," Bralatar announced, setting down his chest. It clinked.

Lorgyn raised an eyebrow at the sound. "*I* went back for my wand and some favorite food . . . I thought *you* were getting your best *spells*."

Bralatar raised a decanter into view. "And some *real* wine, to celebrate!"

Lorgyn chuckled and set down his own coffer to study the four spread-eagled, motionless figures hanging in the webwork of cold fire.

"Hmm . . . see? It drains the mage first," he said, indicating the shrunken, nearly skeletal body of Mortoth the Mighty.

"Is that because we put him in it first, do you think, or because he wields the most magic?"

Lorgyn shrugged. "We'll have to gather some more wizards to see . . . and we'll need more, anyway, to keep this open. If these apprentices here don't work properly or hold enough life-force, we could be stranded here after just one more back-and-forth trip."

"Plenty of time to go mage-gathering after we've mastered a little more magic and had some fun," Bralatar said, picking up the chest again and starting toward the door.

He stopped and turned, indicating the female apprentice with a jerk of his head. Irendue stared endlessly and sightlessly at the privy wall, her mouth agape. "Shall we free her for a little dalliance tonight?"

"I don't know if that's such a wise idea," Lorgyn said with a frown. "I thought of that myself—she could show us the magic of this place, for one thing—but then I thought of the chance it would give her to turn some spell we don't know about against us. There're so many enchantments in this place, one overlaid atop another, that I can't see any way to keep clear of them all."

"We still have to find a way out past those things in the moat," Bralatar pointed out, "and the stone golem, and the cat on the lawn, to say nothing of whatever servants he's got in the house, and any magic they can call on! I think we've no choice but to pull this one out of the thrall and question her."

"What's to stop her hurling a dozen spells at us the moment her wits're her own?"

Bralatar frowned. "Strip her to take away any magic she carries, tie her hands together to stop her casting spells, and with the same rope hang her down the privy shaft. Dangle her just above the water, where we can threaten her with the things in the moat. Then each of us stretch a tentacle down there with her; mine with an eye to watch her closely—so she knows we're seeing what she does—and yours to hold your wand trained right on her!"

Lorgyn thought about it, then began to smile slowly. He looked over at the unseeing female apprentice and said, "First, we'll have to find some rope . . ."

* * * * *

Shadowdale, Flamerule 27

"*Shadow*dale . . . a fitting name indeed," Argast said, peering through the leaves of the last tree on the west bank of the river Ashaba. "Where the Great Foe lived," he mused, "and so many of our kin died. We'll conquer this place first."

"And rule it as a slave farm, anon," Amdramnar agreed, looking across the water at the twisted spire of the Tower of Ashaba. "Pretty, this . . . all these trees, and the water. . . ."

Argast looked at him. "That's not what you said when we were in the swamp."

Amdramnar snarled. "If I hadn't shifted fast enough, I'd be dead now. What *was* that?"

" 'Quicksand,' they call it. Didn't you hear the nice man who hauled me out?"

"Not until he screamed when you started to eat him," Amdramnar replied archly. "I was too busy washing the mud off . . . I can feel grit inside me, even now!"

"We only lost a day," Argast said. "Should we cross the river here?"

Amdramnar shook his head, putting an entire day of floundering through the mud-choked swamp west of them out of his mind . . . hopefully forever. "Let's work our way around and come in from the east. That man I talked to most of the night—"

"Before *you* ate *him*," Argast reminded, just as

archly.

"—was from Hillsfar. I can talk as he did, and say the same things about Great Lord Maalthiir and the cursed Zhents and all that. We have to talk our way past guards no matter how we get in."

"Why not just turn to eels and swim down to the millpond? Up onto the bank, take human shape, and—"

"Get challenged by the first guards we meet, or a wench in the tavern, or a shopkeeper," Amdramnar finished the sentence for him. "I *want* to talk to someone, to confirm that Elminster's dead . . . and this Hillsfar place is east of here, so we'd best be coming from the east."

"And doing what?"

"Going to ask Elminster—about some strange shapeshifting beings our master Dundifolus of the Sixteen Unlit Black Candles saw. He'd come himself, but they changed both his feet into fish fins, and he hasn't yet managed to reverse the strange enchantment!"

Argast smirked. "You expect them to believe that?"

"I'll tone it down . . . but we *should* ask for Elminster, and say we've been sent by some mage. How will they know we aren't telling the truth? Their magics can't read the minds of any of the blood of Malaug!"

Argast nodded slowly. "Your plans are sound. Lead on."

And so it was, not long after, that two footsore wizard's servants from Hillsfar trudged into Shadowdale along the Voonlar road—and passed by three leather-armored folk who were quietly taking a woodcutter's trail out of the dale due east into Myth Drannor. The three rangers were refreshed and reprovisioned after a day-long sleep and a bath personally administered by Lady Shaerl of Shadowdale. With heavy packs on their backs, they were setting out on another patrol and wondering when they'd meet with lurking Malaugrym. By the humor of the gods, neither band saw the other.

* * * * *

Tower of Mortoth, Sembia, Flamerule 27

"M-Mercy," Irendue sobbed as they hauled her up through the privy hole she'd sat above so many times before, holding her bound wrists back behind her, over her head, so that she could barely keep her balance. "Mercy!"

Bralatar smiled at her as his tentacles took her by the throat and around both elbows, holding her so tightly she could barely breathe through her aching throat. Her eyes were large and dark in terror as Lorgyn's tentacles untied the ropes that cut into her wrists. He thrust her back, back once more into the cold embrace of the flames that did not burn. . . .

Irendue's body trembled as the spell energy raced through it, and she whimpered once before the surging energy drove away her wits once more. "You see?" Bralatar told her as the light in her eyes slowly died, "you are untouched. This *is* mercy."

He chuckled coldly while Lorgyn arranged the apprentice's limbs apart as they had been earlier. The endless hum of the spell flames grew stable once more.

"The gate is unharmed," he said at last. The two Malaugrym exchanged a smile and went to the study, snaking out tentacles ahead of them to uncork the wine and bring out some roast shadowbeast.

"Profitable, that," Bralatar said, flopping down in an old armchair that until recently had been the exclusive preserve of Mortoth, and raising one of Mortoth's best glasses in salute to Lorgyn. "The wench certainly knows how to talk with a wand nearly down her gullet."

"More to the point, she's seen Faerûn shrewdly, and knows what lies behind what can be readily seen," Lorgyn replied, sipping at his own glass.

"Ah," Bralatar said slyly, "do I hear the tones of a Shadowmaster looking for a mate?"

Lorgyn looked at him levelly. "No," he replied, "you do

not. I merely meant that what she knows makes her too valuable for us to destroy. How else would we have found out all that about the Realms and the wizards in less than a day?"

Bralatar nodded, levity gone. "You speak truth . . . she yielded much to us, and swiftly. Enough for me to conclude we'd best avoid Thay, the islands Lantan and Nimbral, and the slave keepers—Calimshan, that was the name—until we know a lot more about Faerûn. These Red Wizards'll bear a lot of watching. They could be almost as much trouble as Elminster was. The Zhentarim, on the other hand, seem more persistent than competent. Would you say that sums up what she said?"

Lorgyn nodded. "I would . . . and so long as we keep these things in mind, and keep humans from realizing that there are shapeshifters among them, nothing and no one stands between us and our ruling any part of Faerûn that we please. You'll take your preferred lands, and I'll take mine."

"I want to see those lands for myself first," Bralatar replied as they shared a grin. "And what better way than to have some real fun hunting this time, across half Faerûn!"

"Chasing down wizards?"

"Chasing down and slaughtering," Bralatar said with a sudden flame in his eyes, "any humans we fancy."

16
Shadows So Sharp

Only the eyes of the two guards moved to follow him as Lord Mourngrym of Shadowdale strode past the door of the forecourt, heading for the kitchens. He'd come straight in from a patrol in the northern reaches of the dale, and there was fresh blood—Zhent blood—on his mud-spattered armor. He was bareheaded and unshaven, and his reddened, sunken eyes told of little sleep and hard going.

"Belmer!" he called back, turning, as he went on. "Get something hot from the kitchens, and a bottle of zzar, and take it to the Old Skull as quick as you can. A lady guest is giving birth, and the father needs a good meal and a walk with someone who's been a father not long past—so the gods've chosen you!"

"Aye, Lord," Belmer said with a smile, and left his post just inside the front doors to rush down the hall. Guthtar, who'd heard the exchange, was already moving to take his place.

Mourngrym stuck his head through the kitchen door, dipped a flagon into the stew pot, brought it out dripping, put a towel underneath it, and turned back down the hall, armor rattling in his haste.

"That too, Lord?" Belmer asked, hesitating.

"No, this is *my* evenfeast," Mourngrym told him with a grin. "Syluné tells me the audience chamber is full of folk with troubles, so I'll be eating on the throne again. Just tell the cooks to send someone to the chamber a little later on to see if any of the supplicants are in need of something hot to eat."

Belmer turned pale at the mention of the Witch of Shadowdale, and muttered some prayer or other under his breath as he went into the steam-filled, noisy, bustling kitchens.

For a moment, Mourngrym stopped beside Guthtar with the steaming flagon in his hand. "Good Guthtar— tell Thurbal from me that I want all of you men to do half shifts until I order otherwise. You've been done out of a lot of sleep, and it's time someone gave some back to you."

The normally terse Guthtar practically bounded into a salute. "Aye, my *lord!*" he said.

Mourngrym chuckled and clapped him on the shoulder. "I thought you'd find those orders rode easier than most." He turned to the forecourt and nodded to his two new guards as he stepped between them. They stiffened in salute.

When the double doors of the audience chamber boomed closed and they heard the guards within thunk their spears on the stone floor, Argast turned his head to be sure the forecourt was now empty. Finding it so, he said to Amdramnar, "In spite of myself, I begin to respect this young lordling. If one is to be a weakling, why not go all the way and *serve* the people rather than commanding them?"

Amdramnar nodded. "I like him, too—but 'tis too early to tell . . . until we can spend a session or two in there, hearing him sit in judgment."

They fell hastily silent as Guthtar moved closer to open the door for the departing Belmer. Though they'd slain two of the newly hired Westgate men and taken their shapes, the two Malaugrym hadn't had a chance to hear either of their victims speaking—in a sober state, at least—and didn't want anyone to overhear them now and think the speech of Aunsible and Haratch had suddenly and curiously changed.

Belmer went out of the tower, and a magnificently robed, bearded man of middling years came in, with the Lady Shaerl on his arm. The holy hammer of Tyr, worked in silver, rode on a heavy chain around his neck. "I find Shadowdale dispirited for the first time since the Knights of Myth Drannor rode into it for *their* first time," he was saying in a rich, sonorous voice, "and that is ill. Have you had much trouble in this time of strife?"

"We are only days away from turning back the armies of Zhentil Keep, good justicar," Shaerl said gently, "a victory that cost us greatly. The Witch-Queen of Aglarond—"

The two guards clearly heard the priest's hiss of indrawn breath as he was turning to walk between them at that moment. He looked awed.

"—tells us that the Zhent troops were led by the god Bane himself. In the fight against him, the temple of Lathander, which formerly stood across the way, was destroyed, along with the archmage Elminster and, some have testified under oath, the goddess Mystra, herself."

The priest came to an abrupt halt. "You credit this to be true?" he asked, his voice incredulous.

"I do, holy lord, and can produce witnesses whose testimony will, I know, impress you," Shaerl said firmly.

The priest waved a dismissive hand. "Well enough, so let us grant that the tales are true. Bane, Mystra, and Elminster all destroyed along with that temple over there." He drew a deep breath, shook his head, and bid gruffly, "Say on."

"Over half of our soldiers fell in defending the dale," Shaerl told him, "and are now pyre ashes; scarce a farm in this dale did not lose someone. Moreover, magic has gone wild here, and Storm Silverhand, the Bard of Shadowdale, has been missing for five days."

The priest suddenly looked very old, and felt behind him for the bench he knew was there. Shaerl smoothly guided him to it, keeping hold of his hand as the justicar of Tyr sank down onto the bench and whispered hoarsely, "Storm. I . . . we were very close, once. I'd hoped to see her this night, after my audience with the youn—with your Mourngrym."

Shaerl patted his arm. "She told us she was looking forward to your visit, because you had been so noble to her," she said softly. "She spoke of your valor and kindness."

For just a moment, the proud priest looked like a young boy—a young boy on the verge of tears. "She did?" he asked, his voice rising in wonder.

"Yes," Shaerl said, "and I've never known her judgment to be wrong yet. I feel as if you are an old friend."

Argast leaned a trifle closer to Amdramnar and muttered, "She's smooth, this one."

Amdramnar agreed with the slightest of nods, but just then the doors between the audience chamber and the forecourt scraped open and three farm folk came out. "The gods bless him!" the stout old woman in the forefront was saying.

"If he keeps his promise," her hired hand said doubtfully as they went out, not even seeing the two people on the bench.

The old woman turned and poked out a bony finger. "Now ye list and learn, Thurton! If there's one thing this young lord of ours does, it's keep his word! When my man, Undlejack, was still alive, he won a hand of cards off Mourngrym, playin' the night away at the Old Skull, and the lord asked him his price. . . . A new roof, my man says, as bold as anything—'cuz that's what we needed, in truth—an' the next day, gods be blowed if the lord doesn't show up with half a dozen guards, n' do the roof right then! The lord himself, up on our cottage, sweatin' along with the rest of 'em! And when he's done, he asks if we want the fence set straight, seein' as they're here . . . an' up comes a cart, after, when we're talkin'—and out of it he serves us a feast, an' the neighbors what come to watch, too! Tells us it's no more'n we deserve!"

She turned and marched out of the forecourt, then pivoted back to face the astonished Thurton. "Ye find me another lord anywhere as does that for me—an' others what ain't high and mighty, an' can't do him anything great in return! Ye'll be lookin' from the Sword Coast to the weird lands past Thay, an' not be findin' one, neither!"

Another two dalefolk strode out, one of them weeping, and the other walking awkwardly beside her. "Now, Nan—he can't raise to life someone he can't find! He did say he'd walk you around those laid out in the temple for burial, to see if we can find him. No one could do more."

The next person to come to the door was Mourngrym, his face pinched with sorrow. Shaerl leapt up and threw her arms around him. "My love," she said in a low, tender voice as their arms tightened around each other. He kissed her gently, as if they were alone in the room, before lifting his head and saying, "Shaerl, ask Thurbal to pass the word. No one's seen Aglyn's grandsire since the battle, and Nan's beside herself not knowing. If anyone . . ."

Mourngrym's gaze fell upon the priest of Tyr, waiting patiently to be introduced, and his face lit up. "Most Holy Arbeth! Be welcome, please, in Shadowdale! I'm sorry I didn't see you at once! Have you eaten?"

"If we could talk for just a few breaths, Lord Mourngrym, I'd be delighted to dine with you and your beautiful lady. I'd hoped also to meet the Lady Storm, but I hear she's . . . not to be found."

"That is so, I fear," Mourngrym said, "but come in, and we'll talk, the three of us—oh, yes: my lady and I rule as one." The priest's eyebrows were still raised as the doors of the audience chamber swung shut behind the three of them.

"He's a good ruler," Amdramnar said grudgingly.

"All the better for us, then," Argast said. "Let him manage our cattle until we're ready to rule here."

"Our foes the three bold rangers seem to have just departed on patrol . . . do we chase after them?"

"No, let them go. They'll return to us—and then we'll feed."

"Eat them?"

"Yes—I mean to eat them alive, limb by limb, slowly, while they plead. We'll use our everfire wand to seal the joints and keep them living. They may last several days."

"And then?"

"Then we'll reveal ourselves, and start on the rest of these cattle."

They had just time to fall silent and look as if they'd been that way for some time when a tall, silver-haired figure strode through the front doors, exchanged a salute, a wink, and a blown kiss that left old Guthtar blushing, turned into the forecourt, and strode to the audience chamber doors.

Argast turned. "Ah, my La—"

"Hist!" Amdramnar and Guthtar said together, reaching to silence him. Storm turned, gave them all a cheery wave, and flung the doors wide.

"That's Lady Storm!" Guthtar snarled in a whisper. "*Never* stop her going anywhere!" By common accord, the three guards had moved hurriedly to look through the closing doors—in time to see Storm, with a joyous laugh, sweep the justicar of Tyr up into the air as if he was a boy, then bring him down to her lips.

"Ye gods," Argast said, for Guthtar's benefit. "Guarding folk around here's going to be a lot more interesting than I'd dared hope!"

"A lot more fun, too," Guthtar whispered hoarsely, and trotted back to his post.

The two Malaugrym exchanged glances. These folk of

Faerûn seemed to care for each other a lot more than any of the blood of Malaug ever had . . . and laughed a lot more, too. . . .

* * * * *

Tower of Mortoth, Sembia, Flamerule 29

Cold fire flickered, and Irendue was free of the endless nothingness and blinking away tears to stare into the darkly handsome face of one of the cruel shapeshifters . . . a human face whose eyes were two dark flames.

Irendue swallowed as he took her hand and lowered her gently to the privy chamber floor. The air was cool on her bare skin. She shivered as the monster smiled at her.

"You won't hurt me?" she pleaded, voice quavering despite herself.

"Not yet, Lady." He drew her firmly out of the room, past the humming lines of white fire that held the suspended bodies of the master and her two fellow apprentices.

"My name is Bralatar," he said as he guided her into the study and sat her in the master's chair. Once she was seated, two tentacles slid gently around her wrists, and another captured both of her ankles, but their coils held her loosely, almost gently.

"What do you want of me?" she whispered. "And where is . . . the other one?"

"Not far away, exploring this impressive estate," Bralatar replied, "but we can speak more freely later . . . after you've shown me how to do a certain something with *this*."

He held up Mortoth's crystal ball. The glossy sphere, larger than a man's head, shone back the fire of his eyes. His smile was not a pleasant thing to see.

"You won't hurt me?" she pleaded, trembling under

his tentacles as she fought for calm.

The Malaugrym smiled softly. "Not yet, so long as you are obedient, Lady . . . not yet."

* * * * *

Blackstaff Tower, Waterdeep, Flamerule 29

"I understand Storm's concern about their living on to rise behind her and slay again after the battle seems won," Khelben muttered in exasperation, "but when one uses Mystra's fire on anything, not a lot is left to work with!"

"Alassra turned a dozen or more Malaugrym into mushrooms at Irythkeep," Laeral reminded him, "and they fell from a height to shatter on rocks. Surely some residue remains there, however small, that we could use. . . ."

"Then go to the Cavern Perilous and cast whatever is needful to bring some of that residue here!"

Laeral glided close to plant a fond kiss on the ear of the lord mage of Waterdeep as he stood staring and sweating into the heart of a slowly spinning magical construct in the air before him. She left the chamber.

The construct wavered, billowed varicolored smoke, and collapsed, flying apart into spreading motes of dust and light. Khelben "Blackstaff" Arunsun gave the scattering residue his best scowl, sighed, and strode to his favorite armchair. For more than a day now, with Laeral at his side, he'd been working feverishly on a spell to trace Malaugrym or prevent them from shapeshifting freely . . . preferably both.

He sipped at the elverquisst in his glass, turning it slightly so that the flecks of gold in the smooth, iridescent heart of the ruby liquor sparkled in the light of Laeral's latest spell—a spell that conjured a ring of dancing radiances that looked like candle flames.

Briefly he wondered if he should watch over his lady,

to see that nothing ill befell her in the Cavern Perilous, a vast cave in the heart of Mount Waterdeep, which they used when working magics that might prove damaging to the surroundings. Nowadays, with magic gone wild, Khelben thought sourly, just about *any* spell could prove damaging to the surroundings.

He'd barely had that thought when the air across the room shimmered and sparkled. His beloved smiled at him as she crossed the room, a stone in her hands, the black spatters of long-dried mushroom clear upon it.

With a smile, Khelben bounded up out of his chair, feeling the familiar excitement of the chance to work truly new magic.

Then he saw the brightness of unshed tears in Laeral's eyes, and looked a wordless question at her as he came forward, arms out to hold and comfort her.

His lady sighed as she came into his embrace. "I wish Elminster were still with us. Even more than holy Mystra, his presence—gruff ways and all—made me feel all was right in Faerûn, underneath the troubles of the day."

* * * * *

Elven Court woods, Flamerule 30

"I'm sure I saw someone walking through the trees just about . . . here," Shar whispered. The three rangers crouched together amid a close-grown stand of massive dark trunks—shadowtops that had stood on this slope for nigh a thousand years.

""What sort of someone?" Itharr asked her. "Human?"

"A youngish man, in robes, going from down there, along this slope, toward somewhere that way. I think he was on his way back after a call of nature."

"On his way back to a camp, or a halted group of wayfarers," Belkram mused. "Either way, we'd best be cautious when going where this knave you saw was headed, for fear of being seen by a sentry—or blundering into the heart of a group of foes."

Sharantyr laid a silencing hand on his arm and pointed back the way they'd come. All three strained to see and hear something. After a moment, Itharr caught sight of a furry animal moving away and said reassuringly, "Badger . . . a big one, but a badger."

"That's not reassuring," Shar said, her face inches from his, "because I saw it, too . . . and what I saw go behind that tree stood on two legs and had several eyes, on stalks."

"Malaugrym," Belkram said bleakly. "Hunting us?"

"Why else would it be here, in the depths of the Elven Court woods, where creatures to devour or hide among are relatively few?" Shar replied. "Doppelgangers like cities, where there's prey in every alley and folk to hide among on every corner. Of course it's after us."

"I'm vastly reassured to know we now know what's going on," Itharr said with a grin. "I'll be ecstatic if someone details what, by the skulls of the Seven Lost Gods, we do *now?*"

Behind them, from just about where they'd been peering at the probable Malaugrym, there came a sudden shout of alarm and the sharp 'whump' of a spellburst, followed by a crackling of brush and somebody crying out an incantation in desperate haste.

"That's easy," Belkram said with a wolfish grin. He waved a hand in the direction of the commotion. "We sit and watch."

* * * * *

Thuruthein Tlar was determined to impress his master. Orth Lantar was the wisest Red Wizard Thuruthein had ever met—and wise Red Wizards guarded and rewarded those who were truly loyal to them, for there was no more rare commodity in all of Thay.

Prestym, Iyrit, and the others were the sort of

ambitious, scheming apprentices that surrounded every Red Wizard; a seething mass of fawning back-stabbers who were little better than fodder. Thuruthein suspected Orth Lantar knew their true worth—and probably intended to spend the lives of more than a few of them in his stated attempt to penetrate the ruined elven city of Myth Drannor and find some of its fabled magic. Thuruthein was determined not to be counted among the expendable.

So when three humans in leather armor came skulking around the camp—brigands, for certain—in his watch field and during his sentry duty, Thuruthein knew just what to do.

He'd stood up behind his tree and was aiming the wand very carefully at the face of the woman, humming in anticipation and noting her wild beauty with the briefest of appreciative regret—when he heard the smallest of sounds close behind him and whirled about, heart leaping into his throat.

To see himself grinning back at him! A Thuruthein Tlar with tentacles instead of hands. Those tentacles were stretched out an impossibly long way, like two hungry snakes, so as to be almost around Thuruthein's throat!

Orth Lantar's senior apprentice trembled, swallowed, and fired his wand with commendable calmness—only to have his foe collapse like a felled tree before the spell-burst, falling beneath most of its harm.

It gathered itself and lunged at him with a forest of tentacles.

Backing away in sudden real terror, Thuruthein stammered the most powerful incantation he knew.

The blazing beam of destruction seared the body that so resembled his own almost entirely away to ashes—but something dark and huge and very fast indeed reared up out of the leaves right in front of him, and seven mouths opened hungrily.

Thuruthein had barely time left to scream, "No! Noooo! I was loyal, Master! I was loyaaaaaah—"

* * * * *

"A loyal Red Wizard's apprentice?" Belkram asked, raising his eyebrows. "A rare gem indeed!"

"Belt up," Shar hissed at him, "and let's get out of here! *I* don't want to get caught between a Malaugrym looking for us and an angry Red Wizard!"

"You don't?" Itharr asked as they sprinted frantically away through the woods. "Where's your sense of adventure?"

* * * * *

The map held in midair before him, in the teeth of four floating skulls, was finally beginning to make sense. If one placed the balefire rune in the emptiness within the circle of nine black blades, a sequence of directions was revealed, leading to . . . what, by the fires?

Orth Lantar's head snapped up from the map as his crystal ball flashed a blinding red and began to shudder, rattling in the carved cup that formed the head of his staff. At the same time, a binding in his mind shifted uneasily—then snapped, flooding his thoughts with a brief, fading pain and a frantic calling. . . .

Thuruthein? By the Seven Serpents! Orth Lantar whirled, snatching up his most mighty wand from the table. "To me!" he called, and flung up his hand. His most powerful staff was leaping across the tent toward it when he felt an inward tremor, and sighed. His best apprentice was dead.

The staff smacked into his palm, and the Red Wizard spun around again to fix the crystal ball with coldly furious eyes. Under his steady glare the scrying sphere quieted and cleared—and in its depths he saw a wolf lift bloody jaws from Thuruthein's torn face. The creature twisted horribly and become a larger thing, like a bear with four long, spidery arms, shaggy hair, and piercing talons. It raised its head and sniffed the air, gave a horribly human laugh, and shambled purposefully away, not even glancing back at the apprentice's sprawled body and vainly lifted hands.

"An attack that robs me of something so valuable must be swiftly avenged," Orth Lantar told the nearest skull, "lest some rival behind it misread it as weakness and send all sorts of petty annoyances in its wake."

"Swift strikes the avenger, and towers topple toward the sunset," the skull intoned. The Red Wizard stiffened and stared at it in amazement. He shook his head, feeling suddenly dangerously close to tears. This must be one of Thuruthein's last pranks!

He set the warding rod to guard the magic in his tent from interlopers and shot a last look at the scene in the crystal. Rings winked on his fingers—and he vanished. Four skulls tumbled to the floor, the conjured map fading away to nothingness once more. There came a startled exclamation from the apprentice on watch outside the tent.

"Master?" an anxious male voice called. "Master?"

At the lack of reply, its owner was emboldened enough to part the tent with the rod that bore the hand of a dead man, and peer within. In eerie silence, four human skulls rose to face him. Radiances deep within the rod on the table and the crystal ball atop its staff winked in unison, faster, and faster. . . .

Prudently, the apprentice withdrew, letting the hangings fall.

"Craven dullard," one of the skulls murmured as it sank down to the carpets again. Thuruthein Tlar had been busy in the idle time he'd had earlier this day, when the tent was up and his master was busy setting the wards around the camp. Now his time was all gone.

The crystal sphere flashed a sudden scarlet, and another of the skulls began to moan.

* * * * *

"Where, by the beard of Elminster, are we running to, anyway?" Belkram gasped as they topped a rise and headed down a fern-choked gully. "What makes one part of this old forest any safer than another?"

"Ask her," Itharr grunted as, side by side, they rounded a riven stump. He jerked his hand back at Sharantyr, who was watching their rear, ready blade in hand. "She's t—"

The rest of his words were lost in a sudden rush from the side of the gully, a plunging fury of flashing talons and dark hairy bulk and gleaming fangs.

Belkram was thrown off his feet to crash heavily through thorns and dead branches, and heard Sharantyr scream as she charged. He snatched at his blade as something large and dark and hairy clawed him . . . something that was crouched atop Itharr, raking its talons and surging forward to bite down at the ranger beneath it with a horrible wet crunching sound that made Belkram wince as his blade finally grated free of its scabbard. Too late.

17
All Too Much Magic

The fire was so cold, so utterly . . . cold. Its chill made her limbs tremble, helplessly and endlessly, as it rushed through her and on around the web. Irendue gasped at its icy searing, feeling her teeth chatter uncontrollably as she stared at the all-too-familiar walls and ceiling of the privy chamber . . . and wished she could die.

The one called Bralatar had promised her death . . . after he and his companion were finished with her. She could still feel the cold slime of his tentacles slithering into her ear and out her nose, and the casual way in which he'd pointed out, as she gagged and wept, that simply expanding his tentacle at this moment would cause her head to explode like a rotten fruit, giving him his most favorite of meals . . . still-warm human.

Irendue swallowed, sick at the thought, and almost let her head sink back into the endless white fire. It would be so easy to just surrender. . . .

Aye, surrender and die in slow, screaming agony while the two shapeshifting monsters gloated over her . . .

Irendue swallowed again, and looked beside her at the master, hanging slack-jawed and unseeing, virtually a skeleton, his hair falling out in clumps from a shriveled scalp. Mortoth had been vigorous and strong, brusque even, but when he took her to his bed, he'd shaken with passion long pent up. . . . She looked again at his shriveled ruin and shuddered at what he'd become.

It was the first time she'd been free to see or think about anything without one of the shapeshifters ordering her about. The one called Bralatar had been careless in his haste, so confident of her trembling fear that he'd thrust her back into the web of fire and simply pushed at her face as he turned away. But her head had passed between two strands of the enchanted everfire, and so remained free.

His eagerness to be ahunting had let Irendue Nuentar, most favored but least powerful of the apprentices of Mortoth the Mighty, keep her wits, but she could take no advantage of that while she trembled in the grip of the spell. She was caught in some sort of gate that took the two monsters to and from their home. Even more chilling than the thoughts that her life— and that of the master and Turnold and Lareth—kept the gate open, that it sucked energy out of them to do its work, was the thought of how many more shapeshifters might dwell at the other end of that gate . . . free to spill into Faerûn at any time, to take the shapes of kings and merchant princes and wizards alike, and ruthlessly rise to rule all.

And what if they disagreed, as men always seem to, and fell to war? They could change shapes like flitting leaves to suit their purposes. The men, so helpless by comparison, would fall in their thousands and stain all Toril dark crimson with their spilled blood. . . . She had to get free.

So much depended on her. She simply must win free of this evil spell, but how?

Even now, one shapeshifter must be tiring of the hangings and statues and little carved things Mortoth had gathered in his long life of sorcery and be turning back through the labyrinthine ring-shaped house, toward this tower. The other must be hunting down the three grim rangers she'd seen him watching on their cautious creepings through an ancient forest.

The ball! The master's scrying crystal! She'd never dared do this for fear of Mortoth's wrath, but . . . She looked at the thing of bones beside her, then looked away again.

Slowly and carefully, Irendue lifted her head and called, "Buldimer! To me!"

There was a thrumming sound from the unseen doorway behind her, and Irendue's heart leapt. It pleased Mortoth to give names to the items he'd personally enchanted, that he might summon them in need. With this evil spell linking her to the master, it seemed the items would answer her call!

"To me!" she called again, putting all her will behind it this time. The sphere of crystal sailed into view around the fiery web, flying smoothly through the air to come scudding to a stop in the air before her, a little to one side—the master's side.

She could see into its depths, where there was a forest and tiny running figures, and the flash of swords, and . . . a bear that grew a human face and hands. One of those hands rose from a fold of pelt holding something she knew well: the master's wand of pain.

She'd seen him use it on the cat that prowled the garden, and on Lareth once. She'd even felt its peculiar burning sting herself when she'd disagreed with Mortoth on what beast shape he'd change her into, and what use of her he'd make then. She'd never forgotten its lash, or the softly spoken word the master had used to make it hurt her so.

She spoke that word now. "Anamauthree," she said, softly but clearly, staring into the crystal, and feeling a sudden surge in the white fire around her as the crystal flickered.

The only flesh the wand was touching as she spoke

was the grasping hand of the creature called Bralatar—and so, of course, its magic was visited upon him. She saw him stiffen and stagger. From out of the forest beyond, something came roaring. Something blue-white and deadly, which washed across the crystal with blinding fury, sending out a lance of light through the web beside her.

The endless fire faltered for a moment—and with a sob of desperation, Irendue flung herself forward through a moment of twisting, churning agony . . . and fell free.

She'd never thought falling on her face on the cold, hard privy chamber floor would be such a welcome thing . . . even with the sick, weak feeling in her right arm. She looked at it, shuddered, and bit her lip as fresh tears came.

Her once smooth, shapely arm was now wrinkles of skin over bones, from forearm to shoulder . . . a thing of death. She lifted it, and watched it move normally. She flexed the fingers of her unblemished hand, beyond the ruin, and watched them respond as usual. She touched the floor with one . . . and felt nothing.

Irendue swallowed and looked back up at the web of fire, a thing of stars through the tears on her lashes. The master hung there more dead than alive, and Turnold and Lareth, too.

She knelt on the floor below it and shuddered, gathering all her strength for what she knew she must do. The crystal ball flashed and spun silently above her, but she did not bother to look at it. Whatever befell in that distant battle, she must prevail here and now.

Here, and—now. Grimly she wobbled to her feet, unbalanced by her shriveled arm, and swayed, fighting for calm and stable footing. If she fell back into the web, this would all be for naught.

She wept anew when she stared into the master's sunken face. It was little better than a skull, a skull with staring white eyes, no pupils to be seen in those deep-sunken sockets.

Irendue swallowed. With her good arm, she reached out and tugged at his hair. A good handful of it came away; she flung it aside in revulsion and tried again, twisting her fingers into what little hair was left and shaking him. His scalp began to tear . . . and no blood welled forth!

"Master! Brave Mortoth! My master! Irendue calls thee!" she cried desperately, her face inches from his own. His lips moved slightly, but no sound came forth. He made no further reaction. She shook him again, and patted at his forehead and shoulder—the only other places in the flowing fire that she dared reach, earning an almost painful tingling in her fingertips as she did so. There was no response at all this time.

Irendue stepped back. Tears fell unheeded to the floor at her feet, and she regarded her master soberly. "Fare better than this, Mortoth," she said formally, once she'd fought down sobs to find a voice. Then, with a last great sigh, she turned away. The great wizard was beyond her help.

His hands were spread, the fingers awash with white fire. There was no way for her to get them free to open the spellbooks that would respond only to his touch. The only spell she knew to banish magic was in one of those books . . . and without its touch, this web of fire remained a doorway for legions of shapeshifters, and Faerûn stood unguarded.

The words seemed to echo in her head, as if declaimed as a doom by a great herald. "Faerûn stands unguarded," she whispered aloud, and looked wildly around the room, half-expecting shapeshifters to curl out of the air in all corners.

Nothing happened. The cold fires raged on, humming endlessly, and the crystal ball hung in the air beside her, flashing and flickering. She looked once into its depths, then at her two fellow apprentices, spread-eagled and sightless in the grip of the spell.

Lareth's hair was long enough, and one of Turnold's knees projected out of the streaming fire. She stepped forward, calling their names in a soft but insistent whisper, shaking them until the very flames around them snarled in protest. She was rewarded at last with eyes swimming open, questing dully about for a moment before fixing on her.

"Lareth! Turnold!" she hissed. "I need you!"

Lareth's mouth worked silently, but Turnold licked his lips and said, slowly and carefully, "I have always suspected this."

The words were followed by the faintest of smiles. Irendue would normally have answered such a gibe with stinging words, but now it made her eyes fill with tears. Turnold's wits were still his own . . . something, at least, was as it should be in the Tower of Mortoth.

"Turnold," she said, ignoring the tremor in her voice, "do you know where the master keeps scrolls or items to dispel magic?"

Turnold's eyes held sorrow. "In his grimoires, only. He didn't want us unweaving his wards and getting into things he wanted undisturbed."

"How can I get you free?"

Turnold managed the smallest of shrugs in his bonds of flame and said, "I know not, but this gate must be destroyed—or all Toril stands in danger."

Irendue nodded and with an impatient hand wiped tears from her cheeks. "But how?" she asked, thinking of all the unusable staves and rods and floating scepters in the rooms around her. Either one of the shapeshifters might step into the room at any moment. She had no time.

"The web," Lareth said haltingly, his voice sharp and high with fear at what he was suggesting, "lives through our life. Slay us, and it will fade."

Turnold's eyes blazed with sudden fire. Irendue looked helplessly from one imprisoned apprentice to the other until her eyes were snared by those of the older, wiser apprentice.

"Do it," Turnold whispered hoarsely, transfixing her with eyes of steel. " 'Tis the only way."

"I can't!" Irendue hissed helplessly, standing nude before him, tears rolling down her cheeks once more. She could not look away from his blazing eyes.

Hanging in the web of fire, Turnold said carefully, "You must. Know, Irendue, that I have always loved you—'tis why I baited you so often."

"I can't harm anyone!" she wailed, clenching her fists.

"Take the sword the master keeps behind the door," Turnold said faintly. "Put it in my mouth—and then push. Please."

Her tears almost blinded her as she found the sword in the study, fumbled its heavy length back through the passage, and came to face Turnold once more.

"I can't do this to you," she whispered. "I just can't."

"You must," he said fiercely, straining forward in the web of flames, "and you will. Put the blade in my mouth."

Irendue shook her head, weeping wildly. The sword point danced and glittered wildly in front of his face until he growled, "I suppose one of my eyes would do as well, but I hardly think taking off my ears will suffice."

His familiar sarcasm steadied her. Irendue slid the steel between his teeth. Resting it there, she asked quietly, "Turnold, are you sure?"

"Of clorse hlyime shlure," he managed to say around the tip. "Do it!"

Irendue swallowed, blew him a kiss, closed her eyes—and thrust the blade forward.

"Gods greet ye, Turnold," she said huskily, giving him the formal farewell. Her stomach heaved, and she almost flung the blade away in her haste to tear it free. When she opened her eyes again, she tried not to look at the limp thing that had been Turnold, but his blood was blazing up around him in flames of orange and red, and the web of white fires was dim, fading as she watched!

Irendue let out a tremulous breath and looked at Lareth. "Can—Can you pull free?" she asked him, and watched his face tighten as he struggled. Cold fire flickered around his trembling limbs, but after a long, silent battle he gave up, sagging forward. His teeth were chattering in fear as he raised a gray face to her and said, "D-Do it."

She did. It was easier the second time . . . and as the apprentices' bodies slumped, the web of fire faded silently away, gone as if it had never been. Its passing was marked by the hollow clatter of Mortoth's bones bouncing on the floor.

With dull eyes, Irendue stared at his grinning skull. She went to her knees among the dead men, and the dust that had been the skin of her master eddied around her. The bloody sword was cold and heavy in her hands as the world dissolved in tears again. . . .

The voice, when it came, was menacingly quiet. "What have you done?"

Irendue lifted her head and the sword together, glaring up through tangled hair at the other shapeshifter. He wore the form of a handsome, sandy-haired man with a mustache . . . but his eyes glittered dark and deadly, like those of a hawk.

"Freed us," Irendue gave him her fiercely whispered answer. "Freed us all."

"You shall die for this," Lorgyn said softly.

"I know," the woman replied calmly, embracing the sword as if it was a babe in her arms. "Kill me, then, and have done . . . monster."

Lorgyn showed his teeth in a smile. "Ah, no," he said in almost friendly tones. "Death need not be so fast and easy as all that. I shall use your sorcery to help me raise another gate . . . and your body to power it. Of course, that body need not be whole . . . "

Still wearing that terrible grin, he advanced on her.

* * * * *

Elven Court woods, Flamerule 30

"Die!" Belkram roared in fury, forgetting all thoughts of stealth and nearby wizards as he thrust his blade repeatedly into the shapeshifter's hairy, many-taloned bulk. If only it were still silver, he thought fiercely as he drove his steel home once more and struck something hard within, making the Malaugrym quiver.

It snarled and shrank away, and Belkram lunged after it, catching sight of Sharantyr's blade flashing on its far flank. The lady ranger's blade glistened as it rose and fell with a green-hued, translucent slime that must be the monster's blood.

"Right," Belkram snarled, "let's see all of your blood, beast! *All of it!*"

His blade thrust down to its hilt into the shifting bulk before him, and the Malaugrym recoiled, drawing flailing tentacles back into itself in struggling spasms of pain.

As it receded, it left Itharr behind, writhing weakly on the ground, his lifeblood drenching the moss and dead leaves around him. The Harper's mouth worked, and his eyes were blood-red; Belkram knew his friend was sorely wounded.

Delude yourself not, Belkram told himself sourly, he's dying.

Frantically he chopped and slashed at the shapeshifter, hearing Sharantyr's sobbing as she did the same thing. Her hair swirling around her, and she leapt high to throw all her weight behind her blade.

Something blazed with sudden fire behind her. A rolling wave of force, like a wave she'd once waded through on the beaches of Sembia, took her behind the knees and flung her forward onto the Shadowmaster.

Gray flesh opened up around her, seeking to suck her down in and smother her. Sharantyr screamed in fear and fury, clawed her way clear, and wriggled off the beasts's far side.

She came up wild-eyed, with blade in hand and

breast heaving—and gaped in astonishment at a cold-eyed man in the robes of a Red Wizard, who stood over Itharr with staff in hand, glaring at a rainbow-hued radiance in the air around him.

"Must *all* spells go wild?" he snarled, leveling his staff in both hands as if it were a lance. Sparks raced down its length, and from its end burst brilliantly blue butterflies.

Belkram was still cutting at the heaving, roiling tentacled mass that was the Malaugrym, but trying at the same time to keep watch on this newcomer. The shapeshifter rose into a pillar of flesh, reached spade-shaped arms toward the Red Wizard, slimmed those arms into needlelike pincers . . .

The Red Wizard said something soft and brief—and fire seemed to be born within the Malaugrym, hurling its flesh and tentacles apart in an eruption of hissing steam.

The riven body fell back onto scorched moss, dwindling into something that was almost human. Something faceless and sprawled, which blazed with many small fires.

Shar faced the Red Wizard across their smoke and asked in a shaking voice, "Why . . . why did you aid us?"

The wizard's cold eyes met hers, and Sharantyr was suddenly aware of how easily he could destroy them. Even with magic fraying wild, he bore several wands at his belt, something longer and more impressive sheathed like a sword at his hip, and the staff. Lights winked here and there along its carved length, and were answered by glows from among the many rings on his fingers. The Knight swallowed and stepped back, raising her sword. Belkram moved to her side, his blade also ready.

The Red Wizard smiled thinly. "Another day we might be foes to the death," he said in a voice strong with confidence and power. "But against such a one as this . . ."

The sorcerer gestured down at the collapsing ashes that had been the Malaugrym, and went on, "Against such a one, all must stand together—or no man in Faerûn will know freedom, in the end."

He did something to his staff, and a glass vial appeared in the air above Sharantyr's hand. As it came to rest gently in her palm, he bowed to them both and turned away.

The flash of his departure lit up the rune graven in the glass. "A healing potion of the utmost power," Sharantyr said wonderingly. She went to her knees beside Itharr.

Blood was bubbling at his lips with every breath. She unstoppered the vial with infinite care and tipped it deep within, feeling his teeth tighten on the glass as a sudden spasm racked him.

"May the gods ascend to their rightful places, so that we can pray to them once more," she said feelingly, holding the vial firmly in place as Itharr bucked and writhed in Belkram's arms.

"May these accursed shapeshifters return to *their* rightful places," Belkram said to her, "so that we don't have to!"

"Gnorlgh," Itharr agreed weakly, from beneath them. "Gut thlisgh out ou my—*mouth!*" He spat out the vial and struggled to sit up.

"Itharr!" Shar said joyfully, and embraced him, covering his lips with her own.

"Some men," Belkram said, watching her weep and meeting one of Itharr's eyes through her hair, "are far luckier than they have any right to be." Then he discovered something must have gotten into his own eye. The world suddenly glimmered and blurred and a sound large and raw rose in his throat. . . .

* * * * *

Tower of Mortoth, Sembia, early Midsummer Day

A crystal ball spun unheeded in a darkened room in the Tower of Mortoth. It flickered fitfully, then came to a sudden halt. As its inner glow died and it crashed to the privy chamber floor, a woman screamed nearby, high and despairing, and drowned out the sound of the crystal shattering. . . .

* * * * *

Tilverton, early Midsummer Day

A solitary lantern guttered outside the gates in the gray hour before dawn, but its light was enough to reveal the Purple Dragon emblazoned proudly on the wrinkled surcoat of a yawning sentry. The armsman came alert with a grunt and stepped back to lower the tip of his spear. Something small and sleek and dark slid around the gatepost.

He relaxed and gave it a grin. Surmalkin back from mousing . . . and irritated at a lack of success, by the look of him.

"How now, little one?" the armsman growled, bending over fondly. The cat gave him a warning, defiant look and minced past. The guard watched him go. Grinning, the man leaned on his spear. It must be a nice, soft life, being a cat. . . .

Something that was strong and swift instead of nice and soft smashed him across the back of the head. He stumbled forward, dazed—and was still gathering wits and breath to shout for aid when the same something took him by the throat. It wrung his neck.

Blood ran from the armsman's nose and mouth as the Malaugrym propped him against the gatepost, hooking the shoulder straps of his armor upon the gate so he seemed to be leaning on it, lost in slumber.

After that, it was the work of a few breaths to scale the crumbling stone walls of the mansion that served the visiting high and mighty of Cormyr as home in Tilverton. From its high site, Lorgyn could see the lamps of the town winking below as his tentacles pulled him onto the balcony. He slid easily into human form . . . or at least, the appearance of an elegant old Cormyrean courtier he'd once seen, but with hands like large, flexible webbed paddles—akin to the hind feet of a beaver. He glided into the room.

The small blue glimmering of the lady's ward spun her awake in alarm.

But he was already bending low over the bed and whispering, "Good morning, my dear. Alambrara, isn't it?"

With one of those broad hands, he smothered whatever reply she might have made. His iron strength held her down until her sudden struggles subsided.

When she fell limp under him and the tiny lightnings of her collapsing ward had finished jittering through him, Lorgyn checked that she yet breathed. She was alive.

He nodded in satisfaction and set about stripping away the gems she wore at her ears, throat, and ankles. Who knew what sort of tracing magic could be linked to the jewelry of a powerful war wizard?

Her own bedclothes—soft samite sheets, no less—served admirably to gag and bind her, and he was gone from the room before the first light of dawn broke the eastern sky, low beyond the gray walls of Tilverton.

Breaths later, that wan, rosy light fell upon the wagon marked "Pendle's Fine Meats." Lorgyn unlatched its side door and thrust his bundle inside.

It was his wagon now, he thought as he melted into the heavy, grizzled form of Pendle once more and undid the sheet that had covered his prize from the eyes of any overly curious early risers.

Carefully drawing the door closed, he tore the sheet into strips and bound the war wizard Alambrara beside the fat Amnian, Gorluth the Great. He chuckled at the contrast between the shapely limbs of the Cormyrean, the fat and hairy little mage from Amn, and beyond him, Irendue's slim beauty. She was awake, her eyes blazing at him over the gag that was her only garment.

Lorgyn winked at her as he tightened a lashing and stood back to survey the three naked people bound to the meat bars.

The beginnings of a fine collection. If more folk collected wizards thus, there'd be less trouble all over Faerûn, to be sure. Still, he'd be needing more if a new gate were to be a truly lasting thing. Two gates, with a hidden one only he knew about, would be even more secure.

Two mages that would be easily found were Jhessail and Illistyl, Knights based in Shadowdale.

Giving Irendue a cheery wave and miming the biting off of a finger (he'd devoured her thumbs thus far, while punishing her, and planned to make of her fingers a long-lasting snack), Lorgyn replaced the padlock that only he had a key for, and went to the next wagon to rouse his men. He wondered briefly how they could sleep through each other's snoring.

"Up, lads," he said, shaking and slapping with brisk enthusiasm. " 'Tis time we set off for Shadowdale. I think we're all due for a little rest . . . and that's the place."

"Urggh," his cook said, "ye want dawnfry first?"

Lorgyn shook his head. The cook eyed him for a moment, then shrugged. Pendle *never* refused an early meal, even when it was only cold partridge from the night before—but this was three days now. . . .

Lorgyn gave the man's back a soft smile, and resolved to eliminate him as soon as the wagon was rumbling along the last stretch, between Shadowdale and the Tower of Mortoth. Yes—roasted alive on a spit in his own oversalty brown sauce would be fitting, too.

The gate guards were almost as sleepy and surly as his own grumbling men, but at last they did their work with bars and chains. Pendle's three wagons rumbled out of Tilverton, the first farers forth onto the road.

Even the horses complained as their burdens groaned and bumped along east toward Shadowdale. Pendle's men rode all around them with ready weapons and sleepy faces, wondering what madness had taken their master this time. Pendle smiled back at them all, and more than one man shivered at the soft promise in that smile.

* * * * *

The Castle of Shadows, Shadowhome, Midsummer Day

The glimmer of the scrying portal faded as it sank into the shadows, spinning away into nothingness. The face above its dissolution was a mask of wiggling, questing worms, but owned eyes that blazed like two lanterns of raging spellfire. Worms beneath them parted, and a calm voice said to the vast, long-empty chamber of the Castle of Shadows, "It is time to move at last. Let the hunt begin in earnest."

* * * * *

Faerûn, Shadowdale, Midsummer Day

The horn had cried out peace and parley, so the guards at the bridge over the Ashaba had not roused the folk of the tower in swift earnest. Lord Mourngrym and Lady Shaerl had been in the morning room over a leisurely dawnfry when their heralds brought word of the coming of a special envoy of Cormyr, Sir Tantor Dauntinghorn.

Just as they were, the lord and lady hastened down to the sward outside the tower, intent on welcoming the envoy and seeing to the needs of his large escort of Purple Dragons and war wizards.

With a glint in his eye, Mourngrym assured the stiff and magnificently mustachioed Sir Tantor that he was not now standing in a holding of Zhentil Keep, and that all minds in the dale were free of insidious Zhentarim spells. He thanked Cormyr for its obvious intent to do battle with the Zhent evil, given the handsome array of battle might and ready sorcery, come so long and dusty a way from the Forest Kingdom to Shadowdale—still proudly independent. He added that he hoped there would always be warm friendship between Cormyr and Shadowdale—coupled with mutual respect for each other's views, aims, and continued freedom.

The lord of the dale invited all of Cormyr into the Tower of Ashaba for a highsun meal as he made himself and his lady available to Sir Tantor, to hear the most important of messages and views from the Forest Kingdom.

The invitation was accepted. Bells rang to bring servants flooding into the feast hall just steps ahead of the hard-striding armsmen of Cormyr—and transform the already-bustling kitchens into a frantic whirlwind of steam and rushing folk and shouts.

"Pray come up to my morning room," Lord Mourngrym said to Sir Tantor. He led the way up the stairs. Shaerl followed beside the envoy's personal escort, a senior war wizard, as they ascended from the tumult below.

"If we can speak bald truth for a breath or two—" Mourngrym added as they stepped into a room still aromatic with the odor of buttered bread, sausages, roast pheasant in sauce, melted cheese with mustard on biscuits, and the other dishes of a light dawnfry, and he drew the door firmly closed "—pray tell me plainly why you're here."

Sir Tantor drew himself up to his full height and growled, "My lord, this is most irregular! While a free and open exchange of views is—"

"Mourngrym," said the old, gaunt war wizard standing at Shaerl's side, "I am Luthtor of Suzail, empowered to speak to you with the voice of Azoun and the candor of Vangerdahast. We're here to investigate rumors of Elminster's death, to make sure Zhentil Keep hasn't gained control of, or influence over, this dale—and to strongly put forth the sixtieth or so offer from Azoun that Shadowdale become a protectorate of Cormyr."

"My thanks for your candor," Mourngrym said dryly. "Let us gently refuse Cormyr's kind offer once more, at once, so that no unpleasantness need follow between us. I want to be Azoun's friend—but not his subject. He cannot have me continue as the one if he must insist on the other."

"Well, *if* we're being quite candid," Sir Tantor growled, "what's to stop us from simply seizing Shadowdale?"

"Me," Shaerl said sweetly. They all turned to stare at her. "I have Azoun's personal promise," she told them, "that I'd have a free hand in Shadowdale, and that no Purple Dragon nor war wizard of fair Cormyr would meddle east of the Ashaba until I gave them leave to do so."

"My lady," Luthtor said sternly, "you know very well that Azoun's word held only so long as you were on your promised mission for the crown . . . a mission Vangerdahast considers you abandoned on your wedding day, cleaving to this man"—he bowed to Mourngrym— "rather than your sworn duty."

"My lord," Shaerl said, her eyes gleaming with a dangerous light, "you are obviously unaware of the precise wording of Azoun's bidding and my promise, so I'll not argue the point with you. Be assured that if you move against us, Azoun will be foresworn."

"And if we know nothing of these ah, private words, and present the throne of Shadowdale to him anyway?" Sir Tantor huffed.

"It will be my duty to resist you," Mourngrym said, "and that of all the Knights of Myth Drannor."

"Their fame is not inconsiderable," the war wizard Luthtor granted. "But do you seriously think a handful of adventurers, however bold, can stand against the forces accompanying us? More than a dozen war wizards are watching over more than two hundred and sixty veteran armsmen in your feast hall right now."

"And just how long, Lord Luthtor," Shaerl asked sweetly, "do you think all of them would last against the Queen of Aglarond?"

Both Cormyreans paled slightly. The war wizard shrugged and asked, "And what evidence can you give us you can even contact her, let alone command her to battle at your bidding?"

"None," Shaerl said softly. "As with other armed endeavors in life, goodsirs, you'll just have to take that risk and find out the hard way. Or back down, as is far more prudent, and go home wondering for the rest of your lives if we were bluffing." She seemed to think of something, and added calmly, "Of course, the second way, you will *have* a 'rest of your lives' to wonder in."

"Moreover," Mourngrym said pleasantly, "the second way preserves our friendship, whereas the first loses forever any hope Cormyr may have that Shadowdale will not ally with Hillsfar, say, or Sembia, against the Purple Dragon."

"I . . . " Sir Tantor seemed unsure of how to proceed. He looked quickly to Luthtor.

The war wizard nodded, smiled, and said, "Perhaps, indeed, we've speculated with extreme imprudence. Permit me to tender our deepest apologies, and pass on to the other matters we mentioned, to whit—"

"What?" The envoy had turned a dangerous shade of purple. He glared at Luthtor, and snarled, "You're just going to—back down? Abandon our mission, just like that? Well, be advised that *my* first recommendation, upon seeing Vangerdahast at our return, will be to repl—"

"Enough of this," Shaerl snapped in tones that brought the envoy to instant silence. "Why don't we involve Azoun and Vangy in this discussion directly? I'd like to hear just what they intend." She held up one finger, and turned a ring upon it so that its black sapphire caught the light. It winked with a blue-white radiance as she stroked it—and both Cormyreans stared at it in surprise.

Like two coldly leveled spears, Shaerl's eyes caught those of the war wizard. "Shall I speak to them myself, Lord—or will Vangy stop merely listening through you, and have the grace to introduce himself?"

Sir Tantor stared again at the war wizard, and Mourngrym looked as if he were hiding a smile.

Luthtor sat very still, his eyes suddenly older and sadder than they had been. When he spoke, his voice was deeper and rougher than before. "Well played, li—"

Suddenly the scene before them melted away into swirling mists of gold and gray, and left the two Malaugrym staring at the fetid insides of a dungeon.

"By the blood of Malaug!" Argast snarled, "is every spell you cast going to twist wild?"

Amdramnar shrugged. "I've another." He strode across the cavern and muttered an incantation, raising his hands to trace intricate gestures. The golden mists returned. They swirled around him for a moment—and then turned into bunches of grapes and fell.

Argast watched the fruit splatter on the stone floor and cast a quick look behind him. The torch in its sconce blazed as before, and there was no watching helmed head nor shout of alarm. They were alone in the dungeons of the tower, on the worst guard duty one could draw . . . unless one were really a Malaugrym, and wanted a little privacy for some spell-casting.

That is, if any spell would work. Amdramnar looked up from the grapes and muttered, "We don't have time to study that spell again—half their talking'll be done before we're ready."

Argast growled in slow anger, and said, "Then it's time for you to take the shape of two guards for a while."

Amdramnar lifted a questioning eyebrow. His fellow Malaugrym was already blurring and dwindling . . . until a rat blinked at him, winked once, and then turned to dash away into the darkness.

Amdramnar sighed, sat down, and stretched into the semblance of two bored guards sitting together on a crate, down here in the storage cavern. He arranged weapons and armor to conceal the place at the thighs where the two bodies were joined, and settled down to wait, hoping Argast wasn't making a fatal mistake.

18
A Gathering in Shadowdale

From the dungeons, old and dusty rat holes led up to the pantry. In the confusion of all the cooks and scullery maids working in frantic haste and doors everywhere propped open to keep the heat down, the rat was able to streak through the kitchens and outside. The yard behind the tower was crowded with youngsters peeling potatoes and carting away greens, but no one noticed a rodent scuttling around the corner, into the tall grass.

In a trice, the rat became a pigeon, and ascended in a flutter of wings to an open tower window.

The casement gave in to the end of a hall lined with tapestries, paintings, and closed doors. At the far end of the corridor, where it opened out into a meeting with other passages, daylight gleamed on the armor of a tower guard. The guard turned his head as the pigeon's wings blocked the sunlight, but Argast hastily landed on the windowsill. The guard gave the pigeon a glance, then looked away again.

It was sheer mischance that he yawned and looked back down the hall as the pigeon was rising up into a man.

"Hold!" the guard bellowed, leveling his spear as he broke into a charge.

Argast snarled in disgust and ducked behind the nearest tapestry, shifting shape as fast as he could.

All too soon a spear point thrust through the hanging, its point skittering along the stone wall—but the Malaugrym had shrunk down into a wadded mass by the floor to watch the spear strike sparks overhead. He surged upright as it withdrew. As he'd expected, it reappeared more cautiously, drawing the hanging aside. By then he was ready.

The guard found himself blinking at a buxom, very bare female . . . the most beautiful woman he'd ever seen. He swallowed as she smiled at him, and blinked again as she held out her arms, beckoning. . . .

An inconspicuous taloned tentacle that had snaked across the floor rose up behind his head, reached around, and tore his face off.

Argast stared down at the twisted, blood-spattered body, satisfied the death had made little noise. But what now? If he posed as the guard, he'd be attacked if he left his post and was seen listening at doors . . . and this body would be found soon enough. He positioned it against the wall behind the tapestry, using the spear as a prop, but anyone who even glanced into the passage was sure to see the bulge . . . and the blood all over the floor.

He shrugged then, and became a rat again. They were only humans, after all. . . .

* * * * *

Blackstaff Tower, Waterdeep, Midsummer Day

Khelben looked up from his work, startled, as Laeral stiffened and laid a hand on his arm. "Malaugrym!" she snapped, eyes closed, and clutched at her forehead, listening to an inner voice. "Jhessail's found a guard murdered in the tower and suspects Malaugrym did the killing. He was torn by talons on an upper floor, where no beast could reach unseen and no strong magic has been worked lately. . . ."

The sending ended, and Laeral raised her head, her eyes grave.

"Aye, it would be in Shadowdale," Khelben said gloomily, reaching out to stroke her long, curly silver hair. "Have you never noticed: nothing much in Faerûn happens anywhere *else.*"

Laeral gave him a tight smile, but said nothing. She was already bustling about the room, gathering cloaks, wands, and boots.

Khelben stared down at his scribblings and litter of material components, and admitted to himself what they both already knew: his Malaugrym spell was going nowhere, right speedily. He pushed back from the table and sprang to his feet. "I'm not trusting teleporting in this, mind," the Blackstaff told his lady irritably.

"I know," she replied brightly. "That's why I'm rushing about gathering things instead of being there already." She held out a wand.

Khelben stared down at it for a long, silent breath. Then the corners of his mouth curled up slightly, and he took it from her. Stepping into the boots she was holding ready, he took both their cloaks over his arm, strode without pause to the door, and held it wide. Laeral gave him a twinkling smile and brushed his cheek with a kiss as she went out.

One of their younger, newer apprentices, Paershym Woodstoke of Neverwinter, was trotting excitedly along a passage, his head down and a precious spell tome clutched in his hands. Its covers, two polished plates of ever-bright silver, flashed suddenly as the lord and lady mage of Waterdeep stepped out of a side door, spilling light into the dim hallway. They leapt across the passage like a pair of pranksome apprentices. With a softly spoken password, they opened the door of a closet that had to be tiny, crunched between two flanking rooms, and crowded into it together, giggling.

Lady Laeral winked at Paershym just before the door closed behind her—leaving the apprentice, who'd halted to gape in astonishment, quite alone in the passage. He blushed a brilliant crimson and stared in disbelief at the closed door of the tiny closet. Slowly, almost reluctantly, he stole up to it and tried the handle. It was locked.

He turned away feeling almost relieved—and stiffened as the doorknob behind him emitted a faint, girlish giggle.

Clutching the book very firmly, he hurried away, wondering how his father would take the news if he wrote a letter home explaining that he'd changed his mind about becoming a wizard. . . .

* * * * *

In a chamber deep within Twilight Hall, a lady laughed. "We've more than earned this, beloved," she purred to the person in the heart of the canopied bed. His reply was a wordless growl that left her giggling— until the closet door beside the bed burst open.

"Please excuse the intrusion," the lord mage of Waterdeep said gravely to the astonished Harper couple as he marched briskly across the room to the closed door of another closet.

Laeral mouthed, "Sorry," to the shocked faces above the covers, waved a farewell, and stepped into the closet behind Khelben.

There were a lot of dusty cloaks inside, and she sneezed more than once before Khelben found the catch on the secret door and led her on into a lightless passage that zigged, zagged, and opened into the back of yet another closet.

As the Blackstaff briskly opened the closet door, they saw a bored Harper guard sitting in the room beyond, sharpening his blade. No intruders ever got this far, after all, and . . .

The guard sprang up as the wizards strode into the room. He waved his sword menacingly. "Halt, by the silver Harp and the blood spilled for it!" he charged sternly—but the two mages were already past him, heading for one of the doors across the room.

The Harper gaped. "But you're—you're Khelben!"

The archwizard sighed. "Has the disguise spell failed again? Oh, dear . . . " He rolled his eyes theatrically.

Laeral chimed in breathlessly, "We've tried *everything*. . . ."

As she spread her hands in despair, Khelben touched the door in a certain spot—and it flared into a blinding glow. The Harper threw up his hand to shield his eyes, just in time to see the two mages fade away. . . .

* * * * *

The Castle of Shadows, Shadowhome, Midsummer Day

In a room where shadows were rarely still, two tentacled things met, exchanged grunts of recognition, and rose into manlike forms.

"It's even worse than I'd thought," Hulurran said without preamble or greeting. "Since Dhalgrave was slain and the intruders first came, over sixty of the kin have perished or disappeared . . . perhaps as many as seventy!"

"Seventy!" Gathran sighed gloomily. "Will we live to see the House of Malaug dwindle to nothing, and the shadowbeasts finally slither in to tear the last few of us apart?"

Hulurran shrugged. "There's just one good thing," he said. "Milhvar was working on a cloak that shielded him from the prying magics of the mages of Faerûn . . . a 'cloak of shadows,' he called it in his notes. If anything's befallen them, the secret of its making is gone with him."

"You saw his notes?" Gathran did not bother to hide his astonishment.

Hulurran smiled. "Milhvar was so old that he sometimes forgot that others of us have seen just as many years. . . . He hid some of his notes—and the finished cloak; I saw him testing it—in a hideaway Anduthil created for safe storage. Since Anduthil's passing, I believe he thought only he remembered its existence." He turned slightly, and made a gesture. "It's right here," he added, "and—"

Hulurran fell abruptly silent. Gathran peered over his shoulder to see why. The hideaway was a small room with a cot, a chair, a desk, and a chamberpot. A few blank scraps of parchment were strewn on the desk, but the cot—where his companion was probing emptiness—was quite bare. " 'Twas right here," Hulurran said, frowning, "and he wasn't wearing it when he met his end—I saw him die."

"Then where is it?" Their eyes met and held in silence for a long while.

Hulurran sighed. "Let us hope one of us is wearing it in Faerûn right now."

"A prudent one of us," Gathran agreed.

They both sighed then, and left that place.

* * * * *

When the world stopped whirling, they were sitting together on a bench in Shadowdale, with Elminster's Tower rising crookedly in front of them—and a startled guard scrambling up from where he'd been lounging on the bench beside them. He swung his gleaming pike down.

Khelben calmly struck it aside and twisted it out of the armsman's hands.

Laeral said mildly, "Perhaps it's the clothes we're wearing. . . ."

* * * * *

"With all due respect, sir merchant," the guardcaptain said firmly, "no one brings wagons into Shadowdale without our looking inside them."

The paunchy, unshaven merchant glared at him. "Aye, I know your sort of searching. What's the point o' my coming all the way from fair Cormyr"—one of his men gave him a strange look, and the guardcaptain almost smiled—"if you steal half my stock, eh? Pendle's Fine Meats are known from Suzail to Selgaunt, and I'll be damned by all the gods if I let some uniformed thugs in a backwater dale rob me of what I've worked so hard for!"

"Then turn your wagons about, merchant, and go around Shadowdale," the guardcaptain said softly, his hand on his sword.

"This one's open, sir," one of the guards spoke out, pointing at the second wagon back. Without taking his eyes from the guardcaptain, Pendle grew a tentacle thirty feet long that snapped like a lash around the armsman's throat.

There was a collective gasp of horror and fear from men on both sides of the roadblock. The guardcaptain stared hard at Pendle as his sword flashed out. "What are you?" he asked, white to the lips.

Lorgyn smiled a wintry smile at him as two tentacles smashed the man's sword away, and a third rose with a bony spear to stab him in one eye. "I wondered when you'd get around to asking that," he said softly.

Men were screaming on all sides now. There was a general rush from the wagons into the woods. Pendle's outriders turned their horses and spurred westward as fast as the horses would go.

The Malaugrym reached out and calmly slew another man, and another, reaching always for those trying to flee or raising horns to arouse the dale. Some of the guards got their bows out, and arrows hissed and hummed. Lorgyn ignored them as he went on killing.

By the time all the guards were dead, lying twisted

and broken in the road around him, the Malaugrym was feathered with many arrows. Heedless of the blood streaming from him in a dozen places, Lorgyn shifted to oxen form to drag the lead wagon aside; its draft horses had taken even more arrows than he had, and lay dead in the traces.

The wagon of wizards was all that mattered now. Lorgyn led the frightened horses past all the blood, into Shadowdale. The time for skulking was past . . . now, let all in Faerûn beware the Malaugrym, and cringe in fear!

* * * * *

"There it is again," Belkram said, pointing at Sharantyr's pack. "You'd better see what it is!"

The lady ranger set down her pack with more haste than grace, and drew her sword.

"I'll open it," Belkram offered, "and you keep blade ready, right?"

She nodded, and Itharr stood back to keep watch on the woods around as Shar bent over her pack. Something had quivered in its depths . . . at least twice now. Belkram was cautiously turning out the kindling, her candles, her spare boots and undershift, her gloves . . . "There!"

Two blades flashed down—to hover above a small cloth bundle. "Lhaeo was holding that before we left," Shar said slowly. "What is it? And why would he put it in my pack?"

The tip of Belkram's blade touched it very cautiously. Then the ranger grinned, reached over, and unwrapped it, revealing—a stone.

A ghostly vapor swirled up from it as it said, "Finally! Draw together, all of you, and bide here until I return— I only hope we're not too late!"

Open-mouthed, the three rangers watched Syluné of Shadowdale fly off through the trees.

"She can leave her stone?"

"Storm or Lhaeo must have worked some magic," Belkram said, grunting as he reached beyond comfort's stretch to pluck up Shar's gloves. "Let's get you packed again," he said. "When a mage tells you to stay together, she usually means it's teleport time."

Itharr nodded agreement—then they all gaped again as the air shimmered. The Red Wizard was standing before them again, Syluné's head floating above his open palm. He gave the three a curt nod of greeting.

The Witch of Shadowdale asked crisply, "Have we a bargain, then?"

Orth Lantar nodded again. "We do."

"Right. Know then that the Lost Ring of Blaestarn lies beneath the third flagstone south of the unicorn fountain, in the house where you've been searching; the white dragon Glandananglar is no more, and her treasure lies under her bones in a cave on the east side of Mount Ahaeragh—its mouth is covered by an illusion, but lies below the tallest horn; and the ioun stones of Thavilar Halcontar are buried a long pace to the south of the duskwood tree in the northwestern corner of his garden. I'll tell you where the rest of the treasures lie after you've sent these three safely to Shadowdale."

The Red Wizard bowed. "It will be my pleasure to so serve." He raised his hands and began, and the three rangers saw a blue-white radiance stream from Syluné to surround his head and shoulders, steadying him against the magic twisting wild.

Soberly and carefully the Red Wizard worked a mass teleport spell, and the world began to whirl into blue-white mists.

"Holy Mystra, aid us," the three rangers heard Syluné say as the magic took effect.

Then the floating head of the Witch of Shadowdale gasped, and her ghostly eyes widened. "Wh-Who are you?"

"Midnight," came the reply, echoing in all their

heads.

Sudden force flooded into Syluné; her fading spectral form flickered, and then grew strong and bright. "But you can call me Mystra—for so I am, henceforth."

Syluné gaped at a face only she could see—and beside her, the Red Wizard went to his knees, babbling a prayer.

He had not prayed to the Lady of All Mysteries since he'd been a young apprentice, and that had been very long ago.

* * * * *

The world danced, and the three rangers suddenly found themselves standing at the crossroads by the Old Skull Inn in Shadowdale, with startled armsmen and villagers staring at them from all sides.

They peered around, wondering why Syluné had been so suddenly adamant that they be here, now.

"Is that the Blackstaff?" Itharr asked, eyes wide. He pointed toward Elminster's Tower.

Belkram peered. "Aye—I spoke to him once, and to Laeral several times; that's her, too, beside him."

Khelben Arunsun was casting a spell—or rather, miscasting it. A shower of blue furry jungle plants abruptly rained down around him. He cursed loudly, like any merchant who's made a mistake, and strode toward the road. Two laborers, who were walking along it with heavy hods on their shoulders, looked back.

They let the hods fall, and boiled up into things out of nightmare.

A small forest of tentacles reached for folk all around, and the street became a chaos of screaming, fleeing people, with armsmen trying to wade through them. Tentacles grew many-fanged mouths and bit down mercilessly.

"Malaugrym," the three rangers shouted, breaking into a run.

Laeral hurled a spell—and the two monsters were

girt with an amber radiance, out of which darted dozens of butterflies.

Laeral stared in disgust at the clouds of insects, unbelted her robe, and let it fall to the turf behind her. Beneath it she wore a short kirtle bristling with daggers. Drawing one in either hand, she raced across the meadow toward the road, Khelben lumbering along beside her.

Horns were ringing out from the Tower of Ashaba, and armored men were streaming from its gates—men who wore the Purple Dragon of Cormyr.

The Malaugrym were undulating along the road toward the three rangers. As the three hefted their blades and eyed reaching tentacles, they heard the deep, bubbling voice of one tentacled monster ask, "Argast, what's *that?*"

They all stared at what was rising up from the road in front of the tower—a gigantic black dragon, clutching a wagon in its claws!

"By all the blinded, crawling gods . . . " Shar cursed in disbelief, watching the dragon spread its great wings. One beat sent it over the meadow, where it set the wagon down as tenderly as a newly laid egg. It banked and roared down at the crossroads, jaws gaping. . . .

* * * * *

Jhessail looked up sharply as a roar split the air outside. "What was that?" she snapped.

Illistyl beat her to the window. "Gods!" she gasped. "A dragon!"

Jhessail thrust her head past her apprentice's shoulder and glared out. "Out of nowhere? Impossible!"

She snatched something out of her bodice and tugged. A fine gold chain parted, and Jhessail held up a pendant that was shaped like a sphere, with windows enclosing a smaller windowed sphere—and another, and yet another.

Illistyl stared at it. Elminster had given her that, and she'd never said what it was for. . . .

Jhessail thrust it out the window and whispered a single word—and the pendant was gone in a flash of spreading light that all but blinded them both.

The swooping dragon flashed with that same light, and was suddenly no huge black scaled wyrm at all, but a small, manlike thing trailing tentacles as it fell from the sky.

Laeral leapt desperately out of the way as the twisting, changing thing crashed to earth.

Both Malaugrym hissed, "Lorgyn!"

Around the cursing lord mage of Waterdeep, spells were going awry in a continuous swirl of radiances and odd manifestations. Laeral scrambled through a shower of green lizards, the snapping fangs of Malaugrym tentacles close behind her.

"Gods," Sharantyr said, her face paling as the three rangers charged together, pounding along the road toward the two gigantic snake-things that were writhing and snapping in earnest now, crushing guards and sweeping horses and men into the air with their lashing tails. "Are we really going into *that?*"

"Of course," Belkram shouted merrily. "We're reckless, crazed heroes, remember?"

"More than that," Itharr bellowed, "we're the Rangers Three!"

"The Rangers Three!" they shouted in chorus as their blades struck home.

The world rapidly became a place of constant slashing and hacking, with Malaugrym tentacles smashing and slapping from everywhere as armsmen shouted and died.

The lady mage of Waterdeep was stabbing with silverbladed daggers, and Malaugrym tentacles were shriveling at their touch or cringing away before her. To avoid the bite of silver blades, the monsters began to hurl hapless armsmen and villagers at her, seeking to crush or suffocate her beneath broken bodies. Khelben stood over Laeral, the broken haft of a pike in his hands, trying to protect his lady against too many stabbing tentacles.

An armsman was flung through the air, his broken limbs flailing like smashed twigs. Sharantyr ducked under him, slashed aside one last tentacle, and drew back her blade to plunge it deep into one gigantic yellow Malaugrym eye.

Out of the eye burst Amdramnar's face, pleading: "Stay your blade, Sharantyr! Know that I love you—"

Shar gazed at the Malaugrym in astonished horror, blade raised. She never saw the scorpionlike tail that rose behind her, lifting from a broken thing that had once been a dragon.

The bony spur stabbed down—and burst out through the lady ranger's breast in a rain of blood.

Itharr and Belkram shrieked in horror and went mad with their blades, screaming and stabbing in all directions.

The lady ranger stiffened, and blood sprayed from her sagging lips.

A great roar of anguish rose over the fray as the monster that was Amdramnar cried, "No! Lorgyn, you *fool!* She was to be my mate! *Sharantyr!*"

* * * * *

Storm Silverhand was almost home from patrol now, and contentment welled up within her. The familiar woods rose green and deep around her. She did not hurry. Her boots followed trails she hadn't walked in a while, and chances to relax were few enough, these days.

A roaring sound rose into the air ahead, muffled by the trees. Storm frowned and stopped to listen. Were those shouts? Yes!

Shadowdale must be under attack! With a soft curse, the Bard of Shadowdale drew her blade and broke into a trot, weaving through the trees as quickly as she could.

* * * * *

Laeral darted through a dancing chaos of tentacles, desperately stammering a healing spell. Too late.

The rearing tail of the Malaugrym thrust the limp lady ranger high into the air, then smashed her into the dust of the road. Again it rose, Sharantyr dangling, and again flung her down.

Itharr and Belkram all but clawed their way through a forest of writhing tentacles to get at that tail.

A tentacle struck Laeral. She rolled in the dust herself, slashing her way free and scrambling up—to find the air in front of her shimmering! She drew back her hand to hurl a spell of searing destruction . . .

But two white-faced women in robes appeared—Knights of Myth Drannor. They raised their hands and snapped out incantations. Their magic twisted wild as they hurled it, and the tentacles swept down at them, too. . . .

"Here!" Laeral called. She tossed two of her silver-bladed daggers to the Knights—who fielded them expertly, waved in thanks, and set to work.

The Malaugrym Amdramnar was writhing under the blades of the two furious Harper rangers, and the other one—the one he'd called Argast—was shrinking into a xornlike beast with many massive clawed arms instead of tentacles. The shifting body of Argast was flickering with strange magics as Khelben Blackstaff struggled to control spell after spell hurled at the shapeshifter.

Itharr was weeping incoherently now. He stood hip-deep in a gory hole he'd hacked in Amdramnar, and stabbed down endlessly.

None of the armsmen of Cormyr saw Storm Silverhand burst out of the trees, running hard, but they all saw her swarm up the scorpionlike third Malaugrym and plunge her sword deep into one of its eyes. It shuddered and convulsed madly under her, and she grimly clung to it as she tumbled to the ground, one arm around Sharantyr's broken body.

"Burn it! Burn the things with oil!" she bellowed at the armsmen. She found her feet amid writhing ropes of shapeshifting flesh—ropes that rose to fling Khelben and Belkram together in a helpless tangle into the gathered armsmen.

The soldiers stared at Storm; who *was* this woman? An old woman staring at the fray from the door of the Old Skull suddenly tossed away her tankard, plucked down one of the lanterns from beside the inn door, and flung it.

It shattered, spilling oil down the tentacled bulk of Amdramnar—and Illistyl murmured the simplest fire spell she knew.

Flames flared. The oil caught, boiling up with a roar. The Malaugrym convulsed and reared, shrieking, and the air was suddenly full of oil as every armsman scrambled to find and fling any lamps they could.

The Malaugrym shrieked as flames rose around them, and through the growing roar of the flames, Belkram cried, "Khelben! Can't you do something for Shar?"

He practically dragged the lord mage of Waterdeep to his feet. Khelben blinked at him, then said grimly, "Er—eh—well, I'll try."

The archwizard looked at Sharantyr's sprawled body and raised his hands to cast a spell—only to pitch forward, falling on his face in the dirt.

Belkram stared at the man whose pike had struck Khelben down from behind: a warrior of Cormyr, who smiled coldly, shivered slightly for an instant . . . and became someone else.

Someone who wore doomstars at his wrist, and answered to the name of Dhalgrave.

19
We, the Rangers Three

Blue stones flashed and pulsed, spitting out beams that cut the air to strike Laeral and Storm. The two silver-haired women stiffened as blue fire raged around them—and then fell limply to the ground, their eyes dark.

"With the Chosen out of the way," Dhalgrave said almost pleasantly, "I can really enjoy what I came for."

The Shadowmaster High ignored an armsman's sword that thrust through him, and when another warrior thrust a torch in his face, he grew a bone spur and casually stabbed the man through the face. All the while wearing that deadly smile, the senior Malaugrym advanced leisurely toward the weary, panting rangers.

Belkram and Itharr watched him come; they grimly stood their ground, leaning on battered blades. The three Malaugrym burned behind them, and from the flickering flames a weak voice called, "Shadowmaster High! Aid, please, in the name of Malaug! I'm burning! Great Dhalgrave, aid me!"

Dhalgrave never took his eyes from the two rangers, and never paused in his slow, menacing advance. Argast soon fell silent . . . and joined Amdramnar and Lorgyn in death.

* * * * *

Deep in the Castle of Shadows, in a place where thinking shadows glided, was a grotto. At its heart were two stone seats that faced each other in the bone-white glow. On one of them, something blazed briefly, then burst.

A hand promptly reached down out of darkness to pick up the largest of the fragments and sweep the seat clean . . . and a soft chuckle echoed through the grotto.

* * * * *

Dhalgrave stopped just beyond the reach of the two weary rangers and smiled a gloating smile at the fearful warriors, noting many Purple Dragon surcoats. "All the way from Cormyr, just to die?" he asked in mock sorrow, shaking his head.

From among the warriors, lightning lashed at the Malaugrym, and on his other flank something that looked like a white mist driven by churning human bones rose and drifted speedily toward him.

Dhalgrave simply watched those deaths come for him. The spells faded away as they reached him, and he sketched a mocking bow.

"My thanks, Ladies," he said. "Jhessail and Illistyl, isn't it?" He gestured lazily down at himself. "Unfortunately for your valiant endeavors, I wear a cloak of shadows that wards all your spells . . . and hides me even from the Chosen. I had to 'die' for a time to get it, but watching my underlings scramble to try to take my throne was richly entertaining compensation."

The doomstars lashed out again, and four armsmen were hurled back against their fellows, their bodies trailing blue fire. Blades fell from their hands . . . blades that shone with silver. Sir Tantor Dauntinghorn peered at the dead and trembled with anger, reaching for his own blade.

"No, envoy, keep your life," the Malaugrym told him. "I shall need your services to inform Azoun that the

Purple Dragon throne is mine now. My realm will take in Sembia, too, of course . . . but you won't be bored. I'll be sending all the brave warriors of both lands against Zhentil Keep—and none of you shall rest, nor fail me, until that city and all its folk are eradicated."

He took another slow pace forward. "Before all of that, however, I must attend to the business that brought all of the blood of Malaug lately to Faerûn . . . a little matter of revenge."

Dhalgrave looked at Belkram and Itharr and smiled again. "Your deaths will be slow," he said softly, "very slow." A frown crossed the handsome human face he wore, and he asked the world at large, "I wonder if I can transform them to mushrooms, as that woman did?"

He raised his hands slowly, nodding in sudden satisfaction, and said, "Yes!"

The doomstars hummed, dimmed, and grew still. The Malaugrym began the gestures of a spell—and the two Harper rangers erupted into a last desperate charge, swinging their blades as they came.

The cloak Dhalgrave wore spoke.

"Yes, indeed," it agreed, and two gnarled old hands grew out of it on the shapeshifter's flanks, and dug fingers deep into Dhalgrave—fingers that blazed with spellfire!

The Malaugrym screamed. His hands faltered, the doomstars winking wildly, and the hands literally tore him apart.

Dhalgrave convulsed, struggling to throw out a tentacle here and an eyestalk there amid the spreading spellfire—and as the two Harpers came to hasty halts, blades held ready, the Malaugrym sported the long, jagged jaws of a crocodile for just a moment . . . before collapsing into a swirling cloud of ash. What remained was a raging, man-high column of spellfire, with the hands that had slain Dhalgrave protruding from it.

The doomstars spun and winked by themselves in midair for a breath, then drifted obediently into one of those old, waiting hands.

As they settled, all of the spellfire seemed to roar down into them—and burst in a flash that made unwary men cry out and clutch at their eyes.

Those stricken did not see the beams that lanced out from the destruction of the doomstars to touch Storm, Laeral, and Khelben, and awaken them to vibrant life.

As the Bard of Shadowdale came unsteadily to her feet and reached down to help her sister up, a familiar voice said disgustedly, "Do I have to do everything myself, look ye?"

"Elminster!" Laeral cried delightedly.

The Old Mage puffed one last time on his pipe before calmly tapping out its coals onto the ash that had been the Shadowmaster High.

"But you—you died!" Mourngrym said, laughing, as he shouldered through the armsmen, Shaerl at his side.

"Reports of my death," the Old Mage said solemnly, "have been—ahem—greatly exaggerated."

*   *   *   *   *

The scrying portal shook as Hulurran's rage almost ended his control over it. "No!" he snarled, but the other two who stood in the shadows with him kept silent. One of them laid a silent tentacle against his cheek for a moment.

After they'd stood staring into Faerûn for a long time, Gathran stirred.

"If we could get that cloak," he began, "we—"

He fell silent again as, below, Elminster stirred the ashes, held up a tattered scrap—and firmly burned it to nothingness with a jet of spellfire from his finger.

"By the blazing blood of Malaug," Hulurran raged in a voice that trembled with emotion, "I'll never rest un—"

"Hold your wind!" snapped the youngest and smallest of the Malaugrym. "This disaster is born directly of reckless overconfidence . . . even on my father's part."

Huerbara's eyes blazed with resolve as she scattered the scrying portal with one slim tentacle. "We must not act—we must *never* act—against folk of Faerûn until we are strong, and prepared . . . even for the unexpected. Revenge can be won, yes . . . but it may take years. We must rebuild the House of Malaug first. To do it, I'll need your help."

"*You?*" Hulurran asked, slack-jawed in disbelief.

Gathran, however, said quietly, "Command me, daughter of Ahorga."

Huerbara nodded to him before turning to the elder shapeshifter. "Are you with me also, Hulurran of the Winds?" The query was soft with menace.

After a long silence, Hulurran nodded. "Aye. Aye, you have fire enough to be Shadowmaster High. I am yours." He turned to meet her gaze squarely, and added, "But we must move very carefully, lest our house be torn apart by strife between you and rivals for the throne."

"Teach me, then," Huerbara said to them both, gliding nearer, "how to move very carefully. . . ."

"Lady, we will," they agreed in chorus, and three sets of eager tentacles met and entwined.

* * * * *

The folk in Shadowdale fortunate enough to survive the events of that morning had seen wonder upon wonder . . . but there were still gasps and mutterings and a shrinking back as a ghostly, silver-haired head came floating over the grass. Gawking dalefolk and weary Cormyreans alike melted out of its path, and stared at the three naked, bedraggled folk who followed it.

"It seems one of the Malaugrym was collecting wizards," Syluné told Elminster. "And as both you and Mystra seem to be back with us, we'd best be using these three to bring Sharantyr back."

The Old Mage stared searchingly at the short, fat

man and the two women, and they all nodded their agreement. Jhessail and Illistyl pushed through the crowd, and Sir Tantor was jostled aside by Lord Luthtor, firmly leading a line of war wizards.

"What did you say?" Itharr hissed to Syluné.

Belkram put an arm around his shoulder. Weeping, the rangers watched Khelben, Laeral, and even Storm join the circle of wizards. The mages joined hands around Sharantyr's broken body, then looked to the Old Mage.

Elminster said softly, "Do it."

For a breath or two, it seemed nothing was happening. In silence the wizards stood, unmoving, as warriors craned their necks to look. Next came gasps here and there as folk noticed the radiance silently forming in the air above the circle. Small motes of light twinkled, grew, and shone more brightly. Swiftly the light swelled until a great sphere of white radiance blazed above the wizards.

They heard Elminster and Khelben grunt in unison—and a shaft of light stabbed down from the sphere to strike the still form of Sharantyr.

The wizards trembled, and on the bodies of the three unclad mages the watchers could see sweat streaming. The wizards strained as the beam slowly rose from the ground, taking the lady ranger's body with it.

Through their tears the two Harpers held each other, wild hope leaping within them, and saw the body of their lady disappear into the light.

One of the war wizards cried out, and slumped over, but Luthtor firmly held one of his hands and Irendue clung like grim death to the other, and the circle was not broken. The mages wavered. More than one sagged to his knees, but held fast to the hands of the chain.

Then a great, collective gasp went up from them, the light faded, and out of its heart something sprang.

Something soft and shapely and whole—and alive!

Sharantyr fell from the sky as naked as the day she

was born, and something seemed to boost her abruptly sideways—of all the assembly, only Mourngrym saw Elminster's momentary grin—in her fall, so that she landed, heavily, atop Belkram.

He went to the ground with a startled "Whumpf!" A moment later, Itharr, Belkram, and Sharantyr were rolling over and over in a happy embrace, weeping and kissing and laughing for joy.

Khelben looked down at them and frowned. "Must they?" he complained to his lady. "And her without a stitch on, too!"

Laeral grinned happily up at the lord mage of Waterdeep through the sweat glistening on her face—and bowled him over with her own sudden embrace.

"Whumpf!" Khelben said as he hit the ground. "Get off!" he shouted when he had breath enough to speak again. Grinning faces of armsmen and dalefolk surrounded him. "I said get *off!*"

* * * * *

Shadowdale, Midsummer Night

The fire spat sparks in the kitchen hearth, and Sharantyr put her bare feet up on Storm's kitchen table, crossed one shapely ankle over the other, and sighed in satisfaction. A huge tankard of strong home brew was ready at her elbow, and she was leaning back against Belkram. Itharr smiled and reached out a hand to stroke her foot.

"Ahh," Sharantyr said happily, "all this, and we're done with the Malaugrym for now, too!"

"We are," Storm agreed. "Elminster rode the shadows through their castle this afternoon, and tells me it is a place of confusion and back-stabbing disorder. Only three of them know what befell here, and plan any sort of revenge."

"Oh, joy," Belkram said, raising his tankard.

"Oh, joy, indeed," Storm said with a smile, turning from her cooking cauldron and crossing her arms. Itharr decided not to tell her that her ladle had decided to drip all down her hip. "That means, Harpers bold," she continued briskly, "that it's time for your next assignment."

Belkram choked, and brought his tankard down onto the table with a crash as he sputtered and coughed. There were titters from some of the other Knights at the table.

"Which is?" Itharr asked, giving his companion an amused look.

Storm noticed the spill, ran a finger up her hip, and licked it. "Aid embattled Randal Morn in Daggerdale," she told her ladle.

"A simple matter," Belkram said with airy dignity.

"Well, after battling Malaugrym, aye," Mourngrym agreed, "but you'll no doubt have the lord-devouring Sir Tantor and Luthtor's war wizards to contend with." Shaerl dealt her lord's shoulder a mock blow, and he put an arm around her with a chuckle.

"Does this mean your students are taught, and they'll be leaving Shadowdale?" Sharantyr asked quietly.

Storm nodded. "It does."

Sharantyr swung her feet down from the table and stood up. "Then I have to tell all of you something." She looked around the table at the assembled Knights, from Florin and Dove at one end to Jhessail and her new apprentice, the shyly silent Irendue, at the other. "Whether it costs me my place among you or not, I will go with Belkram and Itharr . . . because"—her voice sank almost to a whisper, but she stared across the room at Elminster's encouraging smile, where he sat in a dark corner, and continued steadily—"I can't bear to be parted from them."

And as the room erupted with cries of "Well said!" "Of course!" and "A Knight forever, wherever you go!" the tears came.

Sharantyr leaned on the table and wept until two pairs of strong arms went around her, and Belkram and Itharr said into her ears in unison, "The Rangers Three—forever!"

* * * * *

The crystal ball glimmered, and Laeral turned away from it with misty eyes and a sigh of satisfaction. "She did the right thing," the lady mage of Waterdeep told Khelben happily. "She's following her heart."

"That's nice," Khelben said absently, his attention deep in a spell tome. Laeral looked at him, shook her head fondly, and grinned impishly as she rose.

Three gliding steps brought her to the table, and a little jump and turn brought her behind down firmly atop the open book, even before her arms went around her man in a fierce embrace.

She fondly kissed the balding pate of the lord mage of Waterdeep, and felt his muffled roar as he snarled into her bosom, "Get off! I said, get *off!*"

* * * * *

It was very late when the floating, disembodied head said to Elminster, "You promised me another body of my own, Old Mage."

"Aye," he said as they stood together in the dusty, paper-choked main room of his tower. "Would n—"

The front door flew open, startling them both, and a wild-eyed woman, garbed in the black tatters of a once fine gown, strode in. Without slowing, the Simbul smiled at Syluné, took Elminster's hand in her own, and practically snatched him up the stairs to the bed-chamber.

"My body?" Syluné asked softly.

"It will be the first act I set him to when we awaken," the Simbul told her sister as they vanished around the first curve of the stair. "I'll see to it."

"Perhaps I should get to it now," Elminster's voice came floating down the stairs, sounding a trifle anxious.

"I have other uses for you first," the Simbul told him fiercely. "Gods, El, I've missed you!"

Her arms went around him hungrily. In the room below, Syluné listened, a smile growing on her face. Then she chuckled softly, and flew out into the night.

Lhaeo bid her a pleasant night as she drifted down the path. The floating head turned to face him. "Lhaeo? I thought you were abed!"

"I was," Elminster's scribe said dryly, "until the Queen of Aglarond arrived. Then I suddenly found myself dressed, awake, and out here—with this bottle of elverquisst to keep me company." He sipped at the glass in his hand and sighed appreciatively. "Superb stuff."

Syluné hesitated, looking out over the moon-drenched, placid pool toward the flickering torches on the walls of the Tower of Ashaba. "Would you mind if I stayed to talk for a bit?"

The scribe looked up at her. "Lady," he said softly, "I would be honored. Stay with me so long as it pleases you." He drained his glass and added slyly, "You can tell me what it's like to get a head in this world!"

The floating head growled at him. "You may be surprised to learn," the Witch of Shadowdale said sweetly as she drifted nearer, "that I *can* still tickle."

"Ah, no," Lhaeo said with a groan, putting his glass carefully out of harm's way. "No . . ."

* * * * *

The farmhouse shook, and the night outside was briefly as bright as day.

"What was *that?*" Mourngrym snarled.

There was a confused snatching at weapons and a rush to the door.

The Rangers Three, Storm, and the lord and lady of

Shadowdale reached the flagstone path outside Storm's house in time to see a bright stream of stars rising from Elminster's Tower, in the wake of a radiant orb in which two familiar figures danced and swam. They heard a happy, wordless cry before the sphere that held Elminster and the Simbul turned suddenly and streaked away northward, into the stars.

"Gods above," Itharr said wonderingly. He turned his head and saw Sharantyr's awed face looking up into the sky beside his. Leaning close, he asked quietly, "Do you think we could try that?"

Still watching the distant sphere dwindle into the night, Sharantyr drew back her arm and punched him enthusiastically.

Shaerl and Storm hooted with laughter.

* * * * *

The moonlight of another night washed down over the ruined pillars and walls of Irythkeep. Itharr looked up at Selune, yawned, and said, "High time for slumber."

A slim lady rose from banking the fire beside him, took his chin in her hands, and kissed him fondly. "The watch is mine, of course, O King of Snorers," the Witch of Shadowdale told him, and patted his arm. "Go on."

"Are you sure?" Belkram asked sleepily, coming out of the tent with Sharantyr's leathers and his own, to drape them over a line for the night.

"I don't need to sleep, remember?" Syluné told him.

Both Harpers nodded, more asleep than awake, and said, more or less in chorus, "May the night be good, then." They turned together to go into the tent where Shar was already lost in slumber—and bumped together.

"Ugliness first," Belkram said, indicating the tent mouth.

"Stupidity first," Itharr countered, waving his friend

toward the sleeping furs.

"Pigheaded Harpers first," a smiling Syluné said in both their ears, and shoved at their backs. They fell into the tent in a chuckling heap, and the Witch of Shadowdale turned away to look out over Daggerdale, a smile on her face.

"Sharantyr's first child, at least," Azuth said softly as the two gods stood together by the fire, magically hidden from mortals and Chosen, "will be thine."

Midnight nodded. "She'll need to be strong, and soon . . . magic may be biddable again, and the gods back in their places."

The goddess sighed then, and added almost in a whisper, "More than that: Elminster cannot last forever."

FANTASTY ADVENTURE

R. A. Salvatore
Siege of Darkness

The new Drizzt Do'Urden novel by *The New York Times* best-selling author of *The Legacy* and *Starless Night*

Revenge sought! As a ruling matron of Menzoberranzan prepares a venemous assault on Drizzt Do'Urden and Mithril Hall, the laws of magic take a horrific turn. The metropolis of the dark elves is thrown into chaos and Lloth, the Spider Queen, roams the streets!
Hardcover Edition
Available August 1994
Sug. Retail $18.95; CAN $23.95; £10.99 U.K.   ISBN 1-56076-888-6

Starless Night
Paperback Edition
Available August 1994
ISBN 1-56076-880-0

The Legacy
Paperback Edition
On Sale Now
ISBN 1-56076-640-9

Dragonlance® Saga

The sweeping saga of honor, courage, and
companions begins with . . .

The Chronicles Trilogy

By *The New York Times* best-selling authors
Margaret Weis & Tracy Hickman

Dragons of Autumn Twilight
Volume One
Dragons have returned to Krynn with a vengeance.
An unlikely band of heroes embarks on a perilous
quest for the legendary *Dragonlance!*

ISBN 0-88038-173-6

Dragons of Winter Night
Volume Two
The adventure continues . . . Treachery,
intrigue, and despair threaten to overcome
the Heroes of the Lance in their epic quest!

ISBN 0-88038-174-4

Dragons of Spring Dawning
Volume Three
Hope dawns with the coming of spring, but then
the heroes find themselves in a titanic battle
against Takhisis, Queen of Darkness!

ISBN 0-88038-175-2

THE ICEWIND DALE
T r i l o g y

By R. A. Salvatore
The New York Times best-selling author

Follow the adventures of an unlikely quartet of heroes – the dark elf Drizzt Do'Urden, the halfling Regis, the barbarian Wulfgar, and the dwarf Bruenor – as they combat assassins, wizards, golems, and more in a struggle to preserve their homes and heritage. The Icewind Dale Trilogy is a fascinating tale filled with mystery, intrigue, and danger you won't want to miss!

The Crystal Shard	**Streams of Silver**	**The Halfling's Gem**
Book One	Book Two	Book Three
ISBN 0-88038-535-9	ISBN 0-88038-672-X	ISBN 0-88038-901-X

ON SALE NOW!

DragonLance® Saga

THE HISTORIC SAGA OF THE DWARVEN CLANS
Dwarven Nations Trilogy
Dan Parkinson

The Covenant of the Forge **Volume One**
As the drums of Balladine thunder forth, calling humans to trade with the dwarves of Thorin, Grayfen, a human struck by the magic of the Graystone, infiltrates the dwarven stronghold, determined to annihilate the dwarves and steal their treasure. ISBN 1-56076-558-5

Hammer and Axe **Volume Two**
The dwarven clans unite against the threat of encroaching humans and create the fortress of Thorbardin. But old rivalries are not easily forgotten, and the resulting political intrigue brings about catastrophic change. ISBN 1-56076-627-1

The Swordsheath Scroll **Volume Three**
Despite the stubborn courage of the dwarves, the Wilderness War ends as a no-win. The Swordsheath Scroll is signed, and the dwarves join the elves of Qualinesti to build a symbol of peace among the races: Pax Tharkas. ISBN 1-56076-686-7